GODDESS

OF

VENGEANCE

Lucky Santangelo Novels
by Jackie Collins

Drop Dead Beautiful
Dangerous Kiss
Vendetta: Lucky's Revenge
Lady Boss
Lucky
Chances

Also by Jackie Collins

Poor Little Bitch Girl
Married Lovers
Lovers & Players
Hollywood Divorces
Deadly Embrace
Hollywood Wives—The New Generation
Lethal Seduction
L.A. Connections—Power, Obsession, Murder, Revenge
Thrill!
Hollywood Kids
American Star
Rock Star
Hollywood Husbands
Lovers and Gamblers
Hollywood Wives
The World Is Full of Divorced Women
The Love Killers
Sinners
The Bitch
The Stud
The World Is Full of Married Men

GODDESS
OF
VENGEANCE

Jackie Collins

ST. MARTIN'S PRESS ♏ NEW YORK

GODDESS OF VENGEANCE. Copyright © 2011 by Chances, Inc. All rights reserved. Printed in the United States of America. For information, address St. Martin's Press, 175 Fifth Avenue, New York, NY 10010.

www.stmartins.com

Library of Congress Cataloging-in-Publication Data

Collins, Jackie.
    Goddess of vengeance / Jackie Collins. — 1st ed.
        p. cm.
    ISBN 978-0-312-56746-0
  1. Santangelo, Lucky (Fictitious character)—Fiction.
  2. Businesswomen—Fiction.   3. Las Vegas (Nev.)—Fiction.
  I. Title.
    PR6053.0425G63 2011
    823'.914—dc22

                                            2011019512

First Edition: September 2011

10 9 8 7 6 5 4 3 2 1

This one is for all my fans and loyal readers around the world.
On Twitter, Facebook, my Web site—
you all rock!
Keep on reading . . .

GODDESS
OF
VENGEANCE

CHAPTER ONE

It was early evening and the garden restaurant was only half full. The patrons were trying to play it cool, because after all, this was L.A. and stars abounded. However, most of them couldn't resist an occasional surreptitious glance over at Venus, the platinum-blond, world-famous superstar, as she picked at a chopped vegetable salad.

Sitting at the table with her was Lucky Santangelo, a dark-haired beauty who'd experienced her own share of controversial headlines and scandals over the years. Lucky, the former owner and head of Panther Studios, was a businesswoman supreme who currently owned the luxurious hotel, casino, and apartment complex The Keys in Las Vegas.

The two of them made a formidable couple. In Hollywood, where looks were everything, Venus and Lucky ruled. Venus with her in-your-face blondness, startling blue eyes, and toned and muscled shape. And Lucky—a dangerously seductive woman with blacker-than-night eyes, deep olive skin, sensuous full lips, a tangle of long jet hair, and a lithe body.

"I'm beginning to think you're a sex addict," Lucky said lightly, smiling at her close friend.

"*Excuse* me," Venus retorted, raising a perfectly arched and penciled eyebrow. "Last week you called me a cougar, and *now* I'm a sex addict. *Seriously*, Lucky?"

Pushing back her mane of unruly black curls, Lucky grinned. "Yeah. I'm so wrong," she drawled sarcastically. "It wasn't *you* who slept with your twenty-two-year-old costar last week, and it wasn't *you* who screwed your sixty-year-old director two days later."

"Oh *please*," Venus said, dismissively waving her hand in the air. "I'm getting a divorce. What do you expect me to do, join a convent?"

"That might be a touch extreme," Lucky said, smiling as she thought about Venus wreaking havoc in a convent. "But anyway, I'm sure you know what you're doing."

"You bet your fine ass I do," Venus answered vehemently. "Billy is all over the Internet and the magazines with that juvenile skank he's supposedly hooked up with. Just like Cooper before him." She paused for a long thoughtful moment. "Another cheating rat. I sure know how to pick 'em."

"You certainly do," Lucky agreed, thinking that Cooper Turner, Venus's husband before Billy Melina, was a whole different ball game. Cooper was a much older movie star with a Warren Beatty–style track record, and everyone had known that Cooper would eventually cheat. Billy—not so much. Even though Billy was thirteen years younger than Venus, he'd seemed thrilled to be with her. And why not? Like Madonna, Venus was a true original with legions of fans worldwide.

"I cannot believe Billy turned out to be such a loser," Venus said, determined to verbally trash her soon-to-be ex.

"Hardly a loser," Lucky couldn't help pointing out. "His current movie has grossed over a hundred million. Not too shabby."

"Yeah, yeah, rub it in," Venus snapped irritably. "Billy's career is on fire, but I can assure you that as a man he turned out to be a big waste of space." She narrowed her eyes. "And what's up with *you* today? Shouldn't you be agreeing with me, not regaling me with his box office?"

"Hey—don't say I didn't warn you about marrying a much younger man," Lucky responded.

"Billy isn't *that* much younger," Venus insisted. "Anyway, it's sure working for Demi and Ashton. Besides, I thought you liked him."

"I did," Lucky said carefully. "I mean I still do. Only, marrying a younger guy . . . it's kind of a given that they're bound to cheat."

"Oh thanks!" Venus said, frowning. "When did *you* turn into Ms. Cynical and a Half?"

"Not cynical, merely practical."

"Says you," Venus snorted.

"You know I tell it like it is," Lucky said, picking up her wineglass and taking a sip.

"Oh yes, we all know that about you. Nothing's off-limits."

"I believe in the truth."

"And I guess it works for you."

Lucky regarded her brilliant friend, and wondered why any man who was fortunate enough to be with Venus would ever *want* to stray. Venus had it all—beauty, brains, and talent.

"Exactly why *are* you divorcing Billy?" she asked.

" 'Cause he—"

"Cheated!" They finished the sentence together, then broke up laughing.

"Well," Venus said sagely, "it was fun while it lasted. Eighteen months together and six months married. Now I'm almost free again, and believe me, it's not such a bad thing. I enjoy being on my own. Living with Billy was like doing time in a frat house. It's such a pleasure that I don't have to pick up dirty socks and underwear from the floor, there are no endless midnight snacks everywhere, *and* I get full control of the remote."

"Surely you always had that."

"Actually, I didn't. You know me—when I wasn't working, I was busy playing wifey to the hilt, and you can see where it got me."

"Free to fuck your costar, *and* your director," Lucky pointed out. "Not so bad."

Venus gave a wicked smile. "I know. Shame we just finished shooting."

"You should fly to Vegas this weekend," Lucky suggested. "It'll take your mind off all things Billy."

"What's going on in Vegas—apart from your fantastic hotel?"

"A board meeting of all my investors. And since you were one of the first, it would be great if you showed your face. Everyone would really love it. And—even better—I've decided to throw an eighteenth birthday party for Max, although the brat is driving me crazy. She's still carrying on about moving to New York."

"I cannot believe that Max is about to be eighteen. Little Maria, all grown up."

"Tell me about it." Lucky sighed. "Time goes too fast."

"You do realize that now there's no way you can stop her from doing anything she wants?"

"Unfortunately, I understand that," Lucky said, nodding. "And if I know my Max, she'll take full advantage."

"Hey—*you* were married at sixteen," Venus said brightly. "So maybe she'll turn out to be street-smart like you."

"Married *off* you mean, by dear daddy Gino," Lucky said, shaking her head as if she still couldn't quite believe that Gino had forced her into a marriage she didn't want. "Can you imagine that Gino thought he was protecting me from my wild ways? What a joke *that* turned out to be!"

"How come you didn't fight it?"

"I was sixteen," Lucky said, remembering the overwhelming rush of helplessness and dread she'd felt on her wedding day. "I guess I considered myself powerless to say no."

"C'mon, Lucky, it didn't do you any harm," Venus said. "Just look at everything you've accomplished. You've built hotels, run a movie studio, had three kids, *and* you're married to Mister Amazing. Admit it, you're a goddamn superwoman!"

"No," Lucky answered after a thoughtful pause. "I'm a woman who took chances every inch of the way. I had to fight for my independence. Believe me, it wasn't easy."

"Right," Venus said. "And that's exactly why you and I understand each other so well. We both know that being a strong, successful woman in this town can be a lonely and difficult path."

"Agreed," Lucky said. "You gotta kick ass like a guy, *and* get called a bitch for your trouble."

"Ain't *that* the truth," Venus said, nodding vigorously.

"But you know something?" Lucky added. "I know who I am—and I wouldn't have it any other way."

"Me too!"

"I think we should drink to invincible women," Lucky said, raising her glass.

"You got it, sister," Venus murmured.

They clinked glasses and smiled at each other.

"I've been meaning to ask you," Lucky said. "Who's getting the apartment at The Keys, you or Billy?"

"Me, of course," Venus answered firmly. "I've already told my lawyer there's no way I'm giving it up. It's mine. Billy can go piss in the wind to get his hands on *that* piece of real estate."

"Glad to hear it. In this world you gotta claim what's yours."

"Hell, yes. The apartment is in *your* hotel, and you're *my* friend, so screw Billy."

"Right on!" Lucky said, nodding her agreement.

After coffee and more conversation—mostly about what an asshole Billy was—Lucky signaled for the check.

A young waiter who'd been watching them all night edged toward their table and presented it to her. Lucky threw down her black American Express card.

"I guess that means it's your turn," Venus said, removing a small gold compact from her oversized Chanel tote and inspecting her flawless image. She knew there'd be a pack of paparazzi waiting for her exit, and there was nothing they liked better than catching a celebrity looking like crap. She wasn't about to give them that pleasure.

The waiter hovered and cleared his throat. Although he was nervous, he saw an opportunity and he was seizing it—even if it meant getting fired should the manager catch him bothering a guest.

"Excuse me, Miz uh . . . Venus?" he ventured, stammering slightly. "I've, uh, written a script that is *so* right for you. I was, uh, hoping you might find time to read it."

Venus threw him a look—the famous cool-as-an-iced-martini look—her blue eyes raking him over.

Oh no, Lucky thought. *Here we go. The diva is on the loose.*

Venus didn't disappoint. "Do I *look* like an agent?" she purred. "*Really?*"

The waiter blanched, quickly picked up Lucky's credit card and the check, and slunk off.

"Poor guy," Lucky said sympathetically. "He was merely taking a shot."

"Well, let him take a shot elsewhere," Venus said grandly. "I can't stand being harassed when I'm trying to relax."

"Oh my God—you can be such a queen bitch!" Lucky admonished. "Wouldn't want to get on *your* wrong side."

"So be it," Venus said with a wry smile. "Shall we go?"

~ ~ ~

Seventeen-year-old Max Santangelo Golden could somehow or other wrangle her way into any club she wanted. Fake ID? No problem. Lavish tips to the doormen? No problem. Cultivating a friendship with one of the promoters? No problem.

"When it comes to getting in anywhere, I rule!" Max often boasted.

Her two closest friends, Cookie, the chocolate-skinned daughter of soul icon Gerald M., and Harry, the gay son of a TV network honcho, agreed with her. Ace, her on-again, off-again boyfriend, was not so pleased. The L.A. club scene failed to enthrall him. He wasn't into drinking, drugging, and spotting out-of-control celebrities. But Max loved every minute. Not that she drank much or did drugs, but she did get off on people-watching and dancing on tables. Music was her special thrill—especially rap and unknown British groups with wasted-looking lead singers. Oh yes, she was totally into lean and mean. Ace was way hot and sexy, but sometimes Max considered him too nice a dude, and she often craved a more edgy relationship. Besides, Ace didn't live in L.A., so he wasn't always around when she wanted to do something with him.

"Where're we goin' tonight?" Cookie asked as she sat cross-legged on her messy bed, picking at her green nail polish.

"There's a rave for some old rock group at the House of Blues," Harry said, speaking up. "S'pose we could crash if you're up for it."

Harry was the palest boy known to man, pallid-faced and skinny, with gelled and spiked hair dyed a ruthless black. It was only recently that he'd emerged from the closet, although Max and Cookie had always known and totally accepted that he was gay. He had yet to come out to his controlling father, who would probably disown him.

"No can stand the House of Blues," Max opined, her brilliant green eyes flashing disapproval. "It's always full of major wannabes. Besides, we'll never make it into the Foundation Room."

"Why not?" Cookie inquired, leaning over and reaching for a can of 7-UP balanced precariously on the edge of a table.

"Yeah, why not?" Harry repeated. "Thought you could get in anywhere."

"Anywhere I *want* to," Max answered pointedly, tossing back clouds of wavy black hair. "Who needs the freaking Foundation Room? It's always full of ancient rockers gulping down handfuls of Viagra. *So* not cool."

Cookie let forth a manic giggle. "I bet my dad takes Viagra," she said, swigging 7-UP from the can. "Bet he pops those little blue pills by the dozen."

"All old guys do," Harry said with a knowing smirk. "They can't get it up without 'em."

"Gross-out!" Cookie squealed. "Don't wanna think of my dad with a boner!"

Max decided that sometimes Cookie and Harry could be too much of a good thing. The three of them had grown up together, attended the same school, and shared some interesting, sometimes frightening, experiences, but in a way she felt she'd outgrown them. As soon as she was eighteen, she planned on making a break for New York and freedom. Not that her parents weren't great, but the two of them were a lot to live up to. Lucky, who'd achieved absolutely everything she'd ever wanted. And Lennie, a multitalented writer/director who helmed all his own independent movies. Max was tired of being referred to as their daughter. Fed up with the pressure it put on her to do something spectacular with her life.

Her big brother, Bobby, was her role model. Bobby had escaped and made his own way. He was definitely her inspiration—she adored him. Although now he had a permanent girlfriend, Denver Jones, and as much as she reluctantly admired Denver, a Deputy DA, she missed having Bobby all to herself when he was in L.A.

"Got it," Max said at last. "Whyn't we hit the Chateau for dinner? There's always something going on there."

"'S long as I don't bump into my old man," Cookie said, wrinkling her nose. "He's got himself another dumbass girlfriend, an' I think she stays at the Chateau when she's in town."

"What's the deal with this one?" Max asked.

"English, complete with uptight accent and a bug up her ever-so-tight British ass," Cookie said, making a disgusted face. "She thinks she's like the second coming of Keira Knightley. As *if*."

"Your old man sure covers the waterfront," Harry remarked, pulling up the collar of his long, Goth-like coat.

"Tell me about it," Cookie said with a weary sigh. "I've had more almost-stepmoms than you've had filthy thoughts about Chace Crawford!"

"Okay, okay," Max said, interrupting them. She was into making fast decisions, not screwing around and vacillating about what to do. "We could check out a new club that opened a couple of weeks ago. River. I'm sure we can get in."

"Let's do it," Cookie said, fiddling with the chocolate-brown dreadlocks that framed her exceptionally pretty face.

"D'you think Chace Crawford'll be there?" Harry asked hopefully.

Max threw him a look. "Calm down," she said. "Surely you know Chace Crawford is *so* into girls."

"That's what they all say," Harry muttered. "But I know better."

~ ~ ~

"Lucky has invited us to Vegas next weekend," Bobby Santangelo Stanislopoulos said, stretching his six-foot-three frame on Denver Jones's shabby-chic couch. "She's planning a party for my sister Max's eighteenth birthday, one of her big family events."

Denver regarded her boyfriend of several months with slight trepidation. Oh, man, the longish black hair, dark eyes, Greek nose, and strong jawline got her every time. If only he weren't so damn handsome. If only she hadn't harbored a crush on him since high school. If only he weren't such a fantastic lover, with all the right moves.

"Your mom intimidates me," she said at last, stroking the belly of her dog, Amy Winehouse, who lay on her back making happy sounds. Amy was a mixed breed that Denver and her ex, Josh, had found wandering on Venice Beach. They'd named the dog

Amy Winehouse because of her low, throaty growl. Plus, the fabulous Miz Winehouse was one of Denver's favorite singers.

Bobby laughed. He had a fantastic laugh. Naturally. "C'*mon*," he chided. "I'm sure Lucky thinks you're the greatest thing that ever happened to me."

Denver raised an eyebrow. "'Thing'?" she said coolly.

"Y'know what I mean."

"The problem is," Denver said, desperately searching for a suitable excuse, "I'm moving over to the drug unit next week, so there's a ton of stuff I feel I should research."

"You'll bring your laptop; that way you can do all the research you want. It's a forty-eight-hour trip, sweetheart. I'm calling for the plane."

She hated it when Bobby said things like "I'm calling for the plane." It was so elitist, so exactly who she wasn't. Some girls might get off on all the luxury, but private planes, lavish parties, and hanging with Bobby's illustrious family was not for her. Plus, she wasn't that fond of Vegas, and she hadn't told Bobby, but she hated spending time at his ultra-happening club, Mood. She especially hated the way women fawned all over him and flirted outrageously, ignoring her as if she didn't even exist.

The truth was, she loved Bobby. But she didn't love the trappings that came with him.

Bobby stretched again and yawned. "Whaddya say?"

"I say I'll think about it."

"Sounds good," he said, reaching up to pull her down on the couch beside him.

She acquiesced. It was early evening and they had no plans, so what was wrong with relaxing for the moment?

They'd been seeing each other on and off for the past three months. The on was when Bobby was in L.A. The off was when he had to spend time at his two clubs: Mood in Vegas, and Mood in New York. The on was the best of times. The off was missing him and wondering what he was doing, and trying to have some decent phone sex, which left them both in a hysterical state of laughter.

Neither of them had uttered the L word. Although they *had* conducted the talk about being exclusive.

Both of them were wary about getting too involved. Secretly they couldn't wait. But playing it semicool seemed to be the name of the game they were currently into.

Bobby began stroking her hair. Denver felt good about her hair; it was long and thick, chestnut brown with natural golden highlights. She knew that her hair was one of her best features, along with her widely spaced hazel eyes and full lips. If she lived in any other big city, she'd be considered a ten. In L.A. she felt she barely made it as a seven.

She was wrong.

Bobby's hands moved down to her breasts, and with a quick move under her T-shirt, he released her bra and began playing with her nipples. Oh yes, unusual for a woman in L.A., her breasts were actually real.

Sighing with anticipation, she leaned into him. It made no difference that they'd already made love in the morning. Desire was desire, and they were both in the mood.

Sometimes she couldn't help wondering how long it would last. Her previous serious boyfriend, Josh, had been a pretty decent lover for the first six months of their three-year relationship, then after that it was a total slump.

"What're you thinking?" Bobby whispered in her ear, giving her a little tongue action at the same time.

"That's such a girly question," she murmured, fiddling with the zipper on his jeans.

"You calling me a girl?" he asked, mock serious.

"You do have *some* female tendencies," she teased.

"Like *what*?" he responded, challenging her to come up with something.

"Oh," she said vaguely, dragging his jeans down, delighted to find that he wasn't wearing underwear. "You have soft lips . . ."

"All the better to kiss you with." And with one swift movement, he flipped her so she was trapped beneath him. "Soft lips and a hard cock," he joked. "How female is *that*?"

"Bobby!" she exclaimed.

Then the banter stopped and the passion began. He had a way of making love to her that forced her to lose every inhibition she'd ever possessed. One moment he was slowly caressing her, the next he was all hard-driving action. The combination drove her nuts. She wanted more and more and more . . .

When it was over, they were spent, wrapped up in each other's arms, sleepy and content.

Denver often wished that those precious times would last forever. Just the two of them. No outside world to interfere.

But the outside world was a big presence, and they both lived in it. Tomorrow Bobby was driving to Vegas before flying to New York for a few meetings. And she had her job, which right now was especially exciting and challenging since she was transferring to the drug unit. Once more they would be separated.

The good news was that she loved her job. It was grueling work, but the end results were incredibly rewarding. She was so glad she'd changed tracks. From working at a high-powered law firm as a defense attorney, she'd scored a job as a Deputy DA, prosecuting people, and she was thrilled with the switch. Why defend the probably guilty (one of her high-profile cases was a movie star who'd arranged his wife's murder, then walked; he was the catalyst for her change of plan) when she could be doing meaningful work—such as putting the bad guys behind bars? How rewarding to go after the dregs who distributed drugs and got kids hooked at an early age. Talk about job satisfaction!

"Hey," Bobby said, "wanna catch a movie and grab a pizza?"

Yes, that's exactly what she wanted to do. Normal activities with her man.

If only things could stay that way.

CHAPTER TWO

Prince Armand Mohamed Jordan rarely used his full title, only when he visited the country of his birth, Akramshar, a small but wealthy Middle Eastern country located somewhere between Syria and Lebanon.

As a naturalized American, and a mega-successful business-man, he felt it more prudent to keep his title to himself, decid-ing it wasn't business-savvy to advertise his heritage.

Most of the people he dealt with knew him only as Armand Jordan, a sometimes ruthless and extremely powerful man who expected everything to go his way and usually got his wish. None of his business associates was aware that his father was King Emir Amin Mohamed Jordan, a man who ruled his small oil-rich country with a stern fist. A man with six current wives and sixteen children.

Armand was suspicious of friendship. The only person he trusted was Fouad Khan, the right-hand man whom he'd im-ported from Akramshar many years previously. Fouad knew all of Armand's secrets and kept them to himself. He was Armand's sounding board and confidant, always there to do his bidding.

Fortunately or unfortunately for Armand, he was the king's ninth son, and therefore considered not at all important. So when his American mother—Peggy, a former Las Vegas dancer— had begged to take her son back to America when he was eight, the king had offered no objections. King Emir was bored with the leggy American redhead and her strident accent. Happy to see her go. And much as Peggy had enjoyed the adventure of living in a harem and being lavished with expensive gifts, enough was enough, and she knew it was time to return to civilization. At twenty-six, she had the rest of her life ahead of her, and she planned to live it. The king's only request was that the boy be returned every September to Akramshar so that young Armand could celebrate the king's birthday—the most important day of the year in Akramshar.

Peggy complied. The cash payoff she received was compensation enough for her to do anything the king required.

So Peggy and her son relocated to New York, and Armand soon adapted to the American way of life. It didn't take him long to love everything about America. The endless TV shows full of fun and adventure, the violent action-packed movies, the loud, vibrant music, and the girls. Ah yes, especially the girls; they were far more forward than the girls in Akramshar.

Every September his mother dutifully put him on a plane back to Akramshar, and for several weeks he played the role of a young prince, mingling with the half brothers and sisters he barely knew anymore. They failed to get along.

The juxtaposition of his two lives was exciting. It made him feel special, different from the other kids who attended his private school in Manhattan. He was a prince, and they were nothing. He felt superior to all of them.

When he was thirteen, on one of his yearly visits to Akramshar, his father had taken him aside and informed him it was time he became a man. Immediately, one of the king's minions had ushered him into a room where two prostitutes lounged on a bed waiting for the young prince.

The following experience with the two older women left an indelible impression on Armand. Although he'd fooled around with girls at school, this encounter was quite different. The prostitutes—one Russian, one Dutch—were in their twenties and heavily made up. They wore sexy lingerie and high-heeled shoes, and they introduced him to a variety of sexual acts, some of which he enjoyed, some of which disgusted him. When they felt he was fully initiated, they informed him that all sexual acts should be paid for. Not that they were asking him for money— the king's people had already taken care of them—it was simply something they thought he should be aware of. "Women have to be paid for sex," they said, exchanging amused glances. They were words of wisdom he never forgot.

When he emerged several hours later, his older brothers jeered and laughed at him. He'd ended up fighting one of them, and had gotten a broken nose for his trouble. He hated his siblings. They were all jealous of him because he was different.

His mother remarried a month after his eighteenth birthday. This time Peggy chose wisely: she married Sidney Dunn, a very successful investment banker twenty-five years her senior.

Armand respected Sidney. He felt he could learn a lot from the old man, and learn he did. He chose to get a business degree, and Sidney was always there with his wise counsel.

On Armand's twenty-first birthday, the king summoned him

to Akramshar for a special visit. Armand went—reluctantly, for surely once a year was enough. However, it turned out to be a memorable trip, because the king's closest adviser informed Armand that in the future the king might—from time to time—need him to take care of various business transactions in America.

Armand, eager to please his father, agreed. And as a twenty-first birthday gift, the king presented him with a check for a million dollars, money he immediately put to good use. On Sidney's advice, he invested in a parcel of derelict buildings in Queens, which a year later he turned into several apartment complexes, eventually selling them and tripling his initial investment.

After that there was no stopping him. He formed Jordan Developments and began buying up properties, renovating them, and selling them for a large profit. He was also taking care of business for his father, who needed large sums of money legitimized. Apart from Jordan Developments, he formed several subsidiary companies, including an import/export business that he had nothing to do with except in name. By the time he reached the age of thirty, he was acquiring hotels and apartment houses up and down the East Coast.

On his yearly visit to Akramshar, his father looked on him kindly and beamed with pride. "You are the son I can be proud of," the king boasted. "You are smart, and clever, and trustworthy. You are the son who one day should be inheriting my kingdom."

These words did not sit well with his half brothers, who now regarded him with suspicion and, even more, hatred.

But one thing puzzled the king. "Why have you never married?"

he demanded. "At your age it is tradition that a man should have many wives and children."

Armand shrugged. To him, a relationship was a distraction he didn't need. His sexual desires were fully met by a series of call girls who serviced his every whim whenever he picked up the phone and summoned them. Women were inferior human beings, something his father had taught him at a very early age. "Females are merely vessels to be used for gratifying one's sexual urges and bearing children," the king had informed him. "Never trust them. And never give them your heart."

His father was right. Women would do anything for money— absolutely anything. And they were stupid creatures too.

A year after his father questioned his marital status, he'd arrived in Akramshar for the usual birthday celebrations, and the king had immediately whisked him off to one of his private palaces. Once there, the king had announced that Armand's birthday gift to him would be to marry the daughter of a close family friend with whom the king conducted business. "You'll have no responsibilities," the king had assured him. "Your wife will stay here and, God willing, bear your offspring. This is my desire for you, my dear son. This is my gift."

The girl was fifteen and a beauty. Her name was Soraya.

Later that day there was a lavish wedding ceremony, and that night Armand deflowered the innocent Soraya. She was trembling and scared, which didn't faze him because he had no intention of going against his father's wishes. Her nervousness was not his problem. She was there to do his bidding, and that was that. He rode her hard, ignoring her startled cries of pain. She was merely a vessel for him to fill, and that was the extent of her usefulness.

A week after his wedding ceremony he flew back to America.

Upon returning to Akramshar one year later, he was surprised to discover that he had a son. Eleven years later he had fathered three more children, all girls, which didn't particularly please him, but it made the king happy.

In his mind he regarded Soraya and her brood as his fantasy family. They lived in a place called Akramshar. A place where women were docile and obedient and did as they were told. A place where men ruled.

He lived in a Park Avenue penthouse in New York, where money was his aphrodisiac and women were his paid playthings. The two worlds only came together in September, when the king celebrated his birthday. And that was as it should be.

Now Armand was forty-two and becoming restless. He'd conquered the East Coast, and he desired more. His latest plans were to cement a firm position in Las Vegas, a city he'd spent some time in. He was an avid gambler, and the call girls in Vegas were raunchy and used to fulfilling any request, however decadent. Besides, he had family ties in Vegas. His mother had danced at Caesars Palace, and the king had spotted her there and whisked her back to Akramshar. Family ties had to mean something.

His people had done a financial analysis of most of the big hotels. While Steve Wynn's empire was intriguing and lucrative, and the Palms, the Four Seasons, and the Harrah's hotel groups were a possibility, the hotel complex he'd finally decided he had to have was The Keys.

Yes, The Keys was perfect. A magnificent structure built to extremely high standards less than two years previously. Not Vegas flashy, but incredibly luxurious and classy. A stunning casino. World-class restaurants and stores. Exquisite gardens, and park-like grounds. A magnificent apartment complex. Multiple swimming pools. Two spas. A man-made lake. A lush golf course. And then there was the hotel itself.

The Keys was it for Armand.

He wanted it, and therefore he would have it.

CHAPTER THREE

By the time she drove her distinctive red Ferrari down Pico and along P.C.H. to Malibu, Lucky had forgotten about Venus and her man-related issues. Her mind was more focused on Max and her imminent departure. Lucky was wise enough to realize that there was no holding her smart, gorgeous, green-eyed daughter back. Max was going out on her own whether Lucky and Lennie liked it or not. And the truth was, Lucky didn't like it, but there was nothing she could do. As everyone was quick to point out, she herself had been running wild at sixteen. After she ditched her strict Swiss boarding school and took off to the South of France, Gino had tracked her down and hurriedly married her off to the irritating and boring Craven Richmond— Senator Peter Richmond's son. Craven was a weak loser whom she hadn't loved, and even worse, had no respect for. But she'd refused to be trapped. She'd bided her time, and when Gino left the country on a tax exile, she'd broken all ties with the

Richmond family and swiftly moved in to take over Gino's lucrative hotel business. She'd succeeded, gotten a divorce, and
never looked back.

Now Max was ready to fly, but did her only daughter possess
the street smarts to survive all the sharks who'd be circling
such a major catch? And if Max chose to move to New York, how
was Lucky supposed to protect her?

"You're not," Lennie had informed her, always the voice of
reason. "You gotta let Max go. She's ready to make her own mistakes and learn from them."

Even Gino agreed. "Let her loose, kid," he'd said. "She'll find
her feet just like you did."

So be it.

Even though it was past midnight, Max was not home.

Determined not to worry, Lucky picked up the phone and
called Lennie, who was on location in Utah. They talked for a
while; he soothed her fears about Max, told her not to obsess
and that he'd see her in Vegas for the birthday party.

Lucky decided that for once she'd listen.

One big Vegas party, coming up. And after that she'd send
Max on her way with her blessing and hope that everything
worked out.

~ ~ ~

"Frankie?" Max yelled, making a wild dash toward the guy emerging from a Grand Sport convertible Corvette. "Is it really you?"

Frankie Romano stopped mid-stride, slowly lowering his mirrored Ray-Bans—an unnecessary accessory because it was dark
out. The shades were merely an affectation.

"Jesus!" he exclaimed, after scrutinizing her up and down. "Little Max?"

"Not so little anymore," she answered boldly, remembering the last time she'd seen her brother's friend, the irascible Frankie Romano. He was thinner than she remembered, but his outfit was cool—all leather, retro shades covering his eyes, his dark hair pulled back into a tight ponytail. Very L.A.

She gestured toward the entrance of the new club, where a restless gathering of girls dressed to seduce and a rowdy bunch of guys hoping to get laid attempted to talk their way past three burly security doormen. "Can you get me and my friends in?" she asked, throwing Frankie a winning smile.

"Hey," Frankie said, with a nod of his head, "if I can't, nobody can. Follow me."

Max grabbed Cookie's and Harry's arms, and without hesitation, they marched in behind Frankie.

The doorman gave Frankie a respectful salute.

"Wow!" Max exclaimed, suitably impressed. "They're acting as if you own the place or something."

"I do," Frankie boasted, although not truthfully. "It's mine, all mine."

Max widened her eyes. The last she'd heard of Frankie, he'd been dumped by Annabelle Maestro, his longtime girlfriend, and was looking for a job. Now he claimed to own this happening new L.A. club. She wondered if Bobby was aware of it, because as far as she could recall, the two of them had fallen out due to Frankie's over-the-top drug habit. Too bad. She'd always sort of liked Frankie in a weird way, even though he'd tried to letch after her when she was sixteen and staying with Bobby in New York.

"Does Bobby know you're in the club business?" she asked as Frankie guided them straight to a booth.

"You think Bobby has dibs on running clubs?" Frankie responded, his left eye twitching beneath his shades. "I was deejaying before he ever got into the whole club scene. I would've given him a chance to invest in River, but we've been out of touch. His loss."

"Guess he missed out," Max said vaguely, checking out the club, which resembled a poor rip-off of Mood.

"Since your brother hooked up with that lawyer bitch, you gotta know he's totally pussy-whipped," Frankie said gruffly. "She's got his balls in a clench. Came between us big time."

"I thought it was—"

"What?" Frankie said, shooting her a sharp look.

"Nothing," she mumbled, biting down on her bottom lip. Bobby had told her that Frankie's addiction to coke was not something he could deal with anymore, especially since Denver was a Deputy DA.

"So . . . little Max, all grown up," Frankie said, moving close, his thigh pressing up against her leg. "Haven't seen you in a while. How've you been?"

"Amazing," Max replied, edging away because the last thing she needed was Frankie coming on to her.

"You're looking hot," he continued. "Smokin' hot."

"Thanks," she said, feeling uncomfortable. Was he stoned? Probably.

"Wow!" Cookie exclaimed. "This place is totally bangin'."

Frankie turned his attention to her. "You like?" he said. "I designed the place myself." Another lie.

"We like," Cookie answered, nudging Harry while wondering how old Frankie was, and if he was too old for her. "Can we score a drink?"

"You got it," Frankie said, snapping his fingers, grabbing the attention of a half-naked waitress with long talonlike nails and a fixed smile. "You all have your fake ID's on you, I hope."

"Wouldn't be without them," Cookie replied, licking her generous lips and fluttering her purple-tipped eyelashes.

"That's what I like to hear," Frankie said, thinking that this one might be young, but she was certainly ready.

And what the hell? Young was his flavor of the night.

~ ~ ~

Pizza and a movie turned out to be sushi at Matsuhisa, a favorite of Denver's.

"I love this restaurant," she said, helping herself to a California roll.

"Why do you think I chose it?" Bobby said, reaching for her hand across the table.

"'Cause you wanted to surprise me?"

"Ah, but she's so smart," he said, dazzling her with one of his special smiles.

"And she's dressed for pizza and a movie," Denver said ruefully.

"*And* she looks gorgeous," he assured her.

"Thanks, Bobby," she said, taking a sip of warm sake.

"For what?"

"For always making me feel good."

"That's easy."

"It is?"

"You *know* it is."

"Don't *you* always know the right thing to say."

"Speaking of the right thing—you *are* coming to Vegas with me next weekend for Max's party, yes?"

"I . . . I'm going to try," she said, still hesitant.

"Whaddya mean, try?"

"Well . . . y'know, work . . ."

"I told you," he said insistently, "we'll go Friday, come back Sunday. You won't miss a thing."

"You have to understand, Bobby, transferring to the drug unit is kind of a big deal. I want to be fully prepared."

"Like I said, you'll bring your laptop. We'll have plenty of downtime."

"Can I think about it?" she asked tentatively.

"She'll think about it," he said, exasperated. "Have I ever told you you're one stubborn woman?"

"Simply because I don't say yes to you all the time . . ."

"No, you don't, do you?" he said, giving her a long, intent look. "Is that why I like you?"

"Hmm," she said thoughtfully. "I guess you're used to women saying yes at all times."

Bobby started to laugh. "What *women* did you have in mind?"

"Remember high school? You and M.J. had it all going on. Girls falling out of trees."

"Oh c'mon, Denver," he said with a quizzical expression. "Now we're reverting to high school? How come you're remembering that now?"

"'Cause watching Mister Football Star score was the main entertainment of the day."

"Then aren't I glad it's all behind me, an' now I've got you."

"Really?" she teased. "You've got me, have you?"

"Don't I?" he said, grinning. "We've been together *how* long?"

"I dunno," she said, knowing exactly how long. "Three months, maybe."

Bobby shook his head. "'Maybe,' she says! You're supposed to tell me to the minute."

"I am, huh?"

"Yes, you am."

They smiled at each other, savoring the moment.

One of the reasons she enjoyed spending time with Bobby was because they always had so much to talk about. He often regaled her with stories about his deceased father's family, who all resided in Greece, apart from his niece, Brigette. Brigette lived in New York and had once been a top model. Along with Bobby, Brigette had inherited most of the Stanislopoulos fortune. Although he was uncomfortable talking about money, Bobby had informed her that he'd chosen not to touch his inheritance, preferring to make his own money from the success of his clubs.

She admired him for his desire to make it on his own. Only occasionally did he indulge in any kind of extravagance—such as using the Stanislopoulos plane.

Sometimes she told him stories about *her* family, a family he still hadn't met. She was reticent about introducing him to her political activist mother and maverick lawyer father. Not to mention her three brothers. They'd all been very fond of her ex, Josh, and she didn't think she should add Bobby into the mix until she was sure they'd stay together for longer than a few months.

Bobby laughed about it. "Not good enough to meet your family, huh?" he teased.

"You will," she assured him.

And yes, one day she would definitely bring him to meet them. But not yet. It was too soon.

"Bobby!" an exceptionally pretty model type exclaimed, stopping by their table. "Oh my *God!* I haven't seen you since Graydon's party in New York. How *are* you? What are you doing in L.A.?"

"Uh . . . hey," Bobby managed. He didn't have a clue who she was, and he didn't much care. "Do you two know each other?" he said, gesturing toward Denver.

The girl threw Denver a cursory glance, then proceeded to ignore her. "We must get together," she purred, leaning toward Bobby. "I miss you. Call me, I'm at the Mondrian."

Then she tottered off on her six-inch heels, looking pleased with herself.

"Nice," Denver remarked.

"I swear I don't know who she is," Bobby insisted.

"That's okay," Denver said, determined not to throw a jealous fit over nothing. "I have exes too."

"She's not an ex," he said firmly. "No idea w*ho* she is."

"It doesn't matter, Bobby."

"No, it doesn't," he agreed. "All that matters is that I'm sitting here with you."

The thing about Bobby Santangelo Stanislopoulos was that he always knew the right thing to say.

~ ~ ~

Max was ready to go, and so was Harry, but Cookie was putting up a fight. "I wanna stay," she said stubbornly. "Frankie'll look out for me."

"You can't stay," Max argued. "We're in Harry's car."

"I'll get a ride," Cookie said.

"Oh, like who you gonna get a ride from?" Max snapped.

Cookie shrugged. "I'm sure Frankie'll drive me home."

"For shit's sake!" Max exclaimed. "Don't you know that all Frankie wants is to get into your pants?"

"So?" answered Cookie with a slightly tipsy smile. "Is that such a bad thing?"

They were arguing in the booth several mojitos later. Frankie was off meeting and greeting, playing the genial host, and Max wasn't feeling it. She wanted out. So did Harry.

"We can't leave you here by yourself," Max said, looking to Harry for some support.

"I told you, Frankie'll look after me," Cookie said, leaning back in the booth.

"Frankie's a cokehead, an' he's old," Harry sneered. "You don't wanna hit that."

"He's *so* not old, an' he's hot," Cookie insisted. "You two better get the fuck outta here, 'cause *I'm* stayin'."

Max decided not to argue. She knew what Frankie was like, and if Cookie was intent on taking that road, there was nothing she could do about it. Cookie was hardly a virgin; she'd been around Hollywood all her young life.

"Whatever you do, don't screw him," Max warned. "He's not someone you wanna hang with. Believe me, I *know*."

"Thanks for the advice," Cookie responded sarcastically. "I'll call you guys later."

"You do that," Max said, checking her watch. It was already two A.M. "An' don't do anything you'll regret," she added.

"Good-bye." Cookie giggled. "Shift your asses outta here."

Max grabbed Harry's arm. "You cool to drive?" He nodded. "Then let's go."

Sometimes one had to quit on an argument one wasn't about

to win, something her dad, Lennie, had taught her when she was five.

She'd learned a lot from both her parents, and there were times she appreciated their wisdom. But still, she couldn't wait to get out on her own.

CHAPTER FOUR

Freedom suited Billy Melina just fine. Being married to a superstar was a major kick for about fifteen minutes, but after a few months of everyone worshipping at her feet, the thrill was gone. *He* was a huge movie star, but when he was out with Venus, nobody gave a crap. This was not a big ego booster. Oh no, not at all.

When Billy wasn't with Venus, the attention came fast and furious. Girls galore. Fans everywhere. Respect from agents, managers, and lawyers who realized his potential. After all, he had only just hit thirty; his entire career lay ahead of him, and his latest release was already breaking box office records.

Billy was over six feet tall, with bleached-by-the-sun hair and a surfer's tan all over his ripped and taut body. Abs were his thing. He worked out two hours a day to make sure they were rippling perfection. He liked seeing himself in the magazines under the heading BEST BODY ON THE BEACH. Eat your heart out, Matthew McConaughey. Go crap yourself, The Situation. Billy Melina was King of the Abs. And with his upcoming divorce from the Queen of the Divas, he—along with his soon-to-be ex—was currently on the cover of every magazine.

Covers were satisfying. Covers validated his existence. Covers gave him a positive vibe.

So did blow jobs. There was nothing like a polished blow job to put a smile on his face. Lately, now that he was free, his big kick was picking up some random girl, taking her back to his rented house, and having her blow him out by the pool. There was something about strange lips enclosing his cock, with the shimmering blue of the swimming pool in the background and the sun beating down on his body, that really got him off.

Venus was under the impression that he'd hooked up with his recent costar Willow Price—a bodacious young blonde with pillowy lips and a burgeoning career. But that was not the case. Willow was good to be seen with at parties and award shows, but they were in no way involved. Willow preferred her sex served lesbian-style, and he was not attracted to her, so being seen together suited them both.

Feeling horny, Billy hopped on his Harley and set off on a hunt.

It didn't take him long to find exactly what he was looking for. The girl he spotted was walking along Melrose wearing a denim skirt that barely covered c-level, a skimpy tee with *I Like It Fast and Sweet* emblazoned across the front, and wedge-heeled sandals.

"Yo," he greeted her, pulling up alongside her on his bike. "Didn't I see you last night at Soho House?"

She stopped, checked him out, recognized him, and couldn't

believe her luck. Twenty minutes later she was in front of him, on her knees beside his pool, servicing him as best she could.

When it was done, he called her a cab and sent her on her way.

Billy never had any trouble finding girls.

~ ~ ~

Breakfast in Malibu was Lucky's favorite time of day. She loved to sit out on the deck overlooking the ocean with a glass of fresh orange juice and a dish of cut-up papayas, figs, and mangos. Since she was an early riser, always up before the rest of her family, she took advantage of the solitude. Early morning was her time for making plans, deciding what she wanted to do next. Right now everything about The Keys satisfied her. Even Gino was impressed with what she had managed to achieve. She'd built the ultimate prize, the most magnificent complex in Vegas, encompassing everything from a major casino to a one-of-a-kind hotel and luxury condominiums. "Put in a racetrack an' you're all set," Gino had joked.

She'd smiled. Not such a bad idea. But then Gino always thought big.

She decided that her next project would be persuading Lennie to take a well-deserved break. He was such a workaholic, skipping from one movie to the next. They had a fantastic marriage, but spending more time together would not be a bad thing. There were days and nights she really missed him.

Her cell rang. It was her New York attorney, Jeffrey Lonsdale.

"Yes, Jeffrey, what's up?" she asked, wondering why he was calling her so early.

"Have you been putting out the word that you want to sell The Keys?" Jeffrey inquired.

"*What?*" she said, frowning. "Why would you say that?"

"Because I keep getting calls from a man representing Jordan Developments. He claims you're prepared to sell, and that Jordan Developments is ready to buy."

"That's total bullshit," Lucky said. "And who the hell is Jordan Developments?"

"A big real estate company. I'm looking into it. Just needed to make sure."

"Jeffrey," Lucky said patiently, "surely you know that if I were prepared to sell, you would be the first to know."

"Of course. But Fouad Khan, the Jordan Developments representative, seemed very sure and very persistent."

"Well, tell Mr. Khan to go persist elsewhere. The Keys is not for sale. Not now or ever."

"Message received loud and clear."

"Glad to hear it."

"I must say, Lucky, I thought it had to be a joke. Everyone knows you put your heart and soul into building that complex, so I was certain there was no chance you'd be putting it on the market."

"You got that right."

"I'm glad we've cleared that up."

"We have."

"Then enjoy your day."

"You too, Jeffrey."

"Unfortunately, it's raining in New York."

"Sorry to tell you, but it's brilliant sunshine here," she said, gazing out at the vast expanse of blue ocean.

"Ah, Lucky, you always know how to stick it to me."

"You're the lawyer," she said, smiling. "You should be used to people sticking it to you."

"Trust *you* to point that out."

"You're flying to Vegas for the board meeting on Friday, you'll get plenty of sunshine then."

"In a boardroom?" Jeffrey said dryly.

"Stay the weekend," Lucky suggested. "I'm throwing a birthday party for Max. It'll be fun."

"Maybe."

"Not maybe, Jeffrey. Say yes. Bring your wife."

"We're getting a divorce."

"Then bring your girlfriend."

"I don't have one."

"Okay, okay, enough about your love life. But if you do decide to stay over, let my assistant know. He'll take excellent care of you."

She clicked off the phone, thinking what a crazy way to start the day.

The Keys was her ultimate achievement. She would never sell. Never.

~ ~ ~

Bobby got up early and left the apartment before Denver was awake. He had an important meeting in Vegas with Russian investors who, according to his partner, M.J., were ready to close on a deal to put up all the money for branches of Mood in Miami and L.A. He'd decided to personally show them the star that was Mood, Las Vegas. The Russians were not easy to deal with, but they were the ones with the money to do things the way he wanted. After finishing with the Russians, he had more meetings in New York, then after that he'd hop a plane and be back in time to pick up Denver and take her for a romantic Vegas weekend.

He was getting in way deep with Denver. The more time he spent with her, the better he liked her. She was so damn normal, and smarter than any girl he'd been with. *And* she was beautiful—inside and out. There was an incandescent quality about her that he couldn't get enough of.

He wanted her to spend more time with Lucky, so that the two of them could get to know each other. It was important to him that his mom approve of the girl he was becoming serious about. Not that he'd told Lucky anything; it was up to her to discover how great Denver was, and the birthday party weekend would be the perfect time.

The next step he planned was buying a house in L.A. where they could live together. Denver's apartment was too small for him. He needed more space. He'd brought the subject up a couple of times, whereupon she'd informed him that it was too soon to think of living together.

"But sweetheart, I live here when I'm in L.A.," he'd pointed out.

"No, you *stay* here," she'd corrected. "That's not the same as living together."

Man, she could be difficult. Most girls would go nuts if he offered to buy a house for them. But part of Denver's charm was that she was not most girls, and that was another thing he loved about her.

Flooring his new silver Lamborghini Murciélago LP 640, he blasted Jay-Z and headed for Vegas.

~ ~ ~

"I fail to understand your problem," Denver's best friend, Carolyn, said, rocking the stroller next to her in the garden of her small West Hollywood house, situated behind Pavilions supermarket on a quiet street. "Bobby is a fantastic guy, and it's blatantly obvious he's wild about you."

"You think?" Denver said, sipping from a mug of coffee.

"I *know*," Carolyn responded, pushing back a lock of honey-blond hair. "He's great, and he's been so nice to me."

"Why wouldn't he be?" Denver said, placing her coffee mug on a rickety outdoor table. "Let's not forget you were caught in a terrifying situation. Kidnapped, taken hostage, and pregnant . . ."

"Then along came you and Bobby like the cavalry—rescuing my sorry ass," Carolyn said, making light of what had been a very perilous situation.

"Couldn't have done it without Bobby," Denver said. "He was a big help."

"Without the two of you . . ." Carolyn trailed off, trying not to think about the ordeal she'd survived. Working in Washington as an assistant to the very married Senator Gregory Stoneman, she'd become involved in a torrid affair with him. Just like most married men, the senator had promised to leave his wife, but of course he'd had no intention of doing so. And when Carolyn had informed him that she was pregnant, he'd panicked, and set up her kidnapping in the hope that she would lose the baby. Thank God for Denver and Bobby; they'd found her just in time.

After spending a few days in a hospital recovering, she'd fled Washington to L.A. She gave birth to her baby—a boy she'd named Andy—and vowed that she would never speak to Senator Stoneman again. Not that he was exactly running after her; she hadn't heard a word since she'd left. And she didn't care. Andy was all hers. She would never allow Gregory anywhere near her son.

"My problem is Bobby's mom," Denver ventured, anxious to vent her feelings. "She's so . . . well, how can I describe her?"

"Go ahead and try," Carolyn said briskly.

"For a start, she's drop-dead beautiful," Denver began, attempting to paint an accurate portrait of the incredible Lucky Santangelo. "I mean, she's tall, olive-skinned, with incredible dark eyes and hair. She's an absolute knockout in a very earthy Italian way."

"What's so bad about that?" Carolyn remarked. "She certainly passed on the good genes to Bobby."

"She's also extremely accomplished," Denver continued, wondering how she could possibly live up to the force of nature that was Lucky Santangelo. "She builds her own hotels, once ran a major movie studio. She gave birth to three children, and if that isn't enough, she's an insane cook, does everything herself, and has a long-lasting and apparently very happy marriage to Lennie Golden."

"The movie star?"

"He was. Now he writes and directs extremely successful independent movies."

"Sounds as if *Bobby* has a lot to live up to."

"Lennie's not his father," Denver explained, picking up her coffee mug. "I thought I told you—his father is a deceased Greek billionaire ship owner. Hence the company plane whenever Bobby wants it. Something else to intimidate me."

"Stop it, Denver," Carolyn said firmly. "Nothing should intimidate you."

"So," Denver said, grimacing, "Bobby's mom is perfect and I'm not."

"Oh my *God!*" Carolyn said, throwing up her hands in exasperation. "Will you listen to yourself?"

"*What?*" Denver said, aggravated that Carolyn wasn't getting it.

"*You're* incredible, Denver. You have a terrific career doing something meaningful. You're young, smart, and beautiful, *and* you have a great boyfriend." Carolyn paused for a moment, then added, "It's a given that your cooking skills are nil. But I've got a strong suspicion Bobby is not with you for your culinary assets."

Denver couldn't help laughing. "I'm not beautiful, and I'm not so young anymore, but I *am* smart," she admitted.

"Oh yeah," Carolyn said. "Twenty-seven is *really* getting up there. And let me correct you—your beauty is not magazine perfect, it's warm and natural, made all the better 'cause you damn well have no clue how great-looking you are."

"Thanks, but you should see the girls that hang out in Bobby's club. Not to mention the ones that come up to him when we're out. They're all over him."

"What do you care? He's with you, isn't he?"

"I guess . . ."

"She guesses," Carolyn exclaimed, rolling her eyes. "The man is crazy for you; everyone knows it. And about those random girls? Let me take a shot—size zero 'cause they never eat. Huge boobs—fake. Huge lips—fake. High cheekbones—fake. And—"

"Stop!" Denver said, breaking into laughter. "They're in the entertainment business; they have to look their best."

"Bull!" Carolyn exclaimed. "And don't take this personally, but I'm changing the subject to *me*."

"Good," Denver responded. "What's up with you?"

"I've decided to become gay," Carolyn announced.

Denver choked on her coffee. "What?" she spluttered. "You can't just *decide* to become gay. It's something you're either into or you're not."

"I'm into it," Carolyn said matter-of-factly. "Met this lovely woman at yoga. She's invited me out on a date. So guess what? I'm going."

"Why would you do that?"

"Because I'm off men forever. First I was with Matt, who cheated on me. Then Gregory, who turned out to be a lying, despicable piece of crap. I've had it with the male sex—I don't want anything to do with them anymore. Not so hard to understand, right?"

"Well . . ." Denver began, but before she could say anything else, Andy began to cry, and glancing at her watch, she realized that if she didn't get a move on, she'd be late for work.

"Then you think I should go to Vegas?" she asked, grabbing her car keys and hurrying toward the door.

"Damn right you should," Carolyn said, reaching down to pick up her son.

"Okay, I'll do it," Denver said, deciding that she definitely would. "And you have fun with . . . uh . . . who?"

"Vanessa," Carolyn said, smiling. "And yes, I promise I will."

~ ~ ~

Groping for her cell while still asleep was nothing new for Max. "What?" she mumbled into her BlackBerry.

"Guess where *I* am?" came the whispered reply.

"Cookie?"

"Yes, it's me," Cookie giggled. "Little ole me."

Max opened one eye. "Where are you?" she asked, although she had a horrible suspicion that she already knew the answer.

"Guess!"

"Don't wanna guess," Max said irritably, kicking off her duvet. "Where the fuck are you?"

"I'm in Frankie's bed, and it was *amazing!*" Cookie sighed. "Like, totally random, amazing sex!"

"Crap!" Max exclaimed, sitting up. "You didn't screw him, did you?"

"Course I did," Cookie said with a triumphant giggle.

"*Oh my God!*" Max scolded. "You're not supposed to screw someone like Frankie."

"Why not?"

"'Cause you're just not. He's way too sketchy, *and* a total druggie."

"But it was *soooo* great," Cookie enthused. "Wanna hear the sex-drenched details?"

"No thank you," Max said primly. "I'd rather not."

"You're no fun," Cookie complained. "I'm gonna hav'ta call Harry. He's *so* into details."

"Do that."

Jeez! Frankie Romano, Bobby's former drug-addict best friend, and Cookie. This was not welcome news. And it was all her fault because she should never have left Cookie at the club. Frankie was a certified lowlife who'd been running call girls with his previous girlfriend, Annabelle Maestro. He'd use Cookie, cast her aside, and the fallout would be a total pain. She'd have to listen to Cookie moan and groan for weeks on end.

What a bummer! Why had she gone and hooked them up with Frankie simply to get into his stupid club? She should've known better.

Grabbing an oversized T-shirt, she fell out of bed, wondering what she could do to rectify the situation.

Unfortunately, nothing came to mind.

~ ~ ~

Bobby was all business as he pulled into the private parking sector of The Keys. M.J., who was not only his business partner but also his closest confidant, came strolling over to greet him. They exchanged a macho hug.

M.J. was African American and handsome, although slightly short. He was married to Cassie, a young singer with big ambitions. They'd gotten married in Vegas on a whim, and now, just under a year later, Cassie was pregnant. M.J., who'd moved to Vegas from New York to oversee the launch of Mood, was delighted. Cassie was not. At almost nineteen, she wanted a career, not a baby. M.J.'s affluent parents—his father was a renowned neurosurgeon and his mother a former opera singer—were perched on the sidelines, waiting to see what happened next. Cassie was not the girl they'd envisioned for their only son, nor was a career opening nightclubs, however successful they might be.

M.J. didn't care. He was crazy about his young wife, but now with a baby on the way, there was a catch, something he couldn't wait to discuss with Bobby.

"Great wheels!" M.J. exclaimed, checking out Bobby's Lamborghini.

Bobby nodded. "Yeah—since I've been spending so much time on the West Coast, I decided I needed to buy me a car. It can get up to two hundred eleven miles per hour, man. It's insane, and I love every minute of it. Denver doesn't."

"No shit," M.J. said, walking around the car, giving it a full inspection. "I wonder why."

"Thinks it's too flashy and fast."

"Well, bro, low-key it ain't."

They laughed and exchanged an enthusiastic fist pump.

"How *is* your low-key girlfriend?" M.J. asked as they entered the enormous glass-enclosed lobby. "Still putting away bad guys?"

"Denver's great," Bobby said. "She's a special kind of girl."

"I'm gettin' you feel that way. I've never seen you so caught up."

"What can I tell you?" Bobby said with a big grin. "The woman makes me happy."

"And that, my man, is all that matters."

"Right on!"

"An' talking of happy," M.J. said, "I got some news of my own."

"Wanna tell me?"

"Cassie's pregnant."

"Jeez, M.J. You ready for that?"

"Ready as I'll ever be."

"Told your parents yet?"

"Haven't got around to it, but I will."

"You'd better."

"Don't think I don't know it."

"They'll be happy for you."

"Yeah?"

"Sure they will. Now let's go kick some investor butt. And later we gotta get together an' celebrate."

CHAPTER FIVE

Once Armand Jordan decided he wanted something, there was no going back, whether it be a woman, an unobtainable painting, a special delicacy, a one-of-a-kind car, or a building. Nobody ever said no to Armand, and if they did, he merely upped the price.

Usually he favored high-class call girls—hookers had tricks that other women did not possess. Little tricks. Dirty tricks. Filthy things a man can only dream about.

Once in a while he came across a woman who was *not* for sale. This did not faze Armand, for they all had a price. And sometimes it wasn't monetary.

On occasion it intrigued him to discover what that price might be. It was a game he played for his own enjoyment, and when Armand played, he played to win.

His latest conquest was Nona Constantine, the wife of Martin Constantine, one of his rivals in the real-estate business, a man some considered to be almost as powerful as Armand.

How wrong they were!

Nona was exactly the kind of challenge he craved. Married, with a young child, she was a former beauty queen from Slovakia, with high cheekbones and slanted eyes. Her husband doted on her, but Armand's canny instinct allowed him to guess that ever since she'd given birth, Martin was not fucking her the way a woman yearned to be fucked.

Armand worked on her slowly, and since they moved in the same New York social circles—art gallery openings, charity events, small dinner parties—it was quite easy to get close to her. Especially as he always had a girl on his arm. Only *he* knew that his so-called "dates" were bought and paid for. That way they never gave him any trouble or made any demands. His unbreakable rule was never to use the same girl twice.

New York hostesses considered Armand Jordan a huge catch; they were always trying to fix him up. But he eluded their attempts. He was attractive in a slightly mysterious way, with a neat black mustache, thick eyebrows framing brooding eyes, and an impeccable dress sense. Only the best for Armand. He wore socks and underwear once, then threw them away. Shirts he might wear twice, but that was it. And his hand-tailored suits never stayed in his closet longer than a month.

The hostesses persevered, for not only was Armand mega rich, but it was rumored that back in the small Middle Eastern country he originally hailed from, he possessed some kind of title.

He never spoke of that.

It took him a couple of months to get Nona to his penthouse, on the pretext of showing her a rare Picasso he'd recently acquired. He did not mind the wait; in fact, he quite enjoyed the anticipation of the conquest.

She arrived at eleven in the morning, an innocent time of

day. She had on a pale pink Chanel suit with a lacy blouse underneath, and beige Louboutin heels that clicked on his highly polished marble floor as he led her around his penthouse, giving her the grand tour. Finally they ended up in the master bedroom, a masculine room, all deep burgundy leather couches and black cashmere throws covering the oversized bed.

"No family photos," Nona said, glancing around his stark bedroom. She laughed coquettishly. "Armand, you are *such* a man of mystery. And why do I always see you with a different girl? Surely you wish to meet a woman you can share your life with."

"Why would I want to do that when I can have a woman like you?" he said, gazing into her eyes as if he meant it.

And just like that, all his hard work paid off. All the compliments and sly attention and flattery, flattery, flattery.

She was his. All his to use and abuse and humiliate.

Because that was his pleasure. That was his kick.

First he kissed her, roughly forcing his lips down on hers, thrusting his tongue into her mouth, giving her no chance to object. Then, without warning, his hand swooped under her skirt, and his thick fingers slid past her panties into the soft mound of flesh that was wet and willing and waiting for discovery.

No foreplay for this one. She was turned on the minute she'd walked into his apartment. Nona Constantine wanted it. And he was about to give it to her. Hard.

Navigating his thick fingers through her wiry pubic hair, he was excited by the furriness. He wound strands of hair tightly around his fingers until she cried out in pain. This pleased him. If he wanted a woman shaved like a child, he would have a child.

"Oh, Armand," she gasped, flushed and breathless. "We shouldn't be doing . . ."

It was a little late for objections. Too late.

He shoved her down onto the bed and thought about Martin Constantine and the concealed camera recording every moment. His thoughts made him as hard as he'd ever been.

Dipping into his bedside table drawer, he withdrew a glassine bag of cocaine and sprinkled some of the white powder on her erect nipples.

She writhed beneath him as he snorted the powder from her breasts. Then, as she begged him to fuck her, he gave it to her hard, ramming his penis into her with considerable force, then turning her over and taking her from behind—ignoring her objections and sudden cries of pain.

Realizing this was not going the way she'd hoped it would, she struggled to escape his relentless attack, but he was having none of it as he rode her hard, punishing her with his penis for being an unfaithful bitch.

He felt invincible and powerful. He was the man, and once again a woman had proved to him that all women were dirty whores.

Except perhaps his wife. But who cared about her? He certainly didn't.

~ ~ ~

Later, after relentlessly fucking Nona Constantine in every possible way, he informed her that she was a cheating, filthy prostitute, physically dragged her from his bedroom, and threw her out.

The shock on her face was palpable as he hustled her out his front door, flinging her designer clothes after her.

"What? What did I do?" she sobbed, red in the face as he slammed the door on her.

He didn't bother replying.

It was satisfying to know that there was nobody she could complain to, nothing she could do. She was fucked in more ways than one.

Once rid of his conquest, Armand snorted more coke and summoned Fouad, who worked downstairs in a different apartment. "Come up here," Armand commanded. "Right now."

Fouad hurried to the penthouse.

"What's happening with The Keys?" Armand demanded as soon as Fouad walked in.

"There is a half-naked woman crying outside your door," Fouad remarked, noting that the prince wore only a bathrobe, and that there was a telltale residue of white powder under his nose. Armand's use of cocaine was escalating, and it worried Fouad as he watched Armand become even more irrational and moody.

"I trust you ignored her," Armand said, striding purposefully toward his palatial bathroom.

"Who is she?" Fouad asked.

"Martin Constantine's wife," Armand boasted. "I told you I can have any woman I want. They're all whores."

Fouad shrugged and followed him into the bedroom. He was well aware of Armand's predilections when it came to women. Privately, he considered it a sickness, but he would never dare say anything. Although lately Armand's sickness, coupled with his excessive use of drugs, was becoming almost dangerous.

"That crying bitch deserved everything she got," Armand said, dropping his robe. "I took care of her in ways she won't soon forget."

"Does it not worry you that she might tell her husband?"

"Don't be ridiculous, Fouad. She came here of her own free will. She wanted it. She was begging for it. Now remove the DVD from the camera, make two copies, and put them in my safe."

"Yes, Armand," Fouad said. He would make three copies and keep one for himself. Nothing like insurance when dealing with a man like Armand.

"And The Keys?" Armand said, unabashedly naked as he stepped into the all-marble shower. "What's happening?"

"I have several calls in," Fouad said, not wishing to reveal that he'd spoken to the owner's attorney, and that he'd been informed that it was highly unlikely The Keys was for sale.

"What is taking so long?" Armand demanded as four powerful showerheads rained down on his body.

"You only told me you wanted to buy it two days ago," Fouad pointed out. "There are times it is prudent to be patient."

Armand stepped out of the shower dripping wet. "I am not a prudent man, Fouad. You above all people should know that."

Fouad noted the prince's large appendage and attempted to avert his eyes, even though he'd seen it many times before. The prince, like his father the king, was not shy.

"I understand, Armand," he said evenly. "I am on top of it."

"You'd better be," Armand responded, vigorously toweling himself dry. "Whatever the price, I am prepared to pay."

"Of course," Fouad agreed, because agreeing was simpler than arguing.

"How is your wife?" Armand asked, abruptly changing the subject.

Fouad hesitated for only a moment. He had no wish to discuss his wife with Armand. He was well aware that Armand did not approve of his marriage. Armand thought he had made a mistake marrying an American girl. But Fouad adored his wife and two little children, and nothing Armand could say would ever change that.

"Alison is very well," he answered carefully.

"Hasn't cheated on you yet?" Armand said with a spiteful smirk.

Fouad maintained a steely silence.

"All American women cheat on their husbands eventually," Armand stated. "Look at the whore I just threw out. She's a classic example of a rich bitch with an itchy cunt."

Fouad chose to ignore Armand's crass remarks. Sometimes he found them difficult to understand, considering that Armand's own mother was an American. But then Armand's relationship with his mother had always been something of a problem.

"Go make some phone calls," Armand said, abruptly dismissing his faithful right-hand man. "And before the end of the day, I wish to know that The Keys is mine."

CHAPTER SIX

"What's going on today? Anything I should know about?" Denver asked Leon, a young detective with whom she'd become friendly. It was Leon who had encouraged her to transfer to the drug unit, a move she was excited about.

Leon was African American and quite laid-back. He was excellent at his job, and had helped her get acclimated when she'd first arrived. They had a good buddy thing going on, which she hoped would last because sometimes she had a sneaking suspicion that Leon was on the verge of asking her out.

Please don't, a little voice whispered in her head. *I'm taken. Besides, it would be awkward.*

Not that Leon wasn't attractive. He was. He had a kind of chill Will Smith vibe going for him, and the ladies were always giving him the look. Denver ribbed him a lot. He acted bashful, but she knew he was a stud at heart.

"There's a hostage deal happening," Leon explained. "Some Mexican drug pusher grabbed his baby and barricaded himself in his house with an arsenal of weapons. I'm goin' over there now. They've had to clear the neighborhood an' close the street."

"What else is new?" Denver asked, immediately thinking how blasé she sounded. And well she should, because if it wasn't a hostage situation, it was a random shooting or a gang initiation or a murder or a high-speed car chase. Things were going on all the time, and she could not believe how isolated she'd been working at a top Beverly Hills law firm, where the main excitement of the day was some coked-out Hollywood starlet with two DUIs trying to dodge jail time, or a boring client lunch at Spago.

"Not enough for you, huh?" Leon said with a wide grin. "An' how come you was late this morning?"

"I . . . uh . . ."

"Boyfriend in town?" he asked, leaning his elbows on her desk.

"Yes. Bobby's here," she admitted, a touch sheepishly. "But that has nothing to do with—"

"Morning sex," Leon said, his grin spreading. "Now, *that's* what I'm talkin' about."

"Excuse me?" she said, pretending she had no clue what he was alluding to.

"You got the glow, girl," Leon teased. "Comin' off you in waves."

Damn! She knew she did, and there was nothing she could do about it. Whenever she had sex it was written all over her face for everyone to see. How annoying was *that?*

"I have to work," she said, powering up her computer. "So if you'll—"

"I'm outta here," Leon said, throwing up his arms. "Out. Gone. Good-bye. Adios."

"Be careful," she said.

"Always," he said.

As soon as Leon left, her thoughts drifted to Bobby. It was ridiculous, but whenever she wasn't with him, all she could do was think about him. So juvenile. It was almost as if they were back in high school, and who could forget those days? Bobby Santangelo Stanislopoulos, the most popular boy in school. Football star, major jock, head of his class at everything. All the girls lusted after him, including her. But he'd never noticed her, hadn't even realized she existed. And now, ten years later, she was his actual girlfriend. How weird was that?

Stop thinking about Bobby and get to work.

Okay, okay, I will.

~ ~ ~

"You're up early," Lucky said, regarding her daughter as Max came wandering outside onto the patio. The girl was all long bronzed legs, with a coltlike body. Her green eyes were still sleep-filled, her dark hair a cloudy mess. "Hard day's night?" Lucky questioned, thinking what a beautiful child she and Lennie had created. Although Max was no longer a child; she was a young woman getting ready to take off.

"What?" Max mumbled.

"A Beatles reference."

"Wow, Mom, you can be so obscure," Max complained, flopping into a chair.

"And good morning to you too," Lucky said dryly.

Yawning, Max reached for a jug of orange juice.

"What were you up to last night?" Lucky inquired.

"You're not gonna question me, are you?" Max said, flashing her a disgusted look. "That would be so lame."

"Why? You got something to hide?" Lucky replied, faintly amused.

"Oh yeah, like anyone could hide shit around you."

"Nice," Lucky said, thinking how much Max reminded her of herself as a teenager. Restless, full of sass, yearning for adventure, determined to do things her way yet still not quite sure of herself.

"Sorry," Max allowed after a few moments of silence. "Crappy night."

"That's okay," Lucky said, taking the understanding route. "By the way, I spoke to your brother yesterday. He sends much love."

"Bobby?" Max said, perking up.

"No, your other brother, Gino Junior. He's loving their trip; so is Leonardo. They're currently in Switzerland, skiing like mad. Apparently they're having a fantastic time."

"Where *is* Bobby?" Max asked, wondering if she should tell him about Frankie. Or not. He'd probably be furious at her for taking Cookie and Harry to River in the first place. But how was *she* supposed to know it was Frankie's club? She wasn't a mind reader.

"Not sure," Lucky said. "However, I do know he'll be at your birthday party in Vegas."

"Mom . . ." Max ventured. "I've been thinking about it, and I'm not certain I want a party."

"Do *not* even attempt to back out," Lucky said firmly. "You're going to be eighteen. It's a big deal. Everyone will be there. Gino, Lennie, Bobby . . ."

"Is Bobby bringing his girlfriend?"

"Which one?"

"You know perfectly well which one. Denver. They're like a major hookup."

"They are?" Lucky said vaguely.

"Oh *please!*" Max said, laughing. "You know it."

"No, actually, I don't."

"Wow! Then you're the only one who doesn't. Why do you think Bobby keeps coming to L.A. when his clubs are in Vegas and New York?"

"How do you know he keeps coming to L.A.?"

"'Cause I just do."

Lucky was silent for a moment. She hadn't realized that Bobby was getting serious with anyone. She'd always thought that Bobby was the love 'em and leave 'em type, like his grandfather before him. He was still in his twenties, too young to tie himself down. She'd met Denver maybe once, but she hadn't taken much notice of the girl since—like all the others before her she hadn't thought Denver would be around for long. Apparently she was wrong. Therefore if Bobby was bringing her to Max's party, she'd better make some kind of effort to get to know her.

What really surprised her was that Bobby was—according to Max—spending a lot of time in L.A. and not even calling.

Who was this girl? And what kind of hold did she have over Bobby?

It was obviously time to find out.

~ ~ ~

"So you're gonna have a baby," Bobby said as he and M.J. made their way into the art deco glass elevator that led them upstairs to Mood. "That's really something. Daddy M.J. Never thought the day would come!"

"Yeah," M.J. said ruefully. "Kinda weird, huh?"

"Getting married in Vegas overnight was kinda weird," Bobby

pointed out. "Starting a family goes right along with marriage. But what the hell, 's long as you're happy."

"Couldn't be happier," M.J. answered without taking a beat.

"You're sure?" Bobby said, shooting M.J. a quick look and thinking that he didn't seem exactly ecstatic.

"Course I'm sure," M.J. said, hesitating for a moment before adding, "except for maybe one minor detail."

"An' that would be?"

"Cassie doesn't want to have a baby right now," M.J. blurted. "She keeps on threatenin' to get an abortion."

Bobby frowned. "You're screwing with me, right?"

"'Fraid not. An' what the fuck am I supposed t' do about *that*?"

"Shit, man," Bobby said, shaking his head. "How would *I* know?"

"It's a problem," M.J. admitted. "A big fuckin' problem."

"You got plans to solve it?"

M.J. gave a helpless shrug. "I'm playin' it strong. Tellin' her if she goes ahead an' does that—we're over."

"Seriously?"

"I'm dead serious."

"Well," Bobby said, finding himself at a loss for words, "I gotta wish you luck, man. Seems like you're gonna need it."

The elevator came to a stop and they stepped into the reception area of Mood.

Bobby glanced around. It always gave him a feeling of achievement to note what he and M.J. had accomplished. Their club was sleek and sexy; it featured spacious booths with muted gold leather banquettes imported from Italy, Brazilian wood tables, smoky-mirrored walls, and clever lighting supplemented with glowing candles. And in the middle of everything was the pool, surrounded by private dinner cabanas—*the* place to be seated.

And of course a state-of-the-art sound system, the best that money could buy. The entire vibe screamed style and class, comfort and fun.

Since its opening, Mood had become *the* club of choice for visiting Hollywood celebrities, high rollers, affluent Vegas locals, and showbiz performers when their shows finished and they were looking for somewhere to hang and relax. Tourists had a hard time getting in. Privacy was the name of the game.

Yes, Mood was banging—the very best.

"Remember Sukie in high school?" M.J. ventured, heading toward the bar. "The girl I knocked up?"

"Turned out to be a false alarm, right?" Bobby said, following him.

"Uh, no," M.J. said. "I didn't tell you 'cause you were taking off to spend the summer in Greece with your other family. Besides, Sukie swore me to secrecy."

"Man, why didn't you say something?" Bobby said earnestly. "I would've been there for you, you know that."

"Yeah, I know," M.J. said, going behind the bar and opening one of the fridges. "But we had to do something fast, 'cause by that time, Sukie was almost four months."

"What *did* you do?" Bobby asked, perching on a bar stool.

"The janitor at school told us 'bout this midwife downtown," M.J. said, extracting a couple of cans of Diet Coke. "He told us that for five hundred bucks, she'd take care of it. No problem." He slid a can of Diet Coke across the bar to Bobby.

"And?" Bobby said, opening the can.

"We drove to a run-down house in some shit neighborhood, where an old Chinese woman took us inside, bundled Sukie into what she called her 'operation room,' an' demanded the cash."

"Jeez! Did you even have it?"

"Uh-huh. I stole it from my dad's dresser that mornin'. Had no other way of getting the money."

"Then what?"

"For a start, we were both scared shitless."

"I bet you were."

"Anyway, I handed over the cash an' waited. After a while the old crone comes walkin' back into the room where I'm sitting. This time she's carryin' a big bucket, an' in it was the dead baby. She fuckin' *showed* it to me, like it was some kinda prize. 'You see,' she says—like she's proud or somethin'. 'All done.'"

"Oh, *fuck!*"

"Oh fuck is right. I swear to you it was a sight I'll never forget. Jesus, Bobby, I threw my guts up." M.J. shook his head as if he couldn't stand remembering, then after a long beat he said, "I couldn't wait t' get us out of there. I got Sukie into the car, but on the way home she started getting major pains. She was bleeding, so I panicked an' called my dad. He put her in the hospital. I guess he saved her. I'll never forget seein' that baby," M.J. added sadly. "It was a boy. *My* boy. The image burned itself into my eyeballs."

"I can't believe you never told me this before."

"Too painful, Bobby. I was too ashamed of what I did."

"Yeah, I can understand that. But now you gotta tell Cassie, explain how you feel."

"No way. She wouldn't get it," M.J. said, vigorously shaking his head. "An' don't go repeatin' the story to anyone."

"C'mon, man," Bobby said. "You were a kid—sixteen. You didn't know any better. You got nothing to feel guilty about."

"I guess," M.J. said miserably. "Only I still get fuckin' sick when I think about what we did. It wasn't right, it simply wasn't right."

"I get it," Bobby said sympathetically.

"It's somethin' I gotta live with," M.J. said, adding a determined, "But believe this—I'll *never* let it happen again."

"Then you *gotta* tell your wife," Bobby insisted. "She'll do the right thing when she hears your story."

"You don't know Cassie."

"*Make* her listen to you. Seems to me you got no choice."

CHAPTER SEVEN

Lunch was a daily ritual for Armand. He always selected a different restaurant and a different guest, and he always made sure to pick up the check. Armand had no wish to be beholden to anyone. He was in charge, and let nobody doubt it.

Today he was anticipating his luncheon engagement more than usual, because today his guest was Martin Constantine, and how satisfying it would be to sit across the table from Martin and reflect on his morning activities with Martin's lovely, unfaithful, whorelike wife.

Martin and he had come up against each other in various business deals, and usually Armand managed to come out on top. But the last deal they'd both been trying to close had gone in Martin's favor, and that infuriated Armand. Hence the assignation with Martin's wife. A satisfying punishment toward his business rival. And the secret knowledge that he'd had her in every sexual position he could think of.

Martin Constantine was a puffy-faced New Yorker in his sixties, with ruddy cheeks, a weak chin, and red-rimmed eyes. He was also a billionaire, although Armand suspected on paper only.

The two men shook hands and settled into a corner table. Martin had come to the lunch only because he was curious to find out what Armand wanted. It had to be something, for the two of them were hardly best friends—more like polite enemies. Not that Martin considered Armand polite. Actually, he couldn't stand the man. He abhorred the way Armand swaggered around town, always with a different woman on his arm—the way he attempted to give everyone the impression that his real-estate holdings were the cream, and that everyone else's were inferior. As far as Martin was concerned, Constantine Holdings could buy and sell Jordan Developments and not even notice.

Lunch was uneventful. Small talk. Business talk. A derisive chat about Donald Trump's television career, and how neither of them would ever sink that low. Reality television was for peasants, not for men of substance.

Armand was under the distinct impression that Martin would give his left ball for the public recognition of Donald Trump, whom Martin very much admired, but he would never admit it.

Over coffee, Armand contemplated telling his lunch guest about his morning activities. He had an urge to do so, but then he realized it was more prudent to wait until he needed something from Martin.

"How is your beautiful wife?" he asked when they stood up to leave. *I fucked her this morning. I shoved my cock up her tight ass while she screamed like a banshee. I violated her in every way I could. She loved it. I did things to her that you would never dare do.*

"Nona is a fantastic woman," Martin boasted. "I am so fortunate to have found her. She is the light of my life." He paused for a moment before continuing. "You should try marriage some-time. It might surprise you, being with one woman."

"Ah yes," Armand replied, keeping a straight face, because he'd discovered that before Martin had "found" Nona she was work-ing as a call girl in Amsterdam. Armand had his spies. "I am certain that marriage is an honorable institution."

They shook hands and parted company. Armand got into his Mercedes smiling to himself. What an old fool Martin Constan-tine was. He'd divorced his wife of thirty years and married a call girl.

The satisfaction was in the not telling.

And Armand would not tell. Not until it suited him.

~ ~ ~

Later in the day, Armand summoned Fouad to his study. "De-velopments regarding The Keys?" he demanded, leaning back in his leather desk chair, tapping his fingers impatiently on his desktop.

Fouad paused a moment before answering. He knew Armand was preparing to throw one of his screaming fits. With the news he was about to deliver, there was no avoiding it.

"Unfortunately . . ." Fouad began.

Armand glared at him. "'Unfortunately'?" he questioned, his eyes becoming narrow slits. "Did you say 'unfortunately'?"

"Indeed I did," Fouad said, small beads of sweat decorating his forehead. "Because unfortunately, I have learned that The Keys is not for sale."

There was a long moment of deadly silence before Armand began to yell.

"What do you mean it's not for sale?" he shouted, banging his fist on his desk. "Everything is for sale. Every person, every building, every damn thing in the world."

Fouad remained silent. There was nothing else he could say.

"Who told you it's not for sale?" Armand continued. "What fool uttered those asinine words?"

"The owner's lawyer, Jeffrey Lonsdale."

"What *owner?*" Armand said with a derisive sneer. "The Keys would not have an *owner.* The Keys would belong to a company. And that company should be prepared to sell. To me. I will pay whatever it takes, Fouad. Do you hear me? Whatever it takes."

Typical Armand behavior, Fouad thought. Show him something he can't have, and he will move heaven and earth to get it. Fouad recalled the case of the exquisite baby-faced call girl Armand had used on occasion. One night he required her services, and it turned out she had left the business and married a rock star. Armand was incensed. He wanted her and he would have her, so he'd devised a complicated plan that involved setting the rock star up with a paid-for call girl, making sure babyface walked in on her cheating husband, and then flying her to New York for a reunion fuck. It had cost him plenty, but to him it was well worth it.

"The Keys is owned by a private company. And the company belongs to a woman, Lucky Santangelo," Fouad said. "I spoke with her lawyer, who informed me that there is no way she is prepared to sell, whatever the price."

"A woman," Armand said disdainfully. "A mere woman." He shook his head in disgust. "I can see I will have to deal with this matter myself. Tomorrow I go to Akramshar for my father's birthday, and upon my return we will travel to Vegas or wherever this Lucky Santangelo woman is, and you will watch me convince her to sell me The Keys. Set up a meeting. And find out everything there is to know. Sometimes, Fouad, I wonder at your ineptitude. It seems there are times that if I don't do it myself, nothing gets done. Perhaps marrying an American woman has blunted your business acumen. Your wife addles your brain—such as it is."

Once again Armand was making disparaging remarks about Fouad's marriage. It infuriated him, and one day in the not-so-distant future, Fouad knew he would have to leave Armand's employ, but until that day came, he would simply be forced to suffer the insults aimed at his wife and his marriage in silence.

"It is done, Armand," Fouad said, always calm, always polite. "I will make sure all arrangements are in place for us to fly to Las Vegas."

"The Presidential Suite at The Keys," Armand stated. "And you will see—soon it will be all mine."

CHAPTER EIGHT

It was noon when Frankie Romano hauled himself out of his oversized bed with the clichéd black satin sheets and regarded himself in the mirror above his bathroom sink. He considered himself a good-looking son of a bitch. Not in the classically handsome sense, but he had an edgy style and plenty of attitude, plus he knew how to present himself. And he certainly knew how to score with the ladies. Oh *yes!* Frankie Romano was a first-class cocksman, and nobody could argue that.

Last night he'd mega scored with Cookie, Gerald M.'s sexy little offspring. A teenager with real tits and real enthusiasm. Not some tired old twenty-something Hollywood blonde who'd had more hot cocks than hot dinners. Oh no, Cookie was something else—a real prize.

Frankie made his way into the living room of his apartment, all chrome and leather furniture, the full-length windows overlooking the Sunset Strip. He laid out a couple of lines of coke on his mirrored coffee table and rolled a twenty-dollar bill.

Was he living the dream or what? After splitting with his longtime live-in Annabelle Maestro, he'd figured he was done for a while. But after watching her shine as a TV personality, he'd gotten pissed and reconnected with Rick Greco, a former teen idol who'd parlayed his dead career into a successful gig as a club promoter. "We gotta open a club together," he'd informed Rick. "We can fuckin' own this town between the two of us. Who do you think got Bobby Santangelo's New York club off the ground? It was fuckin' me, man. All me."

Which was not at all the truth, but what did he care? Frankie could spin a masterful story. The truth was, he'd been a deejay in Bobby's club, and that was about it. He'd also had a lucrative sideline selling overpriced designer drugs, and then there was the very successful business he'd created with Annabelle, running call girls. But eventually everything had crashed and burned. Luckily, he was Frankie Romano, and therefore nothing fazed him.

Rick Greco had taken to the idea of going into business with Frankie. Frankie had a big mouth and a big personality, and that's what the club business needed—a front man who knew everyone and made them feel important.

Frankie didn't know everyone, but he was a fast learner, and he certainly knew the club business. So Rick had put together a group of investors, and River was born. It was a new club, but Frankie was determined to make it as successful as Mood in New York and Vegas. Screw Bobby and M.J. They'd both deserted him just when he'd needed them. Bobby all cozy with his Deputy DA girlfriend, and M.J. with his hot, sexy little wife. Fuck 'em both.

Unfortunately, Rick had not made him a full partner. Rick had come up with the weak excuse that since Frankie wasn't putting up any money, it wasn't possible. So he'd had to settle for a percentage. But he'd soon figured out a way to make his own personal score.

Seeing Max Santangelo had made his night; he'd always had eyes for Bobby's hot little sister. But when he sensed he wasn't about to get anywhere with her, he'd switched his attention to her cute friend, which wasn't a bad thing, because Cookie had a famous father—soul icon Gerald M. And it soon occurred to Frankie that if he started dating Cookie, the tabloids would immediately latch on, and he too could hit the rags.

It was a plan.

Frankie liked having a plan.

~ ~ ~

"I'm giving you my schedule," Lucky informed Max. "I'll be taking off for Vegas tomorrow, staying there until after your party. I've got a board meeting of investors on Friday, and other business to take care of."

"Sounds like a fun time."

"Don't knock it, Max, 'cause one day you'll understand how much fun it can be running your own business."

"Not me," Max said, vigorously shaking her head.

"What *do* you want to do, then?" Lucky asked, slightly exasperated that Max didn't seem to have much drive.

"Dunno," Max said with a casual shrug. "Gonna live life an' find out."

Sure, Lucky thought. *You'll find out, all right. Things are not always as easy as they seem.*

"Anyway," she continued, "you'll find three e-tickets to Vegas on your computer for you, Cookie, and Harry. The five o'clock flight on Thursday. Are you sure you'll be okay in the house by yourself?"

Will I be okay? Max thought. *Hot shit! This is totally rad. I'm planning my own party. No parents. Lose the housekeepers. It's all one big green light. I cannot wait.*

"Mom," Max said scornfully. "It's only for, like, *one* night. I think I can manage *that*."

"Is Ace coming into town?" Lucky inquired.

Why was Lucky always carrying on about Ace? Did she think he was such a good influence? "Dunno," she muttered. "Maybe."

"You should invite him to your party in Vegas."

"Sure," Max said, checking out a text from Harry on her phone. "I'll do that."

"You could come to Vegas before Thursday if you felt like hanging out," Lucky suggested. "What do you think?"

"That's okay," Max said, thinking she'd like nothing less. "I'm into being by myself. It'll give me a chance to consider my future."

"Ah," Lucky said. "Your future."

"Yeah, Mom, my future. Can we, like, *not* discuss it now?"

"Do you still want to move to New York?"

"Maybe, maybe not," Max answered vaguely. "I told you—I'm gonna decide."

"And you're absolutely certain you have no interest in going to college?"

"*You* didn't do the whole college thing," Max said, irritated that Lucky kept on bringing it up. "Why should I?"

"Those were different times," Lucky pointed out.

"Yeah. The Dark Ages," Max said, rolling her eyes.

Lucky shook her head. No use getting pissed off. Nothing to be gained.

"Strangely enough," she deadpanned, "we had phones during

the Dark Ages. Instead of texting, we actually talked. Can you imagine?"

"What a thrill," Max drawled.

Brat, Lucky thought. *Spoiled Beverly Hills brat. But she's my brat, and one of these days she'll grow up, just like I did.*

"I'm off," Lucky said, standing up. Sometimes playing the concerned mom was not for her. She loved her kids, but once they reached a certain age, it was best to let them fly. "Are you home for dinner?"

"Don't think so," Max replied. "Gonna hang with Cookie and Harry."

"Okay, then. We'll see each other in the morning before I leave. Oh, and if you hear from Bobby, tell him to call me."

"Will do."

Max waited until Lucky was out of sight, then she called Harry. "Party time at my house tomorrow night," she announced. "Alert the troops, and grab as much booze as you can from your dad's liquor cabinet. Got it?"

Harry got it.

~ ~ ~

Once every few months Lucky had lunch with her old friend Alex Woods, the legendary and unpredictable film director. They shared a history, a long friendship, and one night of twisted passion a long time ago when Lennie was missing and Lucky thought he was dead. Alex had never gotten over her, and she knew it, but she wasn't prepared to give him up as a friend. He was loyal and insane and incredibly talented and forceful and sincere when he felt like it. During the time she'd owned Panther Studios they'd produced a movie together, and when she'd embarked on building The Keys, Alex had come in on the project as one of her major investors.

If Lennie weren't around, she would be with Alex, and they were both aware of it, although it was never discussed.

In the meantime, Alex dated Asian women. They came. They went. Sometimes they stayed longer than a few weeks. He didn't care. Like Lennie, he lived to make movies—women and love affairs were secondary. Except for Lucky, who, in his eyes, became even more wildly beautiful as each year passed.

He studied her as she walked into Mr. Chow. She wore white pants, a casual jacket, and plenty of gold gypsy-style jewelry. She strode in like a panther, all sleek movement, her dark eyes flashing, her trademark mass of tumbled jet curls as wild as usual. Alex stood up from the table.

"Such a gentleman," she teased as he moved forward and kissed her on both cheeks, inhaling the exotic fragrance she always wore. "How are you, Alex?" she asked, sitting down. "Working hard?"

"What do *you* think?" he said with a wry smile. "I'm in post on the war movie I recently finished shooting in Morocco, and my editor is driving me nuts. Plus, we're way over budget, and the studio is throwing a shit fit. Fuck 'em."

"Are you pleased with it?" she asked, scanning his face. He looked a little ragged around the edges. Alex drank too much; that and his excessive smoking were not good for him. He was still an enormously attractive man, though, and she loved him dearly—as a friend.

"Am I ever pleased with anything?" Alex said, picking up a tumbler of Jack Daniel's. "You know me, Lucky. You probably know me better than anyone."

"Isn't it a little early for the heavy stuff?" Lucky inquired, indicating his drink.

"Jesus!" Alex said. "Since when did *you* become the AA rep? Whyn't you leave it to my girlfriends to be concerned about my drinking? They're the ones who get off on bitching."

"How sweet."

"Sweet is the last thing I'm looking for."

"Well then," Lucky said briskly, "you should stop picking actresses and try finding a girl—I mean a woman—you can have a decent relationship with. It's about time you gave up the chasing."

"Believe me, honey, it's them who do the chasing," he said dryly.

"Don't call me honey."

"Why not?"

"Save it for your one-nighters."

"You were a one—"

"Alex!" She stopped him with a deadly look. He was venturing into forbidden territory, and she didn't like it one little bit.

"Yeah, yeah, I get it," he said, taking another gulp of Jack.

She ordered a bottle of Evian and leaned across the table. "Tell me about your movie."

"Don't want to bore you."

"Why would I be bored, Alex?"

"'Cause you know exactly what I'm going to say."

"And that would be?"

"I'm gonna regale you with stories about what a bunch of fucking assholes my actors are."

"Then why do you hire them?"

"Got no choice. Unfortunately, I need 'em."

"How inconvenient for you."

"Yeah, robots are more my style," he said with a cynical laugh.

"Imagine that!"

Alex smiled. It didn't matter what kind of a mood he was in, Lucky could always make him feel better.

"Did you hear that Venus is in the process of divorcing Billy?" she asked.

"Should I be surprised? Working with Billy was like slogging up the Himalayas with no Sherpas. That little prick took 'asshole' to new heights."

Lucky laughed. "Billy's major box office. The public seems to love him."

"We all know that the public has no fucking taste."

"That's what I like about you, Alex."

"I knew there was something," he said with a wry grin.

"You tell it the way you see it."

"That's me, Lucky. No bullshit."

"You're unique."

"Takes one to know one," he said, signaling the waiter to bring him another drink. "How's Lennie?"

"Lennie's fine."

"Shame," he said with a resigned shrug. "I was hoping he'd slipped off a cliff."

"Stop!" she said sternly.

"You know that'll never happen," he countered. "And I do mean never."

They stared at each other, a long intent stare that Lucky finally broke.

"Okay," she said, taking a deep breath. "I want you to come to Vegas."

"I fucking hate Vegas," Alex said vehemently. "Especially after what happened there with Ling."

Lucky flashed onto the memory of Alex's former live-in girlfriend, who had been sending her threatening notes and hatch-
ing a plan to shoot her. It was all so bizarre, but when Alex
caught Ling with his handgun in her purse during the opening
festivities of The Keys, he'd gone berserk and thrown Ling out.

"There are two reasons I need you to come to Vegas," Lucky
said as persuasively as she could.

"Go ahead," Alex said. "Try to convince me."

"Reason one, it's Max's eighteenth birthday next weekend,
and I'm throwing her a party. You know she'd love you to be
there. After all, you've known her since she was a baby."

Alex groaned. "Blackmail," he said flatly. "Psychological blackmail."

"No such thing," Lucky said crisply.

"Reason two?"

"A board meeting of all the Keys investors."

"Jesus! I'll send my business manager. He handles that kinda
shit."

"I'm sure Max would be thrilled to see him, but I'm expecting
you."

"Will Lennie be there?" Alex asked, shooting her a meaningful look.

"Of course."

"What kind of incentive is that?"

"Knock it off, Alex. You're doing this for me. Okay?"

"Whatever the Lady Boss says."

"Fuck you, Alex."

"Anytime, Lucky."

"Then you'll come?"

"If only," he said with a lascivious grin.

Lucky ignored his double entendre. "I'll book you a suite. Don't let me down."

"Jesus Christ! You're so fucking bossy," Alex complained. "But I guess I'll be there. For you, I'll always be there."

"Thank you, Alex."

~ ~ ~

As soon as Max was sure that Lucky had left the house, she began texting friends about the Malibu party she was planning. Never mind Vegas, she'd have her own crazy celebration, and with the house all to herself, it should be a major blast.

To invite Ace or not to invite Ace, that was the question. She wasn't sure what to do about him. Ace could be totally great or, as Cookie and Harry had pointed out, totally controlling. Besides, it wasn't as if she was in love with him.

Max had imagined she was in love only once, and that was in high school with a boy named Donny Leventon, who'd broken her heart and left her crushed and disillusioned.

She'd never told anyone he'd broken her heart. She'd laughed off the fact that she'd caught him in Houston's, of all places, with another girl.

She was sixteen at the time. Donny was seventeen, and they'd never slept together, although they'd done plenty of other things. Experimenting with sex was fun. Going all the way was not an option, not until she found The One.

Discovering that Donny was seeing another girl was a shattering experience. It had driven her to the Internet, where she was determined to hook up and lose her virginity to a suitable candidate—whether he was The One or not. She'd set up a meeting with a twenty-two-year-old boy who'd posted a majorly hunky photo. After arranging to meet him in Big Bear, she'd turned up, only to find that the major hunk was a disgusting, ugly perv, who'd then kidnapped her and locked her up in some deserted cabin in the woods.

She shuddered at the memories. Thank goodness for Ace, who'd come along at exactly the right time and rescued her.

She wasn't in love with Ace. She liked him in small doses, and that was okay because he didn't live in L.A. They hadn't slept together, but as with Donny, she'd done plenty of other things with him.

Yes, she was still a virgin, and it was becoming an embarrassment, especially as Cookie had slept with an army of guys and boasted about them constantly.

But she wasn't Cookie, and she didn't want to be.

She was waiting—for what?

She didn't know, but when it happened she'd be all over it.

CHAPTER NINE

With Bobby in Vegas, Denver decided to have a night at home by herself. She was happy when he was in town. But she was also happy when he wasn't.

I'm confused, she thought. *I love him but I don't want to love him. I don't want to get hurt. I don't want to make myself vulnerable.*

BUT I LOVE HIM!

She thought about calling Carolyn, then remembered that her friend was out on a gay date. How random was *that*? Carolyn had never indicated a yen for the same sex, but everyone had their secrets . . . and if taking the lesbian route was what she wanted, then so be it.

She put on the TV and checked out the news. The standoff with the Mexican man and his baby—the two of them barricaded in a house—was all over the news. Denver hoped that Leon was all right. She'd grown quite fond of him, and everyone knew that a crazy man with a gun was always a dangerous situation. She'd worked with Leon on a couple of cases—both drug-related—and won both of them. They made a good team. He caught the bad guys, she prosecuted them. Currently Leon was tracking a drug trail that he was hoping would lead him to the big guys, and then she would really have an important case to work on.

Throwing open the freezer door, she inspected the contents. Ice cream, frozen pizza, a half-open packet of waffles, and some spaghetti sauce in a plastic container with ice forming a suspicious film on the top.

Damn! Nothing she wanted for dinner, so maybe a quick walk to the burger place on Santa Monica.

Amy Winehouse was giving her a look as much as to say, *Are we taking a walk or what? I need some activity.*

"Yes," Denver said out loud, returning Amy's baleful stare. "We're taking a walk."

Amy's tail began to wag. The dog understood English perfectly.

After quickly changing into jeans, a tartan shirt with rolled-up sleeves, and sneakers, Denver grabbed Amy's leash and set off.

Amy was in fine form, dragging her down the street at a fast pace. By the time they reached the burger place, Denver was out of breath. She stopped for a moment, thinking she needed to spend more time at the gym.

Ah . . . if she only had more time. Work took up most of it, and Bobby the rest. Not that she was complaining; spending nights and weekends with Bobby was always the best. But a weekend in Vegas with his family was not something she was looking forward to.

"Denver?"

Somebody spoke her name and she spun around.

"Sam?" she countered.

They both grinned and hugged.

"What are *you* doing here?" she questioned, flashing on the last time she'd seen Sam, her New York screenwriter friend with the lean body, crooked teeth, and disarming sense of humor. He'd been standing outside her front door in L.A. when she and Bobby had returned from rescuing Carolyn in D.C. Just standing there with an overnight bag and an expectant expression, which totally threw her, because it wasn't as if he was her boyfriend. They'd shared one very pleasant night of passion in his New York apartment and a delicious breakfast the next morning. That was it.

After Bobby had taken off, she'd asked Sam in for a drink and told him she was kind of involved. They hadn't spoken since.

"They're making my movie," Sam said, his wacky smile going full force. "Remember I told you I sold my screenplay?"

"You mean it's actually in production?" she asked, surprised, because she honestly hadn't imagined he was a successful screenwriter.

"Can you believe it?" he said modestly. "And they've made me a creative consultant. Which means I stand around the set making incredibly smart comments, and nobody listens to me, including the actors."

"You're the writer," she said succinctly. "Why would they?"

"You got that right," he said, bending down to pet Amy. "Hey, buddy."

"He's a she," Denver pointed out as Amy basked in the attention.

"That's me," Sam said wryly. "Always confusing the sexes."

Denver smiled. She had fond memories of Sam; he was a really interesting and funny guy.

"What are you doing right now?" Sam asked. "Can I buy you a burger?"

"No," Denver replied. "But I'll buy *you* one. Kindly take into account that L.A. is *my* city. You're merely a visitor."

Sam held up his hand, "My mom taught me that when a beautiful woman wants to buy you *anything,* go for it."

"Your mom's a smart woman," Denver said, liking the "beautiful" comment.

"She is," Sam agreed, ushering her to a seat at a plastic table on the outdoor patio. "She taught me a lot of things."

A waitress, balancing her out-of-work actress body on roller skates, appeared and handed them menus.

Denver hid behind hers for a moment, studying the list of various hamburgers. Mexican, Puerto Rican, Southwestern. She wondered if Bobby would mind her sharing a meal with an old friend.

Hmm . . . an old friend she'd slept with. But only once, and it wasn't as if she was planning on sleeping with him again.

Sam was just a friend. Period.

~ ~ ~

Now that he was getting a divorce from the Queen of the Divas, Billy was determined to enjoy his newfound freedom. It was about time. He felt like he'd escaped from a gilded cage and was finally able to do whatever he wanted.

And what *did* he want?

To ride his Harley.

Get blow jobs beside his pool.

Wake up late when he wasn't working.

Flirt with anyone and everyone without Venus checking out his every move.

Never wear a tuxedo again.

Fart in bed.

Drink milk from the carton.

Play video games all night long.

Watch wrestling at midnight.

And porn whenever he felt like it.

Yeah, being free was a good thing. He liked it a lot.

His lawyer had recently informed him that Venus was going for the jugular. She was under the misguided impression that he was sleeping with his costar, and nothing could be farther from the truth.

The breakup of their marriage had come about because Venus never trusted anything he said anymore. She'd taken to checking his e-mails, pouring over his Tweets, going through his pockets, reading his texts.

He *was* faithful. She simply hadn't believed him.

One divorce, coming up.

He was relieved.

Freedom meant he had his life back.

~ ~ ~

Max, Cookie, and Harry were working on texting big-time.

"This is gonna be one flat way-out cool rave!" Cookie decided. "We should have In-N-Out burgers come by. I'll organize the truck. I can use my dad's credit card, he'll never notice."

"And we should get pizza," Harry said. "Everyone's always up for pizza. My dad has a charge at Cecconi's. I'll order from there."

"No deadbeats or losers," Max instructed. "It has to be kids we know an' trust. An' I don't want anyone hangin' around in the house—they can only use the patio, the pool, or the beach."

"Whatever," Cookie said, waving her beringed hand in the air. "I'm telling Frankie he can only bring way hot guys."

Max frowned. "You're inviting Frankie?" she said, not happy at the news. "Why are you doing *that?*"

"'Cause why shouldn't I?" Cookie responded, immediately combative. "He's cool. He'll fit right in. Besides," she added succinctly, "he could be my future boyfriend."

"Gimme a fuckin' break," Harry muttered, snorting with disgust.

"What if I wanted to invite Bobby?" Max argued. "You know they kind of fell out."

"Bobby? Here? At our party?" Cookie said, pulling on her dreadlocks. "No way. Bobby's a killjoy. He'd stop the booze an' all kinds of crap. He's like your *way* too protective big brother. Forget 'bout inviting *him.*"

"Cookie's right," Harry said, fingering his spiked hair so it stood up even higher. "Bobby's always checking out what you're drinking an' watchin' out for you. It's sick."

"That's 'cause he *cares* about me," Max said, getting all defensive.

"Well, you don't want him *caring* when we're tryin' to have ourselves a time," Cookie remarked. "What fun is *that?*"

"Yeah," Max admitted. "I suppose you're right."

"You askin' Ace?" Harry wanted to know.

Max thought about it for a moment. Should she ask Ace? Or

would he do the Bobby thing and prevent her from having fun? And she *really* wanted to have fun, maybe even get a little crazy. Why not? It was about time. "Dunno," she answered vaguely. "Maybe."

"Or maybe not," Cookie said with a knowing smile. "I'd keep it loose if I was you. Who knows what tomorrow night will bring. Let's go for it all the way. Let's PARTEE!"

~ ~ ~

M.J. and Bobby's Russian investors consisted of two burly men and an exceptionally tall woman in her fifties with yellow vampirelike teeth, thick legs, and an overbearing, critical attitude. Not to mention a hideous fuchsia masculine-style business suit. She spoke in her native tongue to her two companions and practically ignored Bobby and M.J., who were showing them around the premises.

Bobby was getting aggravated. The woman was a rude piece of work, and he couldn't stand her. However, these investors represented major money, so he attempted to stay cool.

M.J. calmed him down. "They've already agreed to put up all the money for the L.A. and Miami clubs," he said in a low voice. "This is just a courtesy visit. I got the contracts all ready for them to sign."

Fuck 'em, Bobby thought. *I don't need their money. I could finance both clubs with my own money.*

If he wanted to.

Which he didn't.

Long ago he'd made up his mind that his success could not depend on his inheritance. For some insane reason he had it in his head that he had to make it on his own. It was something he felt strongly about.

The Russians finally finished their tour, whereupon M.J. suggested they sit in a booth so they could sign the contracts that both sets of lawyers had already approved.

"We sign, we sign," Vampire-Teeth said, scarlet lipstick caking on her thin lips. "Later. We come back later, see club full."

"Sure," M.J. said, all easy charm as he guided them toward the glass elevator.

"Sure my ass," Bobby grumbled when they'd left. "I'm supposed to be on a plane to New York tonight. I've got meetings."

"Don't sweat it," M.J. said. "I can look after them."

"No," Bobby said. "You've got too much on your mind. I'll take an A.M. flight an' stay here with you. This is too important to screw up."

"Are you sayin' I'd screw it up?"

"No way, man, but we both need to be here. We have to make sure they sign the contracts tonight."

"You're right," M.J. said. "I'll have the office change your flight."

Bobby nodded. The last thing he wanted was to be stuck in Vegas without Denver. But some things had to be done, and this was one of them.

~ ~ ~

In between texting and making calls about their upcoming rave, Cookie expected to get a call from Frankie, and when it didn't come, she was pissed.

"I'm callin' *him*," she announced.

"Don't do that," Max warned.

"Why not?"

"'Cause it'll make you look desperate."

"Screw it. I'm doin' it."

The three of them, Cookie, Max, and Harry, were holed up in Harry's room at the top of his father's Bel Air mansion, a sad place since his mom, a born-again Christian, ran off with her pastor. They now resided in Arizona.

Harry's room was all dark and creepy, with heavy purple drapes to keep out the sunlight, and walls painted black. He'd actually painted the room himself, and he was so pleased with it that he'd painted his bathroom black too.

"Your living quarters suck," Max complained, staring around at the gloomy surroundings. "It's so, like, *depressing*. I dunno why we're here."

"To load up on booze," Harry reminded her. "My old man won't be home till midnight, an' I can't move a dozen bottles of tequila an' twelve cases of imported beer by myself."

"Right," Cookie said, distracted, as she was still hoping Frankie would call.

"How come a dozen bottles of tequila?" Max asked.

"Some actor sent them to him to try to score a part on one of his shows. He's always getting suck-up gifts. He won't even notice they're missing."

"Cool," Max said.

"Bribery," Harry responded. "And the douche actor didn't even get the job."

"If Cookie can separate from her phone, we should load up," Max suggested, ready to get going.

"Whose car we gonna put it in?" Harry wanted to know.

"Mine," Max decided. "That way we can unload it all when Lucky's left."

"What time's she going?" Harry asked.

"Early in the A.M., I hope. The sooner she shifts outta L.A., the quicker we can get goin' on the party."

"An' you're certain your old man's not gonna spring a surprise an' come home unexpectedly?" Cookie questioned.

"Who, Lennie?" Max replied. "No way. Once I give the housekeepers the day off, we're free—totally free! And I for one cannot freakin' wait!"

CHAPTER TEN

Armand did not own a plane—too much trouble. He preferred hiring a private plane to fly him wherever he wished to go. On his yearly visit to Akramshar, he enjoyed stopping off for twenty-four hours in London, where he spent all his time at the Dorchester Hotel, ordering in a series of call girls. He insisted that his madam of choice—a titled woman who resided in a mansion in Belgravia and was forever recruiting new girls—send him only the best. Well-bred English girls with clipped upper-class accents, slim bodies, and excellent pedigrees.

Humiliating English women appealed to him. He plied them with drugs and watched them prostitute themselves while doing anything he commanded. It made a pleasant change from dealing with American whores, who sometimes acted as if they were faking it.

Recently, Armand's cocaine habit *had* escalated, just as Fouad suspected. At first Armand had simply enjoyed watching the women lose all their inhibitions on drugs. But after a while he'd found he enjoyed the enhanced sensation of sexual power he felt when high on coke. And why not? He was invincible. He could do anything he wanted.

He especially enjoyed snorting cocaine off the women's bodies—using them, toying with them, debasing them in any new way he could think of.

With his sexual appetite well sated, he was finally ready to spend forty-eight hours in Akramshar, avoiding Soraya and his four offspring, whom he barely knew. He only made the yearly trek because of his father and their shared business interests.

When King Emir Amin Mohamed Jordan passed on, there would be a huge fortune to be divided between the king's sons (the women of the family would inherit nothing), and Armand had to make certain he received his rightful share. Not that he needed it, but he was damn well going to see that he received it. Plus, the companies he'd formed with the king would be all his.

He was fully aware that his father considered him the favorite among all of his sons, who now totaled eleven. He was the one who got away and made a huge success in America. He was the only one worth shit. And he was the one the king trusted to funnel his money into America in case he ever needed it.

Returning to Akramshar was always a jarring experience. Leaving the Western world and entering a city where men ruled supreme was quite primitive and yet strangely satisfying. Subservient women behaved the way all females should. But try telling the Americans that.

A black Mercedes met him at the airport and ferried him to his palace. Yes, he had a palace, on loan from the king. Sometimes he wondered how the stringy, social-climbing New York hostesses would feel if they knew he was a prince and lived in a palace. They would slit their skinny throats to get a piece of him.

Servants abounded, but Soraya was not there to greet him. As if he cared. The children were confined to their quarters—another plus.

Upon his arrival, he shed his clothes and enjoyed the comfort of the traditional male robe that all men wore. Most of the women in Akramshar were expected to be covered at all times, and rightly so. His mother had told him that under their burqas the women in the harem wore expensive clothes purchased in Rome and Milan, where King Emir sometimes took a select group of his wives for a long weekend. The king especially favored lacy lingerie, and on these trips he encouraged his wives to spend, spend, spend.

Peggy had needed no encouragement to do exactly that. She'd amassed an impressive collection of jewelry during the years she'd spent in Akramshar, and several trunks full of designer clothes.

Armand tried not to think about his mother too much. Sidney Dunn had died a year previously, and it annoyed him that since then Peggy had become quite demanding—phoning him at all hours, claiming that she didn't see enough of him, wondering why he'd never married and given her grandchildren. Since she had no contact with anyone in Akramshar, she knew nothing of his wife and children.

Armand was well aware of what a nightmare it would be if she ever found out that he already had a family. A nightmare he was not prepared to deal with. She would insist on being involved, and when Peggy insisted on something, there was no stopping her.

Fouad was the only person who knew about his family, and he trusted Fouad to keep his silence. Fouad would never betray him; it was in his blood to remain loyal.

After changing into his robe, he retired to a males-only ter-race room, far away from Soraya and the children. A manservant immediately brought him a cup of strong black tea and a plate of sweet biscuits. Another servant asked if he required a massage.

Yes, a massage was exactly what he required.

He sipped his tea, then entered a side room where soft music played. Two young women helped him out of his robe and, when he was fully naked, onto a massage table.

These women were not whores, they were servants who treated him like the prince he was. They trickled hot oil over his chest and stomach, moving slowly down to his groin area with their soothing hands. They wore white robes, which after a while he instructed them to remove. They were young—but not too young to service him with their soft lips. He felt aroused, and lay still while they brought him to orgasm. They were too young to humiliate; he couldn't be bothered.

When they were finished, he required nothing except soli-tude and time to think about the prize he was about to acquire when he returned to America.

The Keys.

His hotel.

A place where he'd decided he would be forever content.

CHAPTER ELEVEN

Spending time with Sam was nice. Denver really appreciated his slightly skewed sense of humor. He was so laid-back and un-threatening, and not overly good-looking, although he was attractive in an Owen Wilson quirky kind of way. Also, he didn't hail from a high-powered family, or at least she didn't think he did, and that was another plus. Her brothers would love him; he was their kind of guy. Bobby—not so much. They'd find Bobby a bit out of their league.

Out of my league too, she thought wryly. *Way out of my league. Or not.*

Lately she'd found herself trying to talk herself out of being with Bobby. It was almost as if she didn't feel she deserved him, which of course was ridiculous.

Or was it?

He'd never even noticed her in high school, so why was he with her now? She was the same person. Well . . . almost. Minus the braces and bad hair and chubby curves.

Sam had walked her back to her apartment, and she hadn't invited him in.

"Are you still seeing that guy you were with last time I was here?" he'd asked, striving to sound casual.

"Kind of," she'd replied.

Kind of! Bobby would throw a fit if he heard how offhand she sounded about their relationship. Why hadn't she said, "Yes, we're together. Very much so. I love him and he loves me. So sorry, Sam, *that's* why I'm not inviting you in."

"Okay then," Sam had said. "Maybe you'd like to come by the set one day—watch them all ignore me." She laughed. "I can offer you a fine lunch off the catering truck," he added. "Whaddya think?"

"Sounds irresistible. Only please remember I'm a working girl."

"We're shooting all next weekend," he said, determined not to give up. "How about dropping by Saturday or Sunday?"

"I, uh, think I might have to go to Vegas," she said, keeping it vague. "But, uh, I'll call you."

Great, Denver. Getting all friendly with an ex would not go down well with Bobby. What's wrong with you?

Nothing. Or everything.

Suddenly she missed Bobby like crazy.

~ ~ ~

Finally Frankie returned one of Cookie's seven calls. Max and Harry exchanged a relieved look. Cookie had been driving them nuts with her endless stream of comments about Frankie, all about what a stud he was, and how she could definitely fall for a guy like him, and WHY THE FUCK WASN'T HE CALLING HER BACK?

"He wants me to go to the club," she announced, shooting Max and Harry a triumphant look. "Wanna come?"

"No thanks," they chorused.

"Why not?" Cookie demanded, already trying to decide what to wear.

"'Cause I have to get everything ready for my party," Max said.

She was excited about the party. It was actually the first time she would have the Malibu house all to herself. And it was an amazing house, so perfect to throw a fantastic party. As long as she could keep everyone out of the house, what harm could anyone do? She planned on locking all the bedrooms, the screening room, and Lucky's and Lennie's private studies. The enormous patio, the infinity pool, and the sandy beach would be more than enough space for everyone to have a great time. She estimated they'd invited around thirty people, who would probably all bring a friend or two—so maybe they'd end up with seventy or eighty. Just the right number of bodies.

Harry was busy organizing a deejay he knew, and Cookie had already booked the In-N-Out hamburger truck to arrive at ten P.M., so it was all systems go.

Max had still not made up her mind about whether to invite Ace. He'd be a last-minute decision.

Cookie took off, and Max decided an early night wouldn't be a bad idea, so after she and Harry had finished loading up her trunk with as many boxes of beer and tequila as they could fit in, she gave Harry a hug and headed for home.

Tomorrow would be a very busy day indeed.

~ ~ ~

Bobby was not happy. He'd had to postpone his flight to New York, and now he was sitting in a strip club with M.J., the two male Russian investors, and the lone female, who was obviously a raving lesbian the way she was stuffing hundred-dollar bills into the strippers' almost nonexistent G-strings.

Fuck! He wanted out. But he couldn't leave M.J. to handle them on his own. They were a tricky trio. First they'd requested dinner and a show. Then they'd spent ten minutes in Mood— thank God it was only ten minutes. Finally M.J. had gotten them to sign the papers, at which point they'd insisted on celebrating at a famous Vegas gentleman's strip club to cement the deal.

Bobby had a strong aversion to clubs that featured strippers. He wasn't one of the guys when it came to a bunch of bored, vaguely desperate females taking off their clothes for the public's pleasure. He felt sorry for the girls, and even sorrier for the usually drunk guys who sat there with their mouths hanging open, hoping for a stray tit to come their way.

The strippers immediately gravitated toward Bobby and M.J.—two handsome, apparently sober guys.

"Wanna go private, honey?" a breast-enhanced redhead whispered in Bobby's ear, her tasseled nipple grazing his cheek.

"Uh . . . not tonight," he managed.

"You won't regret it, sweet thing," she purred, licking her lips. "I got moves you ain't gonna see on *Dancing with the Stars*."

"I bet," he said, backing away and indicating Miss Russia, who had shed her jacket and stern expression and was eyeing a small blonde with lustful eyes. "Take *her* private. I'll pay."

"Spoil sport," the redhead whispered, but she moved over to the woman, grabbed her by the hand, and led her back to one of the private champagne rooms.

Bobby leaned over to M.J. "They've signed the papers. You think we can get the hell out of here?"

Before M.J. could answer, Bobby's cell rang. He almost didn't hear it, what with Lady Gaga screaming about paparazzi on the sound system, and the general noise.

It was Denver. He'd tried to reach her earlier to tell her he hadn't left for New York yet, but she hadn't picked up.

"Hey," he said.

"Hey," she responded. "What's all that noise?"

"Long story," he said, delighted to hear her voice.

"Are you in New York?" she asked.

"Got delayed," he answered, waving off a determined blonde with painful-looking nipple rings enhancing her overly large fake breasts.

"What? I can't hear you."

"I'll call you back."

"No. I'm going to sleep. Call me tomorrow."

"Will do."

He clicked off. Nothing worse than an unsatisfactory end to the evening.

CHAPTER TWELVE

An army of hardworking executives made sure that The Keys ran as smoothly as possible, considering there was a workforce of thousands. From the head of security to the woman in charge of guest relations, everyone pitched in, for Lucky had made sure there were plenty of incentives for every employee—whatever their position—to do their best.

When she'd built the hotel, she'd put together a syndicate of investors, who all held equal shares in the private company she'd created. Very soon, she hoped, her investors would begin receiving money back. The Keys was doing well, but the initial investment was monumental, and the downturn in the economy was not helpful. However, the casino was one of the most successful in Vegas, thanks to a band of casino hosts who were the best in the business. The hotel was usually at 90 percent capacity, plus the apartments had all sold for record-breaking prices.

Lucky was satisfied with the way things were going. The Keys was her child—her love child—created from her desire to build the perfect oasis in Las Vegas, the city where she'd first made her mark when she'd taken over the building of Gino's hotel after he'd been forced to leave the country on a tax exile.

There were good memories and bad ones. Gino's moneymen had refused to deal with a woman, so in the middle of the night she'd paid one of them a visit, held a knife to his balls, and demanded he pay up—otherwise she'd be back to cut 'em off!

Surprise, surprise, he'd paid! Oh yes, that was a fun memory.

Not so funny was remembering Marco, her fiancé, who'd been gunned down next to the hotel swimming pool. And her brother, Dario, murdered and tossed from a moving car.

Lucky refused to dwell on the past. After taking a suitable revenge, she'd moved forward. It was the only way to survive.

The Keys was her tribute to Marco, Dario, and her beautiful mother, Maria, another victim of a brutal crime.

Lucky often wondered if Max had any idea about their family history. Max never asked questions; she didn't seem interested. One day Lucky planned on sitting her down and telling her everything. Max needed to know the battles the Santangelos had gone through, from which they'd emerged triumphant. And she had to be made aware of their famous motto—*Never fuck with a Santangelo.*

So far Lennie had prevented her from filling Max in on the family saga. "Let her grow up first," he'd said. "There's plenty of time."

Lennie Golden. Her husband. The best man on the planet. When she'd first met him, he was a stand-up comedian at her hotel. She'd propositioned him. He'd turned her down. And when they'd next run into each other, she was married to Greek shipping billionaire Dimitri Stanislopoulos, and by some weird coincidence, he was married to Dimitri's spoiled daughter, Olympia. A crazy situation.

But in the end it had all worked out, and she could honestly say that Lennie was the love of her life. They were compatible in every way. True soul mates.

Before setting off for Vegas, she peeked in on Max, who was still asleep. Her child appeared so innocent when she was sleeping. Long-lashed eyelids covering brilliant green eyes, dark curly hair fanning out over the pillow.

Lucky stared at Max for a moment, remembering the day she was born, and Lennie's expression when he'd held his daughter for the first time. They'd named her Maria after Lucky's mother—a name Max changed in her teens because she felt Max was more her. So little Maria had become little Max. The new name suited her style; she'd always been an assertive child and quite a tomboy. Max Santangelo Golden.

Lucky sighed. Soon Max would be out on her own. They all grew up too quickly. Time moved at such a lightning pace.

"Bye, sweetheart," she whispered, bending down to kiss Max on the forehead. "See you soon."

~ ~ ~

The moment Lucky left her room, Max—who'd been faking sleep—jumped out of bed and ran to the window to witness her mother's departure. She'd pretended to be asleep because she hadn't wanted to get involved in a conversation about what she was going to do while everyone was away. Too risky, considering she was not the world's greatest liar, and unfortunately, Lucky possessed an extraordinarily keen bullshit detector.

Soon enough she observed Lucky striding out of the house and getting into a waiting town car to take her to the airport.

Max immediately reached for her cell and called Harry and Cookie, giving them the all clear. "Get your asses over here, we've got much to do," she said excitedly.

Her next job was getting rid of the two housekeepers, who might present a problem. They were recent hires, sisters from Guatemala. Fortunately, twenty-four hours of freedom suited them just fine. Lucky did not believe in keeping a large staff around—she was very down-to-earth in that respect, preferring to do things for herself. She'd also never cared to raise her children in a pampered environment.

Cookie arrived at the house first, a blissful smile on her pretty face. "No more *boys* for me," she announced with a dismissive wave of her hand. "It's men all the way."

"Oh, for God's sake!" Max responded, rolling her eyes. "It's *Frankie*. Get a grip. He's a major loser."

"He is *so* not," Cookie argued. "You don't know him."

"I've known him longer than you, thankyouverymuch," Max retaliated.

"Not in the way *I* know him," Cookie said with a secretive smile.

"Don't tell me you had sex again?" Max said, hoping she was wrong but sure that she wasn't.

"Wouldn't *you* like to know." Cookie giggled.

"Not really," Max said, hurrying over to the window to make sure the two young housekeepers got into the cab she'd ordered to take them to their families. She'd instructed them not to return until noon the next day, and she'd given them each fifty bucks cash, plus cab fare, to make sure they understood. The older sister had been worried about Lucky finding out, but Max had assured the girl in her best high school Spanish that Lucky would never know.

Once the housekeepers were gone, the three of them hurried downstairs and began unloading the booze from Max's car and lugging it out to the bar by the swimming pool.

"Who's going to make everyone drinks?" Cookie asked, filling the outdoor fridge with bottles of beer. "Frankie kinda suggested we could borrow one of his bartenders. Whaddya think?"

"So you *did* invite him?" Max said, turning on her accusingly.

"Told you I was," Cookie said.

"But we didn't agree," Max objected. "Seems you're forgetting it's *my* party."

"Get over it," Cookie snapped. "You're just jealous 'cause I'm getting it an' you're not."

"That's crap," Max said, although maybe she was a little bit put out that for Cookie, sex seemed so uncomplicated. "And by the way, you stink of weed."

"Want some?" Cookie offered, digging into her purse.

"I do," Harry said, darting forward with an eager gleam in his eyes.

Max threw him a withering look. "No thanks," she said to Cookie. "And no bartender either. Everyone can help themselves. I'm dropping by the market and buying a ton of plastic glasses we can throw away later."

Cookie yawned, feigning boredom. "Whatever," she muttered. "It's *your* party."

"Okay, girls," Harry said, thinking it was time he butted in. "We've got work to do. Let's get to it."

~ ~ ~

The hostage situation worked itself out, and Leon was by Denver's desk early in the morning. For several weeks he'd been tracking a dealer who'd been selling his wares to a local high school, and he was close to making an arrest. But they both knew it wasn't the small-time dealer he was out to nail, it was the supplier, so his plan was to not Mirandize the guy, to get him to talk, then set him free.

Denver was in on the plan, and she fully approved. Getting the big-time supplier into court was their ultimate goal, then, after a triumphant victory, throwing him into jail, where he belonged. She couldn't wait to get in on the action.

"What didja do last night?" Leon wanted to know, hovering by her desk.

"Nothing much," Denver replied. "And you?"

"Went on a date with a Cuban girl who was into having sex in the elevator of her apartment house."

"Excuse me?" Denver said, raising an eyebrow.

Leon laughed. "She was one of those danger freaks. Y'know, let's see if we can get ourselves caught."

"Lovely."

"I hadda say no, an' then she blew me off."

"In the sexual sense?"

"I wish," he said, laughing again. "Bitch called me chicken an' told me to get out."

"Because you wouldn't have sex with her in an elevator?"

"You think I wanna get arrested for indecent exposure? I can see myself comin' up in court with *you* prosecuting my ass."

"If that ever happens, I'll be gentle," she promised, smiling.

"Bullshit!"

They both laughed.

"Seriously, Denver," Leon said. "I gotta say I like workin' with you. You're kinda one of the boys."

"I am?" she said, taking it as a compliment.

"Yeah. All the guys think so, an' believe me, that's high praise."

"Well . . . I'm not sure what to say."

"You don't hav'ta say nothin'."

"Then I won't."

Leon circled her desk. "Y'know, this weekend, my partner, Phil, an' his wife are throwin' a barbecue. Nothin' fancy, but a lot of the guys are goin', an' I thought you might wanna tag along. Get t' know everyone."

"That's so nice of you, Leon, but this weekend I'll be in Vegas with my, uh . . . boyfriend." She felt stupid saying the word *boyfriend*, but that's exactly what Bobby was. Anyway, she needed to let Leon know she was taken, even though she was sure he already knew.

"Vegas, huh?" Leon said, hiding his disappointment. "Now, doncha go runnin' off an' sealin' the deal in one of those Elvis impersonator weddin' chapels."

"I promise I won't."

"Then I guess I'm gonna hav'ta let you go."

"I have your permission, do I?" she said, amused.

"Yeah, Denver. Put it all on lucky seven, an' don't come back without a big score."

"Yes *sir!*"

Her cell rang. It was Bobby. Leon took the hint and left.

"Where were you last night?" she asked. "I couldn't hear a word you said."

"Long boring story," Bobby replied, deciding he didn't need to mention the strip club. "Those Russian investors I told you about dragged everything out, and I ended up having to stay in Vegas."

"Poor you."

"Got on a plane early this morning, and just landed in New York." A beat. "But never mind about me. How are *you?*"

"Lonely."

"That's what I like to hear."

"Missing you."

"Even better."

"When will you be back?"

"Thursday night. Then Friday we'll fly to Vegas. Please tell me you're saying yes."

Alternatives: Visiting Sam on a movie set. Attending a cop barbecue with Leon. Seems like no contest. "I'm saying yes, Bobby," she said softly.

"That's my girl. I'll call you later. Have a good one."

~ ~ ~

Checking out a couple of gossip sites on his computer, Frankie was delighted to find several shots of himself and Cookie leaning all over each other at River. She looked hot, kind of like a young Janet Jackson.

He quickly scanned the copy:

Eighteen-year-old Cookie, daughter of soul icon Gerald M., getting thisclose with her new boyfriend, Frankie Romano, at his club, River.

Perfect! Exactly what he'd planned. He'd given access to a paparazzo, who'd gotten the shots in the club and then sold them. Of course, Rick Greco would be pissed that they'd called River his club, but hey—he *was* the front man. *He* was the one bringing the crowd in. Yeah! They all loved Frankie Romano. He knew how to satisfy everyone's decadent cravings. Nothing bad about *that*.

Unbeknownst to Rick, Frankie had a secret to assuring happy repeat customers, and that secret was a lucrative drug business he ran on the side. Coke, pills, Ecstasy, crystal meth, pot. You name it, Frankie could supply it. His rich and famous customers loved the convenience of having a virtual pharmacy at their disposal. Frankie had all his connections down, and now he was starting to make real money.

Too bad Rick hadn't made him a full partner; he might've considered sharing.

CHAPTER THIRTEEN

After spending some time with his father, who was resting before the next day's wildly extravagant birthday festivities, Armand returned to his palace and the family he had not yet seen.

This time Soraya was waiting to greet him. They had been married for eleven years, and he had to admit that from the fifteen-year-old girl he'd wed, Soraya had turned into a striking woman. She was tall and slender, with a sweep of long, straight black hair and large sad eyes. Her body was covered by the traditional burqa.

He found himself wondering what this woman he hardly knew would look like in Western clothes, and if, when he wasn't around, she actually wore them. The truth was he didn't care, even though she had given birth to four children—*his* children.

Soraya rarely spoke when she was in his presence, only answered him when he directed a question at her.

"Where is Tariq?" he asked, naming his only son.

"I will fetch him if you wish," Soraya replied.

He'd noticed that she never looked him directly in the eyes; she avoided any kind of contact, including physical. He'd stopped sleeping with her several visits ago. He had no desire for yet another daughter, and it seemed that every time he touched her, she ended up pregnant. Not that sleeping with her gave him any enjoyment. The few times he'd had sex with her, she'd lain beneath him like a stone statue, unmoving and unresponsive.

So be it. There were many women who would do anything he requested—no request too bizarre. Only yesterday in London he'd had two women crawling around his suite on all fours wearing leather dog collars, serving him dinner and then pleasuring each other for his amusement, while he sat back and snorted coke until he got bored and sent the whores away.

Soraya left the room and returned with Tariq, a tall, skinny boy of eleven. The boy was clad in an American Lakers T-shirt, jeans, and sneakers.

Armand was incensed. "Why is Tariq dressed like this?" he demanded. "It is disrespectful to me. Have him change immediately."

"Yes," Soraya murmured, shooing her son from the room.

"When I come here," Armand said, his voice a harsh command, "I expect obedience and respect. Do you understand me?"

Soraya hung her head, still refusing to look at him.

Armand didn't care. When the king died and he inherited what was his, perhaps he would abandon Akramshar and never come back. For it was not his country, not his home. America was his home. And Soraya and her brood were not his family.

~ ~ ~

King Emir Amin Mohamed Jordan embraced tradition—his own personal tradition. Every year it was the same thing: an elaborate parade put on by his legions of grandchildren, of whom he was extremely proud, followed by a public proclamation to the citizens of Akramshar, who revered their generous king. Then there was a series of more private celebrations. First a massive feast of roasted lamb, goat, and various other animals. The men on one side of the huge tent erected for the festivities, the women and children on the other. For entertainment, a dozen or so plump belly dancers jiggled their wares for several hours, until eventually the women and children were sent away and a parade of exquisite Eastern European women appeared, dressed in tight, low-cut cocktail dresses, with soaring high heels on their bare legs, and an abundance of makeup.

The women formed a line, and the king chose the ones he wished to sit with him and his sons. Later the king would pair off with a woman or three of his choice, and after he had chosen, it was his sons' turns to pick whomever they wanted. Since Armand was not the eldest son, he had to wait. This infuriated him. He felt that because of his business dealings with his father, he should be next. But tradition ruled. When his time came, he selected a sultry honey-blonde from Ukraine. She reminded him of Nona Constantine, and he enjoyed reliving the ravishing of Nona. The high-class call girl didn't complain, but she was paid a small fortune not to, so Armand had his fun with her, humiliating her in every possible way. When he finally dismissed her, he could see the hatred in her eyes. It did not bother him. She was a paid whore; why would he care?

Year after year, the king's celebrations were a repeat performance. And the next morning Armand was on a plane out of there, back to civilization; back to the life he preferred.

Good-bye, Akramshar.

Good-bye, Soraya.

Good-bye to the family he'd never wanted.

CHAPTER FOURTEEN

Driving along Pico on her way home from work, Denver checked in with Carolyn. She was curious to find out what had taken place on Carolyn's date with a woman. It seemed such a random thing for her to do—changing sides for no particular reason.

"Is Bobby in town?" Carolyn asked.

"No. He's in New York," Denver replied, pulling up to a red light. "Why?"

"'Cause I was thinking you might feel like picking up a Chinese chicken salad from Chin Chin and coming over."

"Sounds like a plan," Denver said, happy to do so. She hadn't felt like spending yet another evening home alone, and although she wasn't really into babies, she had to admit that Andy was extremely adorable.

Sam had called and left a message. She hadn't called him back; she didn't want to encourage him. After all, she'd told him she was still involved—sort of. Maybe he hadn't taken her as seriously as she should've.

After stopping by Chin Chin, she headed straight for Carolyn's house.

Carolyn was sitting out in her back garden, Andy balanced on her knee. The two of them made a perfect picture, straight out of *Modern Mother* magazine.

Denver wondered whether her friend was thinking of going back to work anytime soon. Andy's dad, the cheating Senator Stoneman, was certainly not sending her any child support. Who knew if he was even aware that he had a son? And since Carolyn's parents had split up, they were probably not prepared to give financial aid to their daughter forever. Besides, Denver reckoned it would be therapeutic for Carolyn to find a job and put all the Washington trauma behind her.

"Hey," she said lightly. "I left the food in the kitchen. Don't you ever lock your front door? I walked right in."

"Nothing for them to take except me and Andy," Carolyn remarked, completely unconcerned. "And I'm sure nobody wants us."

"How about your TV, your computer, your camera?" Denver pointed out. "All valuable items."

"I'm hardly ripe for a robbery."

"Everyone should take precautions," Denver admonished. "Crime is all around us."

"Spoken like a true DA."

"So," Denver said, throwing herself into the empty lawn chair beside Carolyn's, "I'm dying to know—how was your walk on the wild side?"

"Interesting," Carolyn said as her front doorbell chimed. She stood up and handed Denver the baby. "*Some* people ring before entering," she commented.

"*Some* people haven't known you since you were twelve," Denver replied tartly. "Are you expecting someone?"

"You'll see," Carolyn said, vanishing into the house.

"I only brought enough salad for two," Denver yelled after her. "And I'm starving, so I'm not in the mood for sharing."

Andy let out a big burp, and a dribble of drool slid down the side of his mouth. Awkwardly, Denver tried to wipe it away with the back of her hand. She wasn't used to babies; somehow the maternal gene had yet to kick in.

And then a vision appeared. A gorgeous woman with soft, naturally curly blond hair, kind eyes, and a bountiful figure.

Carolyn was right behind her. "Denver, meet Vanessa," she said briskly.

Denver was surprised and shocked. Somehow or other she'd imagined Vanessa to be big and butch with cropped hair and no makeup, dressed in a manly leather jacket. This lovely, feminine woman was the complete opposite.

"Uh, hi," Denver said, embarrassed that she'd had such a cliché view of what a lesbian should look like.

"Hello," Vanessa said, proffering a firm handshake and a friendly smile. "Carolyn talks about you a lot. It's such a pleasure to finally meet you."

Finally? One date and now Vanessa was acting as if they were in a relationship. *What the hell?*

"Vanessa works for a TV production company," Carolyn said, smiling blissfully at her new friend. "Documentaries and the like."

"Really?" Denver said, suddenly feeling as if *she* was the odd one out.

"Yes," Vanessa said, swooping down to steal Andy out of Denver's arms. "I'm hoping to convince Carolyn to come join us. With all her Washington experience, she'd be such an asset. Will you please talk her into it?"

"I'll try," Denver said with a weak smile.

Carolyn giggled. Carolyn was *so* not a giggler. "I'm thinking about it," she said coyly. "Nobody has to talk me into anything."

"Well, think faster," Vanessa chided, and the two exchanged an intimate look.

Oh my God! Denver thought. *They're acting as if they're already a couple. Who knew?*

~ ~ ~

Lucky's apartment in The Keys was her dream home. Not that she didn't love the Malibu house and spending time with her kids, but her haven in Vegas was her special place. Whenever she was there, she felt at peace. Sometimes she needed to be alone, and sitting in her penthouse above the Strip—looking out at the sparkling lights of the city—gave her immense satisfaction. It also reminded her of so many Vegas memories. Sometimes the memories were overwhelming, good and bad.

Picking up the house phone, she called downstairs to Danny, her personal assistant. Danny was the eyes and ears on everything Vegas when she wasn't in residence. He'd only worked for her a year, but he was quite possibly the best assistant she'd ever had. He was young, twenty-something, gay—in a long-term relationship with Buff, his high school buddy. She trusted him implicitly.

"Did Gino arrive yet?" she asked.

"He's here," Danny responded. "Feisty as ever. I cannot believe how old that man is!"

Lucky smiled, thinking of her ninety-something father, who never slowed down. "Yes, he's remarkable, isn't he?" she said. Gino had his own suite at The Keys, and there was nothing he liked more than sitting in a lounge chair outside his private cabana at the pool, watching all the pretty girls pass by. He had not acquired the nickname Gino the Ram for nothing. Over the years, he'd certainly lived up to his reputation. Now married to his fifth wife, Paige, a woman decades younger than him, Gino seemed to have more energy than anyone.

"Is everything set for the board meeting on Friday?" Lucky asked.

"Of course," Danny replied. "It's all in order."

"I think I've persuaded Alex Woods to come. Make sure he has the right accommodations. And arrange to have cars meet everyone at the airport."

"Got it, Lucky."

"Okay, then," she said, tossing back her long jet-black hair. "I'm on my way to see Gino. We'll talk later."

~ ~ ~

The Malibu party started off slowly. A trickle of friends hanging out by the pool drinking beer and Coke from cans, laughing and talking and generally getting loose.

Max glanced around and wished she *had* invited Ace. Maybe this would've been the night they consummated their relationship, shifting it to another level. Since she was about to be eighteen, wasn't it time to do something about taking things all the way?

She took a quick peek at her watch and realized it was only just past eight, so if she called him now he could probably make it in a couple of hours. But then he'd be annoyed that she hadn't told him about it before, so it was best to leave it alone.

Cookie was busy draping herself all over the deejay Harry

had gotten. The guy was Latin and a major hottie straight out of a Calvin Klein ad. Maybe Frankie wouldn't show, and Cookie would settle for this guy. He certainly knew his stuff—rocking everything from Usher to Drake to Miley to old eighties soul and Beatles classics.

This is going to be a perfect evening, Max thought. *A mellow way to celebrate turning eighteen. And after I'm eighteen, I'm moving to New York, far away from parental concerns. I'm going to be exactly like Bobby and make my own life.*

Doing what?

I haven't decided.

She darted inside the house to check that she'd locked up all the main rooms. She certainly didn't want anyone coming into the house. Lucky would *so* not appreciate it.

Harry followed her, his spiked hair gelled higher than ever. "You gotta tell Cookie to lay off Paco," he said, sounding flustered. "She's such a greedy bitch. If it's got a dick, she wants it."

"Who's Paco?"

Harry's pale skin reddened. "The deejay."

"Why d'you want her to back off?"

"'Cause I gotta wild hunch he's gonna be way more into me than her," Harry said.

"Oh crap!" Max exclaimed, getting the message.

"So *do* something about her," Harry pleaded.

"I'll try," Max promised. "But you know Cookie. . . ."

Yes, everyone knew Cookie. If there was a party, she was there. If there was a hot guy, she was there. Cookie had lost her virginity to one of her famous father's friends when she was fourteen, and she'd never looked back.

It kind of irked Max that she lurked so far behind in the sex stakes, but then again, she didn't want to give it up to just anyone. The first time had to be special, and she was making sure that it would be.

~ ~ ~

Back in New York, Bobby stopped by his apartment, checked his e-mail, took a shower, put on fresh clothes, and headed for Mood.

It was past ten by the time he arrived, and the place was packed, as usual. Wednesday nights were usually extra happening, as it was guest deejay night, and everyone enjoyed the change of pace. His manager, Paulo, a suave Italian, assured him things were going well.

Bobby did the rounds, stopping by tables, buying people drinks, complimenting the women. He wasn't crazy about playing the genial host, but he did it because he knew it was good for business.

Martin Constantine—the real-estate mogul—insisted that he join him and his wife, Nona, for a glass of champagne. At one time Bobby had considered asking Martin if he'd be interested in investing in future clubs, but then he'd decided against it, because Martin wouldn't simply put up the money; he was the kind of man who'd expect to be involved.

Nona, an ex–beauty queen from Slovakia, was not her normal flirty self. Bobby was relieved. He'd never quite figured out how to deal with the horny wives of rich men, and it was surprising how many came on to him. Horny wives were a business hazard he tried to avoid.

After having a quick drink with Martin and Nona, he moved on to sit with Charlie Dollar and Cooper Turner, two old Hollywood stalwarts who still attracted a parade of beautiful girls.

There was something about weathered movie stars that prevented them from being perceived as dirty old men. It was the Jack Nicholson/Al Pacino syndrome.

After a while, Paulo approached and whispered discreetly in his ear that the outrageous superstar Zeena was requesting his presence at her table.

Ah, Zeena! They'd had a few run-ins, the last one in Vegas, where she'd unexpectedly appeared in his shower and given him head, later practically announcing it onstage in the middle of her concert, while he was on his first date with Denver. Not easy explaining *that* little incident to Denver. It had gotten them off to a rocky start. But fortunately, everything had worked out, and the last thing he needed was Zeena screwing things up again.

He instructed Paulo to make sure there was no one taking any photos in the club—one had to watch out for cell phones— then reluctantly made his way over to Zeena's table, where she was holding court with her usual entourage of hangers-on and her latest boyfriend, an emaciated English actor famous for playing a blood-crazed vampire on TV.

Zeena was her usual over-the-top self—she was half Brazilian, half Native American, and her exotic beauty could be mesmerizing.

"Bobbee," she purred in her low-down husky voice. "Zeena hasn't seen you for too long. Where has my Bobbee been?"

He stared into her catlike eyes and realized that the crush he'd once had on her was long gone. "Around," he said casually, shaking the hand of her pale-faced boyfriend.

"Maybe Zeena should come visit you," Zeena suggested. "You like?"

Vampire boyfriend spoke up. "No," he said firmly. "He wouldn't like, and neither would I."

At last! Zeena had finally hooked up with someone who wasn't afraid to stand up to her.

Bobby laughed, easing the sudden tension. "Zeena, always the joker," he said smoothly, patting her boyfriend on the shoulder. "I'm sending your table more champagne. Enjoy."

And before she could respond with another unwelcome come-on, he was on his way to the next booth, where Adrien Brody and his friend Dieter Abt were ensconced with a group of beautiful models, male and female.

A fast escape. The best kind.

~ ~ ~

"Y'know," Lucky said affectionately, "if I didn't know any better, I would swear you weren't a day over seventy! You're amazing!"

Gino roared with laughter. Remarkably, he still had all his teeth, and although his hair was gray, it was still there. Age had not bowed him. "I'm in my nineties, kiddo," he said. "Outlived 'em all. An' I don't regret a minute of the life I lived. 'Cept maybe when you an' me wasn't talkin'."

"Well, that didn't last, did it?" she said, remembering their many famous fights over the years.

"Naw. Knew it wouldn't," Gino answered, grinning. "You're easy."

"Sure I am," Lucky replied sarcastically.

They were sitting together in Lucky's favorite restaurant at The Keys, a cozy Italian place tucked away in a corner spot, aptly called Gino's. The restaurant served all the food Gino loved. Meatballs with garlic and a rich tomato sauce. Penne pasta. Tasty veal chops with roasted Tuscan potatoes and myriad vegetables. Plus an assortment of pizzas named after various members of the Santangelo family.

Paige had elected not to join them, claiming she was tired, but Lucky knew it was because Paige was smart enough to know they enjoyed spending time together, just the two of them.

"How's little Max?" Gino wanted to know. "Still plannin' her escape?"

"Oh yes," Lucky said ruefully. "There's no stopping that one."

"Just like you, Lucky, huh?" Gino said, nodding at the memories.

"I hope not. I was a wild one."

"You still are, kiddo, you still are."

"Thanks, Gino, but I don't know about that."

"Yeah, well, I do. You inherited the Santangelo balls; that's what makes you such a winner. An' you gotta teach Max how t' deal."

"She's pretty smart, Gino."

"Not as smart as you when you were her—"

"There's plenty of time for her to learn," Lucky interrupted.

"Time goes quickly, kiddo. You'd be surprised."

"Not for you it doesn't."

"Y'know," he said, lowering his gruff voice, "if ya wanna know what goes on in my head, I'm gonna tell ya—I got this thought goin' on that I'm only thirty." A big grin spread across his face. "How's about *that*?"

"Right," Lucky retorted. "And I'm sixteen, getting my ass married off to some dumb senator's son 'cause my daddy thought it would control me. Lotsa luck with *that*."

"Here she goes," Gino groaned. "Always dredgin' up the past."

"Just f-ing with you, Gino," she said lightly. "Nothing I like better than watching you squirm."

And once again she smiled, realizing there was nothing more satisfying than spending time with her father, for who knew how long he'd be around.

~ ~ ~

Willow Price and her posse of nubile young women—all various shades of blond and bubbly—decided they would like to go clubbing. And since Billy had nothing better to do after buying them all dinner at an expensive restaurant, he thought he might as well tag along. After all, his image was out of control and he kind of liked it. Leaving BOA with the darling of the tabs, Willow Price, and her blond entourage guaranteed a major media blitz, and since Venus had been seen out and about with her young costar *and* the grizzled director of her current movie, it was only fitting that he do the same.

Also, Venus's lawyer had informed *his* lawyer that she intended to keep their Vegas apartment in The Keys, and since he'd paid for half, that really pissed him off. He'd told his lawyer to fight her on that one. Screw Venus. Screw the big superstar who thought she could get anything she wanted.

Think again, sweetheart. He might be thirteen years younger than his soon-to-be ex, but he was no pushover.

Willow clung on to his arm for the sake of the paparazzi. The photographers descended like a pack of rabid dogs, screaming both their names, while the unknown blondes hovered and giggled, and flashed their tits and long legs emerging from tight micro miniskirts, thrilled to be a part of such mayhem.

"If you're a very, *very* well-behaved boy," Willow whispered in his ear, pouting innocently for the cameras, "I'll let you watch me lick pussy later."

He contemplated the future scenario she had in mind. Watching was not his thing. If he wasn't a participant, he wasn't interested.

"That's all right," he mumbled. "Whyn't we get in the car an' stop by River?"

"Oh yes," Willow purred. "I'd like that."

One last pose for the cameras, and they were on their way.

CHAPTER FIFTEEN

Three hours into what seemed like an under-the-radar, mellow party, chaos reigned. Max couldn't figure out how it had happened. From the maybe seventy or eighty people they'd expected, others were pouring in at an alarming rate. Carloads of teenagers she didn't know, didn't want to know, and could do nothing about. And not only teenagers, but a bunch of dirty old men—probably agents or producers—in their flashy Porsches and Bentleys, not to mention flocks of random girls in tiny backless, almost frontless, outfits.

Several people brought booze with them. A boy in a Batman outfit dragged in a keg. Two girls came armed with a margarita machine. Some people were smoking weed, others snorting cocaine. A whole bunch of naked men and women were frolicking in the pool, while others were making out on the patio. It was insanity. And neither Cookie nor Harry was any help. Harry had affixed himself to Paco, the deejay, and refused to move, while

Cookie was snorting and drinking and having herself a fine old time. They were both stoned. Both feeling no pain.

Max rarely drank, and she didn't do drugs. Apparently she was the only one.

People were finding their way into the house. They'd already taken over the living room, and a drunken group of girls was attempting to break the lock on Lucky and Lennie's bedroom door.

Panicked, Max thought about anonymously calling the cops and complaining about the noise, but that wouldn't help, considering they might file a report of a disturbance, and then Lucky or Lennie would find out. Not a smart move.

What was she supposed to do to stop the invasion?

Lucky would go totally ape shit if she ever found out what was going on. Max knew she'd be grounded for weeks, maybe even months. Life as she knew it would be over.

Although, wait a minute, she thought. *I'm about to turn eighteen; they can't ground me.*

Or can they?

What they *could* do was cut off her allowance and not pay for her ticket to New York and the six months' rent on an apartment Lucky had promised her as a birthday present.

Pulling herself together, she confronted the girls trying to force their way into Lucky's bedroom.

They told her to screw off.

She yelled back at them that it was her house and *they* could screw off or she'd call the cops and accuse them of trespassing.

They retaliated with a few obscene gestures and insults, then staggered off.

Max wished she had invited Ace. He'd know what to do. She

didn't. As far as she was concerned, her party had turned into an uncontrollable nightmare, and she was totally helpless to do anything about it.

Lucky would know how to handle it. Lucky knew how to handle anything.

Dammit. Why couldn't she be more like her mom in situations such as this?

~ ~ ~

The insistent buzz of his doorbell awoke Bobby with a sudden start. Groping for his watch, he noted it was four A.M.

Goddammit! Who was outside his apartment at four in the morning? And what the fuck was his doorman doing that he allowed someone to come up unannounced?

Muttering to himself, he rolled out of bed and headed for the door in nothing but his Calvins.

Then he stopped. Dead still. There was only one person who would have the balls to come calling at this time. Zeena.

Of course!

The doorbell continued to ring, and he stood silently in his hallway trying to figure out his next move.

It suddenly occurred to him that there was only one answer, and that was to do absolutely nothing and hope the predatory superstar would slink away into the night. It wasn't the first time she'd turned up at his apartment at some unearthly hour. She was one hell of a persistent woman, who when she wanted something, expected to get it. And tonight she obviously wanted him.

They had a history. Once upon a time he'd harbored a slight crush. She'd turned up at his New York apartment and they'd gone at it like a couple of wild things. One time was enough. Crush over. But the unfortunate thing was that she'd continued to pursue him, culminating in the embarrassing shower scene on the night of his first date with Denver. That was some memory.

He'd had no contact with her since, and tonight he'd been pleased to note she was with her latest conquest.

Apparently her latest conquest wasn't enough to satisfy Zeena, for now she was on *his* doorstep.

And what was he supposed to do about *that*?

Exactly nothing.

~ ~ ~

"Who wants to come to a party in Malibu?" Frankie asked Billy, Willow, and their assorted hangers-on.

"Whose party?" Billy wanted to know.

"Does anyone care?" Willow retorted, always up for a fun time. "It'll be *our* party when we get there, no doubt about that."

They'd all been hanging out in the club for a while, during which time Frankie had presented them with primo weed and made sure all their drinks were comped. Willow's crazy girlfriends were dancing on the tables to Katy Perry, while Willow watched them cavort, a secret smile playing around her glossy lips as she anticipated the scene that would take place later.

Billy sat back, downing a vodka or two. He looked bored. He *was* bored. The session with the girl he'd picked up on Melrose had not satisfied him. Momentarily, yes. But somehow he craved more than a fast blow job beside his pool. Lately he'd been thinking that it might be refreshing to find someone he could conduct an actual conversation with.

Willow was certainly not that person, nor were her nubile groupies. But that's what he seemed to be stuck with—for now.

Meanwhile, Frankie was buzzing. Having celebrities in his club was a plus, especially as he got off on spending time with anyone famous. Celebrities validated his existence.

Cookie had phoned several times asking when he was getting to the Malibu party. The last time she'd called he'd assured her he was on his way, and since Cookie was his pathway to bigger and better, he wasn't about to let her down. Arriving with Willow and Billy—two of the hottest stars around—would definitely impress her.

After a while he rounded up Billy, Willow, and the girls. "Got a couple of limos downstairs. Time to bounce," he informed them. "Refreshments in the limos," he added with a knowing wink, wondering if he stood half a chance with Willow—although rumor had it that she was a tried-and-true carpet muncher.

But hey, he was Frankie Romano. Who knew *what* could happen?

~ ~ ~

Feeling out of her depth, Max grabbed a bottle of beer and fled down to the beach. She didn't know what else to do. Maybe if she stayed away from the chaos, everyone would go home.

Wishful thinking.

Whose dumb idea was it to have a party in the first place?

Mine! Mine! Mine!

As for Cookie and Harry, the two of them were useless. She'd thought they were at least loyal, but they'd turned into party animals, thinking only of themselves. Although she didn't blame

Harry so much. He'd finally found a gay dude he could latch onto, and he wasn't about to let the opportunity go to waste.

Why can't I enjoy myself too? she thought. *Just get stoned and drunk like everyone else?*

Because there's no one I can enjoy things with. Besides, I'm a Santangelo—gotta stay alert.

She slumped down on the sand, closed her eyes, and allowed the hypnotic sound of the waves crashing on the sand to wash over her.

~ ~ ~

After spending an awkward couple of hours with Carolyn and Vanessa, Denver drove home filled with mixed emotions. What was Carolyn thinking? How could she simply decide she was gay and that was it?

They'd been best friends since they were twelve. They'd shared everything—all their thoughts and dreams and problems with the men in their lives. Now Carolyn had taken off down a different road, and Denver couldn't help feeling that somehow she'd been left behind. It wasn't that she didn't like Vanessa; the woman was warm and friendly. Quite lovely, in fact. So what was it?

Am I jealous? she wondered. *Do I feel as if Carolyn is deserting me?*

Or maybe she sensed that their friendship was slipping away, because if Carolyn became a couple with Vanessa, there might not be any room left for her. Sad but true.

She wished Bobby were at home, waiting for her.

But no, Bobby was in New York, so she'd just have to make do without him. And that was one of the problems of having a long-distance relationship: the separations were a bitch.

~ ~ ~

Once they arrived at the party, Billy soon decided that he wasn't in the mood to mix with a bunch of stoned people he didn't know, who were all busy brownnosing him simply because he had a hit movie. If he weren't a movie star, they wouldn't give a shit. He'd be just another good-looking dude searching for a break. And he knew this because of his experiences when he'd first arrived in Hollywood with no money and no foreseeable future. Countless auditions that had taken him nowhere, sleeping on friends' floors, waitering for a living, until he finally got the big break he'd been praying for—not that he was religious, but a prayer or two in the right direction never hurt. The big break was in an Alex Woods movie, *Seduction,* playing opposite the incredibly famous Venus.

And so it had begun. The crazy career. The road to stardom, marriage to Venus, and all the bullshit that went along with it.

The party and the people were getting on his nerves, so after fifteen minutes of meaningless conversations, he made his way over to the steps that led down to the beach, leaving the party behind.

As he walked along the sand, he noticed a girl curled up against a rock. He edged toward her. "Hey," he said, gingerly nudging her with the tip of his foot, hoping she wasn't dead or sick or anything overly dramatic. "You okay?"

Max sat up with a start. Wow! She'd downed a beer, closed her eyes, and zoned out. Talk about an escape hatch!

"I'm, uh . . . fine, thank you," she said stiffly, somewhat embarrassed.

He proffered his hand.

She took it, and he pulled her up.

"What're you doing down here by yourself?" he asked.

"Same as you, probably," she said, pushing her clouds of dark hair off her face. "Getting away from all those morons."

Billy laughed, and took a second look at the sexy young girl with the jet-black curls and the exceptionally pretty face. She was clad in rock 'n' roll torn jeans and a midriff-baring white shirt knotted under her breasts, with multiple silver chains and crosses hanging around her slender neck. He narrowed his eyes. "I *know* you," he said, thinking she looked vaguely familiar.

"And *I* know *you*," she responded, staring at the studly tousled-haired movie star with the piercing blue eyes and rippling torso nicely displayed in a tight black T-shirt. Of course she knew him. Everyone did.

"Saw my movie, huh?" Billy said, thinking that his fame was such a useful conversation opener. And this girl was majorly hot—in a very un-bimbo-like way. He'd left the bimbo squad cavorting naked in the pool with Willow, and he couldn't care less about any of them.

"I didn't, actually," Max lied, thinking that he looked way better offscreen, because she'd seen his latest movie. Twice. But she wasn't about to tell *him* that.

"Then where do we know each other from?" Billy asked, realizing that he'd smoked too much weed and downed too many vodka shots, which was another reason he'd headed to the beach to chill out.

"Um . . . you were married to my mom's best friend," Max blurted.

"Who's your mom's best friend?"

"Venus."

Billy's face registered shock. "You're—"

"Yeah, I'm Max. Lucky's daughter."

"You *gotta* be shittin' me," he exclaimed.

"Now, why would I do that?" she asked innocently.

"Jeez!" he said, his mind taking off in many different directions. "Thought I recognized the house. I must've been here a couple of times. Where's Lucky and Lennie?"

"Lucky's in Vegas. Lennie's shooting a movie," Max said, slightly breathless because this was Billy Melina, and along with Johnny Depp and Robert Pattinson, he was one of her favorites. She'd harbored a secret crush for months, ever since seeing his latest movie.

"Don't tell me this is *your* party?" Billy said, gesturing up toward the distant house where music was blaring and lights were flashing. Someone had added fireworks to the mix, so every few minutes the sky lit up and the noise was out of control.

"Unfortunately, yes," she admitted. "It's a total bad scene, right?"

"Let me get this straight," Billy said, somewhat perplexed. "So even though it's your party, you're down on the beach because . . . ?"

"'Cause I just told you—it's a freaking nightmare," she said with a helpless shrug. "I made a daring escape. Can you blame me?"

"Hmm . . ." he said, giving her a long quizzical look. "Do Mommy and Daddy know you're entertaining?"

"What do *you* think?" she replied, gazing directly into his electric blue eyes.

"I'm taking a wild guess an' saying they don't."

"And you're *so* not about to tell them, are you?"

"Hey," he said with a casual shrug. "We're hardly on speaking terms, what with Venus bad-mouthing me big-time."

"Oh yes," Max said tartly. "Auntie Venus."

"Shit!" Billy mock-groaned. "Don't say that, you're makin' me feel old."

"You *are* old, aren't you?" she said boldly.

"Thirty, chicken. An' you?"

"Eighteen," she answered, which wasn't *such* a huge lie, because there were only three more days to go.

They exchanged a long look, one that sent shivers up and down her spine.

Was this really happening?

Yes. Absolutely.

"Hey," he said, breaking the look. "Wanna take a walk?"

She nodded. Like it was Billy Melina; there was no way she'd turn *him* down.

They started strolling along the sand, close to the shoreline, and after a while, Billy began to talk. The more he talked, the more she found herself really liking him. He told her about the movie he was shooting and a whole load of interesting and funny stories to do with the cast and crew. Soon she began telling him about her plans to move to New York and start a new life away from her parents, and the cool thing was that he actually listened to her, told her it sounded like a great move to make and that she should definitely do it.

Yes, he was way hotter offscreen than on. In the past she'd seen him from afar several times with Venus, and she vaguely remembered watching him laughing and joking with Lucky and Lennie at the opening of The Keys. He'd never taken any notice of her before, but this time was different. This time they were two people with an awesome electric current buzzing between them.

She wondered if he could feel it too.

Suddenly she wanted nothing more than to touch him, feel his skin against hers, experience everything he had to offer.

Oh God! Could this be it? Had she finally met The One?

Billy Melina.

Soon-to-be ex of her mom's best friend.

Red-hot movie star.

What better way to lose her virginity?

~ ~ ~

Sometimes Frankie got into fights. He had his enemies. A club promoter he'd butted heads with in the past was coming on to Willow and her naked nymphs in the pool, calling them names and generally being obnoxious.

Sitting in a lounge chair with a giggly and very stoned Cookie, Frankie felt perfectly content until Cookie hissed in his ear, "Do something!"

So he did, and almost got coldcocked for his trouble.

"Goddammit!" he exclaimed, nursing his jaw. When had he become the protector of dykes? "That prick could've knocked my fuckin' teeth out."

"Well, he didn't," said an unconcerned Cookie as "that prick" was escorted off the premises by two macho gay guys who worshiped Willow Price and would do anything for her.

"Where were they when I needed them?" Frankie grumbled.

"Never mind," Cookie cooed, getting up and leading him into the house. "Let's go do some more blow. You know that'll make you feel *way* better."

It was almost four A.M. and the party was starting to wind down. There were only a few stragglers left in the living room. Harry was around, helping the deejay pack up.

Cookie had no clue where Max was, and she didn't care. It was time for Frankie to give it up, and not only the cocaine.

Cookie was one very happy camper.

~ ~ ~

"Maybe we should get back up to the house?" Billy suggested after a while.

"Sure," Max said, totally aware that something powerful was going on between them, an unstoppable attraction.

"Or . . ." He moved toward her, placing his hands on her shoulders. "We could stay here."

Yes, he senses it too! Oh crap!

She leaned a touch closer to him. "Maybe we *should* stay here," she managed.

"Maybe you're right," he countered.

Then, before she could think of anything else to say, his lips descended on hers, insistent and strong.

She kissed him back, shudders of excitement racing through her body, an excitement so intense that she couldn't wait to rip her clothes off, or have him do it for her.

After a few moments he began unknotting her shirt, pulling it off her, then touching her breasts with his fingertips, pushing them together before bending his head to suck ever so slowly on each nipple.

"Billy," she murmured, rubbing her hand between his legs, stroking him the way Ace liked her to do—although he wasn't Ace, with whom she'd only gone so far. He was Billy Melina, movie star, friend of her parents, soon-to-be ex-husband of Venus.

She didn't care. She didn't care about anything except having him close to her.

Hurriedly, he ripped off his T-shirt and threw it down on the sand, then somehow he maneuvered her on top of it and he lay on top of her. Within minutes they were both naked and enthralled with each other.

Billy was vaguely aware that he shouldn't be making this move with Lucky's daughter. If Venus ever found out, she'd go nuts. But jeez, he hadn't felt this way since the first time he'd had sex with his high school girlfriend. There was something very special about Max. She wasn't just another casual pickup.

Oh yeah, on one hand he knew being with her would cause nothing but trouble.

On the other hand, he didn't give a flying fuck.

Max felt the same way as she gave in to the feelings that were completely overpowering her. This was it. This was the man she'd been saving herself for, and as far as she was concerned, nothing was going to stop the inevitable, and to hell with the consequences.

He began to make love to her, slowly, surely, taking it easy.

She closed her eyes and fell into his rhythm.

He smells so good, she thought. *Like a strong, fragrant soap mixed with his masculine body smell.*

She smells like sweet sin, he thought. *And it's a smell that turns me on to the highest degree.*

He has a body to die for.

She has the kind of body I dream about.

Smooth skin.

Taut surfaces.

Erect nipples.
Hers—deep rose.
His—black like the night.
I think I'm in love.
I think I'm in lust.
First time.
Tactile touches.
A rush of pure sweat.
An avalanche of desire.
Plunging into heaven.
Going all the way.
Feeling his power.
Feeling her acceptance.
Working together.
So gentle.
So soft.
And hard.
Breathless.
Wow!
Amazing.
Forbidden fruit.
Barely ripe.
Heady.
Intoxicating.
Falling into ecstasy.
And finally
Together.

CHAPTER SIXTEEN

Arriving back in New York, Armand was escorted through security by an airport representative, then ushered to a limousine parked at a private entrance where Fouad was waiting. Most times he accompanied Armand to Akramshar, but this time Armand had chosen to go alone.

Before Fouad could say a word, Armand demanded to know what was happening with The Keys.

Typical Armand, thought Fouad. *No time for pleasantries; straight to business.*

"We have a meeting in Vegas tomorrow," Fouad said, clearing his throat. "It was not easy arranging it. As I told you before, according to her lawyer, this Santangelo woman is not interested in selling, so I informed him that we were thinking of perhaps financing future projects she might be open to. Her lawyer seemed to entertain the thought of unlimited investment capitol."

"For God's sake!" Armand snorted derisively. "Why did you say that?"

"It was the only way I could arrange a meeting," Fouad explained.

"Such a fool," Armand muttered.

"In the meantime I had a dossier compiled on Lucky Santangelo," Fouad said, handing Armand a thick manila envelope. "I thought you might find it interesting. I know I did."

"'Interesting,'" Armand sneered. "Show me an interesting woman and I will show *you* a freak of nature."

"She is not your average woman," Fouad said evenly. "I would read it if I were you."

"Unfortunately for you, you're *not* me," Armand replied with a note of disdain, tossing the envelope on the floor of the limo.

Fouad wasn't surprised. Over the past few months, Armand had become even more arrogant and difficult. Fouad realized that this was due to Armand's escalating use of cocaine, and it worried him. At first Armand had used it as a recreational drug, but lately it seemed he needed it all the time.

Fouad deeply disapproved of any kind of drug use, but when he'd tried to tell Armand that the habit he'd acquired was turning into an out-of-control addiction, Armand had thrown one of his angry screaming fits.

There was a time Fouad had enjoyed working with Armand, but ever since Fouad had gotten married and created a life for himself, Armand had treated him less like an equal and more like an employee. Fouad did not like it. Armand continuously disrespected him, it was as simple as that.

"Your mother wishes to speak with you," Fouad said, keeping his expression impartial, because he knew Peggy, Armand's mother, was the only woman on Earth that Armand felt he could not control.

"Did you not tell her I was away?" Armand said, his voice a hostile missile.

"She knows that," Fouad answered quietly. "She is well aware of the date you visit our country each year."

"Your point?"

"She asked that you call her immediately upon your return."

Armand scowled. But he took out his cell phone and made the call anyway.

~ ~ ~

Since the death of her husband, Sidney, Peggy Dunn was beginning to realize that without a rich husband by her side, she was just another lonely Manhattan widow. At first her friends had rallied, making sure that she was still included in dinner dates, events, and parties. But as the months drifted past, she began to notice that the calls became less and less frequent, until she was fortunate to receive one dinner invitation a month. One a month! For a woman who was used to going out five nights a week, this was shocking. She was sixty years old, a decade younger than Raquel Welch, and, like Raquel, she was still an attractive woman. Not as beautiful as the eighteen-year-old girl King Emir Amin Mohamed Jordan had plucked from the chorus of a Vegas show and whisked back to Akramshar to become his fifth wife, but beautiful all the same. Thanks to one of the best colorists in New York, her hair was still flaming red. Her skin, smooth and pampered from weekly facials and twice-a-week massages, was still impeccable. Her body was passable, in spite of an extra ten pounds she couldn't seem to lose.

When Sidney died, she had expected to meet someone else, but that hadn't happened, and being alone did not suit her.

She was angry at her only child, Armand, a man who had made quite a name for himself in business—and only because of the money the king had given him on his twenty-first birthday, plus Sidney's counsel and advice about how to invest it wisely.

Armand was a billionaire simply because of the two men in her life. He had *her* to thank for his good fortune. And how had he repaid her? Not in any way she could see. When Sidney was alive, the three of them had dined together every few weeks, but since Sidney's unfortunate demise she'd hardly seen her son, and every time she called him, he seemed to come up with a work-related excuse. Furthermore, Armand had never married, and therefore had no children. At forty-two years old, he was still single.

Peggy did not think it was right that he had not presented her with grandchildren. For a while she and Sidney had feared he might be gay, but then they'd run into him at various events around town and he'd always had a pretty girl on his arm, so that had assuaged their fears.

"He's merely a late starter," Sidney had assured her. "He doesn't wish to get tied down for now. It's understandable."

Sidney was always so smart about everything. How she missed him!

However, the time had come to do something about Armand, and she fully intended to. If he couldn't pick a wife for himself, *she* would do it for him. As his mother, it was her duty.

When he called, she was ready.

"How was your trip, Armand?" she asked.

"The same as usual," he replied.

"And the king?"

"Nothing changes."

"Any new wives?"

"I do not notice such things."

Of course he doesn't notice such things, Peggy thought, slightly aggravated that her son never had any juicy gossip when he returned from his yearly visit.

"Well anyway," she said. "I wish to see you."

"When I get back," Armand said, wondering what the hell she wanted now.

"You just got back," Peggy said, pointing out the obvious.

"I know," he said impatiently. "But tonight I fly to Vegas for an important meeting."

"What time tonight?"

"Does it matter?"

"Yes, Armand, it does," she said, keeping her tone even. "Because tonight I am coming with you."

CHAPTER SEVENTEEN

Upon awaking early Thursday, Bobby was pleased with himself. He had not answered his door to the four A.M. caller, whom he was positive was Zeena. His only fear was that she might have been accompanied by a bodyguard who would be quite capable of springing the lock on his front door. Fortunately, this had not happened, and after fifteen minutes, the ringing had stopped and he'd gone back to bed. Now it was morning and he was safe.

Man! What an insane situation. Scared of an ego-driven superstar desperate to get in his pants. Who would believe it?

After shaving and showering, he called Denver, who was at work. "I'm hoping to catch a three o'clock flight out of here," he told her. "That means if I don't get delayed, I should be with you around six."

"Uh . . . how do you feel about dinner at my family's house?" she ventured, thinking that the time had come. "Family dinners are a Thursday-night tradition, and since you haven't met them, I thought . . ."

"You mean you're actually going to introduce me to your family?" he teased. "What are you—on drugs?"

She laughed weakly. "Is that a yes?"

"Damn right it's a yes."

"Then consider yourself invited."

"Oh, you bet your ass I will."

Things were looking up. He was finally going to meet Denver's family. He couldn't wait.

~ ~ ~

"Morning," Billy said, fit and tanned, tousled dirty-blond hair flopping on his forehead.

Max rolled across the sand and slowly opened her eyes. There he was, Billy Melina, standing over her holding a glass of orange juice. *So it wasn't all a crazy dream! He's here, and so am I.*

"Where . . . where did you get that?" she asked as he passed her the glass.

"From the house," he said calmly. "Hate to be the one to tell you, but it's a freakin' wreck up there. We're gonna need a cleanin' crew."

We; he'd said we. How exciting was that!

The sun was just coming up and it was chilly. Shivering slightly, she attempted to recall details of the previous night. Getting together with Billy was some kind of wonderful hazy blur. But one thing she knew for sure was that it had been totally great, and she didn't regret one single minute of it.

"You're still here," she murmured, stretching her arms above her head.

"Course I'm still here," he answered cheerfully. "What did you think, that I was gonna run off an' leave you?"

She gazed up into his super-blue eyes and broke into a wide grin. "You wouldn't do that, would you?" she said happily.

He grinned back. "No," he said sincerely. "I wouldn't do that."

"Didn't think so."

"Oh, like you know me so well," he teased, dropping onto the sand next to her and placing his arm around her shoulders.

She snuggled close. "You do know that last night was . . . uh . . . my . . . uh . . . first time," she murmured softly.

"Yeah," he said, nodding. "I kinda realized that."

"And you weren't disappointed?" she asked, dying to hear what he would say.

"Are you kiddin' me?" he said, throwing her a quizzical look. "You made it all the way to eighteen, that's almost a record."

"Uh . . . actually, I won't be eighteen until Saturday," she confessed, deciding that she'd better be honest with him.

"Huh?"

"Yeah, I kinda fudged a little," she admitted.

"Ah, jeez!" he groaned.

"*What?*"

"That means you're not even legal."

"Almost," she said quickly.

"'Almost' doesn't cut it," he said, imagining the headlines if this got out. "You do realize I could get my ass thrown into jail for what we did last night?"

"Who's going to know?"

"You, me, and no one else, right?" he said, swallowing hard.

"Right," she agreed.

"That means you cannot tell anyone—an' I mean *anyone*. Got it?"

"Like who exactly am I gonna tell?" she asked, regaining a little of her composure.

"Lucky, for a start."

"You *have* to be insane!" she exclaimed. "Lucky's the *last* person I'd tell."

"And who'd be the first?"

"Oh, I dunno," she answered vaguely. *"The National Enquirer, Star* magazine, TMZ—"

He lunged on top of her, and they rolled across the sand, laughing. The orange juice spilled, but neither of them cared.

"You're funny," he said.

"I try," she replied, suddenly breathless.

"And a nasty little liar," he added, but not in a bad way.

"Sorry," she said, feeling quite exhilarated.

"But I like you," he said quickly.

"And I like you back," she replied, equally fast.

"Jeez, this is crazy, isn't it?" he said, touching her face.

"Way crazy," she replied, marveling at the intense blue of his eyes and the feel of his hard body on top of her.

Actually, it was beyond crazy. Never mind about the party, if Lucky and Lennie found out about her night of lust with Billy, they would totally *freak!* Her losing her virginity probably wouldn't faze them. But her losing it to Billy Melina was a big huge NO!

Anyway, who cared? She'd just experienced the most fantastic, awesome night of her life. Now all she really wanted to do was be by herself so she could relive every magical, fantastic moment.

"I suppose we should drag our asses up to the house," Billy said.

"I guess," she said, worrying about what kind of devastation she'd find.

"I'd better warn you, you're not gonna be thrilled," Billy said, leaping to his feet and helping her up.

"Is anyone still there?"

"A coupla strays."

She hoped the strays were Cookie and Harry, but she doubted it. Knowing them, they'd both taken off and left her to deal.

"Is it a mess?"

"You'd better believe it."

"What am I gonna do?" she groaned. "How am I gonna fix it?"

"Don't sweat it."

"Well," she said, searching for a solution, "at least the housekeepers are coming back at noon."

"Gonna take more than a couple of maids to fix this," Billy said, shaking his head.

"You think?" she asked nervously.

"Come on," he said, pulling her toward the steps that led up to the house. "I've already called my manager. He's gettin' a crew over here."

"You can't do that," she said, frowning. "I've got to keep this under the radar."

"Don't worry, my manager's a cool dude. Nobody's gonna know whose house it is."

"You're *sure?*" she asked, certain that somehow or other she was going to get busted. Oh God! The wrath of Lucky and Lennie didn't bear thinking about.

"Course I'm sure."

Billy's amazing, she thought, gazing up at him. *He won't let me down. He's definitely a take-charge kinda dude, unlike Ace, who's always vacillating about what he's going to do with his life.*

Still . . . Ace had been her on-again, off-again boyfriend for eighteen months, and now she would have to break up with him for sure. She liked him, she'd just never liked him enough for him to be The One. The truth was, even if she never saw Billy again, she was glad he'd turned out to be The One. It was super karma.

As they reached the top of the steps and approached the once immaculate pool area, she let out a gasp of horror. "Oh my *God!*" she yelled, trying to control a sudden rush of panic. "They've trashed my house!"

A trail of destruction surrounded the pool. There were over-turned loungers, overflowing ashtrays, cigarette butts stamped out on the marble surround by the pool, and empty firework boxes everywhere, plus scorch marks on some of the sun umbrellas. Not to mention crushed beer cans, broken bottles, half-eaten burgers, cartons of French fries, ketchup spilled everywhere, and trash, trash, trash.

The pool resembled a garbage dump—what hadn't ended up around it was in it. A mass of floating debris.

"Lucky's going to *kill* me," Max wailed. "She'll freaking *murder* me!"

"Stay cool," Billy said, in charge and liking it. "It'll all be taken care of."

Venus had *never* let him take charge; she'd had "people" to do everything. This situation was refreshing, made him feel manly and useful.

"When?" Max demanded, thinking of all the ways she could be punished. "How?"

"They're on their way," Billy assured her.

"*Who's* on their way?"

"I told you, I called my manager. A cleaning crew will be here any minute."

"You think?" she said, forcing herself to calm down because she had no wish for him to perceive her as a hysterical kid. That would really be lame. After all, he was used to being with Venus—who was not only a worldwide superstar, but the epitome of cool, even though she was old. Well, not exactly old, but certainly older than him.

"It's a done deal," he said easily. "So calm down."

"If you say so."

"I do," he said, taking her hand and leading her over to the outside bar, where they perched on two tall bar stools.

"I'm, uh . . . going to Vegas later today," Max blurted. "Lucky's throwing me a birthday party on Saturday."

"No shit?" he said, picking up a half-full bottle of Evian and taking a long swig.

"It's not what I want," she said quickly. "Not at all."

"No more parties for you, huh?" he said, thinking what a knockout she was with her dark curly hair, olive skin, and brilliant green eyes. So different from Venus, who was all seductive blond perfection and toned muscles.

But she was young—too young?

Hell no. He was Billy Melina; he could hook up with anyone he wanted.

"Absolutely not," she said, shaking her head. Then after taking a long beat she added, "I don't suppose . . ." Trailing off, she looked at him expectantly.

He caught her drift and hurriedly said, "Sorry—no. Much as I'd like to be there for you, it ain't gonna happen." *No way, babe. Are you kidding? Lucky would have my balls for breakfast.*

"No?"

"No."

"I get it." She sighed.

And then she thought, *But there's no way I'm giving up on Billy Melina.*

No way at all.

~ ~ ~

Once a year Lucky planned a board meeting for all her original investors, hopefully a celebration of how well The Keys was doing in such a downward economy. Generally Vegas had taken a big hit, but not The Keys, oh no. Business was on an upward spiral.

The day before the meeting she gathered a group of her key executives, who early on had each received shares in her company. Being part of the process was the biggest incentive of all, and everyone appreciated Lucky's generosity. She'd learned from Gino that making people who worked for her feel like part of a family was a key move. Actually, it was something she enjoyed; personal interaction couldn't be beat for creating a loyal group of executives who were always there for her.

A lunchtime gathering took place on one of the flower-filled outdoor patios, where Lucky made sure to have a one-on-one conversation with each individual. She had a knack for not only remembering everyone's name, but also remembering the names of their spouses, kids, and family pets if they had any. Lucky was adored by the people who worked for her; they were extremely dedicated, and they too strived for The Keys to be the best it could be.

As Lucky moved between groups, stories were exchanged about difficult guests, high rollers who weren't worth the trouble they caused, con artists, stars and their egos, jewelry thieves, card sharks, petty criminals, fake identities, and beautiful women passing themselves off as high society when in fact they were highly expensive call girls. All Vegas hotels and casinos suffered from the same proliferation of scammers, but Lucky liked to think her security team worked at the top of their game. She enjoyed hearing the stories, always interesting, sometimes bizarre, often hard to believe.

Jerrod, her head of security, was the best, formerly a captain in the Israeli army. Nothing and no one got past Jerrod.

Jerrod was Lucky's rock, and like she did Danny, she trusted him implicitly.

~ ~ ~

Oh my God! What have I done? Denver thought, panicking slightly.

You've invited Bobby to meet the family, her inner voice replied, unruffled and in control.

Why? she asked herself, still panicking.

Because you know it's time.

The problem is, will they like him? And will he like them?

You'll just have to wait and see, won't you?

Fortunately, she was due in court to prosecute a famous actress who was up on a shoplifting charge, so she didn't have much time to think about Bobby and her somewhat eccentric family. But she was anxious all the same. She so wanted them to like him.

And they will.

What if they don't?

Stop obsessing.

On her way into court she got a text from Carolyn asking what she thought of Vanessa.

Hmm . . . interesting question, but she had no time to give her opinion of Vanessa now. She had a high-profile shoplifting case to win, a family dinner to worry about, and an upcoming trip to Vegas.

Briskly she texted back. *Seems nice.* But she didn't add *or not.* Had to keep a positive attitude. It was Carolyn's life.

Then she dived into court with work on her mind.

~ ~ ~

Now that his slippery Russian investors had finally signed on to put up the money for his L.A. and Miami clubs, Bobby was more than ready to meet with the architects and designers he'd chosen to work with. Mood in L.A. had to be a total winner considering the fierce competition. Clubs in L.A. came and went all the time, so Mood had to stand out as *the* place to be.

Bobby's vision was of a rooftop space with panoramic views of the city, incorporating a sixty-foot pool with underwater speakers, a forty-foot stone bar surrounded by a dozen private party cabanas, a kick-ass restaurant run by a world-class chef, and a major dance space—all with a tropical feel. Simple, stylish, the perfect hang.

The meetings took longer than expected, and he was so caught up in the details that when he checked the time, he realized he'd never make his flight.

Damn! Denver was not going to be happy, but there was nothing he could do about it.

Too bad. He'd been looking forward to finally meeting her family.

CHAPTER EIGHTEEN

The cleaning crew went to work like the well-oiled team of professionals they were.

Billy threw Max a triumphant look and said, "Y'see? They're taking care of business. No worries."

She had to admit he was right; they were fast and thorough. By the time the housekeepers arrived back, things were looking a lot better. Although once the women figured out what had taken place, they threw Max contemptuous looks and muttered under their breath because they knew that if anything important was broken or missing, it was them who would get the blame.

Fortunately, Billy spoke a smattering of Spanish, so he moved into action and charmed them into a hypnotized state, then made them assure him they would not utter a word of this to Max's parents. After he was sure they understood, he handed each of them five hundred bucks as insurance.

Max was impressed. He was protecting her, which is more than she could say for Cookie and Harry—who'd obviously both taken off without a thought about how she was going to put the place back together. Man, they were totally selfish! She had a good mind to rescind their Vegas invitation. How dare they run out on her?

Or . . . maybe they'd tried to find her and couldn't, which was a possibility because she'd been sequestered on the beach with Billy.

But if that was the case, shouldn't they have been worried about her?

On the missing list and nobody gave a rat's ass.

Whatever . . .

At shortly after two, Billy glanced at his watch and muttered, "Shit!"

"What?" Max asked, still basking in the glow of his company. They'd been sitting in the kitchen, where she'd fixed him a tuna fish sandwich while they watched the cleaning crew finish up. It was all good. In fact, it was all totally awesome.

"I've kinda blown off a big interview with *Rolling Stone,*" he announced. "My PR's gonna be so pissed."

"Does that mean you have to go?" Max asked, trying to hide her disappointment.

"Yeah, but I guess I can turn up late—what're they going to do, shoot me?" he said with a wry smile. "Problem is I don't got a ride."

"I'll drive you," she said, quick as a flash.

"Nah," he said, with a casual shrug. "I'll call a cab."

"Why would you do that?" she asked, determined to hang on to him as long as possible, because who knew when she'd ever see him again? "Don't you trust my driving?"

"Course I do, babe. But if I ain't in the driver's seat, then I'm your front-seat passenger from hell. Trust me, you'd hate it."

She was beginning to feel slightly desperate. "How about if *you* drive?" she offered. "That way I'll be the one sitting in the passenger seat."

Too needy, Max. Calm down! Stop sounding like a stalker.

"Wouldn't work out," he said. "I gotta get my ass straight to the interview. It's at the Sunset Towers, an' driving up with you in the car is not an option."

"Okay, then," she said, coming up with a plan that would assure her of seeing more of him. "You can take Lucky's Ferrari, and I'll pick it up from you later."

"C'mon," Billy said disbelievingly. "There's no way Lucky would want me driving her car."

"She wouldn't mind," Max lied, knowing full well that Lucky had a thing about her precious Ferrari, so much so that she wouldn't even leave it with a valet parker. "I drive it all the time," she added. "Believe me, Lucky hardly ever uses it."

Big fat fib, but hey—this was major.

"You're sure about that?" Billy said, still hesitating.

"Dead sure," Max said convincingly.

"Then it's a deal," he said, being a big fan of fast cars ever since Venus had bought him his first Ferrari, which he'd recently sold. "Only how're you gonna pick it up if you're flying to Vegas today?"

Darn it! She'd forgotten all about Vegas and her upcoming party.

"Uh . . . actually, I'm not leaving until tomorrow."

Another lie. But if it meant seeing Billy again, totally worth it.

~ ~ ~

Prosecuting a famous actress was an easy road. The woman's defense team (and there were three of them) were highly paid and totally inept. Denver listened to their weak excuses for the woman's behavior, then she swooped in with her witnesses—a series of fed-up sales people and store managers who had been putting up with the actress's stealing addiction for years.

The jury was unimpressed with the woman's fame. Too many high-profile people were getting away with—yes—sometimes even murder.

Denver's immediate boss had told her to go for it with all she had. So she did. And her closing argument sealed the deal. The jury took twenty minutes to come back with a guilty verdict.

Her boss informed her that she'd done a stellar job, then asked if she would care to grab a drink with him to celebrate her victory.

Inappropriate, she thought. *Why, if a woman is single and attractive, do all men feel the need to make a move?*

He was fat and fifty *and* married, plus he was her boss, so why would she even think of putting herself in that position?

She mumbled something about next time. But of course there would be no next time, as she was moving on. "Sorry, family commitments," she added, and made it to her car.

Yes. Family commitments. Introducing boyfriend to Mom, Dad, and the rest of the Jones clan.

Anticipation was the name of the game.

~ ~ ~

Danny gave Lucky the word that Max would not be arriving Thursday night as planned; instead she would be getting there the next day.

Lucky was disappointed. She'd arranged dinner with Gino and Paige, and she knew that Gino was looking forward to spending some time with his feisty granddaughter. Gino got a kick out of joking around with Max.

Family. They were always the ones that felt free to change plans at the last minute, never taking into account that everything had to be shifted. Well, Bobby better be on his way.

Lucky called him to make sure.

"Just getting on a plane," he informed her.

"To Vegas?" she asked, hoping he might make it for dinner.

"No. I'm in New York, on my way to L.A. Heading to Vegas tomorrow."

"So is Max. Maybe you can fly in together."

"Uh . . . I'm using the Stanislopoulos plane," Bobby said, sounding slightly sheepish.

"*Really?*" Lucky said, aware that Bobby only used the plane when it was for something important. "What's the occasion?"

"No occasion," Bobby answered vaguely. "Kinda feel I should use it sometimes, let the relatives know I'm still around."

The relatives Bobby referred to were his late father's two sisters and their respective families, who were all on the board of Stanislopoulos Shipping and resided in Greece. Bobby wasn't exactly close to his Greek relatives. America had always been his home. But he was, after all, along with his niece, Brigette, one of the main heirs to the enormous Stanislopoulos Shipping fortune.

"Okay," Lucky said. "Then you can give Max and her friends a ride."

"Sure," Bobby agreed, albeit reluctantly, because he was so not wanting Max and her cohorts on the plane. He'd planned a romantic trip with Denver, just the two of them. However, saying no to Lucky was never an option.

"I'll tell Max to call you," Lucky said. "And if you get here in time, maybe we'll all have lunch."

"Uh . . . not so sure about that," Bobby said, trying to come up with a fast excuse. He wanted time alone with Denver before the whole family thing took over.

"Okay," Lucky said. "I'll plan on it and hope you can make it. Fly safe."

That settled, Lucky went over her Friday schedule with Danny. An early breakfast with Venus, who was flying in late Thursday, then a meeting with Jeffrey Lonsdale and the people who'd wanted to buy The Keys. Though she refused to ever sell, she'd learned that they were now apparently interested in investing in future projects. Then the board meeting, perhaps a late lunch with Bobby and Max—if they arrived on time—and finally dinner alone with Lennie.

Ah, Lennie . . . They'd been apart for six weeks, way too long, although making up for lost time was always the most exciting.

Friday night was reserved strictly for Lennie. There would be no distractions. No family. Just the two of them.

She couldn't wait.

~ ~ ~

Billy was totally into taking a ride in Lucky's Ferrari, especially as it was one of the latest models, a Ferrari California—sleek and smooth and definitely kick-ass. He'd recently read up on it, and he couldn't wait to drive a car that had a top speed of 193 miles per hour. In fact, he'd been thinking of buying one, so this would be an excellent test run.

"Sweet!" he said, easing himself behind the wheel.

Max hovered beside the car, nervously biting her lower lip. "Uh . . . when should I pick it up?" she asked.

Billy's attention was on the Ferrari, not her. "C'mon by my house around seven," he said, smoothing his hands lovingly over the steering wheel. "Maybe we'll go grab a bite."

Was that a dinner invitation? Cool!

Billy gave her his address, blew her a distracted kiss and took off at full speed.

Please God, Max thought as she watched her mom's car vanish into the distance. *Let Lucky's precious Ferrari survive the ride. Otherwise I am one dead person.*

~ ~ ~

"Where's this Bobby character we've heard so much about?" Denver's father, Derek, asked in his loud—some would say booming—voice. He was a maverick lawyer and quite used to intimidating people.

"I told you, Dad," Denver explained patiently. "His plane from New York is delayed. He'll be here later."

"Will he now?" Derek said in a tone that expressed deep disbelief.

"Yes," Denver said confidently. "He will."

"You're sure about that?"

"Oh, for God's sake, Dad. It's no big deal."

"Someone's gettin' edgy," Scott, her favorite brother, singsonged. "What's so special about this dude, anyway?"

"I never said he was special," Denver retaliated, glaring at him.

"You're sure as shit acting as if he is," Scott said, irritating her even more.

"Language!" intoned Autumn, Denver's mother, a tall, imposing woman with gray hair worn in a low ponytail, no makeup, and a penchant for the hippie clothes she'd favored as a teen-ager. "If you cannot speak properly, then do not speak at all."

As if on cue, Hanna, Scott's five-year-old daughter, raced into the room screaming, "Fuck! Fuck! Fuck!"

Scott scooped up the little girl and shushed her.

"Disgusting!" Autumn shrieked as Hanna's seven-year-old cousin ran in with a fully loaded water pistol, which he pro-ceeded to shoot at Hanna, who immediately began screaming again.

Pandemonium reigned.

Just another normal Thursday-night gathering in the Jones household, Denver thought. *They're all crazy, including the kids.*

And suddenly she wasn't so upset about Bobby not making it.

~ ~ ~

"What the fuck?" Max yelled over the phone to Cookie. "You are *such* a douche."

"Wassup?" Cookie mumbled in her best innocent voice—the voice she used when she knew she was in trouble.

"*C'mon,*" Max complained, having finally reached Cookie after sending four texts—all ignored. And now, miraculously, Cookie had answered her cell. "You ran out on me, left me to clean up a huge freaking mess. You *know* they trashed my house big-time, how could you not?"

"They did?" Cookie said, maintaining her innocent approach. "I didn't know that. I was busy with Frankie."

"Of course you were," Max said heatedly. "In *my* bedroom. Thanks a lot. You left coke residue all over my bathroom sink. *And* you used my freaking bed. You're gross!"

"What makes you think it was me?"

"Oh, I dunno, maybe 'cause you an' Harry are like the only two who knew where I hid the keys."

"Forgive me!" Cookie said, going all pseudo dramatic. "Can I help it I wanted to get laid by my *boyfriend?*"

"Frankie Romano is *so* not your boyfriend," Max scoffed.

"Yes he is," Cookie argued. "Check out RadarOnline and Perez. Our photo is all over the place."

"You *gotta* be delusional."

"Would I make it up?"

"Your dad's gonna freak."

"My dad doesn't give a shit," Cookie said matter-of-factly. "He's too busy being his famous self."

"Anyway," Max said, deciding it was prudent *not* to tell Cookie about her and Billy. Cookie had a big mouth, and it was definitely best not to trust her. "No Vegas today. We're going tomorrow morning. I changed our flight."

"Hmm . . . about Vegas," Cookie ventured, hesitating for a moment. "Here's the thing—"

"What?" Max said sharply. "Don't you *dare* bail on me. I'll freaking *kill* you."

"Is it cool if I invite Frankie?"

"*Why* would you want to do that?"

"'Cause, duh, didn't I just tell you? He's my *boyfriend.*"

"But didn't *I* just tell *you* Frankie and Bobby aren't talking?"

"Then this would be the perfect opportunity for them to chill," Cookie said, perking up. "Frankie told me that he really misses Bobby. It wasn't as if there was a huge fight. They just kinda drifted apart. After all, they *were* best friends."

"I don't know . . ." Max answered unsurely. "I thought M.J. was his best friend."

"M.J., Frankie . . . they were all kind of a team. An' besides, it's *your* birthday party," Cookie said, turning up the pressure. "Which means that basically it's up to you whether Frankie comes or not."

"You think?"

"Yes, Max. An' it's not as if I ever ask you for anything."

"Yes you do," Max objected. "All the time."

"You *gotta* do this for me," Cookie pleaded. "Do it, an' I'll owe you big-time."

Max weakened. Why not? It wasn't as if she hated Frankie or anything. And since it was Frankie who'd brought Billy to the party . . .

"Fine," she said at last, adding a stern "Only no drugs—save that for your quality time together."

"You're *such* a star!" Cookie squealed. "Frankie will be like majorly psyched, and I promise we'll leave all illegal substances at the door. Deal?"

"Deal," Max agreed, hoping that Bobby wouldn't be too mad.

CHAPTER NINETEEN

Naturally, Armand chose to blame Fouad for his mother wishing to accompany him to Vegas. Someone had to be held responsible for her infuriating request. Not even a request, more a statement of intent—"I am coming with you," she'd said in a take-no-prisoners tone of voice.

Dammit! What did she want from him?

Armand was furious, but he'd acquiesced all the same, since he'd never been able to say no to Peggy. Whenever he was in her presence, he felt less of a man, more of a boy. Unfortunately for him, there was nothing he could do about it, it had always been that way.

His childhood memories were not pleasant. A few weeks after his eleventh birthday, Peggy had caught him torturing the neighbor's cat, whereupon she'd forced him to pull down his pants in front of several of her friends and whipped him on the butt a dozen times with a thick leather belt. He'd barely been able to sit down for a week.

The deep humiliation mixed with the intense pain and the fear of his mother had stayed with him for a very long time. After that, whenever he did anything bad, he made sure she never found out.

On their return trip to the airport, Armand had Fouad alert their driver to stop and pick up Peggy. She sashayed out to the limousine accompanied by five pieces of Louis Vuitton luggage. As usual she was dressed for attention, wearing a yellow Valentino suit and matching Louboutins, her flaming-red hair setting off her pale skin.

Armand tried not to breathe in her overpowering scent. The familiar smell sickened him; it reminded him of when they'd moved from Akramshar to New York, and she'd insisted that every morning he jumped into her bed for a cuddle. The cuddle had involved the feel of her soft breasts pressed against him while her strong perfume completely enveloped him. He was eight years old, and the smell had lingered in his nostrils all day long. Childhood memories did not please him.

"Peggy," he said, greeting her stiffly, using her name because the moment he'd hit his teenage years she'd requested that he no longer call her Mother, claiming it made her feel old. So Peggy it was.

"Mrs. Dunn," Fouad said, always polite and proper. "It is so nice to see you again. I feel that it's been too long."

Armand shot him a disgusted look. How dare Fouad encourage her, make her feel welcome? She was not welcome at all.

"Nice to see you too, Fouad. Tell me, how is your lovely family?" Peggy inquired, always gracious.

"Very well, thank you for asking," Fouad replied.

"I only wish Armand would find a nice girl and settle down." Peggy sighed. "You are a shining example, Fouad. I admire you."

"Thank you, Mrs. Dunn."

"Why this sudden interest in coming to Vegas?" Armand asked, his tone brusque.

"Why not?" Peggy said, delighted she'd made the decision to accompany her only child to Vegas. "It was once my home, you know," she added, looking forward to revisiting the city she'd been plucked from as an eighteen-year-old girl.

Forty-two years had passed, but Peggy had never forgotten her life back then. As a dancer in one of the most popular shows in town, she'd received more than her share of attention. With her red hair and delicate white skin she'd been quite the stand-out; men could not get enough of her. And then King Emir Amin Mohamed Jordan had swooped into town and claimed her for himself. He'd plied her with gifts and jewelry, and she'd allowed herself to be swept up in the dazzle. It was mysterious and exciting, like a fairy tale. Without much thought, she'd accepted the king's proposal and gone with him to his country, leaving behind her pit boss boyfriend, Joe Piscarelli, who she'd always suspected was mob connected. When she told Joe she was leaving, he flew into a vile rage, called her a gold-digging cunt, and warned her to never set foot in Vegas again.

She hadn't until now.

Where was Joe Piscarelli forty-two years later?

Probably dead, Peggy thought with a frisson of satisfaction. *Buried in a ditch somewhere in the desert. That would teach him to call her names.*

Back in the day, Vegas was quite the place to be if you were a girl with big dreams. Her dreams had certainly materialized— marriage to a king, an enormously rich second husband, and a billionaire son. Not too shabby for a girl who'd come from nothing.

~ ~ ~

The flight to Vegas was turbulent. Armand was never bothered by things like that, but since becoming a father to his two children, Fouad hated turbulence. He white-knuckled his way to landing, then set about organizing the luggage to be loaded into the stretch limousine waiting on the tarmac alongside the plane.

Armand was annoyed that Peggy had brought so many suitcases with her. He sat in the back of the limo and fumed. "We're only here for a day or so," he muttered. "Why did you feel the need to bring so much?"

"You never know," she answered, with a vague wave of her hand. "I might stay awhile."

Her statement alarmed Armand, for when he purchased The Keys, the last person he wished to have hanging around was Peggy. His mother belonged in New York, and that's exactly where he expected her to stay.

"What meetings do you have here, Armand?" she asked as the limousine sped away from the airport.

None of your damn business, he would say if Peggy were a normal woman.

But she wasn't normal.

She was his mother.

The only woman he had ever feared.

~ ~ ~

Armand was situated in the Presidential Suite at The Keys. Four bedrooms, two living rooms, a sauna, a steam shower, five bathrooms, a fully equipped bar, a pool table, a game room, and a private rooftop swimming pool and Jacuzzi. It was more luxurious than his New York apartment, and he decided that when he bought the place, he would use this suite as his own pied-à-terre while he built himself a magnificent mansion on the property.

There was no doubt in his mind that The Keys would be his. No doubt at all.

"Make certain Peggy stays elsewhere," he'd instructed Fouad before arrival. "Book her into another hotel. Tell her The Keys is full."

"Are you sure?" Fouad had asked.

"Of course I'm sure," Armand had replied, annoyed that Fouad would question him.

Fouad had managed to arrange a one-bedroom suite for Peggy at the Cavendish, a neighboring hotel to The Keys. She was surprised when the limousine dropped her off first.

"No room at The Keys," Armand said brusquely, shooting Fouad a *Why didn't you tell her?* look. Jesus Christ! Did he have to do everything himself?

"The whole point of my coming here was to spend more time with you, Armand," Peggy complained, quite disappointed. "There are things we need to discuss."

"It's unfortunate, but there is a big convention at The Keys," Fouad explained, attempting to smooth things over. "No more suites available. And of course Armand did not wish to put you in a room. He requires only the best for you."

Little did Peggy suspect that Armand would be occupying a suite with four bedrooms. If she'd known that, she would have insisted on staying with him.

"Very well," she said, pursing her lips. "And what time will you be picking me up for dinner?"

Armand had not factored in taking Peggy to dinner. This was Vegas, home of the most expensive and inventive call girls in America. Girls who never balked at any request, however out of line. As long as the money flowed, anything was possible, and he'd been planning on taking full advantage. Armand's line of credit in Vegas was limitless, plus he always travelled with a suitcase full of cash in case of an unforeseen emergency.

Yes, he was ready to indulge himself, and now Peggy expected dinner? Goddammit! This was not the trip he had imagined.

"I thought you would be tired after the flight," he said tersely. "Perhaps room service?"

Peggy threw him a scornful look. "Tired, Armand? Me? How *old* do you think I am? Eighty?"

"I didn't mean—"

"Pick me up at eight," she ordered, cutting him off. "And make sure we go somewhere fancy. I plan on dressing up."

The moment Peggy was out of the limousine, Armand issued more instructions. He handed Fouad an engraved card stamped with the name Yvonne Le Crane, a phone number, and an e-mail address. "Book two women to be in my suite at five. An Asian and a black girl, both under twenty-five," he ordered. "I will keep them for two hours. Then at midnight, three more girls. White, preferably from Texas, with blond hair."

Fouad was almost speechless. Since when had he been appointed head pimp? He was not an assistant, he was a vice president at Jordan Developments, a man who deserved at least a modicum of respect. Now Armand was instructing him to order up hookers? This was a ridiculous situation.

"I suggest you might want to make this phone call yourself," Fouad said, swallowing his anger. "There could be questions I cannot answer. And I wouldn't want you to be disappointed."

Armand considered Fouad's words and, surprisingly, agreed. Yes, he was specific when it came to the women he paid. *He* would call Yvonne Le Crane; that way he would get exactly what he required. No mistakes.

After all, he was a prince among men, and he expected only the best.

CHAPTER TWENTY

A text from Bobby informed Max that she and her friends should meet in the private sector of LAX at noon the next day to take the Stanislopoulos plane to Vegas.

She was excited to go on Bobby's plane, and even more excited to spend time with her big brother, whom she adored.

As luck would have it, after she'd agreed that Cookie could bring Frankie to Vegas, Cookie had announced that they would be driving, since Frankie wanted to have his car there. Max considered this to be perfect, because turning up to meet Bobby with Frankie in tow might've been majorly awkward.

Harry was delighted about being invited on the private plane, and asked if Paco, who had a gig in Vegas, could hitch a ride too.

Max agreed, and then she thought, *Oh, great. Everyone will have someone in Vegas except me.*

No time to think about that; her main concern was planning the perfect outfit to wear to Billy's house. Her closet contained a ton of options, none of them quite right. After rummaging through everything she possessed, she finally settled on skinny black jeans, a simple white tank top, and a black cashmere dance hoodie. Tough but cute. It was her look, especially when she added a dozen thin studded bangles, big earrings, a long leather necklace with crosses and shark teeth hanging from it, and a low-slung belt.

Staring at her reflection in the mirror, she wondered if she looked any different.

Would anyone be able to tell that she'd finally done the deed? No way.

"But I can tell," she whispered to herself. "And it feels so right."

Then Ace ruined everything by texting that he was driving into L.A. so that they could celebrate her birthday together.

Crap! She hadn't told him about Vegas. And she certainly wasn't planning on telling him about Billy. What was a girl supposed to do?

She quickly texted him back, hoping that he wasn't already on the road. *My mom wants me in Vegas,* she tapped out, keeping it vague. *Call you when I get back.*

That should stop him. And when she did get back, she would give him the news that it was over between them.

Sorry, Ace. Too bad. It was fun while it lasted.

Meanwhile, she had Billy on her mind. She couldn't stop reliving their night together: their long conversations, the feel of his body next to hers. It was like some kind of awesome dream, a dream she never, ever wanted to stop.

Billy Melina. Who would believe it?

~ ~ ~

"Billy Melina. Who would believe it?" the reporter said as Billy slid into the booth beside her. The girl was in her late twenties, pretty in an aggressive way, with big boobs and an ultra-short skirt. She was on assignment from *Rolling Stone*, and she didn't seem to care that he was three hours late for their sit-down interview.

Bambi, his personal publicist, cared. So did the studio publicist. So did the groomer—hired for the day to make sure Billy looked his best at all times. They all hovered anxiously by the table, until Billy waved them away and told them to come back in an hour.

Girl reporter, whose name was Melba, repeated her words.

"Sorry I'm late," Billy said, leaning back and ordering a Diet Coke. "Got hung up at the beach."

"Were you getting laid?" Melba asked, licking her lips and giving him a flinty stare, as if she knew everything about him, or was about to.

"'Scuse me?" Billy said, narrowing his blue eyes. This one was determined to be confrontational, and he didn't like it. Dealing with female reporters could sometimes be tricky.

"I always like to start an interview off with a bang," Melba said with a half smirk.

"Really?"

"Yes, I like to get down early on. Move in real close to my subject. The closer, the better."

Was she propositioning him? Probably. Now that he was a big star, all the girls did. And the guys too, because naturally gay rumors abounded—as they did with every other young male star. He wasn't gay. Never tried it. Never had any desire to do so. Not that there was anything wrong with it.

Normally he might've contemplated taking this girl back to

his house for the old blow-job-by-the-pool routine. But after being with Max, he wasn't feeling it. There was something about Max that was incredibly fresh and appealing, and he'd begun to think that it might be nice to get to know her. But there was a big problem—she was Lucky and Lennie's kid, and with the whole Venus divorce drama going on, dating Max was hardly about to fly.

He decided that he'd have to let her down easy. She was young and vulnerable, and seemed to like him a lot. He didn't want to hurt her, so he decided that when she came to pick up Lucky's Ferrari, he'd tell her he had another PR gig to go to and send her home.

"What's on your mind, Billy Melina?" Melba asked, licking her lips yet again. "You're not concentrating."

"What's on yours?" he countered. Sit-down interviews were not his strong suit, and he had a bad feeling about this one.

"Your divorce," Melba said, anticipating a juicy reply. "How nasty will it get?"

"Not at all on my part," he said nonchalantly. "I'm fine with it."

"No gory details?" Melba pressed. "Some salacious tidbit that nobody else knows?"

"Sorry to disappoint—no."

"Shame. I would've thought being married to a controlling older woman would've produced all kinds of problems."

"You heard it here first," Billy said, keeping his cool and wishing he hadn't sent the PRs away. "No problems. And, uh . . . shouldn't we be talking about my movie?"

~ ~ ~

Sometimes Denver felt that she could cheerfully murder her family. They never let up on her all night with questions about Bobby.

When's he coming?

Why is he so late?

Who is this guy?

What exactly does he do?

You like him, you really like him.

She'd received a series of texts from Bobby full of excuses about cancelled and delayed flights, but she was disappointed by the time she headed home. Couldn't he have made more of an effort to meet her family for the first time? It pissed her off that he hadn't done so.

Amy Winehouse greeted her as if she'd been gone a year. A rush of happy barking, followed by wet doggy licks and kisses all over her face. It was comforting to feel wanted.

She took Amy for a walk around the block, and returned to find that Sam had left another message. He was certainly persistent.

And normal.

And attractive.

Why not go for him instead of the dazzlingly rich, too-handsome-for-his-own-good Bobby Santangelo Stanislopoulos?

Interesting question.

Easy answer.

I love Bobby, and that's all there is to it.

~ ~ ~

Prowling around Kennedy Airport was giving Bobby the distinct feeling that he was trapped in a maze of bars, fast-food restaurants, and donut and magazine stands, plus a hundred other useless stores. The flight he was supposed to be on had been canceled at the last minute, while the current flight he was booked onto kept getting delayed.

It occurred to him that he was an idiot not to have had the Stanislopoulos plane pick him up in New York. Such a dumb move. What was he thinking?

After trying to get on an earlier flight—fully booked—he made his way back to the lounge with the latest Harlan Coben thriller and attempted to read and chill out. But he soon found it impossible to concentrate—too much going on in his head. The new clubs he was planning to build were a real challenge. Exciting, but at the same time quite daunting. He'd conquered New York and Vegas with Mood, so bring on L.A. and Miami. After that, who knew?

His big ambition was to create an empire. *His* empire. And maybe, like Gino and Lucky before him, he would eventually move into the hotel business. He had in mind small boutique hotels that would cater to a distinct clientele, people who were looking for somewhere special and private.

"Bobby?"

He glanced up, and there stood Annabelle Maestro, Frankie's ex-girlfriend, now a minor TV personality since the murder of her movie-star mother and the arrest of her action-star father. Annabelle was a true child of Hollywood. She had written a book about growing up in L.A. with famous parents, and then all about the year she'd spent running call girls in New York. Like most people who became stars of reality television, she'd made a career out of simply being seen around, appearing on talk shows, and doing nothing much at all.

"Annabelle Maestro," Bobby exclaimed, putting down his book. "How're *you*, stranger?"

Annabelle immediately sat down next to him without being invited to do so. "I'm doing so well it's ridiculous," she gushed, pretty and powdered in a slightly plastic way, with her very long pale-golden-red hair, high cheekbones, and suspiciously plump lips.

Bobby had known her way before she'd hooked up with Frankie, along with M.J., Denver, and Carolyn; they'd all attended the same Beverly Hills high school.

"My schedule is completely insane," Annabelle continued. "Ever since the success of my book."

What book? Bobby was tempted to say, but then he vaguely remembered Denver mentioning something about it.

"*My Life: A Hollywood Princess Tells All*," Annabelle said, reminding him of the title. "Currently out in trade paperback, which is why I'm in New York doing publicity. I was on *Watch What Happens Live* this week with the adorable Andy Cohen. Did you see it?"

Was she kidding?

"'Fraid not," he said, opening a courtesy packet of nuts. "This has been a quick trip for me."

"Trip?" she questioned, fluffing back her long hair. "I thought you lived in the city."

"Uh . . . yeah, but now I kinda spend most of my time on the West Coast."

"Hmm," Annabelle said, giving him a piercing look. "Don't tell me you're still seeing Denver? That's a surprise."

"Why is that a surprise?" Bobby asked, sensing that a bitchy response was headed in his direction.

"You know," Annabelle said with a dismissive shrug. "Denver's hardly the girl I see by your side."

"Yeah?" Bobby said, not about to put up with her crap. "And who *would* you see by my side?"

A coy giggle. "Someone like me."

Jesus Christ, did she honestly imagine he would ever go for someone like her? All fake—from her hair extensions to her obviously enhanced cheekbones. No freaking way.

"The thing is," Annabelle continued, unfazed by his lack of response. "You and I come from the same background. We're pedigrees, while I guess you would have to call Denver some kind of mutt."

"Jesus, you're a real bitch!" Bobby exclaimed. "Are you listening to what you're saying?"

Annabelle shrugged. "The truth can be a harsh pill to swallow," she said. And then, "Where's your plane? Shouldn't we be taking *that* to L.A.?"

Bobby abruptly stood up. "Go fuck yourself," he said, loud and clear. And then he walked off.

~ ~ ~

Dinner with Gino again, not such a bad thing. This time, Paige, his third wife, was with him. And Jeffrey Lonsdale joined them, along with the owners of the Cavendish Hotel—a lesbian couple, Renee and Susie, whom Lucky liked very much. Renee was a ballsy old broad, and her partner, Susie, was an ex–Hollywood wife. They both had plenty to say for themselves, and Gino always enjoyed their company.

Lucky had organized a window table at François, the best French restaurant in Vegas. Since it was located at the top of The Keys, the view of the sparkling Las Vegas lights was breathtaking.

Sitting across the table from Gino, Lucky couldn't help staring at him and wondering what the hell she'd do without him. They had such a rocky history, but she loved him with every bone in her body, and she was fiercely protective of him, as he was of her. Over the years, they'd fought off many enemies from Gino's past, but in the end they'd reigned victorious, although it had not been an easy ride.

Lucky smiled thinking of the family motto, *Never fuck with a Santangelo.* They were words to live by.

Earlier, she'd called Max at the house to see how she was doing. No answer there. No answer on her cell. Lucky wasn't worried; Max could take care of herself. She'd thwarted that crazy pervert who'd attempted to kidnap her a year ago, and she'd come out a winner.

In her heart Lucky knew that Max was a true Santangelo and could protect herself come what may.

~ ~ ~

Max took a cab to Billy's house. Like most L.A. cabdrivers, her driver barely spoke English and drove as if he were involved in a high-speed car chase with cops inches behind him. The cab stunk of garlic, and the driver kept on muttering under his breath in a foreign language. Several times he applied the brakes so hard that she almost fell on the floor. Lovely!

By the time they reached Billy's, she was nervous and flustered, a combination of the out-of-control ride and the thought of seeing Billy again. She hadn't mentioned what had taken place between her and Billy to anyone, not even Harry, who at times could be relied upon to be fairly discreet. Harry had dropped by her house earlier, apologized for running out on the chaos and mess, then proceeded to smoke a joint and rave about Paco for one full hour. Eventually she'd told him he'd better leave because she had to get ready for a hot date. Interest piqued, Harry wanted to know who her date was. She'd managed not to tell him, even though she was dying to confide in someone.

Arriving at Billy's house, she was horrified to observe a bunch of paparazzi milling around outside the gates. Hurriedly, she instructed the driver not to stop, and had him take her around the corner, where she pulled out her cell and called Billy.

"There's an alley behind the house," he informed her. "Take that, an' I'll make sure the back gate is open."

Her heart was beating fast. She had a date with Billy Melina. She'd actually *screwed* Billy Melina. Or he'd screwed her. Whatever. She'd done the deed, and that was all that mattered.

Man, this was totally surreal.

~ ~ ~

Over coffee and dessert, Lucky grilled Jeffrey about their morning appointment. "Exactly *why* do you feel it's necessary for me to meet with these people from Jordan Developments?" she asked.

"Because they have plenty of money to invest in future projects, and in my opinion it's always prudent to keep that money close," Jeffrey explained. "Who knows what you'll decide to do next, Lucky. And in this economy, investors with actual cash are gold." Jeffrey had worked with Lucky for several years, and he always tried to keep a step or two ahead of her. Knowing the way her mind worked, he was sure she would eventually want to expand, so he was merely putting everything in place should this happen. "I checked out the company," he continued. "It's solid. Armand Jordan is legitimate. He's a billionaire and a useful man for us to know. Fouad Khan is his right-hand man."

"Isn't this the company you told me wanted to buy The Keys?" Lucky asked, sipping a *limoncello.*

"Initially, yes. But they know it's not an option. No harm in seeing what they have to offer."

"I suppose you definitely want me to be there?" Lucky questioned.

"It's a meeting," Jeffrey said firmly. "What's to lose?"

"Fine," she said, downing the rest of her *limoncello* in one quick gulp. "And now it's time to get personal. What's all this about you getting a divorce?"

Jeffrey fidgeted uncomfortably; he hadn't been expecting this.

"Tell me everything," Lucky continued. "Don't hold anything back."

Reluctantly Jeffrey began to reveal every little detail. Lucky had a knack for getting people to talk. She would have made an excellent interrogator.

"Enough," Gino said at last, intervening with a hoarse chuckle. "Give the poor bastard a break. You're makin' him sweat."

"Sure," Lucky said with a half smile. "I'll let Jeffrey off the hook. Only you have to agree that I would've made a great shrink. Oh, and Jeffrey, after the board meeting tomorrow, I expect plenty more info on your marital woes, so be prepared."

"Yeah, and you'd better come up with somethin' juicy," Gino added with a crafty grin. "You know my Lucky, she always goes straight for the goods."

"Ah yes, and guess who I learned it from?" Lucky replied with a wink.

"I do believe a toast is in order," Gino's wife, Paige, announced, lifting her glass of champagne. "To the Santangelos. May they never stop bickering!"

Everyone laughed and clinked glasses.

CHAPTER TWENTY-ONE

"Hey," Billy said, greeting Max at the back gate, barefoot and casual in jeans and a faded denim work shirt.

"Hey," she replied, thinking he truly was so majorly hot that it almost hurt.

Leonardo, Taylor, Rob, take a backseat. Billy Melina is the hottest dude in town—any town.

"Wassup?" Billy asked, heading toward the living room.

"Had a cabdriver from hell," she complained, trailing behind him. "He drove the freeway like a maniac. Thought I'd be, like, *dead* before I even got here."

"That sucks."

"Totally," she said, her eyes darting around his living room, which was all sparse concrete curves and modern furniture. "This is different," she remarked.

"I'm renting," he explained. "Not my style, really."

"Nice pool," she said, moving toward the glass doors that led outside.

For a brief moment he was tempted to take her out to the pool, have her blow him the way he enjoyed, then send her on her way.

But no. Max wasn't that kind of girl.

"I guess when the divorce is finalized I'll be lookin' to buy," he said. "Maybe at the beach. I kinda love Malibu."

"When's that gonna be?" she said, thinking how cool it would be if Billy was her neighbor.

He gave a casual shrug. "Dunno. Soon, I hope."

"Uh . . . how was your interview?" she asked, wondering if she should sit down, or were they going straight out?

"Some pissy uptight girl with attitude. All she wanted to talk about was Venus an' the divorce. After ten minutes of her crap, I cut the interview short."

"What did your PR say? She must've been pissed."

"Who gives a shit," he said, moving to the open-plan kitchen. "Want somethin' to drink?"

"Yes please," she said, testing him. "I'll have a double vodka on the rocks with a twist."

"Very funny."

"You asked."

"A Coke? 7-UP? Sprite?"

"What makes you think I don't drink?"

"Do you?"

"Not much."

He gave her a quizzical look. "So what's it like being Lucky's kid?"

"Don't call me that."

"You get along, don't you?"

"I take after my brother Bobby," she explained. "Of course, I love Lucky, *and* my dad. But I gotta forge my own identity. That's why I'm moving to New York." She hesitated for a second, then added, "Uh . . . maybe." Because now that she'd met Billy, she wasn't so sure she still wanted to make the move east.

"I get it," Billy said, nodding. "That's exactly how I felt being married to Venus. It was a total downer. I was never my own person. However famous *I* got, she was always more famous. It's a drag tryin' to live up to somebody else's success."

"Don't I know it."

"Uh-huh. You got it comin' at you from both sides. Your mom, an' then Lennie."

"That is *so* true," Max agreed, thrilled that he seemed to understand. "Being the daughter of two famous parents is no joke."

Billy opened the fridge, took out a can of 7-UP, and handed it to her. "I'm guessing," he said.

"Good guess," she answered, opening it and gulping down a few blasts.

Billy decided that now was the time to tell her he had something else to do, but somehow he wasn't feeling it. He *liked* having her in his house. He liked spending time with her.

"So . . . are we going out or what?" she asked, immediately regretting her words because God forbid she come across as pushy.

"It's kinda not a cool idea," he replied. "Y'know, what with the paparazzi an' all. They're doggin' my every move 'cause of the divorce."

"Oh yes," she said quickly. "I totally get it."

"But," he added, noting her disappointment, "that doesn't mean we can't send out for food. What d'you feel like?"

I feel like you kissing me, and telling me that last night meant something to you. That I'm not just another notch on your movie-star belt. That you want to see more of me. Much, much more.

"Uh, pizza," she said.

Billy grinned. She noted that he had amazing dimples and extremely white teeth. "Cheap date," he remarked. "Thought you were gonna ask for caviar."

"Caviar's not for me," she said, wrinkling her nose. "It's gross and tastes all fishy."

"Right on!" Billy said, heartily agreeing. "Venus was always trying to get me to like it. 'Caviar's an acquired taste,' she would say. Too bad for her I never acquired it."

Max giggled, wished that she hadn't, wished that he wouldn't keep mentioning Venus, wondered if they were going to do it again, and hoped that he would make a move.

He didn't. He picked up the phone and ordered two large Margherita pizzas from Mulberry Street.

"Uh . . . how was driving the Ferrari?" she ventured.

"Some freakin' car!" he enthused, thinking it was best not to mention that he'd gotten pulled over on San Vicente and that a dozen paparazzi had materialized from nowhere, capturing the whole thing with a thousand intrusive flashes. "Nearly got me a speeding ticket, but the cop recognized me an' let me take off."

Max was relieved that he hadn't gotten a ticket, which would have automatically been sent to the owner of the car. Or maybe not. Was a speeding ticket the same deal as a parking ticket? She didn't know and she didn't care, as long as Lucky's Ferrari was in one piece. That was all that mattered.

"Must be a kick getting recognized," she said, wondering if she'd ever be famous. Not that she wanted to be. Her plan was to succeed in business just like Bobby. Although what business that would be she hadn't quite figured out.

"At first, yeah," Billy said, with a casual yawn. "Then it gets old, *real* old. Fame comes with plenty of downside."

"And plenty of money," she blurted, hoping the yawn wasn't a hint that she should go.

Why did I say such a stupid thing? I don't care if he has any money or not.

"Gotta pay my agent, manager, PR, accountant, business manager, and the tax man. It's not as much as everyone thinks," Billy said. "At least I don't hav'ta pay Venus alimony, an' I want nothin' from her. Our only fight is over a couple of properties."

Once again Max wished he would stop mentioning Venus. Every time he did, it brought her back to reality with a nasty jolt.

"Wanna talk about what happened last night?" Billy asked, startling her.

No! She did not want to talk about last night. Too embarrassing. Did he honestly think they were going to have a casual chat about him taking her virginity? *No thank you!*

She wished she'd never told him it was her first time going all the way. After all, it wasn't as if she was inexperienced with guys. She'd gotten down and dirty with a few of them. Oral sex was nothing new—although Billy hadn't asked her to do that. She and Ace had definitely taken it to the brink on many occasions, stopping just in time.

Anyway, it was no big deal. She was glad she'd waited. And she was thrilled that Billy had turned out to be The One.

When and if she ever confided in Cookie, her friend would say "What the hell were you waitin' for, girl? It's not just the boys who can have fun!"

"Uh . . . last night was great," she mumbled. "What time's the pizza coming?"

He arched an amused eyebrow. "Starving hungry or in a hurry?"

"Both," she answered in a rush.

"Didn't you say you had time to go to dinner?" he said, crinkling his blue eyes.

"Well, we're not doing that, are we?" she said, a touch truculently.

"Disappointed?"

"Why would I be?"

He shrugged, somewhat perplexed that she seemed to be veering toward a bad mood. Had he said something? Done something?

Females. Mercurial creatures, always changing. They were all the same, whether they were seventeen or forty.

"I'll call back an' put a rush on it," he volunteered.

"You don't have to do that."

"Hey, if you're in a hurry—"

"I'm not," she said, feeling like an idiot. Why was she giving him a hard time? It wasn't as if she meant to.

"Then whyn't we go outside, sit by the pool, put on some sounds an' relax," he suggested.

And just when she was thinking how perfect that would be, his doorbell rang.

~ ~ ~

It was past midnight and, finally back in L.A., Bobby used the stealth move to get into Denver's apartment. He made his way in very quietly, but Amy Winehouse heard him at the door and came bounding out of the bedroom, tail wagging.

Hurriedly, he quieted the dog, then began stripping off his clothes before heading for the bedroom.

Just as he thought: Denver was asleep, *au naturel* as usual, with only a sheet covering her.

He slid into bed beside her, edging up against her smooth body. Man, she had skin like satin.

Screw Annabelle Maestro for daring to call her a mutt. What a jealous bitch, because not only was Denver gorgeous, she was smart, thoughtful, and dedicated to her job, but most of all she was real in every way. Every one of her qualities added up to one hell of a lethal combination. Annabelle Maestro should be so lucky.

"I'm home," he whispered in Denver's ear, feeling a familiar stirring.

"Mmm," she murmured, slowly turning over so that she faced him. "It's about time. . . . Why'd it take you so long?"

"Didn't mean to wake you, sleepyhead."

"That's okay," she said softly, all thoughts of being pissed at him vanishing as she reached down under the sheet and began caressing his burgeoning hard-on.

"I really didn't want you to wake up," he repeated.

"Sure you didn't," she drawled, still caressing him. "This fine upstanding member of society wouldn't wake me at all."

"I've been saving up," he quipped, loving the feel of her hands on him.

"How very thoughtful of you," she replied, experiencing a fervent rush of desire. Her man was home, and that was all she cared about.

"Missed you," he said, moving even closer. "*Really* missed you."

"You did?"

"Of course I did."

"Missed you too," she responded, reveling in the feel of him hard and strong against her thigh.

And without any further conversation, his hands began exploring her body, touching her in all the places he knew she liked to be touched. Kissing her breasts, fondling her nipples, kicking off the sheet and moving down her body with his tongue, licking her skin every inch of the way.

Then he was between her legs, slowly parting her thighs, plunging his tongue into her wetness, causing her to throw her arms across her face and groan with pleasure.

After a few minutes, he surfaced for air.

"*Sooo* good." She sighed, feeling the joy. "More, please. I think I've been deprived."

"Is that an order?" he said with a knowing laugh.

Another sigh. "You'd better believe it."

And with no more doubts about whether she should be with Bobby or not, she gave herself up to the moment, luxuriating in his touch.

~ ~ ~

On Billy's doorstep stood his best friend, Kev, a total stoner, fresh from New York with luggage to prove it. Kev was short, with wiry brown hair and a cocky expression.

"Fuck!" Billy yelled, happy to see him because Kev was his friend from way back—before the fame, the adulation, and the high-profile marriage. In fact, when he first arrived in Hollywood, he'd slept on the floor of Kev's one-room apartment, and later—when he'd finally made it—Kev had acted as his chief gofer. They'd been inseparable until they'd both gotten married. Billy's marriage had lasted a lot longer than Kev's. "Why didn't you tell me you were comin'?" he said, giving Kev a manly hug.

"Didn't want you gettin' too excited," Kev joked, making his way into the living room, stopping short when he spotted Max. "Oh, shit!" he exclaimed. "Am I interrupting something?"

"No, man," Billy said. "Say hello to Max."

"Hello, pretty girl with the boy's name," Kev said.

Max rolled her eyes. "Like I haven't heard *that* before."

Billy laughed. "This is my buddy Kev, an' I can see you two are gonna get along just fine."

Max hurriedly checked Kev out. From the two duffel bags by the front door, it seemed Kev had arrived to stay. He reminded her of E from *Entourage,* one of her favorite TV shows.

"We just ordered pizza," Billy announced. "Max is starving and in a hurry."

Max felt her cheeks burn red. Was Billy now dismissing her because his friend had arrived? What a bummer!

"Pizza an' a beer sounds like it's gonna hit the spot," Kev said, flopping down on the couch as if he lived there. And if his luggage was anything to go by—he was about to move in any second.

"So Max," Kev said as Billy handed him a can of beer, "how come a boy's name?"

What an asshole question, but she answered it anyway, because if he was Billy's friend, she supposed she'd better get him to like her.

"My given name is Maria," she answered lightly. "You go figure why I changed it."

Kev looked at Billy as if to say *What the fuck? Maria seems like an okay name to me.*

"Too *Sound of Music*," she explained, thinking they would get it. But from their blank expressions it appeared that neither of them was a movie buff. Lucky and Lennie had organized movie nights since she was a little kid. From *Grease* to *Saturday Night Fever* and *Flashdance*, she'd been exposed to all the popular classics on DVD.

"How long you here for?" Billy asked, turning his attention back to Kev.

"'S long as you'll have me," Kev replied with a jaunty wink.

Max felt her stomach dip. This was not a good turn of events. Not good at all.

CHAPTER TWENTY-TWO

Las Vegas. City of lights. City of sin. A magical mystery town where anything could happen, and usually did.

Take call girls—they were obliging creatures, ready for action at all times. So when Armand called Yvonne Le Crane, a woman he'd dealt with several times before, she immediately sent two of her best girls. Tia, a petite Asian, and Fantasy, a slightly more robust black beauty who'd been told she resembled a young Naomi Campbell.

They arrived at Armand's hotel suite prepared to do whatever it took to make the client happy, armed with a selection of sex toys, handcuffs, whips, rubber bikinis, rolled joints, lotions, Viagra and Cialis, and a bunch of condoms. Between them they had everything that might be needed crammed into their over-sized Gucci purses. The expensive purses were a gift from a Malaysian prince who'd been more than satisfied with their performances. So satisfied that on top of their normal fee, the purses had come stuffed with hundred dollar bills.

Little did they know they were about to service another prince. Not such a generous one, though.

Fantasy had been a working girl for almost two years, while Tia was newer to the game. They'd both come to Vegas hoping to score a gig as a dancer in one of the big shows, only it hadn't happened for either of them. Then along came Yvonne Le Crane, a middle-aged madam always on the search for new girls, and they'd both decided that making plenty of money doing something they usually did for free was a far better prospect than hoofing in a show six nights a week.

So far they'd had no complaints. However, so far they had not encountered Armand.

"Strip," he ordered the moment they entered his suite.

"Where's the bedroom, honey?" Fantasy inquired, in the special sexy voice she reserved for clients. Obviously this was a man who wanted to get straight to business, and that was no problem. The sooner he came, the sooner they'd be out of there.

"Refrain from speaking, and do not call me 'honey,'" Armand said, his voice a sharp command. "Remove your clothes, leave your shoes on, and climb on top of the pool table."

Fantasy and Tia exchanged glances. Apparently this was not about to be the sexy little scene they'd choreographed so many times. They'd got themselves a freaky one, the worst kind.

"Sure, hon—" Fantasy began to say. Then she caught a glimpse of his hard, cold stare, and hurriedly shut up.

Tia was already divesting herself of her clothes. A simple silk dress and a red thong—that was it. She kept her strappy high-heeled sandals on, as requested. Armand's eyes flicked over her nakedness. Too thin for his liking, and her jutting breasts were obviously fake and oversized for her body. He reminded himself to request women with real breasts in the future.

Fantasy, on the other hand, was the kind of nasty bitch he enjoyed humiliating. She would fight back when he instructed her to do certain things. She would entertain him.

As Fantasy stripped off her clothes, a short skirt and a low-cut top, no underwear, he couldn't help admiring her body. Gleaming ebony skin, long legs, a pierced navel, and one pierced nipple. Normally he would watch and instruct—touching hookers was not always for him; he was far too fastidious. But for this one he might make an exception.

"On the pool table," he commanded.

The girls obliged.

"Now get on all fours and play doggie."

"'Scuse me?" Fantasy said.

"Do you have a problem with your hearing?" Armand said. "Lick each other's asses and try to look as if you're enjoying it."

"Fucking perv," Fantasy whispered under her breath. But she did as he asked, like all professionals. The money was waiting at the end of the gig, so did it really matter how she got there?

~ ~ ~

Two hours later, Armand was picking up his mother. Meanwhile, Fantasy was waiting for her car, and bitching to her friend, a valet parker at The Keys, about the kinky customer in the Presidential Suite, a man who'd demanded all kinds of lewd acts *and* anal sex from her and Tia, then refused to pay extra.

"Cheap mothafucker," Fantasy muttered as she got in her car. "Who the fuck he think he is?"

Soon word started filtering up via the staff grapevine about the perverted cheapo in the Presidential Suite. It didn't take long before the gossip reached the ears of Jerrod.

Call girls were not encouraged at The Keys, but since high-end call girls were a fact of life in Vegas, their existence was tolerated. However, Jerrod had certain standards, and if they came to do a job at the hotel where *he* was the head of security, then they should be paid for their services.

Jerrod decided to do some discreet investigating.

~ ~ ~

Armand chose to take Peggy, along with Fouad, to François, a select and expensive restaurant he knew she'd approve of. He needed to make Peggy happy, and preferably drunk. His dear mother was very fond of a bottle of wine. Give her enough, drop her off at her hotel, and she'd sleep it off.

How many times had he watched her do that when he was a kid? Too many to count. His mother, the drunk. Thank God for Sidney Dunn, who'd come along, married her, and taken the pressure off.

Now that Sidney was gone, did she honestly expect to latch onto him again?

Earlier, he'd enjoyed himself with the whores, especially the black one. Women would do anything for money—he'd established that time and time again, and he had the videos to prove it. Two little whores at play. Another shining example to add to his extensive collection.

He stored his videos under certain categories:

Married Women
Whores
Single Women
Famous Women

Yes, he'd had a few famous women sniffing around, all set to land their own personal billionaire—something they imagined would up their pathetic profiles in the tawdry entertainment magazines.

The blonde with the penchant for jocks.

The anorexic brunette who swore she wasn't anorexic.

The girl who'd written about her life as a Hollywood princess.

The stupid blonde with the big boobs.

The drugged-out singing star with a major crack problem.

All one-nighters—his choice, not theirs. There wasn't one of them that he'd care to conduct a repeat performance with.

The restaurant was full. His casino host had arranged the reservation.

Later he would gamble before being entertained by the three Texan blondes he'd ordered up for his midnight entertainment, for when it came to sex, Armand was a true voyeur, a connoisseur of the raw and raunchy.

"I do not like this table," Peggy complained in a high voice. "Why are we not seated at a window table? I would prefer to sit somewhere with a view."

Armand dispatched Fouad to deal with the situation. The restaurant was full, but a five-hundred-dollar tip to the maître d' should certainly make the right table available.

After a few minutes, a group at a well-situated window table got up to leave.

The maître d' had probably told them to get the hell out, Armand thought, satisfied that money could get him anything he required.

"You see," he informed his mother, with a triumphant gleam in his eyes. "Your wish, and it is done."

But Peggy wasn't listening, her attention was fixed on the group making its way out.

"What are you staring at?" Armand demanded.

"That old man," Peggy said, agitated. "I think I know him. Find out his name."

Armand couldn't help himself. "For God's sake," he snapped, curling his lip. "You're ridiculous."

Peggy honored him with an icy stare. "Too much trouble?"

Frowning, Armand turned to Fouad. "Do as she asks."

It was at that exact moment that Fouad decided the time had come to move on and extract himself from the toxic environment Armand had created. He had money, plenty of it. He had copies of most of Armand's explicit sex tapes. And he'd had it being treated like some kind of gofer expected to jump at his master's bidding.

This was not Akramshar, this was America, and as soon as they returned to New York, he was out.

"Certainly, Armand," he said, getting up from the table. "I will deal with it immediately."

~ ~ ~

The three blondes suited Armand just fine. Lithe and lovely with real breasts and mounds of pale pubic hair, they were exactly what he needed after a stupefyingly boring dinner with his mother. Peggy always put him on edge. She was the gift that kept on giving. Lately she'd started lecturing him about getting married and having children. Little did she know . . .

Exhibiting a rare flash of generosity, he'd invited Fouad to join him and the women. It infuriated him when Fouad declined.

How stupid that Fouad remained faithful to his dreary American wife. What a fool.

The blondes did everything he asked. They fucked and sucked, did not object when he ordered them to stick old-fashioned Coke bottles up their asses, licked each other, and complied with his every request.

Fully sated from the two skanks he'd entertained earlier, he mainly watched, snorted a mountain of coke, and issued instructions.

When he was finally ready, he had all three of them take turns going down on him. Then he dismissed them, sending them on their way, never realizing that one of them was a transsexual. If he'd known that, it would have sent him into a royal fury.

After the women were gone, he slept the night through, once again content in the knowledge that tomorrow The Keys would be all his.

CHAPTER TWENTY-THREE

Friday morning, Denver awoke early. She turned her head and there was Bobby sprawled out next to her, lying on his stomach, his lean back exposed. She ran her fingers lightly down his spine, but he didn't stir. For a few seconds she reverted to her teenage years, remembering how she'd crushed on Bobby from afar. Now he was in *her* apartment, in *her* bed, and he was all hers.

Their late-night sex session had been something else. So passionate and emotional in its intensity. The connection they had was unbelievably strong, and it wasn't just the sex. It was more than that. It was love and like with a healthy dose of respect. She only hoped he felt the same way about her.

She jumped out of bed, grabbed a loose T-shirt, went into the kitchen, and put on the coffee. Personally she preferred green tea, but Bobby was a coffee freak—he had to have it strong and black before he was ready to face the day.

Today they were flying to Vegas, apparently on the Stanislopoulos plane.

Denver sighed as she filled the coffeepot. Sometimes she found it odd that Bobby never spoke of his deceased father, or of the huge fortune he'd inherited. She knew he didn't want to touch the money, that it was important for him to make it on his own. She also knew he'd set certain goals for himself, and that he was intent on achieving them.

So why use the plane? It didn't seem to fit into his overall plan.

One day she'd ask him, but not today.

A few moments later Bobby strolled into the kitchen wearing the white terry-cloth robe she'd bought him when he'd first started staying over. He looked so sexy and macho in it with his black curly hair and deep olive skin. Man, he was so damn handsome, he gave her goose bumps.

"Morning, beautiful," he said, grabbing her around the waist.

"Morning, handsome," she responded. "I was just about to bring you coffee in bed."

"Forget about the coffee, how about bringing me *you* in bed," he said, taking her hand and pulling her back toward the bedroom.

"You're insatiable," she said with a dreamy smile, allowing herself to go with him.

"And *you're* irresistible," he replied, tumbling her onto the bed and starting to make love to her again.

His touch was too good to resist. Firm yet gentle. Warm and encompassing. Hard and, this time, fast.

Fact of life: she couldn't get enough of him.

After making out, they headed for the shower together, which led to even more making out, while Amy stood by the glass door attempting to force her way into the shower and under the streaming water. Eventually Amy was successful.

Giggling, they finally emerged, along with a soaking-wet Amy, who, after shaking her fur all over both of them, proceeded to race around the room like a dog possessed.

"Time to get dressed, 'cause it's wheels up at noon," Bobby said, reaching for his pants. "Oh yeah, and I forgot to tell you— little sis is comin' on the plane."

"She is?" Denver questioned, not thrilled at the prospect.

"No avoiding it," Bobby said, buttoning up his shirt. "Besides, you like Max, don't you?"

"Actually, I hardly know her," Denver said, opening up her closet and throwing some things into an overnight bag.

"To know Max is to love her," Bobby said. "She's a wild one."

"Hmm," Denver said, wondering if the party would be dressy and if she should take her one and only Diane von Furstenberg cocktail dress. What was she thinking? Of course she should. It was Vegas and the Santangelo/Golden clan. Whoopee!

"What's with the *hmm?*" Bobby said, his still damp hair curling over the collar of his shirt.

"Well," Denver said tentatively, "I've only met Max a couple of times and she wasn't exactly talkative."

"Max can be shy. Don't forget, she's only a kid."

"Really?" Denver said, loathe to point out that Max had gone out of her way to practically ignore her. And about to hit eighteen was hardly a kid. But maybe Max would lighten up now that she and Bobby had been together a while.

Maybe being the operative word.

~ ~ ~

"Why's your mom's Ferrari all over the Internet with, like, Billy Melina behind the wheel?" Cookie demanded over the phone.

"Huh?" Max said, a sudden chill coursing through her body. "What're you *talking* about?"

"Check it out, girl," Cookie said, unaware of the panic she was causing. "Do you think Lucky *lent* it to him? And why'd she'd do that with his divorce deal goin' on? Isn't Venus like her BFF?"

"I've no idea," Max said, already racing to her laptop and checking out the gossip sites. And there it was: a video of Billy climbing out of Lucky's distinctive customized red Ferrari at a gas station in Pacific Palisades.

He'd stopped for gas! Why would he *do* that?!

And if that wasn't enough, there were numerous photos of him getting pulled over by a traffic cop!

"Seems strange t' me," Cookie continued. "Maybe I'll ask Lucky what's up."

"No!" Max said, totally panicking. "Don't do that."

"Why not?"

"'Cause, uh, maybe she doesn't want Venus to know."

"Ohhh!" Cookie squealed. "D'you think she's hookin' up with Billy? It's always the best friend you gotta look out for. Wouldn't *that* be something."

"You are *so* gross."

"What's gross about it? Billy Melina is a total stud muffin. *I'd* do him in a flash."

I bet you would, Max thought, totally mortified that Cookie was even thinking about Billy in such a fashion.

"Anyway," Cookie continued, "didja know Frankie brought Billy to the party? We think he left with Willow Price. Frankie says she's a raving lesbo. Only *I* think she and Billy are totally doin' it. I got to meet both of 'em."

"Awesome," Max said distractedly, thinking that if Cookie knew the truth, she'd go totally nuts.

"Yeah," Cookie said casually, pleased with herself. "You could've met 'em too if you'd been around. Where *were* you all night?"

"*Now* you're asking. Where were *you* when it was time to clean up?"

"Okay, okay," Cookie said impatiently. "So I flaked on you. Let's not get carried away about it."

"'Carried away'?" Max said indignantly. "Screw you!"

"We're takin' off for Vegas soon," Cookie said, completely unfazed that Max was pissed. "What time are *you* planning on arrivin'?"

"This afternoon," Max said, swallowing hard while attempting to stay calm, for if Lucky saw these pix of Billy with her Ferrari, Max would be in deep shit. "Oh, and Cookie," she added quickly, "do *not* say anything to Lucky about her car."

"Why not?"

"'Cause it wouldn't be cool."

After getting rid of Cookie, Max attempted to think of a brilliant excuse should Lucky come across the video. Not that she was likely to on her own; Lucky was totally uninterested in trolling the gossip sites.

But what if someone showed the video to her? What if *Venus* saw it?

Throw up time!

Wasn't it enough that Billy's best friend had turned up and ruined what was about to be a perfect evening? Kev, with his inane remarks and stupid face. She'd automatically hated him, so after gulping down a slice of pizza, she'd taken off, and to her chagrin, Billy hadn't even tried to stop her. And when he'd walked her out to the car, Kev had come too! What an insensitive *jerk*.

Billy had given her a brief peck on the cheek, warned her to drive carefully, and that was it. No *When can I see you again?* Not even *I'll call you.*

She was furious and hurt and felt like a total idiot. It was apparent that Billy had used her for a quick bang. Just because he was a big freaking movie star, he obviously felt that was acceptable behavior.

Well, screw him. Screw him *big-time.*

Now she was left knowing that Lucky could easily discover that Billy had driven her car. And how exactly would she explain that?

Her dream evening had somehow turned into a disastrous nightmare.

She *hated* Billy Melina.

~ ~ ~

Danny got off on filling Lucky in on all the hotel gossip, scurrilous and otherwise. Danny collected information without even trying; it came to him whether he wanted to hear it or not. Yes, Danny was a magnet for all things juicy. He culled all the latest information over a very early coffee with some of the staff before everyone reported for duty.

It amused Lucky to hear everything that was going on in her hotel, and Danny was always a great source.

Friday morning the news was all about the pit boss caught cheating with a married woman who worked in the catering department. Then there was the delectable and extremely young PR engaged to a croupier, but busy having an affair with a teenage singing sensation who visited Vegas a lot. And lastly the perverted pig in the Presidential Suite who'd refused to pay hookers for extra services rendered.

"Men!" Danny exclaimed, rolling his eyes at his boss. "Why order in if you're not prepared to pay?"

"Ah," Lucky sighed as they made their way onto the terrace of her magnificent penthouse, where a virtual breakfast feast was laid out on a marble side table. "Men can be mysterious creatures, exactly like women."

"You're too kind," Danny said with a snippy edge. "But believe me, most men are nasty little piggies."

"Do you really think that?" Lucky asked mildly.

"Oh, yes indeedy," Danny responded. "I could tell you a thing or two about men. You know, before Buff and I got together—"

Lucky cut him short. "Much as I would love to hear your life stories, Danny, I'd prefer you go pick up Venus and escort her here."

"One day," Danny said, slightly put out that Lucky didn't want to hear what he had to say, "you should listen to my stories."

"One day I will," Lucky assured him. "But not today."

"You're such a machine," Danny said with a knowing nod. "Everything and everyone has to be on time—no room for error."

"And fortunately for you, Danny, you never make errors," Lucky said briskly. "So I suggest you move your tight little ass and go fetch Venus."

"In some circles that remark might be construed as sexual harassment," Danny sniffed. "Besides, you know Venus will keep me waiting. She's such a diva."

"Good-bye," Lucky said, thinking that one of the reasons she got along with Danny so well was that he wasn't scared of her.

Because of everything she'd achieved, some people viewed her as intimidating. Danny was never intimidated; he had a sweet but sometimes perverse nature, plus he was efficient and full of energy. He was the perfect assistant for her.

Danny reappeared fifteen minutes later with Venus, a vision in an all-white workout outfit trimmed with gold braid, her platinum-blond hair piled on top of her head.

Danny escorted her onto the terrace to join Lucky, then left. The two women shared a warm hug. "I'm so glad you made it," Lucky said. "Wasn't sure you would."

"You know I love Vegas," Venus remarked. "And I was thinking we could work out after breakfast." She did an elaborate twirl. "You see, I dressed the part. This is from my new clothing line, Body by Venus. You like?"

"Sensational, but I can't get sweaty today," Lucky said, wishing she had the time. "Got a meeting, followed by the board meeting with potential investors you promised to show your face at. Remember?"

"I did?" Venus said innocently.

"You did," Lucky assured her.

"Damn!"

"Suck it up, superstar," Lucky said, laughing. "You know you get off when everyone's creaming all over you. You're an attention junkie, and it shows."

Venus smiled. It was true; she never tired of being in the spotlight. "I guess Danny can work out with me," she said, checking out the table of food. "Right, Danny?"

"Sorry to disappoint you," Lucky said, helping herself to a plate of scrambled eggs and bacon. "But Danny will be with me, taking notes."

"You're no fun," Venus said, opting for a dish of yogurt and blueberries. "At least you could lend me Danny."

"Don't tell me you flew in by yourself?" Lucky questioned as they sat down. "No entourage to attend to your every need?"

"Do I need one?" Venus questioned, lowering her Dolce & Gabbana sunglasses.

"Apparently yes. You can't go wandering around on your own. Where's your stylist? Your hair person? Your usual glam squad?"

"I thought this weekend was all about family, so I came alone."

"How adult of you."

"Actually," Venus admitted, "got me a surprise package who's even now on his way here."

"Ah!" Lucky exclaimed. "I knew it!"

"Of course you did."

"And who might it be?"

"Well . . ." Venus said, an evil smile hovering on her luscious lips. "Yesterday at the shoot for my new clothing line, they hired a very buff stud to be in the shot." She paused for effect, then continued, "I couldn't let the poor guy go to waste, now could I?"

"You're incorrigible," Lucky said, laughing.

"Oh, like *you* weren't when you were single?" Venus shot back. "I seem to recall you would fuck 'em an' leave 'em quicker than any guy."

"Single," Lucky protested. "I was single. And please, don't *ever* mention that to Max."

"Well, now *I'm* single," Venus said, "which means I will not be wasting a minute of my time."

"As if you ever do," Lucky said dryly.

"By the way," Venus added, "he's twenty, Brazilian, and hardly speaks a word of English." Once again she paused for effect. "I think I'm in love!"

"Does that mean I'll hear no more moaning and groaning about Billy?" Lucky said hopefully.

Venus gave another deliciously evil smile. "Billy who?"

~ ~ ~

Frankie drove his Grand Sport convertible Corvette like a maniac, all the while speaking on his BlackBerry, reaching over to change a CD, texting, and maneuvering in and out of traffic lanes like he was playing dodgem cars.

Cookie didn't care; she was down with a touch of danger, and Frankie offered her all that and then some. When he picked her up they'd done a couple of lines of coke to prep themselves for the four-hour drive, then she'd gone down on him, and promised that when they hit the desert, she'd do it again.

"While I'm driving," he'd said, salivating at the thought.

"What do I get in return?" she'd demanded.

"Depends on how you do it."

"Ha!" Cookie exclaimed. "Who d'you think won the blow job competition at school when she was fourteen?"

Frankie was intrigued. Teenagers indulging in blow job competitions—he'd thought it was an urban legend. Satisfying to know it was true, and that *his* girl was the champ. How about that?

His girl. His first steady since Annabelle Maestro, who in the end had treated him like a piece of shit. He would never forgive her for that. Annabelle had even written about him in her dumb book, and not in a flattering way. He'd thought about suing, but everyone had warned him against it. Not worth the time, money for lawyers, and pure frustration it would entail, so eventually he'd decided against it.

If only he'd had the foresight to make a sex tape while he and Annabelle were together. What a financial bonanza *that* would've been.

But no, he hadn't done that, he'd blown a major opportunity to score. Vivid Entertainment would've paid big. They'd forked out millions for Paris Hilton and the Kardashian broad with the big ass. He could have made a killing. Colin Farrell, here I come!

Too late now.

Then the thought occurred to him—how about a sex tape with Cookie? She was certainly adventurous enough. And if he assured her they were making it just for their own private viewing pleasure . . .

Yeah. Like Annabelle—whose dad was action movie star Ralph Maestro—Cookie had a famous father: Gerald M., soul singer supreme. Although since rap and hip-hop had taken over the airwaves, Gerald M. was not exactly at the top of his game. However, he was still a huge star in Europe. They loved all that Lionel Richie–, Barry White–style of sexual healing.

First order of business when they hit Vegas: buy himself a Flip video and get to work.

Yeah, it was a plan.

~ ~ ~

"Let's work out plan B," Bobby said as they sat in the back of a town car on their way to the airport and his plane. He was feeling bad about letting Denver down and wanted to make it up to her. "When do I get to meet the family?"

"There is no plan B," Denver responded. "You had your chance."

"Not my fault," Bobby objected. "If there's one thing I can't control it's the airlines."

"Apparently you can," Denver argued. And then she couldn't help going there. "Where was *your* plane when you needed it? And how come we're using it today? Isn't it a somewhat extravagant move?"

"Questions, questions," Bobby teased, trying to get her to lighten up. "My girlfriend the DA gets off on asking questions."

"Deputy DA," Denver corrected. "And your *girlfriend* is extremely disappointed you didn't show."

"But sweetheart, I tried," he said artlessly. "My intentions were good."

"Sometimes the best of intentions don't cut it," Denver pointed out, deciding that in spite of the great morning sex, she was still somewhat annoyed that he hadn't made it in time to meet her family. "I really wanted you to be there, and everyone was expecting you. You not turning up made me look stupid."

"C'mon, babe," he said, throwing her a quick glance. "*You* could never look stupid. You're the smartest girl I know."

"Says you."

"You *gotta* stop breaking my balls," he insisted. "This is supposed to be the start of a romantic weekend, so don't go ruining it."

Very romantic, Denver thought. *Surrounded by your entire family, who will be judging me to see if I'm suitable girlfriend material for the heir to—who the fuck knows what?*

She let out a long deep sigh. "Whatever," she murmured.

Bobby couldn't help laughing. "Now you sound as if you're twelve," he remarked.

"Sometimes," she said wistfully, "I wish I were."

CHAPTER TWENTY-FOUR

"Good afternoon!" Bright-eyed and full of good cheer, the two flight attendants, Hani and Gitta, welcomed Bobby and Denver aboard the Stanislopoulos plane.

Denver had flown on it a couple of times before, but not when she'd been Bobby's actual girlfriend. She wondered if Hani or Gitta knew that she and Bobby were now a couple, then she decided that they probably did, because they looked like the kind of women who made it their business to know everything.

Max, Harry, and Paco were already on board. Harry was in a state of delight to be sharing the pleasures of a private jet with his new friend, while Paco was somewhat in awe. Meanwhile, Max had fallen into a depression about the way Billy had ended up treating her. How dare he! She wasn't a one-night conquest. She wasn't some random girl he could screw and walk away from. *And* he'd taken her virginity. Snatched it from her like a thief in the night. She was mortified.

Lurid thoughts of punishment crossed her mind. She could

tell Lucky and Lennie that Billy had forced himself on her. Ha! If Lucky thought he'd done that, she'd blow his balls off. Her mom took no prisoners; everyone knew that about Lucky.

Or . . . she could mention it to Bobby, who was practically ignoring her now that he had a steady girlfriend.

Crap! She hated the fact that Bobby seemed really into this Denver person. Why couldn't he have just gone on being a player? Girls were always chasing after Bobby. With his dark good looks and appealing personality, he could take his pick. So why had *he* picked Denver?

After a while she decided it was time to assert her authority, show Denver who really mattered in Bobby's life. "Big brother!" she squealed, dashing toward him and flinging her arms around his neck. "I haven't seen you in *ages!* I've missed you *soooo* much!"

A startled Bobby extracted himself from her cling. "You remember Denver," he said pointedly.

"Oh yeah, sure," Max said, purposely making it sound like she didn't.

"Hello, Max," Denver said, already sensing trouble ahead. "It's nice to see you again."

"Hey," Max said, with a vague wave in her direction.

Dammit, Denver thought. *Now I've got to deal with a truculent teenager who is not at all thrilled I've hooked up with her brother, whom she obviously adores. Great start to a weekend trip I didn't want to come on in the first place.*

"Everyone please take their seats, turn off their cell phones, and buckle up," Gitta announced. "We are preparing for take-off."

Denver fastened her seat belt.

Bobby reached for her hand. "Happy flying, sweetheart. We're about to set off on a memorable weekend. Prepare yourself for plenty of fun."

The plane roared down the runway, and soon they were on their way to Vegas.

~ ~ ~

"Wassup with you, man?" Kev inquired. "Your mind's like on a trip somewhere in space."

"Yeah," Billy answered distractedly. "I'm thinkin' we might wanna make a Vegas pit stop."

"Vegas!" Kev snapped to attention. Vegas was his kind of town. "I'm *way* down with that. When we gonna do it, bro?"

"Today," Billy said, making a decision on the spot.

He'd been thinking about Max all morning. Truth was, he'd been thinking about her ever since Kev had dragged him out to a club the previous night. As usual there'd been dozens of girls draping themselves all over him, but he simply wasn't into any of them. He'd promised Max dinner, but somehow with Kev arriving unexpectedly, he'd allowed her to slip off, and that wasn't what he'd wanted at all.

It was his own fault. She was so young that he'd gotten kind of scared and guilty; he hadn't quite figured out how to handle the situation. Then Kev arriving had given him a convenient out. But after thinking about it, he hadn't wanted a convenient out. What he'd really wanted was to spend more time with Max. Yes, she was young, but she was special and fresh, and maybe it was too soon to know, but he had this weird feeling that she was his soul mate, the girl he was supposed to be with.

And yet . . . he'd let her go, and now she was probably pissed at him. Girls were sensitive in that way. Especially as the sex they'd had together was her first time.

He was mad at himself. And how to make it up to her?

Vegas. Her birthday. Show her that he cared.

Not that he could simply turn up unannounced at her birthday party; that wouldn't fly at all. He could imagine Lucky's face if she got even a tiny hint that he was screwing her daughter. And Lennie's too.

But . . . he could be in Vegas and meet up with Max on the sly. Lucky didn't have to know.

It seemed like a way to go. He'd do it, and he'd take Kev along for the ride.

~ ~ ~

After breakfast with Venus, Lucky set off for her meeting with Jeffrey Lonsdale and the people from Jordan Developments. Since she didn't have any current projects in mind, she wasn't at all sure why she'd agreed to meet with them. Raising money was never a problem, but Jeffrey seemed to think that they might be useful if, for instance, she decided to build a version of The Keys in Atlantic City or any other big American city where gambling was legal. Jeffrey never allowed her to invest a dime of her own money. Not that he was in control, but she always listened to his sage advice. Jeffrey was smart.

Danny arrived to escort her to her office.

"News flash," Danny announced, looking all pleased with himself.

"What?" Lucky asked, striding to the elevator, chic in black leather pants, boots, and a cashmere shell, her long hair wild and falling around her shoulders, large yellow diamond studs affixed to her earlobes.

"It's juicy," Danny exclaimed, hopping to keep up with her.

"Give it up, Danny, or shut it up," Lucky said.

"The perv in the Presidential Suite I was telling you about earlier is the man you're on your way to meet."

"Huh?"

"Armand Jordan. Jordan Developments."

"You're kidding."

"One and the same."

"Remind me again what the story was."

"Apparently," Danny said, savoring every morsel, "Mr. Jordan hired a couple of expensive call girls, made them do all kinds of unspeakable acts, then refused to pay extra for, ah . . . certain things that require more money."

"Nice."

"Are you sure you should meet with him?"

"Why not?" Lucky replied with a casual shrug. "It's quite likely I can embarrass him into paying up. Wouldn't *that* be fun."

"And you'd do that, wouldn't you?" Danny said, delighted at the prospect of watching his boss in action.

Lucky grinned. "Working girls deserve every red cent they make. Maybe I should consider it my good deed for the day. Whaddya think, Danny?"

"Oh yes, I think definitely yes!"

~ ~ ~

Cruising down the highway with Cookie's head in his lap, and his cock in her mouth, Frankie couldn't have felt more on top of the world.

What could be better than this? Drake loud and sexy on the sound system. The hot sun burning down on them. The smooth thrust of his Corvette as the speedometer hit 80. Plus the insane sensation of holding back what he knew was about to be a mind-shattering orgasm.

Man, Frankie was flying and then some.

Until . . . the goddamn siren. The cop car drawing alongside them. And a red-faced motherfucker of a cop frantically signaling for him to pull over.

He did so, and the cop marched up to his window.

"Sorry, Officer," Frankie said, attempting to seem contrite. "Music too loud?"

"License and registration," Angry Cop said. "And get out the car." He peered suspiciously over at Cookie. "You too."

Cookie, who was busy applying a fresh layer of sticky lip gloss, frowned. "What did *I* do?" she asked petulantly.

"Lewd behavior in a moving vehicle," Angry Cop announced. "I'm thinking of booking both of you."

Frankie tried to remember where he'd stashed the coke and the grass and the pills he'd brought along on the trip—the main reason he hadn't wanted to fly. Then he remembered that all his drugs were in his overnight bag, along with his shaving kit.

Oh shit, this could still be bad.

As Cookie climbed out of the car, Angry Cop gave her a hard piercing look. "How old are you?" he demanded. "And have you been drinking?"

~ ~ ~

Once they were in the air, Denver decided to make an effort to be nice to Bobby's truculent little sister. She moved over to sit next to her. "Bobby tells me you're planning on relocating to New York," she said. "Sounds like an exciting thing to do."

Max grunted.

"Any idea what you want to do when you get there?" Denver asked, persevering.

Another grunt.

"Well, anyway," she continued, "I bet your mom'll miss you. I know my mom was very upset when I moved out, and *we* were living in the same city, so you can imagine."

No reaction at all.

Denver gave up. Screw it. What did she care if Bobby's sister approved of her or not? It was quite obvious that Max felt she had dibs on her brother, and woe betide any girl who came too close.

Bobby was sitting up front talking music with Paco, while Harry sat listening to them, his pale face full of rapt attention.

"If you want, while we're in Vegas, you can spin at my club for a couple of hours," Bobby offered. "I'm always searching out new talent, and a happening deejay makes all the difference."

Harry nodded enthusiastically. "Paco's the best," he announced proudly. "You'll definitely want to hear what he can do."

"I already got a gig in Vegas," Paco said, polite and nervous at the same time. "But spinnin' at your club would be an honor."

"We'll figure something out," Bobby said, grabbing Denver's arm as she came over and settled into the seat next to him. "This girl's into Adele, Winehouse, Mayer. Not me—I'm into every-thing," he added, squeezing her hand.

"Ah yes, that's me," Denver said wryly. "The girl who's into mellow."

"Nothing wrong with that," Paco said earnestly, trying to hide his excitement at actually sitting with these people on a private plane. His family, who all resided in the Bronx, would never believe him. "The mix is what matters. Rap, Cuban, rock, mellow—it all works together. That's the way you get people on the floor."

"You see," Denver said, shooting Bobby a look. "This guy knows what he's talking about."

"Yeah, yeah, I see," Bobby said, still grinning.

Hani came by carrying mimosas in tall glasses. Bobby handed one to Denver, then took one for himself.

"Here's to the weekend, babe," he said, clinking glasses. "We're gonna have a great time."

She smiled and realized that she was hopelessly, happily, deeply, in love.

"I'll drink to that," she said softly.

And suddenly she was delighted she'd agreed to come on this weekend.

~ ~ ~

Once more they were on the move, Frankie's Corvette roaring down the highway at full speed. Somehow or other Cookie had convinced Angry Cop they were on their way to get married, and that the sex thing he thought he'd seen wasn't what it looked like, and that her daddy, Gerald M.—yes, *the* Gerald M.—was waiting to greet them, along with several camera crews and a shitload of paparazzi. Only she didn't say *shitload*; she cooled it with the language.

At first Angry Cop didn't believe she was Gerald M.'s daughter, but she had proof—several photos of them together on her iPad, and his latest CD in her purse. She carried it with her at all times for just such an occasion.

Angry Cop's wife was a fan, so Angry Cop wasn't so angry anymore, and after a short lecture on road safety, he sent them on their way with a warning to be more careful in the future.

"You should be a freakin' actress," Frankie exclaimed, full of genuine admiration. "That little performance you just put on was insane!"

"I know," Cookie said with a less-than-modest giggle. "I'm the real shit, right?"

"You bet your ass," Frankie agreed.

"My dad taught me t' use his name whenever it would get me outta trouble. There's gotta be *some* perks to being his kid."

"Your dad sounds like a smart dude."

"Not so much. When it comes to pussy, he's a total douche."

"I'd still like to meet him," Frankie said, thinking of the possibilities.

"One of these days," Cookie answered vaguely.

"Well anyway, I'm impressed," Frankie said. "I thought we were definitely gettin' busted."

Cookie giggled again. "That's the fifth CD I've used as payoff. It works every time."

"Yeah?" Frankie said. "So tell me, how many dudes you been caught givin' head to in a movin' vehicle?"

"Wouldn't *you* like to know," she murmured mysteriously.

No, actually, he wouldn't. Some things were best left unsaid.

~ ~ ~

Feeling sorry for herself, Max decided a mimosa was a fine idea. So even though she didn't usually drink, she downed two, and immediately felt light-headed.

Nobody cared. Bobby was too busy with his girlfriend to

notice, while Harry was totally locked into Paco, who didn't seem at all gay—so what was *that* about? Was Harry delusional? Or had something actually taken place? She hadn't bothered to ask him; she was too caught up with all the drama in her own life.

Tears threatened to flow. *Snap out of it*, she warned herself. *Get a grip and stop acting like a girl. You're a Santangelo. Suck it up. So you had a one-nighter with Billy Melina. Big freaking deal.*

They hadn't used protection.

Dumb.

Super dumb.

What if she was pregnant?

The very thought shocked her sober, and she moved as far away from everyone as possible, strapped herself into a seat, closed her eyes, and attempted to shut out the world.

~ ~ ~

"I must say, you certainly know how to put me together with the classiest of people," Lucky complained to Jeffrey when they met up in her office adjacent to the conference room.

"What are you talking about?" Jeffrey asked, looking puzzled.

"These Jordan Development people," Lucky said, tossing back her hair.

"Yes?" Jeffrey said, clearing his throat.

"Apparently they're into hooker paradise and not paying."

Jeffrey adjusted the heavy old-fashioned horn-rimmed glasses he always wore to business meetings. "Is there some information I should know about?" he asked, uncomfortable that Lucky apparently knew things he didn't.

"Yes," Lucky said, moving behind her oversized art deco desk and sitting down. "If I know it, so should you."

Jeffrey pulled up a leather chair opposite her desk. "And how do we know this?" he inquired.

"We know," Lucky replied, tapping her fingers on the desk. "Because Danny is the eyes and ears of everything that goes on in my hotel. Right, Danny?"

Danny, who was busy setting up his laptop at a side table so he could recount every detail of the upcoming meeting, nodded.

"What exactly did you hear?" Jeffrey asked.

Danny repeated his story. He really enjoyed being the center of attention; it made a welcome change from hovering in the background.

Jeffrey frowned. This did not bode well for the upcoming meeting. If he knew Lucky, she couldn't care less that the man they were meeting with had entertained hookers. But the fact that he'd stiffed them would definitely irk her.

Before Jeffrey had time to think it through, the receptionist announced that the people from Jordan Developments had arrived.

Lucky smiled a slow, dangerous smile, her black eyes sparkling.

"Let the show begin," she drawled. "This could turn out to be quite interesting."

CHAPTER TWENTY-FIVE

Armand often reflected on what his life would have been like if he'd been raised as a normal boy in America. He wasn't normal; he knew that. He was special. He was a prince. His childhood in Akramshar had been anything but normal. He'd been born in a palace, nursed by women in long black robes who'd barely talked to him. And it wasn't until he and his mother moved to New York when he was eight that he'd finally gotten to spend time with her. Up until then he'd had very little to do with Peggy; she was merely this dazzling redheaded woman who'd occasionally swooped into the nursery wearing low-cut silk gowns and magnificent jewelry.

The king had different rules for the women in his country. Poor females were not allowed to be educated and wore long body-covering robes at all times. Rich females could do whatever they wanted. Most girls from affluent families were schooled in Europe, and many of them chose not to come back, for arranged marriages at the king's request were quite normal. Soraya, Armand's wife, was one of the girls who'd come back.

Armand never gave much thought to Soraya. She was the mother of his children, that pleased the king, and pleasing the great man was all that mattered.

Returning to Akramshar once a year had shaped Armand's life. He was a tried-and-true prince, and one day he might be tempted to let the world know, for he was well aware how impressed Westerners were with titles.

But not today. Today he was buying a hotel, soon to be the jewel in his property empire, the crème de la crème of Vegas.

Armand believed in pampering himself. After doing several lines of coke, he thoroughly showered before applying various lotions to his body, spending an inordinate amount of time massaging his balls and fine shaft of manhood. Thinking of the whores from the night before caused him to become so hard that he had no choice but to attend to his needs. Inconvenient, but far more enjoyable than being with any woman.

When he was finished, he took another shower, applied more lotions, stared at his reflection for a while, and finally got dressed. First a silk Turnbull & Asser shirt made especially for him in London, a $350 tie from Neiman Marcus in Beverly Hills, and finally an $8,000 pinstriped custom suit in pearl gray.

Admiring himself once again in the mirror, he had to admit that he made a dashing figure. It was no wonder women pursued him. The *New Yorker* magazine had recently listed him as one of the city's most eligible bachelors.

New York indeed. How about the world?

~ ~ ~

CHAPTER TWENTY-SIX

"I'm starving," Max whined to Bobby as he exited the bathroom on the plane.

She knew she sounded needy, but she simply couldn't help herself; she had a strong urge to take her frustration out on someone.

"How can you be hungry?" Bobby questioned, eager to get back to Denver. "There's a whole buffet laid out."

"I feel like a hamburger," Max insisted. "Can we go to the Hard Rock when we land?"

"Sorry, kiddo," Bobby said. "I'm busy. Gino's in town; call him when we get there, he'll take you."

"Oh," she said scornfully. "I really want to go get a burger with my *grandfather*."

"Might I remind you, your *grandfather* is one of the greatest men you'll ever come across," Bobby said, frowning. "He practically invented Vegas, so you should try listening to his stories sometime. Maybe you'd learn something."

"Why are you being so mean to me?" Max asked, her eyes filling with tears.

"Who's being mean? Not me."

"Yes you are," she said fiercely. "You're, like, *ignoring* me."

Bobby shook his head in exasperation. "What's up with you today? How come you're acting like a spoiled little kid?"

"I am *so* not," she said crossly. "It's *you* and what'shername."

"Her *name* is Denver," Bobby said sternly. "And you might try being a bit nicer to her."

"Why's that?" Max demanded, narrowing her eyes. "Are you planning on *marrying* her or something?"

As soon as she said it, she wished she hadn't. The last person she wanted to alienate was Bobby. She was hoping he'd forget what she'd just said, hug her, and act all big brotherly. Why couldn't he do that?

Instead he threw her a hard-ass look and returned to his seat, whereupon Gitta made the announcement that they would be landing in fifteen minutes, and everyone should please buckle up.

Max slunk back to her seat, her mind racing. What was Billy doing? Was he out and about shagging some other unsuspecting female simply because he could?

Being a movie star meant getting laid anytime you wanted. And she should've known that. Coming from such a high-profile family, she was hardly naïve.

But no, she'd so fallen for his nice-guy shtick. *Stupid! Stupid! Stupid!*

Ace, where are you when I need you?

~ ~ ~

Ace was actually behind the wheel of his truck, heading full speed toward Vegas. He was feeling pretty upbeat about surprising Max on her birthday. There was no way she'd expect him to leave the construction job he was working on in Big Bear; it would be a real shocker, especially as she was always urging him to loosen up and be more spontaneous.

The two of them had a long-distance relationship, which seemed to work, although one day he hoped to save enough money to make the move to L.A. Then they could see how things panned out when they were living in the same city.

Max was his addiction. One moment she was the vulnerable, thoughtful girl he'd first met. The next, she was some kind of tough party animal who liked spending all her time dancing on tables in L.A. clubs with her somewhat sketchy group of friends. Harry was a weirdo, with his dyed black hair and white face. And Ace especially couldn't stand Cookie; she was definitely a negative influence, with her flashy lifestyle and obvious coke habit.

The problem with Max was that she hadn't figured out what she wanted her life to be. But at least she didn't sleep around like Cookie; she had that under control.

As far as sex was concerned, he'd never pushed her to go further than she felt she was comfortable with, although now that she was about to turn eighteen . . .

Ace was almost twenty-one, and he wasn't about to wait forever for them to take it to the next level. He had his needs, and if Max didn't meet them, then maybe it was time to rethink their situation.

~ ~ ~

Striding through the airport, Billy attracted major attention. Paparazzi dogged his every step, girls excitedly texted about spotting him, airport personnel treated him like royalty, ushering him and Kev to the front of every line. Of course, Kev loved it; why wouldn't he?

"We should do something together," Kev suggested, fully basking in the attention.

"Like what?" Billy said, signing autographs for three overweight security women who'd all abandoned their posts and were gazing at him adoringly.

"I dunno," Kev answered vaguely. "Maybe I could produce your next movie. Like I'm a real winner at dealing with actors an' shit. I could totally nail it."

Billy knew full well that Kev's social skills were nonexistent, but Kev was a loyal friend, who unfortunately couldn't seem to keep a job, even though he'd tried and failed countless times.

"Producing's not for you, Kev," Billy said as he was hustled through a private security door with an officious airport escort.

"Then how about I write a script?" Kev said, trailing behind them. "Like, y'know, kinda a buddy-style comedy. Somethin' like *The Hangover*. An' here's the kicker—*you* can star in it."

"Hate to break it to you," Billy said briskly, "but I'm booked solid for the next five years."

Kev's eyebrows shot up. "Holy jeez! Are you shittin' me?"

"'Fraid not. Signed, sealed, an' delivered."

"I could be your manager, then," Kev ventured, not prepared to give up. "That'd work. I'd be a kick-ass manager."

"Got one of those," Billy said, wondering where this was going.

"I need a job, Billy," Kev said, suddenly becoming serious. "Gotta pay alimony to that cooze I was married to for five min-

utes. An' I got debts up the wazoo in New York. I figured if I
came back to L.A., you'd be able to hook me up. . . ."

"No worries," Billy said, remembering the days he'd slept on
Kev's floor when he was stone-cold broke with no future prospects. "I'll come up with something."

"You will?" Kev said, his face brightening.

"Leave it t' me," Billy assured him. "There's no way I'd ever
leave you hangin'."

And with that they entered the VIP lounge, where Billy was
besieged by even more autograph requests and adoring females.

~ ~ ~

And while Billy was catching a plane, Venus was catching up
with her Brazilian stud from her photo shoot. His name was
Jorge, and he was quite a specimen.

The moment he sauntered into her apartment, macho strut
going full force, smoky eyes sending out major sex signals, she
was ready for action. Venus had never been slow about coming
forward.

Jorge wasn't quite sure what had hit him. One moment he
was a penniless wannabe model working as a busboy at Cecconi's who'd been in L.A. less than a month, and the next he
was plucked from obscurity by a randy old agent who'd gotten
him the gig on the Venus photo shoot. And before he knew it,
Venus had invited him to Vegas for the weekend, and now here
he was.

Venus greeted him with kisses on each cheek as she led him
into her sumptuous apartment at The Keys. It was quite a
place—all white leather furniture and luxurious throws. A giant
Buddha sitting in the hallway welcomed guests. Low lighting

cast a magical glow, for Venus had all the shades drawn shut. Incense-infused candles wafted scent into the atmosphere.

They hadn't made love yet, but they both knew it was inevitable.

Venus didn't believe in wasting time. After Jorge had been in her apartment for a few minutes, she said, "Come with me. I'll show you the bedroom." Taking his hand, she led him to her bed, and without words they both began stripping off their clothes. Jorge took a moment to catch his breath when he saw Venus naked. She was magnificent.

"Do something!" she commanded.

Jorge jumped to attention, manhandling her breasts before pushing her onto the bed in a take-charge kind of way, a move she was definitely into. His nude body hovered over her like a falcon trapping its prey before he plunged into her, keeping up a mind-blowing series of thrusts for a full twenty minutes.

Their sexual encounter was a marathon of tongues and wetness and acrobatic positions. It was all that she'd hoped for and more, for what Jorge lacked in technique, he made up for with pure brute strength, and a staggeringly beautiful uncircumcised cock. Jorge was a stud and then some, plus his lack of English only heightened the excitement she experienced.

When they were finally done, Venus decided she was perfectly delighted with her new plaything. He far surpassed her two previous conquests. She couldn't wait to put him on parade.

Screw you, Billy Melina. I have officially moved on.

~ ~ ~

The landing in Vegas was extremely bumpy. Tightly strapped into her seat, Max seriously considered the possibility of the plane crashing and them all facing a fiery death. Or maybe only Denver would suffer a fiery death, and she and Bobby would be miraculously saved.

Yes, that was a way cool scenario. Billy would hear about the crash and rush to her side, full of apologies for the shitty way he'd treated her. Then they'd immediately run off and get married at one of those crazy wedding chapels with an Elvis Presley look-alike officiating.

Cool. Bobby would be their best man. And Harry's deejay friend would come up with a majorly badass sound track for the occasion.

She giggled at the thought.

The plane touched down, skidded along the runway, and finally shuddered to a stop. No fiery death for anyone today.

Bobby unclicked his seat belt and came over to her. "Glad to see you're smiling," he said, bending over her seat. "It's going to be a great weekend. No fighting, right, sis?"

Little did he know the reason she was smiling. Denver was dead. Billy was back on the scene. And all was well in the world.

"Sorry, Bobby," she said, meekly. "You're right, it's gonna be a way cool weekend. And I promise I'll behave." Her smile widened. *Not!*

CHAPTER TWENTY-SEVEN

Lucky took the power position behind her desk, with Danny somewhere behind her, getting ready to take notes on his computer. Jeffrey was seated across from her.

She gave Armand a long cool stare as he entered her office. What she saw was an arrogant man, impeccably dressed, not bad-looking, with a small, neat mustache and cold, hard eyes. The man accompanying him was much more low-key, and seemed slightly uncomfortable. Lucky considered herself an expert at reading body language, and she immediately got it—Armand Jordan was the boss, and Fouad Khan his faithful lackey.

After announcing the names of the two men, Jeffrey said, "May I present Ms. Lucky Santangelo."

Armand did not proffer his hand; instead he gave her a dismissive nod of his head, making no eye contact.

Fouad spoke up. "It is a pleasure to meet such an accomplished businesswoman," he said, causing Armand to shoot him a furious glare.

Lucky did not miss the energy passing between the two men. It seemed that Fouad was happy to be present, while Armand was certainly not.

"Thank you," she said, picking up a silver letter opener with the inscription *Never fuck with a Santangelo.* Bobby had given it to her last Christmas, a reminder of the family motto. "Gentlemen," she said coolly, "kindly take a seat."

"We should get down to business," Armand said, addressing Jeffrey as he sat stiffly in a high-backed leather chair. "I have no time to waste. I am sure neither do you."

Lucky was amused by this man's obvious difficulty in dealing with a strong female presence. She'd encountered men like him before. Men who were basically scared shitless by powerful women. Men whose balls shriveled at the mere hint of a female being in charge. Men who always had to pay for it, otherwise they were incapable of getting it up.

Ah yes, she'd come across men like Armand Jordan many times. They were unemotional, pathetic creatures who obviously needed help.

It occurred to her that Jeffrey should never have requested that she attend this meeting, for she had no intention of venturing into any deals at all with the arrogant asshole who sat before her. First of all, she didn't need his money, and second, she certainly didn't need his sexist attitude.

"There is really nothing concrete to discuss," Jeffrey said, instantly realizing that there was no way Lucky would ever enter into business with Armand Jordan. This meeting was useless, and he'd better wind it up as quickly as possible, because knowing Lucky, there was no doubt she would bring up the hooker incident if she felt in the mood to embarrass Armand. "Mr. Khan requested a meeting regarding future financing of any major projects that Ms. Santangelo might want to proceed with," Jeffrey continued. "He thought it prudent that the principles get together, and I agreed. However—"

"Fouad must have given you the wrong impression," Armand said, rudely interrupting, while still not addressing Lucky directly. "I am not here to talk about future financing. I am here today to purchase The Keys. And furthermore, I am prepared to pay whatever it takes to do so."

Lucky flashed Jeffrey a look that said, *Are you fucking kidding me?*

Fouad sunk deeper into his chair.

Danny glanced up from his laptop, well aware that there was about to be trouble. He knew better than anyone how Lucky hated to waste time, and this meeting was definitely a huge time-waster.

"There has no doubt been a big misunderstanding," Jeffrey said, adjusting his glasses. "I made it perfectly clear when Mr. Khan visited my offices in New York that The Keys was not in any way for sale." Jeffrey turned to Fouad. "Isn't that so?"

Fouad fidgeted uncomfortably and opened his mouth to say something, but Armand silenced him with a shake of his head.

"I'm not sure that you are hearing what I am saying," Armand said, speaking very slowly, as if dealing with a backward child. "I wish to buy The Keys, and I will pay whatever it takes. This is not a negotiation, it is an offer you cannot refuse."

Finally Lucky spoke up. "Really?" she questioned, her voice dripping with sarcasm.

Armand made the mistake of continuing to ignore her, once more addressing Jeffrey. "I have no time to waste," he said abruptly. "This deal has to take place immediately."

"Why the urgency?" Lucky asked, playing with him.

"My lawyers in New York are waiting for your call," Armand said to Jeffrey. "I expect you to make that call today."

"Mr. Jordan," Lucky said, willing him to look at her. "Although I realize that you are totally delusional, I think it's about time I set you straight."

"Excuse me?" Armand said coldly. "Are you addressing me?"

"The Keys is not on the market for you or anyone else," Lucky said, her tone as sharp as an ice pick. "Whatever the offer."

Armand threw her a severe look. His lip curled, exhibiting his distaste at having to speak to a woman about business. It was quite obvious to him that she was merely a figurehead, and that Jeffrey Lonsdale was running the show.

"Excuse me?" he repeated, annoyed that a mere female would have the audacity to address him in such a brazen fashion. "We're wasting valuable time," he added, making a controlled effort not to lose his temper. "Surely you realize that my offer is too good for you to turn down. I am telling you to name your price." *So do it, bitch. Do it now.*

Lucky raised a cynical eyebrow. "*Telling* me?"

Here it comes, Danny thought. *And I for one cannot wait!*

Armand refused to back down. Finally locking eyes with Lucky, he repeated his words. "Yes," he said harshly. "Telling you."

"Hmm," Lucky said, remaining surprisingly calm. "Let me give you a piece of valuable advice." She picked up the *Never fuck with a Santangelo* letter opener, balancing it in the palm of her hand. For one wild moment Danny thought she might stab the man. But she didn't, she continued talking. "This is the deal, Mr. Jordan. If you wish to keep doing business, then I suggest you make a supreme attempt to conquer your extremely obvious and very intense fear of women. It makes you seem impotent and weak, and you wouldn't want that, would you?"

Armand glared at her, trying to imagine her naked, crawling around on all fours while he pissed all over her, for that's exactly the kind of treatment the cunt deserved.

"You make it clear why women should be seen and not heard," he said at last. "How *dare* you presume to know me. You know *nothing* about me."

"Ah, but I do know that you're an asshole," Lucky said, rapidly losing patience with the game that was taking place.

"And you," Armand replied, his words laced with venom, "are nothing but a foolish, impudent woman with an extreme lack of brain power."

Jeffrey began to speak, but Lucky silenced him with a wave of her hand.

"As I said before," Lucky said, directly addressing Armand, her blacker-than-night eyes feline and deadly. "You're an asshole with both feet planted firmly in the Dark Ages. So I strongly suggest we end this ridiculous conversation right now. I repeat for the last time: The Keys is not for sale. Get that into your hooker-riddled head and then get the hell out of my hotel. Oh yes, and finally," she added fiercely. "Those two working women you fucked last night want the money you owe them. So be a man for once and pay up."

Danny felt like applauding. Who else had a boss as feisty and perfect as Lucky Santangelo? She was unique.

Filled with unmitigated rage, Armand abruptly stood up and marched to the door. Once there he stopped and turned, in spite of Fouad trying to maneuver him out. Glaring at Lucky, he spat his final words. "I can assure you, *bitch,* this is not the end, it is merely the beginning of a battle you will eventually lose. So get off your high horse and back into the bedroom where you be-long. The Keys will be mine; there is nothing and no one who

will stop me from owning it. Be warned, because I will do anything to get it. And when I say anything, I do mean anything.
And that, my dear, is not a threat, it's a cold hard fact."

Lucky rose to her feet, her dark eyes flashing danger signals.
She'd had it with this expensively clad douche bag. "Get the fuck
out of my hotel, moron. And never bother coming back. Because
if you ever do, I promise you'll regret it."

Before Armand could reply, Fouad managed to hustle him
out the door.

As far as Fouad was concerned, this was one deal that would
never happen.

CHAPTER TWENTY-EIGHT

Arriving at The Keys, Max felt as if she was coming home, for she knew the place as well as their Malibu house. She'd swum in every pool, availed herself of all the spa facilities, eaten in every restaurant, shopped in every high-end shop, and explored the lush gardens countless times. She had her own suite in the hotel, on a special floor reserved strictly for family and friends.

Lucky's apartment was off-limits. "It's my haven of peace and quiet," Lucky had explained when she'd started spending time in Vegas. "It's a no-kid zone unless you're invited."

At first Max was furious when her mom had informed everyone of the rule. But then again, her mom was Lucky Santangelo, and everyone knew that Lucky did things her way. Now Max was totally into the fact that she could come and go as she pleased, *and* have her friends to stay whenever she wanted. It was a way cool situation, except when brother Gino Junior and her half brother, Leonardo, were around. Fortunately, the two boys were gone for the entire summer, traveling around Europe with a guardian. It was Lennie's idea that they get a view of life beyond Beverly Hills and Vegas. Max was psyched to be rid of them; they were both younger than her and majorly annoying, especially when they all ended up having to spend time together in Vegas.

Bobby had arranged to have his Lamborghini waiting for him at the airport, so the moment they arrived, he and Denver took off. A chauffeured SUV collected Max, Harry, and Paco and headed straight to the hotel.

"Are you *sure* Paco is gay?" Max whispered to Harry on the drive to The Keys. "He doesn't seem as if he is to me."

"Shh," Harry scolded, his pale face turning bright red. "That's such a random thing to say."

"Only asking," Max said irritably, thinking that Harry should be a little nicer to her, considering she'd gotten his new friend a ride on Bobby's plane. "No need to throw a fit."

"He's sitting two feet away," Harry hissed. "For crap's sake—shut it!"

Oh great. What a birthday *this* was going to be. Bobby in a mood, Harry acting like a dick, and no boyfriend, plus Cookie would be all over Mister Cokeaholic when they arrived.

Fantastic fun. She might as well drown herself in one of the pools.

~ ~ ~

"How very thoughtful of you to bring my favorite car," Denver said dryly as she gingerly lowered herself into the passenger seat of the Lamborghini. "I love it because it's *so* low-key."

"Hey," Bobby said, with a quick grin, "a boy's gotta have *some* toys."

"And you are *such* a boy," she responded. She couldn't help laughing, because it was true. At times Bobby could be quite serious, but it was his playful streak she couldn't resist. The private plane, the fancy car—all big-boy toys. He'd never admit it, but he had very expensive tastes.

"By the way," Bobby said, revving the engine. "Guess who I ran into at the airport in New York?"

"Hmm, let me see . . . the pope? The president?"

"Very amusing."

"I try."

"Annabelle Maestro."

"Oh my God! Not Annabelle," Denver said, flashing onto her old school friend, who'd always treated her like a poor relation—even though they weren't related. And when Annabelle's movie-star mother had been murdered, and Denver was involved with defending Annabelle's famous dad, she'd *still* been treated like the poor relative, even though she was a respected attorney with a top Beverly Hills law firm. "How is she?"

"The same entitled bitch on wheels, minus Frankie."

Now Denver flashed onto Annabelle's ex—the coke-addicted Frankie Romano, who used to be one of Bobby's best friends. "Well," she said, remembering Annabelle's annoying sense of self-importance, "I hardly think it's likely she'll ever change. What did she have to say?"

Bobby decided it was prudent not to mention that Annabelle had referred to Denver as "some kind of mutt."

"Not much," he said, sliding into traffic. "Carrying on about that book she got published."

"Oh yes, *My Life: A Hollywood Princess Tells All.* What a crock of shit!"

"I take it you're not a fan?" Bobby said, amused.

"Hell, no," Denver said, shaking her head. "Annabelle was always a piece of work. Surely you remember her in high school."

Oh yes, he remembered Annabelle, all right, and it was a memory he'd sooner forget. He and M.J. had double-teamed her—with her consent—on a drunken prom night. Something to never mention, especially to Denver, who he was sure would not appreciate hearing about it.

"I guess Frankie had a welcome escape," Bobby ventured, zipping in front of a Cadillac.

"I think they both did," Denver said, briskly closing the subject. The last person she wished to talk about was Annabelle Maestro. And as for Frankie Romano—a total loser.

"When we get to the hotel," Bobby said, "unpack, an' put on something casual."

"Why's that?"

He grinned. "You'll see," he said, barely missing a jaywalking pedestrian.

"Mystery Man," she murmured, loving that he had such a strong romantic streak.

"Yeah," he said, still grinning. "An' doncha love it!"

Yes, Bobby, I do.

~ ~ ~

"We're here, an' I'm, like, so into it!" Cookie singsonged, sliding her long brown legs out of Frankie's car, flashing the valet parker with her miniskirt, under which she wore no panties.

Frankie hadn't bothered to book a room, because Cookie had informed him they would be well taken care of. He hadn't realized they would be staying on what Max referred to as the Santangelo floor. When they got off the elevator, he was already feeling horny again, in spite of Cookie servicing him in the car. A little sex, a little gambling—Vegas had that effect on him.

A stern-looking older black woman armed with a lengthy guest list sat at the reception desk facing the elevator.

"Hiya, Betty," Cookie said, swooping in for a friendly hug. "Are we in my usual room?"

Betty gave Frankie a disapproving once-over.

"'S okay," Cookie said gaily. "He's my boyfriend."

Betty reached for her glasses and consulted her list. "And his name is?"

Frankie bristled. "Frankie Romano," he said shortly. "An' you can forget about a room; we need a suite. An' make sure any calls get put directly through to me. Romano. R-O-M—"

"I know how to spell, Mr. Romano," Betty said caustically. "And I do believe all the suites are reserved."

"Well, unreserve one," Frankie said, giving her a sharp look. "Lucky would want me to be comfortable."

Frankie and Betty locked eyes. It was not a friendly interaction.

"I'll see what I can do," Betty said at last, shuffling papers.

Frankie reached into his pocket and flipped a hundred-dollar bill onto her desk. "You do that, hon."

Betty picked up the bill and gave it back to him. "Not necessary," she said.

"Take it," Frankie insisted, thrusting it toward her.

"No thank you," Betty said, ignoring him as she calmly handed Cookie her door card.

Cookie grabbed it, and pulled Frankie away from the desk. "Let's go," she singsonged. "Don't mess with Betty, she can be fierce!"

He threw Betty another look. "Suite," he said shortly. "Deal with it."

Betty continued to ignore him.

"Max and me—we come here all the time," Cookie announced, flouncing into a large blue bedroom with a balcony overlooking the main swimming pool. "This is usually my room."

"I hope you heard me," Frankie said, not pleased. "We need a suite. When Max gets here, *you* deal with it."

"Take no notice of Betty," Cookie said. "She's only doing her job. I'll score us a suite. Don't go gettin' your balls in a spasm."

"You'd better," Frankie said, grabbing her ass and squeezing hard. "I do not appreciate slummin' it."

"Here's the good news," Cookie said. "Everything's comped. Spa, restaurants, pool, shows. You name it—we get it for free." She fished from her purse a black-and-gold credit card with her name engraved on it. "*This* is my ticket to ride," she boasted. "Lucky handed them out to special people when The Keys opened. Bangin', huh?"

Frankie decided he wanted one of those. How come Bobby had never offered him one?

The porter entered with their bags. Frankie tossed him the hundred-dollar bill the douche at reception had refused to accept. Always good to get out the word that there was a big spender in town.

He wondered if Cookie's magic credit card covered gambling, then smirked at the thought of losing Lucky Santangelo's money in *her* casino. What a coup that would be.

Thinking about Bobby's foxy mom, he realized he hadn't seen her in a while, ever since he and Bobby had lost touch. Lucky and Lennie had always been laid-back with him, always friendly. They were a major power couple, and a kick to be around. He decided that he should try to see more of them, invite them to his club, get reacquainted.

Yeah. This was going to be some weekend, and Frankie Romano was expecting to take full advantage of whatever Vegas had to offer.

~ ~ ~

"Where we gonna stay?" Kev asked as they boarded the plane.

Billy had been so intent on getting to Vegas that he hadn't bothered to work out the details. Obviously it would not be wise to stay at The Keys. He called Bambi, his publicist, and told her to book him into the Cavendish.

"Why exactly are you on your way to Vegas?" Bambi was curious to know. "Are you going for the big fight?"

"You know I'm not a boxing fan."

"Well, then," Bambi said. "Is something happening that I'm missing out on?"

"Nothing but a twenty-four-hour crazy gamble with my friend Kev," Billy assured her.

"Okay," Bambi said, somewhat put out. "Only please don't forget that you have a cover shoot for *Vanity Fair* on Monday."

"Wouldn't miss it, Bamb."

"You say that now, Billy," Bambi lectured, worried that her star client was up to no good. "However, you kept the reporter from *Rolling Stone* waiting for three hours, *then* you proceeded to cut the interview short. She wasn't happy, and I can't say I blame her."

"The she who wasn't happy was aiming to talk her way into my pants," Billy explained. "You know how it is with some female reporters; they're only around for the perks."

"You're a big boy, Billy," Bambi admonished. "Surely you can handle that sort of thing."

"Hey, Bamb," Billy said, deftly switching subjects. "I got a question."

"Yes?"

"When your parents named you Bambi, did they expect you to be a porn star or a stripper?"

"Billy! That's so inappropriate."

"Just askin'."

"I'll arrange a comped villa at the Cavendish," Bambi said snippily. "Good-bye." And she cut him off with a determined click.

"What's she look like?" Kev immediately wanted to know, conjuring up a vision of a juicy blonde in hot pants and a nipple-revealing tank.

"Think about her name, and then imagine the exact opposite," Billy said. "She's a dragon lady with teeth that could bite your cock off in one fell swoop. So fuhgedaboudit."

"Copy that," Kev said, shuddering at the graphic image.

~ ~ ~

Ace had spent time at The Keys with Max on several occasions, which meant he was aware of the routine. There was a reserved underground parking section for the Santangelo/Golden family and their guests, so he drove his truck right to it. The valet parker greeted him like an old friend. After exchanging pleasantries, he grabbed his overnight bag and headed upstairs in a private elevator that deposited him on the Santangelo/Golden floor. There he was met by Betty, the middle-aged concierge. Betty was armed with a list of expected guests. Fortunately, he knew her, and he quickly informed her that he was Max's birthday surprise, so not a word that he was here.

Betty nodded agreeably. After Cookie and her obnoxious

boyfriend, Ace was a delight, a nice-looking young man, tall and lanky, and always polite.

"Any idea what time Max is getting here?" he asked.

"Soon," Betty replied. "The Stanislopoulos plane landed twenty minutes ago."

"The what?"

"Bobby's plane."

"Oh, yeah," Ace said, suddenly remembering who he was dealing with. Max's brother had the use of a plane, and Max was obviously on it. "I'll wait," he said, groping in his pocket to make sure the box with the present he'd purchased for Max was still there. He'd spent $250 on a gold heart pendant, and he was hoping she'd love it. She'd better; it was the most expensive gift he'd ever bought anyone.

~ ~ ~

"I'm curious," Denver said when they were finally settled in Bobby's suite at The Keys. "What's your mom's fascination with Vegas?"

Bobby moved over to the window and stared out at the staggering view, which never failed to thrill him. "My grandfather on Lucky's side built one of the first hotels here, way back in the forties," he explained. "Gino. You've met him."

"I have?" Denver said, unpacking her bag.

"Maybe not," Bobby said, turning back to look at her. "But you will this weekend. He's some colorful character, my granddad. He used to hang out with Meyer Lansky, Jake the boy, Lucky Luciano—a whole slew of those old-time gangsters. Back in the day, those guys ruled everything, and Gino was right up there. He named Lucky after Lucky Luciano—kind of an homage."

Denver stopped what she was doing. "No way."

"Yeah. Kinda wild, huh?"

"I would say so."

"Anyway, Gino was in the hotel business, and decades later, when he fled America on a tax evasion thing, Lucky moved right in an' took over the building of his latest hotel. She was like twenty or something."

"That's quite an achievement."

"It sure is. But hey, that's my mom. Balls of steel." He chuckled. "Rumor has it she threatened some poor slob in the middle of the night that she'd cut off his dick if he didn't put up the building costs he'd signed on for."

"And did he?"

"What do *you* think?"

Denver was half impressed and half horrified. She'd always admired strong women, but maybe Lucky Santangelo took strength to a new level.

"What about you, Bobby?" she ventured. "How tough was it when you lost your father?"

"I was too young to remember much about it."

"And was Lucky a good mother? Was she always around?"

"What's with all the questions, babe? I feel like I'm on the stand."

"I'd just like to know more about you. Is that okay?"

"Lucky is Lucky. She's the greatest," Bobby said, moving toward her. "Anyway, I'm here, and I ain't doin' badly, so no more questions an' let's get going. You're in for a big surprise."

"And what would that be?"

"Now, if I told you," he said lightly, "it wouldn't be a surprise, would it?"

"Well, if you put it that way."

And Denver realized that he'd completely steered her off track. No more Lucky revelations today. Bobby was closing ranks on *that* conversation.

~ ~ ~

After Armand left, Jeffrey expected that Lucky would have plenty to say, and quite frankly he wouldn't have blamed her. Instead she was silent, and the moment he started to apologize she abruptly cut him off.

"Forget about it," she said coolly. "We all make mistakes."

Although outwardly she appeared calm, inwardly she was seething. Armand Jordan was the kind of man she abhorred—a self-absorbed, egotistical, chauvinistic pig. It infuriated her that Jeffrey had actually put her in the same room with the creep. Perhaps her lawyer was not as smart as she'd thought, or maybe his divorce was addling his brain.

"Danny," she said, all business, "inform the desk that I want Armand Jordan out of my hotel before noon. I don't care how it's done, but I want him out."

Danny snapped to attention. "Yes, Lucky," he said. "I'll make sure it's taken care of."

"And Danny, as soon as you've done that, get me a full dossier on Armand Jordan." She turned to Jeffrey. "Something I probably should have seen *before* the meeting."

Jeffrey looked uncomfortable. He knew he'd let Lucky down, and that wasn't good, considering she was his most important client. "His company is top-rate," he began to say. "Armand Jordan is on the Forbes list. I wouldn't bring you—"

"For my own interest," Lucky interrupted, not wishing to listen to Jeffrey's excuses. "I need to know who I'm dealing with. *Especially* when they threaten me."

"Lucky, once again, I'm so sorry—"

"Time for the board meeting," she said, her beautiful face expressionless, only her deep black eyes revealing her annoyance. "Let's go. I don't intend to keep anyone waiting."

Danny shut his laptop and trotted after them, wondering how Lucky was able to keep her cool. Armand might be a chauvinistic billionaire, but if he, Danny, was in Lucky's place, he would've slapped the man's face, a resounding slap heard for miles.

Ah yes, Danny thought dreamily. *One of those old-fashioned slaps that used to take place when Diva Queens ruled the movies. Bette Davis, Ava Gardner, Joan Crawford.*

Danny had rented and avidly watched all their movies; their outfits alone had sent him into a euphoric state.

"Danny," Lucky said sharply, turning her head. "Stop following us and go deal with getting that person tossed from my hotel. I want you to personally make sure he leaves the premises, and be sure to tell Jerrod to alert everyone that he is not allowed back. *Comprende?*"

"I'm on it," Danny said, once again jumping to attention. "Although surely you need me at the board meeting?"

"Send one of the assistants to cover it."

"Really?" Danny said, disappointed because he hated missing anything.

"Yes, really," Lucky said briskly. "And don't forget that Lennie is arriving at five. Make sure he knows I'm at the apartment. And once he gets here, we do not expect to be disturbed under *any* circumstances. Got it?"

"Got it," Danny repeated.

"Tell Bobby and Max we'll see them for breakfast tomorrow. And organize anything they or their friends might need for tonight. I'm picking up the tab."

Danny nodded. He understood. Whenever Lennie reappeared, Lucky carved out alone time with her husband. And that, Danny decided, was the reason they had such a happy and successful marriage.

Lucky had her priorities straight. Nothing and no one came between her and her man.

CHAPTER TWENTY-NINE

Armand was burning up. He had never—repeat, *never*—been spoken to in such a fashion, and by a woman! He was enraged. He felt as if his head was going to explode with sheer fury. Black spots danced in front of his eyes. He was sick sick sick with anger.

The moment they left Lucky's office he turned on Fouad and began screaming a litany of expletives, as if Fouad were personally responsible for the unfortunate meeting. "Fuck that whore bitch. And fuck you," Armand yelled, the veins standing out in his forehead. "Motherfucking *cunt*."

Fouad wasn't quite sure whether the "motherfucking cunt" insult was directed at him or Lucky Santangelo. It didn't matter. He'd made up his mind about moving on, and as soon as he had all his affairs in order, it would be *sayonara* to Armand Jordan and everything he represented. He couldn't wait to return to New York.

However, in spite of Armand's loathsome anger, he managed to remain stony-faced. He'd warned Armand that The Keys was not for sale, but Armand had insisted on meeting the owner anyway. Had he read the research that Fouad's assistant had gathered on Lucky Santangelo, he would have realized that she was no ordinary woman. Lucky Santangelo was a lethal force. A woman with a dangerous and powerful past. A strong, intelligent woman who seemed able to achieve anything she set her mind to. And a beauty too. Fouad was quite struck by her looks and composure.

"What now?" Fouad asked when Armand finally stopped yelling. "Should I arrange for a plane?"

"A plane?" Armand snarled, clenching his fists. "For what? You think I'm running away? You actually imagine I would leave here without getting my prize?"

Why was Armand still thinking he could gain ownership of a property that was not for sale? Surely, as a businessman, he realized there was no deal to be made. Especially after his confrontation with Lucky Santangelo.

This situation was becoming ridiculous. Armand was behaving like an out-of-control child who'd failed to get a new bike for Christmas. Could anyone respect a man who behaved like that? Lucky Santangelo and her lawyer were probably laughing at them. Armand had made a mockery of the meeting. A mockery of Jordan Developments.

"She's not going to sell, Armand," Fouad said patiently. "You heard her. Not to you or anyone else."

"Fuck the cunt. I want this hotel, Fouad. And it's time you got it into your useless head that we are not leaving Vegas until I get it."

~ ~ ~

Peggy enjoyed a leisurely breakfast out by the pool at the Cavendish. Earlier, she'd phoned her son to see if he would care to join her, but there was no answer from either Armand's cell or his suite. She didn't mind; she was sure that she presented a mysterious and glamorous figure clad in a white sundress, a large straw hat, and Chanel sunglasses, sitting at a table by herself watching the passing parade of tourists and young couples with kids. It was still early; the serious gamblers and bachelor-party groups had yet to emerge.

A middle-aged man in a Hawaiian shirt who was sprawled at a nearby table with his overweight wife couldn't take his eyes off her. Lust was in the air. Peggy could smell lust a mile off.

She smiled to herself. Vegas agreed with her. Being back there was almost like re-visiting her youth. Ah yes, as one of the most desirable and sought-after girls in town, she'd created quite a stir. Many a man had fallen for her obvious charms. She treasured the memory of those times.

Seeing Gino Santangelo had given her a jolt. The fact that he was still alive was a big surprise. She realized that he must be at least ninety-something, because on the one memorable night she'd spent with him, he was in his fifties. Even so, he'd been a vigorous lover, such a powerhouse.

At eighteen she'd considered herself experienced, but Gino Santangelo had given new meaning to the act of making love.

LAS VEGAS 1968

Peggy Lindquest and Joe Piscarelli made quite the dashing couple around town. Peggy was a stunner, and Joe was no slouch in the handsome stakes, with his wannabe gangster movie-star looks. Their relationship was volatile due to major jealousy issues on both sides. Joe, at the age of thirty, had been around and then some, which meant there were quite a few exes in his world. One-nighters, two-nighters, and so on.

Peggy claimed she had been with only one other man— her high school boyfriend. She was lying, of course, but since she was new to Vegas, there was no way for Joe to prove otherwise.

They fought like wildcats. And then they made up as if they were starring in a porno movie.

It was their pattern.

The one thing that scared Peggy was Joe's violent temper, and when it got too bad, she usually spent the night at a girl-friend's house. Joe always arrived to collect her the next morning, and all was quiet on the Western front. But Peggy's girlfriends kept on warning her that Joe's vile outbursts could easily escalate and become physical. Peggy refused to believe he would ever hit her.

One night he did act out, shoving her violently across the room. Shocked, she fled to her girlfriend Veronica's apart-ment in a panic, tears and everything.

Veronica, a statuesque black beauty who was a dancer in the Folies Bergere show at the Tropicana, was on her way to an exclusive party at Caesar's Palace. She insisted that Peggy dry her tears and come with her. Peggy declined, until Veronica whispered in her ear, "There's a rumor Sinatra may show up."

Frank Sinatra. Every Vegas showgirl's dream.

Peggy rapidly changed her mind, and the two girls set off to join the party, dressed to conquer.

Sinatra never appeared, but Gino Santangelo was there, and Gino Santangelo was a legendary figure in Vegas.

Peggy set her charm on high beam and went for it. She'd had no idea it would turn out to be such a heavenly experience. The man was not nicknamed Gino the Ram for nothing.

After a short conversation at the party, he invited her upstairs to a sumptuous suite and asked if her breasts were real. When she said they were, he slowly proceeded to strip her, garment by garment, until she stood before him in her high heels and nothing else.

She wasn't shy. She was almost naked onstage every night.

He admired her body, slowly fingering her in the most intimate of places, and when he decided she was ready, he took her into the bedroom and laid her on the bed with her legs spread. Then he went down on her, slowly, surely, until she was in such a state of ecstasy she was begging him to fuck her.

But he didn't. He forced her to wait until he was ready to make her come with his tongue.

She lay on the bed writhing with passion, desperate for him to ravish her, all thoughts of Joe set aside.

But Gino took his time, exciting her all the more. He pulled her off the bed and led her to the shower, and only then did he divest himself of his clothes and climb in with her, whereupon he proceeded to soap her body until she reached orgasm again, screaming aloud with pleasure.

Finally they returned to the bedroom, where he made love to her for what seemed like hours. At dawn, he sent her home in a chauffeured sedan, and she never heard from him again.

~ ~ ~

Peggy had something on her mind, something she'd conveniently never faced up to but always secretly wondered about.

In the space of one week in 1968 she'd slept with Joe Piscarelli, Gino Santangelo, and King Emir Amin Mohamed Jordan. A month later she'd discovered she was pregnant.

So who was Armand's real father?

Was it Joe Piscarelli, her would-be gangster boyfriend?

Gino Santangelo, her one-night stand?

Or her ex-husband, King Emir Amin Mohamed Jordan?

Surely it was about time she found out . . .

CHAPTER THIRTY

The board meeting was about to start, and after her unsettling and annoying morning, Lucky was pleased to be in a room with her investors—all of whom were full of positive vibes.

Alex Woods was standing in a corner drinking a cup of coffee.

She headed in his direction. "Thanks for coming," she said, touching his arm. "I wasn't sure you would, but I'm glad you did."

"You think I'd miss little Max's birthday?" he replied, giving her a long steady look.

"It's nice of you to make the effort."

"And she's so formal," he remarked, giving her another long look, a look that said *We could be making beautiful love together, but you're still hung up on your goddamn husband.*

"Well . . . I know how busy you are."

"Never too busy for you, Lucky," he replied, his eyes never leaving hers.

"Okay," she said, attempting to lighten things up. "Let's not get carried away."

He fished a packet of cigarettes from his pocket, and went to light one up.

"No smoking!" she admonished.

His look turned quizzical. "Are you fucking kidding me?"

"Please, Alex, for me. I gave it up, and I don't want to be tempted."

"You don't, huh?"

"No thank you."

He put the cigarette back in its packet. "When's Lennie getting here?" he inquired.

"Didn't you just ask me that in L.A.?"

"Is it a crime to ask you again?"

"Knock it off, Alex," she said, suddenly becoming impatient. "I know what you're doing."

"Huh?"

"Why didn't you bring a girlfriend with you?"

"What now?"

"A girlfriend, Alex," she said, repeating herself. "A gorgeous young thing to keep you occupied so Lennie doesn't get the impression that you're still lusting after me."

"Oh, I see," Alex said, squinting slightly. "Is *that* what you think?"

"Actually, it's not what I think, it's what I know."

"Well," he said with a sardonic edge, "glad to note your ego is alive and well and living happily in fantasy land."

"Cut the crap, Alex," she said, shaking her head. "Why don't you do yourself a big favor and send for one of your many women?"

"Why would I do that?"

"Because the last thing I need is any tension between you and Lennie, who incidentally arrives later this afternoon, which I do believe I already told you."

"Screw you, Santangelo," Alex said, scowling.

"And wouldn't you like to," she fired back.

"Jesus!" he complained. "You're out of control."

"Well that makes two of us, doesn't it?"

Before Alex could reply, Gino strolled over. "Y'know, I'm kinda surprised you two never got together," Gino remarked. "You're always at each other's throats. Makes for a combative mix."

"Do I *look* Asian?" Lucky drawled.

"I get it," Gino said, chuckling loudly. "Alex only raises the flag for—"

"Don't even go there!" Lucky warned, well aware of the politically incorrect word Gino was about to use.

"Let him say it," Alex said with a throaty laugh. "He's old, it doesn't matter."

"Who're *you* callin' old?" Gino griped. "It takes balls t' reach my age an' still be standin' on two fuckin' feet."

"And I give you kudos for that," Alex said. "You're my idol, Gino. I want to be just like you when I grow up."

"For God's sake!" Lucky exclaimed. "Why don't the two of you go form a circle jerk and be done with it."

"She's *your* daughter," Alex pointed out.

"Yeah," Gino agreed, with another wicked chuckle. "She's the son I never had."

"You *had* a son. Dario," Lucky reminded him sharply. "And just because he was gay there's no reason for you to disrespect him."

"Kiddo, I didn't mean—"

"You know what, screw both of you," she said, shaking her head. "You're a couple of little big boys, so go ahead—get your kicks playing with each other. That's just about the level of your style."

"Hey," Gino objected. "Is that any way t' talk to your old man?"

Lucky shook her head again. Sometimes dealing with Gino

was like dealing with a little kid. "Where's Paige?" she asked. "Shouldn't she be taking care of you?"

"That'll be the day, when I need takin' care of." Gino snorted. "I might be gettin' up there, but I'm not fuckin' dead. Anyway, she's over at the Cavendish dealin' with beauty shit."

"What's wrong with the salon here?"

"She's got her special girl over at the Cavendish. Do *I* know?"

"Okay, I get it. So I suggest you and Alex take your seats and let's get this show on the road."

And so they did, and the meeting took place, and went extremely well. Everyone was enthusiastic about how successful The Keys was in spite of such a flat economy. The hotel was operating at capacity. The casino couldn't be busier. And there was a long waiting list to purchase one of the multimillion-dollar apartments.

Halfway through the meeting, Venus dutifully put in an appearance, beguiling everyone with her radiant blond beauty and dazzling star power. Venus certainly knew how to captivate a room.

Afterward there was a buffet lunch, during which Lucky managed to avoid another one-on-one with Alex. Too uncomfortable. She wished he'd get married or start living with someone again. Having Alex on the loose was too dangerous. Unfortunately, there was still a deep connection between them. And if Lennie weren't around . . .

No! she told herself sternly. *Don't even think it.*

~ ~ ~

Jorge didn't gamble, but Venus did, and after her appearance at the board meeting she felt like some action. Gambling was always a turn-on, especially when she ended up a winner.

Entering the casino at The Keys, Jorge went into semishock. Such opulence. Such a huge number of people throwing their money around. Not to mention such beautiful cocktail waiters and waitresses attending to the customers' every need.

He immediately wondered if he could get a job here, for he was street-smart enough to know that this thing with Venus wouldn't last, and when she tired of him—which he knew she would—what then? Was he supposed to run back to L.A. and the sex-crazed fat agent he'd been forced to service simply to score a job on Venus's photo shoot?

No, Jorge had not fled Rio and the favelas, where he'd almost raised himself, to become the plaything of a series of horny American women.

Venus was exquisite, but she was too famous for him, and at forty-something, too old—even though she was in impeccable shape, with her perfect body and muscled thighs. Earlier, while he was going down on her, she'd almost strangled him with those thighs. Lost in her juices, he'd had to splutter and grunt to get her to release him.

Jorge hung back as two security guards accompanied Venus around the casino. Soon he noticed a crowd beginning to form, and he wondered what it must be like to be so famous.

One day . . . one day somewhere in the future, he vowed to find out.

~ ~ ~

"Remember that time you got a dose of the crabs from some piece a stray you banged, then you hadda 'splain it to Venus with some bullshit story?" Kev said with a raucous chuckle. "Good times, buddy, good times."

"For you, maybe," Billy responded, cracking a slight smile. "I hadda tell Venus I caught 'em from a crapper. Don't think she believed me."

Kev snorted with mirth. "Yeah, those were the badass days. God, I miss 'em."

They were now settled in a luxury villa at the Cavendish, and Kev was hot to hit the tables. He kept on encouraging Billy to do the same.

"I gotta coupla biz calls to make," Billy said, thrusting a few hundred-dollar bills at Kev. "Go put this on seven for me. An' try to make sure I'm a winner."

"Like when're you ever not?" Kev grumbled, grabbing the money and taking off. "See you in the casino."

"Ten minutes," Billy promised. "Don't forget—number seven."

As soon as Kev left, Billy paced up and down for a minute or two, then he called Max on her cell. No reply. He hesitated about leaving a message, then decided against it. He'd sooner talk to her personally.

Unusual for him, but he was feeling slightly apprehensive about what she'd have to say. Would she be pleased he'd followed her to Vegas? Or would she blow him off?

For now he'd just have to wait and see.

CHAPTER THIRTY-ONE

"You ever thought of dumpin' the dreads?" Frankie inquired as he and Cookie lay side by side on top of the bed in their hotel room, casually sharing a joint.

"Huh?" Cookie replied, immediately tugging on the Caribbean dreadlocks that she considered her trademark. "Never had any complaints before."

"I was kinda thinkin' you might wanna go for a softer look," Frankie suggested.

"You sound like my dad," Cookie said, dragging on the weed. "I'm totally into my dreads. Who wants to look like every other girl in L.A.?"

"*You*, never," Frankie insisted, extracting the joint from her fingers and taking a deep hit. "You're an original."

"Why you even askin'?" Cookie demanded, thinking that for an older guy, Frankie sure had his shit together. He was okay in the sack. He came up with a steady assortment of drugs, and he was a kick to be around. Not boring, like Max's boyfriend, Ace. And not a weirdo like Harry—because even though Harry was one of her best friends, she had to admit he was kind of eccentric at times.

"'Cause every time you give me a b.j., your dreads keep hittin' my balls," Frankie said, exhaling a thin line of smoke.

"Ew!" Cookie giggled. "Wouldn't wanna damage your precious *cojones.*"

"You wouldn't, huh?" Frankie said.

"No, 'cause then you couldn't get it up."

"You got a dirty mouth."

"An' doncha love it," Cookie responded, rolling over and climbing astride him. "Anyway," she added, "who'd you want me to look like?"

"Janet Jackson at her peak," Frankie said with a wink. "You're as pretty as her."

Cookie giggled again and snatched the joint back from him. "A *thin* Janet Jackson," she said pointedly. "With way better tits."

"Now, hold on," Frankie objected, pushing her off him. "You gotta admit the woman's got a dynamite pair. We all saw 'em at the Super Bowl."

"An' I don't?" Cookie said, pouting.

"That goes without sayin', honeytits."

"Honeytits!" she squealed. "Where'd you come up with *that?*"

"Mel Gibson, I think."

"Screw Mel Gibson. An' anyway, he called that cop sugartits."

"Same thing."

"No way."

"I got an idea."

"What?"

"Whyn't you blow me, sugartits, an' shut the fuck up."

Cookie so appreciated being treated like an adult.

~ ~ ~

Bobby's surprise was a private boat on Lake Mead, with a gourmet late lunch and an attentive waiter. Denver could've done without the lunch and the waiter, but she didn't say anything because she was fully aware that Bobby meant well, and it was a very thoughtful gesture.

However, she couldn't help sneaking a peek at her BlackBerry to see what was going on back in L.A. Taking Friday off was not a career-enhancing move, but Bobby had been so insistent, and since she was moving on to the drug unit, did it really matter? She'd won her final case and avoided her horny boss, and Monday she would start fresh.

"What are you doing?" Bobby wanted to know, leaning over her shoulder.

"Just checking on work."

"No," he said firmly.

"No, what?"

"Not while we're on our first vacation."

"Bobby," she reminded him gently "this is not a vacation, it's a weekend."

"And our first one away together," he pointed out, kissing her neck.

"Okay," she said, clicking her phone off. "Whatever my Lord and Master wants."

"Easy!" he laughed. "I'm not *that* bad."

"Well, you *are* being kind of overbearing."

"Thought I was being romantic."

"You're right." She sighed. "I'll leave work alone until later."

"Later I might have more surprises."

"Hmm . . . something to look forward to?"

"You'll just have to wait and see."

~ ~ ~

"I appeared at the Maracanã Stadium in Rio once," Venus informed Jorge, who was now massaging her feet after their stint in the casino. She'd won $25,000 at blackjack, so she was on a high. "Thousands of people, and little old me," she reminisced. "It was a fantastic night. Very memorable."

"Ah, Maracanã," Jorge murmured. He spoke more English than Venus thought, and he understood plenty, but he'd decided it was prudent to pretend he had yet to master English. It was also prudent not to mention that he was ten years old when he and some friends had sneaked into the famous Maracanã Stadium and watched her perform. He could still remember the hard-on she'd given him that night.

Growing up in a two-room shack with seven brothers and sisters, no father, and a mother who lived only for Carnival, Jorge had been forced to take care of himself. At the age of ten he'd started stealing from tourists in Rio, and from fourteen on he'd been robbing and fucking them, picking up a smattering of English along the way. The moment he'd stashed enough money, he'd gotten himself a passport and purchased a one-way ticket to Los Angeles. At least he had ambition.

Now what? He might be only nineteen (Venus thought he was twenty), but he was smart enough to know that being with this platinum-blond superstar might be his only opportunity to score big.

He didn't know what, but this weekend he was determined to do *something* to cement their connection.

~ ~ ~

Determined not to feel sorry for herself, Max entered the elevator, which zoomed her upstairs. Harry and Paco had stopped off at the drugstore to pick up God only knew what. Harry was acting totally lovesick; she could hardly stand it.

Betty was sitting in her usual place. Max gave her a quick hug. "Is Cookie here yet?" she asked.

Betty nodded, a disapproving glint in her watchful eyes. "Indeed she is. With that new boyfriend of hers."

"Oh yes, Frankie," Max said, with a knowing grin. "Cookie hit the jackpot, right?"

"Seems too old for her," Betty remarked. "And smarmy, with a smart mouth."

"Hey, we all know Cookie," Max said, grabbing a handful of M&M's from Betty's desk. "This is *way* better than her dragging random dudes up here every night."

"I have never approved of that girl's behavior," Betty said, tight-lipped. "She needs discipline. Where are her parents?"

"You *know* where they are. We've had this conversation before," Max said. "By the way, be prepared. Harry has a, uh . . . boyfriend too. They'll be checking in any minute."

Betty's eyebrows shot up. "A boyfriend?"

"Oh c'mon, Bets." Max giggled. "You *know* Harry's gay."

"He is?" Betty said dryly.

"Please don't tease me. It's almost my birthday and *they've* both got boyfriends, while *I'm* all alone. Charming isn't it?"

"Don't worry, dear," Betty assured her, thinking of the boyfriend all set to surprise her. "You'll still have a lovely time."

"Thanks, Bets," she said as she headed down the corridor to her suite.

Slipping her entry card into the door, she walked inside.

"Hey," Ace said, jumping up to greet her with a big smile on his face. "Happy birthday, sweet eighteen!"

CHAPTER THIRTY-TWO

Getting thrown out of The Keys was without doubt the most insulting thing that had ever happened to Armand—an offensive affront to his dignity. When Fouad had informed him that they were being forced to leave, Armand had refused to believe him. In his mind it was not possible that this could happen. But happen it did, and when four burly security men arrived to escort him off the premises, he finally understood that it was for real.

Armand did not go silently. He threatened every staff member in the vicinity with expulsion the moment he owned the hotel. He had Fouad take down names, and he let everyone know that they would soon all have no jobs. He radiated a dark, cold fury.

Danny, hovering on the sidelines, was startled by the man's level of lethal anger. He'd never witnessed such frightening rage.

Fouad had a limousine waiting downstairs. Once again he had assumed they would head straight to the airport—he'd even left a message for Peggy that they would be picking her up very shortly.

Armand had other ideas.

"Do you honestly believe that I would run from here like a whipped dog with its tail between its legs?" Armand said, enraged. "How many times do I have to tell you? Are you brain-dead, Fouad? Do you not listen? Are you a complete fool?"

Yes, Fouad thought, *I am a fool for continuing to put up with your verbal abuse. You contaminate everything you touch.*

"Get me the best they have at the Cavendish," Armand instructed. "And attempt to listen to me for once, Fouad." An ominous pause. "We are not leaving Las Vegas until I own The Keys. That whore bitch will not win. I will see her die before she gets the better of me. Do you understand me? I WILL SEE HER DIE."

~ ~ ~

Many years ago Peggy had decided that if she did discover who Armand's real father was, she would never tell her son. Armand considered himself royal born, and she refused to dispel the myth—if indeed it was a myth. If it turned out that he wasn't the king's son, the ramifications would be disastrous. And were the king to find out, who knew *what* he would do? The punishments in Akramshar were harsh, especially toward women. They included the ancient custom of stoning, and long spells in prison for nothing more than disrespecting a male.

Not that Peggy would ever consider going back, not under any circumstances. She'd made her life in America, and that's exactly where she was staying. Maybe even in Vegas if she met the right man.

For a woman in her sixties—however great she looked—the pickings in New York were lackluster. Old men with Viagra hard-ons required women in their thirties, and in a pinch, in their forties. So where did that leave her? In Vegas, with casinos full of rich gamblers who might appreciate an attractive redhead in her prime.

Well . . . maybe a tad past her prime, but so what?

After a leisurely breakfast, she visited the spa, where she allowed herself to be primped and pampered while she wondered how she could get close enough to Gino Santangelo to obtain a DNA sample. She'd watched enough *CSI*'s on TV to know that determining paternity was not difficult. A scrap of hair, a cigarette stub—and there were labs advertised on the Internet where you could simply mail in your sample. She'd even found one in Vegas, which (for a price) promised twenty-four-hour turnaround service.

Peggy was excited. She'd always wondered, and now it might be possible to find out.

"Have you ever heard of a man called Gino Santangelo?" she asked the tall brunette who was giving her a facial.

The girl almost choked. "Gino Santangelo is one of the most famous characters in Vegas," she said, lowering her voice. "His daughter built The Keys. The Santangelos are Vegas royalty."

"Shh," hissed the bleached blonde who was busy giving Peggy a pedicure. "His wife's over there getting her nails done."

"His wife," Peggy said, her eyes darting across the room. She observed a short woman with a mass of frizzy copper-colored hair and a compact body. The woman was well preserved, but Peggy—an expert at such things—decided she was in her late sixties.

Mrs. Gino Santangelo. Perhaps this was the opportunity Peggy had been looking for.

Yes, an opportunity to get closer to the truth, and she was about to take it.

~ ~ ~

Settled into a private and secluded luxury villa at the Cavendish, Armand continued to rant and rave about how sickened and angry he was at the outcome of his meeting with Lucky Santangelo. That a woman could get away with speaking to him in such a crude and vile way was unthinkable. His skin crawled at the thought. Her words reverberated in his head and filled him with even more hate.

"In my country she would be stoned to death for her disrespect," he screamed, pacing up and down. "I am a prince. You hear me, Fouad? A royal man. She is nothing but a whore peasant, and she *must* be punished!"

Fouad stared at Armand and realized that he was no longer a man in control. It seemed he had lost any sense of reality. Had Armand honestly believed that just like that he could fly into Vegas and purchase a property such as The Keys? Was he becoming so convinced of his own importance and power that he'd thought it was possible?

Ever since the incident with Martin Constantine's wife, Fouad had sensed that there was something basically wrong with Armand. He appeared to be unraveling, caught up in a fantasy power trip of huge proportions. Now he was proclaiming himself a prince—which of course he was, but his title meant nothing in America.

"You do know," Armand shouted, fixing Fouad with a manic glare, "that one day I will rule Akramshar. *I* will be king."

"I thought your plan was to stay in America," Fouad said, shocked by Armand's announcement.

"My father will expect me to take over," Armand said, a feverish look in his eyes. "Do you think I would disappoint him? Because if you think that, you're an idiot. A *useless* idiot." He paused, then added, "Lately, Fouad, I have been thinking I should rid myself of your useless existence."

Once again Fouad was shocked. He'd grown up in Akramshar, the son of a palace guard, and he'd heard these slurs many times coming from the king. The word *useless* was one of the king's favorite insults. He used it on wives, workers, his children—anyone he felt deserved the wrath of his tongue. He spat it out like a snake's venom, making it sound worse than any expletive.

Was Armand turning into his father?

Was he suffering from delusions of grandeur?

Did he honestly believe that when King Emir Amin Mohamed Jordan died he could become ruler of Akramshar?

Impossible. The king's other sons would never allow that to happen. Armand might have been born in Akramshar and lived there for all of eight years, but he had left the land of his birth and become a high-powered American business tycoon. He would never be accepted back. Fouad happened to know that the only reason the king paid Armand so much attention was that through Armand's various holdings and companies, he was able to filter money for the king, legitimize it. In America they called it laundering.

"Get me everything you know about Lucky Santangelo," Armand suddenly ordered. "That file you had. Where is it? Give it to me at once."

"Do you mean the file you refused to pay attention to?" Fouad said, unable to resist a small dig.

"I want it *now*," Armand said brusquely. "Immediately."

"I will have it sent up."

"Disrespectful whore," Armand muttered. "She will pay dearly for daring to challenge me."

Fouad couldn't quite figure out how Armand had reached the conclusion that Lucky Santangelo had challenged him. She'd merely turned down his offer to buy The Keys. That was it. But obviously she'd triggered something in Armand that had set him on a revengeful path.

"I should go," Fouad said evenly. "You need time alone."

"No. What I *need* is a couple of whores while I think about what to do," Armand raged, his face dark with anger. "Arrange it. I want them here immediately."

Was this what things had come to—ordering up prostitutes for Armand's perverse pleasure?

No. Enough was enough. Once again he refused to do it.

Moving over to the desk, he picked up a hotel notepad and wrote down a number.

"Here," he said, handing the notepad to Armand. "It's best if you call yourself."

And before Armand could object, he made a swift exit.

Fouad is a pathetic excuse for a man, Armand thought. *Why do I continue to put up with his inadequacies, his American wife and his stupid children?*

Not that he'd ever met Fouad's children. Truth was, he'd only encountered the wife on two occasions. A blonde from Tennessee, she was boring and bland and not even that pretty. She'd ruined Fouad, turned him into a sheep incapable of functioning properly in the world of business. *That's* why the meeting to buy The Keys had failed. Fouad's wife had cut off his balls, rendering him weak and ineffectual. Lucky Santangelo had sensed weakness and used it against him. Conniving whore.

Yes, Armand was sure of it. Now it was up to him to make certain the sale happened.

He paced around the living room of the villa, which was not nearly as luxurious as the Presidential Suite he had occupied at The Keys.

After a while he laid out several lines of coke and soon did all of it. Fortunately, he always traveled with a full supply—courtesy of his New York dealer, who took care of keeping him well stocked.

By the time Fouad sent up the information on Lucky Santangelo, Armand felt ready to rule not only Akramshar, but the rest of the world too. He was flying high, angry and resentful. He needed to vent his frustration at not getting what he wanted.

Picking up the phone, he called Yvonne Le Crane.

Yvonne was not pleased to hear from him. She did not appreciate her girls being stiffed. If they failed to receive the full amount of money they were due, it meant less commission to tuck into her latest Prada purse—Prada being her current obsession. When Armand Jordan got on the phone and demanded more girls, she was less than friendly, especially since a certain important person in Vegas had been asking questions about him.

"You didn't pay my girls everything they were due," she accused.

"The two women whom I did not pay extra were inexperienced and unprofessional," Armand stated coldly. "It does not reflect well on your services."

"My services are the best in Vegas," Yvonne retorted, quite insulted. "My girls are clean, beautiful, and honest."

"Your girls are filthy whores," Armand sneered.

"If that's what you think, then I suggest we cease doing business and end this conversation."

"No. We will not end it," Armand said sharply, his anger building as he leaned over the coffee table to snort another line of coke. "You will send me two girls. Big breasts. Thirty thousand. Cash. Have them here at six. I am now at the Cavendish."

Yvonne was silent for a moment. She didn't trust Armand Jordan, and even though she'd never met him, there was something off about him, something she didn't like. Several of the girls she'd sent to him before had complained that he was a crass pervert, and for them to complain was unusual.

However, it occurred to her that she didn't have to send him her girls. There were other places she could obtain talent. Armand Jordan was a sicko; he wouldn't know the difference, since all he chose to do was debase and humiliate them, so what the hell? Above all else, she was a businesswoman, and $30,000 was a tempting amount of cash.

Yes, Yvonne decided, she would send Armand Jordan exactly the type of girls he deserved.

CHAPTER THIRTY-THREE

After the board meeting, Lucky met with Danny, who filled her in on Armand's furious exit. "What a misogynistic asshole!" she exclaimed. "He's demented. A crazy man. Who *is* he, anyway?"

Danny had printed out everything he could find about Jordan Developments, but as Lucky flicked through the thick file, she discovered there were no personal details about Armand at all. Wikipedia supplied scant information; there was nothing about where he was born, just a brief mention that he'd come to America at the age of eight, the schools and college he attended, and that his socialite mother, Peggy, had remarried an investment banker—since deceased. Who was her first husband? Obviously Armand's father. There was no mention of Armand having a wife or children or any other family members.

It seemed Armand Jordan only existed as the CEO of Jordan Developments, along with several other subsidiary companies.

Because of his far-fetched threat about some kind of future battle, Lucky felt she should find out more about him.

Danny clicked onto various gossip sites and came up with a few photos of Armand at New York City social events—always with a different woman on his arm.

While Danny was doing that, Lucky went straight to the WireImage site on her Mac and typed in Armand Jordan, and up he popped—once again photographed with a series of attractive young women.

The man was a serial dater, although his dates were never named. Odd. A couple of B-list actresses appeared in photos, but they only accompanied him to one event each.

Studying the photos of the girls with no names, Lucky figured they had to be high-class call girls or professional escorts. She recognized the look—sleek, expensive, and bland.

Sure enough, when Danny checked out one of the most exclusive and private escort sites—with a $10,000 entry fee, which Lucky agreed he could put on her credit card—they came across photos of several of the girls Armand had been seen with.

"He's a hooker hound!" Danny exclaimed, deciding that this little investigation certainly made up for missing the board meeting. Danny was so into a bit of intrigue, it made his day.

"He certainly is," Lucky agreed. "Obviously one of their best customers."

"Not a huge surprise," Danny sniffed. "After all, he ordered up girls here, so it's his pattern."

"Do we know which madam he used?" Lucky asked, her curiosity on full alert.

"I'll find out," Danny said, deciding not to mention that during his adventures on the Internet, he'd come across Lucky's Ferrari being driven by Billy Melina. What was *that* about?

"Do it," Lucky said briskly. "And get me in touch with the New York madam. I think I want to find out more about Mr. Jordan."

~ ~ ~

"I gotta go see M.J. before dinner," Bobby said when they finally arrived back at the hotel. "You okay for an hour?"

"Bobby," Denver assured him, "you do not have to babysit me. I'm perfectly fine on my own. Actually, it'll give me some time to work on my laptop."

"Anybody ever told you you're a workaholic?"

"And you're not?" she responded lightly.

"Touché," he said, grabbing his jacket. "I'll see you later. Dinner. Just you and me. We'll make it even more romantic than lunch."

"I thought we were getting together with your family?"

"Not tonight, sweetheart. Tonight is all ours."

"How come?"

" 'Cause I reserved tonight for us."

"I like it," she said, secretly delighted that she wouldn't have to deal with the Santangelo/Golden clan until tomorrow.

"So . . . beautiful," he said, bending down to kiss her. "Wear something sexy."

"Only if you do the same," she teased, affectionately touching his cheek.

"A black thong do it for you?" he joked.

"Get *out* of here," she said, the thought of Bobby in a black thong putting a smile on her face.

As soon as he was gone, she pulled out her BlackBerry and scrolled through her messages. Among them was a text from Sam. It was apparent that he now considered himself back in her life, and he was not giving up easily.

*Having a fine time on set being ignored by actors and direc-
tor alike, except when they need an instant rewrite on a
line. Then I'm king of the hill and they kiss my skinny ass. As
an observer of the human race, you would enjoy every second. How's Vegas? Do u miss my eggs?*

Denver grinned. The *Do u miss my eggs?* line was a reference
to the delicious scrambled eggs he'd made for her in New York
the time she'd ended up spending the night in his apartment. It
was his not-so-subtle way of reminding her that they had shared
a bed. And had sex.

She quickly texted him back.

*Vegas fun. Given up scrambled, moved on to poached. Good
luck with being ignored.*

Then she clicked Send before she changed her mind. They
were friends, nothing more, and Bobby wouldn't mind a touch
of banter between friends. Or would he?

Too bad if he did. It wasn't as if they were married or anything.

Wow! she thought. *Where does marriage enter into this equa-
tion? It's certainly not on my mind.*

Leon had also texted her, but his text was all about work. She
appreciated him giving her a heads-up on what she'd be getting
involved with the following week. Leon was dedicated to getting
drugs off the streets—especially the small-time dealers who set
up shop near high schools, targeting kids as young as ten and
eleven. Leon was a solid guy, and after working at a top level
Beverly Hills law firm defending the probably guilty, it was refreshing to know she was finally getting into something that
really mattered.

~ ~ ~

So there he was. Ace. Her boyfriend. Standing in front of her with a big proud grin on his face, which meant she wasn't about to be alone on her birthday. Ace had apparently skipped out on his job and driven all the way to Vegas to be with her. Ace was fully present. Ace loved her. *Yippee!*

Then why wasn't she happy? Why was she suddenly suffused with guilt? Why was she wishing he hadn't made the trip?

"Wow!" Max exclaimed as he moved forward to hug her. "This is crazy. What are you *doing* here?"

"What do you *think* I'm doing here?" he responded. "Making sure I'm with you for your birthday. Wouldn't miss it."

"That's so cool," she managed, extracting herself from his hug.

"Yeah," he said, still grinning. "Had a feeling you'd want me to be here."

"I do," she insisted. "Only we're not alone. Harry's downstairs with some new friend. And Cookie's hanging out somewhere, and I know you're not wild about being around either of them."

"Thanks for the heads-up," Ace said. "But we can sneak off somewhere by ourselves, right?"

"Can't do that," she said. "They're here for me, so it wouldn't be cool to desert them. Anyway, you *know* they're my best friends."

"And what does that make me?"

"Uh . . . my boyfriend," she said, almost choking on the word.

"That's exactly why I'm not into getting caught up with the crowd," he said restlessly. "Haven't seen you in weeks; don't wanna share you."

Thoughts were flying through her head. Thoughts of Billy, and the offhand way he'd treated her. Thoughts of their one night together on the sand. The way he'd touched her, the blue of his eyes, his kind of half-crazy laugh, and his hard abs.

How could she tell Ace that she wasn't a virgin anymore? Oh man! He'd be so bummed that she'd done the deed with someone else after he'd waited forever.

Bad girlfriend.

Cheating girlfriend.

She wanted to cry.

"Look," Ace said, touching her arm. "Dump the miserable face. If it means that much to you, we'll hang with Cookie and Harry, 's long as they don't start doing drugs in front of me. You know I'm not into that crap."

Her boyfriend, Mister Straight. He wouldn't fit in with Frankie for sure.

"You know what?" she said. "Since we're gonna see them all tomorrow night at my party, I guess we can escape an' do something on our own."

"Now *that's* my girl," Ace said. "Knew you'd see it my way."

~ ~ ~

Lying on the bed, smoking yet another joint while thumbing through a Vegas magazine, Frankie was startled to see that Gerald M.—Cookie's dad—had a one-night engagement at the Cavendish that very evening. "Shit!" he exclaimed, sitting up, wondering why Cookie hadn't told him.

"What?" Cookie asked, entering the room with her key card, fresh from a four-hour session at the hair salon, where she'd had them remove her dreadlocks. A lengthy process but hopefully worth it.

Frankie barely glanced up. "Didja know your old man's appearing at the Cavendish tonight?" he demanded. "A one-off sold-out performance."

She marched over to the bed, stood in front of him with hair that curled softly around her pretty face, and said, "Screw my old man. Whaddya think of my new hairstyle?"

"Oh yeah, your hair," he said vaguely, giving her a cursory once-over. "It's lovely, doll. Told you, no regrets."

"It took *forever*," she complained, flopping down on the end of the bed.

"I bet it did."

"Do you really love it? Are you wild about it? Do I look awesome?"

"Course you do," Frankie lied, because he wasn't sure he liked it. Now she looked like every other pretty young black girl instead of standing out as one of a kind. But at least it had given him a free afternoon to play the tables. He'd taken a beating at craps, although he was confident that tonight he'd win it all back.

After all, he was Frankie Romano. He always came out on top.

"So about the concert?" he said. "I think we should go."

"Seriously?"

"Yeah, seriously."

"I'll see what I can do."

CHAPTER THIRTY-FOUR

Lucky had major connections. She could pick up a phone and get through to almost anyone, and if she couldn't, Gino certainly could. After she'd talked to the New York madam who supplied girls for Armand Jordan, and the Vegas madam, Yvonne Le Crane, a pattern emerged. He booked girls to be seen with, and if sex was involved, his preference was to humiliate and debase them.

I knew he was an asshole, Lucky thought. *Probably can't get it up.*

Then she suddenly decided that she was wasting too much time investigating Armand Jordan's dumb ass; it was getting boring. He was a sick joke, not someone to be concerned about. She informed Danny to cut off any further digging, adding a terse "Just make sure he never gets into my hotel again. Okay?"

"Got it, Lucky," Danny agreed. "I'll have Jerrod circulate his photo."

"Good plan. Did you hear if Max and Bobby got here yet?"

"They've both arrived. And according to Betty, Max's boy-friend, Ace, turned up unexpectedly."

"Nice surprise for her," Lucky said, pleased, because she liked Ace a lot, and he seemed to be a good influence on Max. "Any of them requesting reservations tonight?"

"I'll check with everyone shortly."

"Thanks, Danny. You're always on top of it. I know you'll make sure they're all taken care of."

Danny appreciated getting praise for a job he knew he handled well.

"Well," Lucky continued. "I'm about to throw myself into a sauna, so I'll see you in the morning."

"You certainly will," Danny said, still unsure about whether he should mention Billy Melina being spotted in her car.

Best not to, he decided. His boss was getting ready to greet Lennie. Why ruin her evening?

~ ~ ~

Being a star, in Vegas, with nobody around to protect him except Kev—who was about as helpful as a teenager on crack—was turning out to be a bad idea. Everywhere Billy went, fans surrounded him. Girls with longing and hero worship in their eyes. Couples from middle America who requested he pose for a photo with them because their granddaughter was his biggest fan. Gay guys who simply gazed adoringly. Autograph hounds. And predatory middle-aged women who thought that since he'd been married to Venus, he must be into older women.

Kev got off on every fan-filled minute. He was even collecting digits from the fans with the biggest attributes. "Didn't re-alize you was *this* popular, dude," he announced, happily taking advantage of it all. "They're treatin' you as if you're Johnny Depp or Brad Pitt."

Billy was aware that Kev did not understand the price of fame. The loss of privacy, the way people treated him as if he were simply there for their viewing pleasure, the demands they made. It was all too much.

And then there was the touching. Billy loathed the touching. Random strangers throwing their arms around him as if it was their right to do so. Girls trying to feel his hair. Clammy hand-shakes. Every personal interaction turned him off. It was an intimacy issue he could well do without.

Venus had always surrounded them with bodyguards when they were out in public, and now he realized why. When it came to the PR game, Venus was way more savvy than he was.

After attempting to play blackjack at the casino in the Caven-dish, he finally gave up and went back to the suite, where he played with the remote until he found a sports channel on TV, settled on the couch, and attempted to recover from the fan-fest.

Kev stayed in the casino, basking in Billy's fame.

After fifteen minutes of college football, Billy tried Max's cell again. His call went straight to voice mail.

This street was turning out to be a dead end.

~ ~ ~

"So?" Bobby said, joining M.J. in the coffee shop.

"So?" M.J. retaliated, stirring his coffee, a blank expression on his face.

"You know what I'm asking," Bobby said, signaling the wait-ress, who came hurrying over.

"Yeah," M.J. agreed. "But I don't got an answer yet."

"Are you telling me you haven't talked to Cassie about keeping the baby?" Bobby said as the waitress filled his cup with strong black coffee. "You *know* you gotta do it."

"Uh . . . you could say we're kinda at an impasse," M.J. admitted, staring miserably at the table.

"Impasse not good," Bobby stated.

M.J. gave a weary sigh. "Tell me about it."

"You gotta grow a pair," Bobby insisted. "It's time."

"Comin' from you, that's sweet."

"What does *that* mean?" Bobby said, a frown creasing his forehead.

"Since you hooked up with Denver, the clubs have taken second place," M.J. complained. "You're never here. An' you're sure as crap not in New York."

Bobby could not believe what he was hearing. "You *gotta* be shittin' me," he said, still frowning.

"Just tellin' it like it is," M.J. responded.

"Goddammit, M.J. I was here three days ago jerking off the Russians. You got a short memory."

"Big of you to drop in."

"Fuck *you*. What's with the attitude?"

"So now I got *attitude?*" M.J. said, losing his cool. "I'm here every night bustin' my stones, while you're camped out in L.A. cozyin' up with your girlfriend. We're supposed to be partners."

"Jesus," Bobby said, annoyed that M.J. was taking his problems out on him. "Where the fuck is this coming from?"

"I dunno," M.J. admitted, shrugging helplessly. "I'm gettin' buried here. Don't mean to rag on you."

"Look," Bobby said understandingly. "I get it. You're under pressure, you need a break."

"What I'd like to do is take Cassie on vacation, get into her head an' convince her to do the right thing."

"Then you gotta do it."

"I want this baby, Bobby, an' I know I hav'ta tell her exactly how I feel before it's too late."

"Then like I said—do it."

"I was thinking we could take off after Max's party. Maybe hit the Bahamas."

"Cool with me."

"You'll handle things here?"

"Sure," Bobby said, mentally canceling all his next week's plans. "And as a bonus, you can even use my plane."

"Shit!" M.J. said. "You certainly know how to throw it back."

"Oh yeah," Bobby said, with a wry grin. "I certainly do."

"Thanks, man," M.J. said, relieved. "I've been going crazy."

"Once again, I get it."

"How about dinner tonight?" M.J. suggested. "Just you, me, Cassie, an' Denver."

Bobby hesitated for only a second. M.J. was going through a personal crisis, and when a friend was in any kind of trouble, he was there.

"Sure," he said, wondering how Denver would react to this sudden change of plans. "How about eight o'clock at the steak house?"

"We'll be there."

~ ~ ~

Enjoying another brief casino visit, still closely followed by her bodyguards, Venus ran into Alex on the casino floor. They had worked together in the past and enjoyed a cordial relationship, even though they'd fought like lions on the set of the movie Alex had directed her in.

"Alex," Venus said, throwing him one of her cultivated sultry looks. "Meet my friend Jorge. He's from Brazil."

"Your what?" Alex said rudely, his eyes raking over the studly young Brazilian. "Who is he—your son?"

"Alex!" Venus scolded, mock cross. "Behave yourself!"

"I would if I could, but you always bring out the bad in me."

"Do I now?" Venus replied, flirting slightly because Alex was such a brilliant director and she wouldn't mind working with him again.

"You know damn well you do. Remember our fight-a-minute movie?"

"How could I ever forget?" She sighed, playing with a lock of her platinum-blond hair. "You cast Billy in it. Thanks a lot."

Alex gave a twisted grin. "Sorry about that."

"Well," she said, with a half smile, "I suppose you weren't to know I'd be foolish enough to turn around and marry him."

"Jesus Christ!" Alex said, shaking his head at the many memories he had of dealing with Billy. "That kid was a pain in the ass to work with, but I gotta say—a talented little prick."

"'Little prick' is about the right description," Venus murmured succinctly.

Why is it that whenever a woman gets mad at a man, Alex thought, *the first thing she goes for is the size of his dick?*

Growing impatient, he glanced across the packed casino. "What's your game of choice tonight?" he asked.

"I was thinking roulette," she said as her bodyguards blocked a steady stream of excited autograph seekers.

"Of course you were," he replied. "Nothing like a game of chance to get the juices flowing."

"Hmm . . . don't think I need a round of roulette to do that," Venus replied, with an almost imperceptible nod toward Jorge.

Alex gave a low chuckle.

"I think the three of us should have dinner tonight," Venus said, fluttering her hand on his arm. "Since Lucky is all tied up with Lennie, the least we can do is try to amuse ourselves, don't you agree?"

"What about the boy from Ipanema," Alex asked, motioning toward Jorge. "Does he speak?"

"Not a lot," Venus replied. "But then again, he doesn't have to."

"Will he be joining us?"

"I promise you he'll sit quietly."

"Okay, Venus, we'll dine. I got nothing better to do."

"Where?" she asked, delighted she'd convinced him.

"Asian."

Venus smiled knowingly. "Naturally."

CHAPTER THIRTY-FIVE

Peggy was big on charm. She'd used it all her life to get her own way. The king had fallen under her spell, and then poor old Sidney Dunn, who'd given her the lifestyle she'd desired. Sidney had worshipped her. Peggy's little secret? Lots of flattery and charm mixed with excellent oral sex could keep a man very happy indeed. Sidney had never had cause to complain or look at another woman, Peggy had made damn sure of that.

Sometimes, during her years with Sidney, she'd yearned for the days and nights of her youth. Wild sex with Joe Piscarelli. Parties. Recreational drugs. Her one night with the infamous Gino Santangelo. Not to mention the fervent admiration of so many men as she'd paraded across the stage half naked.

The king had sometimes enjoyed the company of two or three women at a time. Since they were all his wives, it never really bothered Peggy. She'd quite enjoyed the softness of another woman's lips and the silkiness of their skin.

She had never revealed any of this to Armand; he would be shocked. Her son was quite a mystery, not the warm and nurturing man she had hoped he would turn out to be. Armand had a cold personality, and a certain disregard for women she could not understand. Surely she was the perfect role model. She's always been an elegant presence, always available for him.

But no, Armand did not appreciate all that she'd done for him over the years.

Earlier, Fouad had called and informed her of their move, and that they might be staying in Vegas longer than expected. He'd also wanted to know why she'd asked about Gino Santangelo. "I thought it was someone I knew," she'd lied, keeping it casual. "But I was mistaken. Wrong name."

Fortunately for Peggy, her charm worked on everyone but Armand, and after starting up a conversation with Paige Santangelo in the beauty salon, she soon had Paige's attention as she chatted about New York and what an exciting and vibrant city it was to live in.

"We had an apartment in New York once," Paige mused, a tad wistfully. "However, my husband, who's quite a bit older than me, decided we should live in Palm Springs, so that's where we've stayed. It's a little boring."

"You're fortunate your husband is still alive," Peggy said, playing the sympathy card. "I lost my dear Sidney a year ago. He was twenty years older than me. I have to say it's been quite hard being by myself, but with the help of my son and dear friends, I manage. I do not mean financially; Sidney left me set for life. But women of our age, alone—it's not easy."

Before long, the two women found they had plenty in common. After a while Paige asked Peggy if she would care to join her and Gino for dinner.

"I'd be delighted," Peggy responded. "Tell me where and when, and I will be there."

~ ~ ~

Armand flicked through the dossier Fouad had sent him on Lucky Santangelo. The only thing he found interesting was that she had children—two sons and a daughter.

Ah . . . children. A weakness he could use against her if he had to. But unfortunately, they were not little children; two were teenagers, and one a grown man.

But still, children made a person vulnerable. And yes, most people would do anything to protect their offspring. It was a basic human instinct.

Peggy phoned, interrupting his train of thought. He'd forgotten about his mother; she was the furthest thing from his mind.

"What?" he said curtly.

Peggy did not appreciate his tone of voice, but she chose to ignore his gruffness.

"Fouad told me you have moved to a villa at my hotel," she said. "I hear the villas are lovely."

Armand was immediately furious. What was wrong with Fouad? Couldn't he keep his stupid mouth shut about anything? Now he'd have Peggy turning up, infuriating him even further.

"Yes," he said flatly. "However, I cannot take you to dinner tonight. I have business to attend to."

"Not to worry, dear," Peggy said, sounding surprisingly mellow. "I wasn't asking you. I already have plans."

"You do?" he said, quite surprised. "With whom?"

"Old friends from my past have invited me to dine with them."

She paused, then said, "Perhaps I can come by for breakfast tomorrow?"

"We'll see," Armand replied, relieved that he didn't have to bother getting rid of Peggy tonight. It seemed she could look after herself.

"I'll phone you in the morning," Peggy said. "Fouad told me we may be staying longer than anticipated, and I'm open to that. Are your meetings going well?"

"I have to go," he said abruptly. "I'm running late."

"Very well, Armand. Tomorrow."

"If I can," he said, banging down the phone.

Peggy. His mother. Why had she insisted on coming to Vegas? She brought him nothing but aggravation and bad luck. She and Fouad were bringing him down. He hated them both. The two of them reeked of bad karma.

If it weren't for them The Keys would already be his.

~ ~ ~

Armand Jordan had requested big breasts, and Yvonne Le Crane decided she would find him big breasts. And while she was at it, how about enormous breasts? Breasts of a ludicrous size? Fake shockers?

She'd informed Armand she would accommodate him, and dispatched a messenger to pick up the cash. Soon the two women she'd booked would be on their way to his hotel.

She'd ordered them from a strip club in town called Dirty Den's. Yvonne was on cordial terms with the owner, a former boxer. She'd called him up and offered him a thousand apiece for two of his freaks, and he was more than happy to oblige.

It was a done deal.

This would teach Armand Jordan for calling her girls filthy whores when they were the crème de la crème of Vegas talent.

Now she was about to walk away with a $28,000 profit, so Armand Jordan could go piss in the wind.

Once again it gave her extreme satisfaction to know that Mister Sicko was about to get exactly the kind of girls he deserved.

CHAPTER THIRTY-SIX

The secret to a sensual, sexy marriage is knowing when to leave children, pets, family commitments, and business affairs at the door.

Lucky had a knack for being able to do just that. She and Lennie shared a bond that dated back to the first time they'd met, a true bond that neither of them had ever allowed to slip away. Sex was sex, and they'd both decided early on that if they expected their marriage to stay hot, then they had to work at keeping the passion on permanent sizzle. They both knew how to do that. Sometimes it involved role-playing. Sometimes it didn't. But whatever it took, they were into it one hundred percent.

Rule number one: Leave any family problems outside the bedroom.

Rule number two: Remember the first time.

Rule number three: No inhibitions.

And rule number four—the most important rule of all: Absolutely no interruptions.

Anticipating Lennie's arrival, Lucky felt the old familiar excitement. They were never together long enough for either of them to get bored with each other. Their reunions were always going to be something special, she made sure of that. So even though family and invited guests were in Vegas for Max's party the following night, Lucky had decided that tonight family and friends were on their own, for tonight belonged to Lennie. He was her number one priority. Always. That would never change.

By the time he arrived, she was ready to greet him, a stunning vision in a soft black leather dress, slit thigh high, her jet hair framing her oval face, the drop emerald earrings Lennie had presented her with last Christmas her only adornment.

Tonight she was nobody's mommy. She was Lucky Santangelo at her wildest.

The moment Lennie entered the apartment, she strode toward him and handed him his favorite drink—a black Russian.

Lennie smiled. His smile was one of the things she loved most about him. It crinkled his eyes—ocean green, paler than Max's brilliant emerald. And she loved his mouth, and his longish dirty-blond hair. But most of all she loved his warmth, his talent as a filmmaker, and his soul. They truly were soul mates.

"Who are you tonight?" he asked, throwing down his bag.

Lucky gave an enigmatic smile. "Whoever you want me to be."

"You know exactly who I want you to be," he said, moving purposefully toward her.

"Tell me," she whispered as he reached her and began peeling down the spaghetti-thin straps of her dress.

"My wife," he muttered, crushing her to him so tightly that she could barely breathe. "My life, my love, my everything."

~ ~ ~

"You *gotta* come with us," Cookie pleaded over the phone to Max. "Frankie's *insistin'* that we go see my dad's concert. There's no way I can do it without you."

"Ace is here," Max stated, sitting on the edge of the couch in her usual suite, trying to figure out what to do about Ace.

"What's up with that?" Cookie said, sounding surprised. "Thought you weren't inviting him."

"Well, he's here, and I promised we'd hang out by ourselves."

"No freakin' way," Cookie wailed. "I need help, an' Harry's goin' to some shitty gig with his Mexican pal."

"Paco," Max said patiently. "The dude's name is Paco."

"Oh, get you—Miss all Politically Correct."

"Where's your dad's concert?"

"At the Cavendish. Can you freakin' believe it? An' Frankie has to find out about it. *Then* he tells me he's always wanted to meet him."

"That's Frankie—the original star fucker."

"He's so not," Cookie argued.

"Then why's he so desperate to get together with your old man?"

"How would I know?" Cookie said irritably. "Maybe he's into that retro soul shit."

"Really?" Max said unbelievingly.

"Yes, *really*. You gonna do this for me or not?"

"I suppose so," Max said, kind of relieved in a way, because spending the night alone with Ace could've been majorly awkward, considering the circumstances of what had recently taken place between her and Billy.

"You're a star!" Cookie exclaimed. "Can you have Danny score us tickets, an' meet us by the elevator in half an hour? Oh, an' turn your cell on. I was tryin' forever to reach you until I thought of callin' your actual room."

Max hung up and dug in her purse for her cell, which she'd forgotten to take off plane mode. Just as she was about to turn it back on, Ace emerged from the bedroom. He'd taken a shower and put on his usual outfit of jeans and a denim work shirt. He looked hot, but not as hot as Billy.

What was she going to do? He obviously expected to stay in her suite, but as far as she was concerned, everything was different now.

"Here's the thing," she said, waves of guilt washing over her. "I totally forgot. Cookie's dad has a show at the Cavendish, and I promised to go. Sorry—can't bail."

Ace shook his head as if he didn't quite believe her. "That's a drag," he said, scratching his chin.

"I know," she apologized, realizing that she was acting like such a phony. "But what can I do?"

"You could say you're busy," he suggested.

"Can't do that," she said, jumping up.

"Why not?"

"'Cause I just can't, that's why," she said stubbornly. "Cookie's my friend. Gotta help her out."

"There goes our one night alone together."

"Yeah, bummer," she said, trying desperately to sound as if she cared. "Only since I didn't know you were coming, I made plans. Big deal."

"You an' your plans," he said, throwing her a look.

"Gotta go get changed," she said quickly. "We're leaving soon."

"You're expecting me to come too?"

"Well, yeah. Unless you wanna sit around here on your own."

"No thanks."

"I'll be right out," she said, heading for the bedroom.

Dammit! Ace knew her pretty well; did he sense that things were different? That she'd changed? That she'd given it up to someone else?

Oh man! She hoped not.

But she couldn't worry about it now. Later would do.

~ ~ ~

By the time Bobby got back to the hotel, Denver had closed her laptop and was preparing for the romantic evening Bobby had promised her. Just the two of them, no distractions. She was looking forward to it, because maybe it was time to have The Talk, figure out where they were headed. He'd spoken about buying a house in L.A. for them to move into together. Was it the right time to say yes? Had they reached that stage in their relationship?

It was an exciting and scary thought, especially as he still hadn't met her family.

And yet . . . they were so close, and she knew that she loved him, so why wait?

Or was she mistaking love for lust?

They certainly hit it off in the bedroom. The sex was incredible. *He* was incredible.

Stop holding back, she told herself. *You do love him, and it's time to let go and trust that he loves you too. So go for it.*

Yes. Tonight was the night. No more insecurities.

When Bobby arrived back, she ran over to greet him, threw

her arms around his neck, and whispered in his ear, "Guess what? I really missed you."

"You did?" he responded. "Thought you didn't need babysitting."

"I don't. Only that doesn't mean I didn't miss you. *And*, I can't wait for dinner—where are you taking me?"

"Yeah," he said hesitantly. "About our romantic dinner for two . . ."

"What about it?"

"It's, uh . . . kinda turned into dinner for four."

"You're kidding?"

"Sorry, babe, but M.J. really needs us, and there's no way I can let him down."

"Seriously?" she said, disappointed.

"M.J. has a problem."

"What kind of problem?"

"I didn't tell you before 'cause I figured he and Cassie would work it out, but it's big."

"Didn't they just get married?"

"Almost a year ago, and here's the deal—she's pregnant and wants to get an abortion, but M.J.'s against it all the way."

Bobby then proceeded to tell her the full story about M.J. and the girl he'd knocked up in high school.

Denver listened in silence, then finally said, "I don't see how having dinner with us is going to help their situation."

"It's a support thing," Bobby explained. "He's trying to tell Cassie that if she gets rid of the baby, their marriage is over."

"That's pretty harsh."

"Maybe, but it's the way he feels."

"And is the way *he* feels the only thing that matters?"

"No, but—"

"How old is Cassie?" Denver interrupted.

"I dunno. Maybe a year or so older than Max."

"Maybe *that's* the reason she isn't ready to have a baby now. It's frightening for her. She's so young—and having a baby is a huge responsibility."

"I understand. But M.J. is entitled to feel the way he does."

"Of course he is. But surely he's prepared to listen to what *she* wants. Her needs are just as important as his."

"Like I told you, sweetheart, M.J. had a life-changing experience that turned him against abortion. He doesn't believe in it."

"Do you?" she asked, suddenly realizing that she didn't know as much about Bobby as she thought she did.

He shrugged. "Dunno," he answered carefully, because it struck him as a loaded question. "Never really thought about it. Unless you find yourself in that situation, it's difficult to say."

"Interesting," Denver said, giving him a long hard look.

"Interesting how?" he said, knowing they were venturing onto dangerous ground.

"Well, I'm assuming you believe in a woman's right to choose?"

"Huh?"

"You heard."

"Look," he said, sensing a fight looming if they continued with this line of conversation. "They're taking a trip right after Max's party. Hopefully they'll work it out."

"You think?" she said, a tad sarcastic. "A trip'll solve everything, right?"

"Who knows?" he said, deciding it was definitely time to change the subject. "What I *do* know is that I'm having to stay in Vegas to keep an eye on things."

"Well, I can't stay. You know I have to get back."

"I wasn't expecting you to, sweetheart. I'll be putting you on a plane to L.A., and we'll speak every day. It's only for a week."

Denver nodded. It looked like The Talk would have to wait, along with their romantic dinner for two.

Suddenly she wasn't so sure about anything anymore.

CHAPTER THIRTY-SEVEN

"What've you done to your hair?" Max gasped when they all met by the elevator.

Self-consciously, Cookie reached up and patted her new-found curls. "Felt like a change," she mumbled.

"It's, like, a way big change," Max exclaimed, thinking how weird it was seeing Cookie without her trademark dreadlocks.

"My idea," Frankie boasted.

"I bet," Max retorted, flashing him a look.

"What? You don't like?" Frankie said, a touch aggressively.

"It's . . . different," Max said as the elevator arrived and they all piled in.

Danny had booked them a limo, even though the Cavendish was within walking distance.

Now it was Ace's turn to look at Max, as if to say, *A limo on top of everything else. What a joke.* But they all got in, and five minutes later they were there.

The Cavendish was nowhere near as luxurious or glamorous

as The Keys. But its two owners, Renee Falcon Esposito and Susie Rae Young, made sure the hotel was a fun alternative. When Lucky built The Keys there'd been bad blood between them—at least on Renee's part. Renee had imagined The Keys was her competition, but it had turned out to be quite the opposite. Being located next to such a magnificent new hotel complex had revitalized the Cavendish, and business was booming. Renee and Susie adored Lucky, and would do anything for her. Lucky often came to their hotel and hung out, especially since they'd adopted a five-year-old Vietnamese orphan who was the light of their lives.

When Danny had called to get front-row seats for Max and her friends to attend the sold-out Gerald M. concert, Renee was happy to oblige, although why she was supposed to do it when one of Max's friends was Gerald M.'s daughter, she wasn't quite sure.

Gerald M. was quite a draw with middle America. The ladies were all agog—he represented old-fashioned sexy. Quite a few of them stashed an extra pair of panties in their purse, for when the opportunity arose they planned on tossing them onto the stage in the hope of attracting his attention, at least for a second or two.

Max and her group arrived at the theater in the hotel with minutes to spare. They were led to their seats by an enthusiastic attendant, also a big Gerald M. fan.

"I want to go backstage after," Frankie said to Cookie as they took their seats. "He does know we're here, doesn't he?"

"Uh . . . yeah," Cookie lied. She was hoping that by the time the concert was over and if they took their time getting backstage, her dad would've taken off to the airport and the private plane he always had waiting. She was not thrilled about the prospect of Gerald M. meeting Frankie. Not that her dad would object to her having an older boyfriend, but she knew it was quite possible the two of them would bond—smoke a joint together, snort a little coke. And that thought horrified her.

Once they were settled in their seats, Ace reached for Max's hand. She held his reluctantly, still struggling about what to do. Should she tell him about her and Billy? Or just carry on as if nothing had changed?

It was a dilemma she couldn't quite work out. Eventually she would, because it wasn't as if Billy was still in the picture, and Ace *was* a major hunk.

However, Lucky had always taught her to be honest. Tell the truth. Accept the consequences.

What to do? It was a difficult decision.

"Who's this dude Cookie's hooked up with?" Ace asked in a low, disapproving voice. "I've seen him somewhere before."

"He's an . . . uh . . . ex-friend of Bobby's," Max replied. "You probably ran into him at the opening of The Keys. He used to go out with Annabelle Maestro."

"Who?"

"It's not important."

"I'm not getting a good vibe from him," Ace said.

"You're not?"

"He's got that rich dude sleaze factor goin' on. Not to mention that he's too old for her."

"Whatever." Max sighed. "You know Cookie. It won't last."

"After the concert we're taking off on our own, yes?"

Saved by the announcer, who planted himself center stage and instructed everyone to turn off their cell phones, which reminded Max that she had yet to turn hers on since the plane ride.

Then, to thunderous applause and plenty of screaming fans, Gerald M. sauntered onstage, resplendent in tight purple leather pants and a blowsy white shirt unbuttoned to his waist, diamond medallions vying for space on his exposed chest. More Tom Jones than Usher, he immediately launched into a medley of his many hits—albeit most of them a decade or two old.

The mostly female audience erupted into hysterical sighs of joy as they leapt to their feet. Soon the panties would start flying.

Cookie shot Max a look that said *Kill me now!* while Ace groaned, and Max giggled.

Frankie wondered if he could sell Gerald M. a supply of pharmaceuticals. Why not? Had to invite him to River. Make him a regular customer. Get him to hang out there with some of the gorgeous girls he was always photographed with. Cookie could arrange it; it was about time she made herself useful. Sometimes a man required more than just an enthusiastic blow job.

"You didn't tell me we were gonna have *this* much fun," Ace whispered in Max's ear. "This dude's got one foot firmly planted in the eighties. Does he know he's a relic?"

"Shh," Max scolded. "He's Cookie's dad. Be nice."

Ace squeezed her hand. "You really are a loyal friend, aren't you?"

Suddenly Max remembered why she liked Ace. He always had her back, and he was always kind. The last thing Ace was into was being Mister Hollywood. He would never dump a girl after taking her virginity. No way.

She squeezed his hand back. "Glad you're here," she whispered. "Wouldn't want to go through this slow torture without you."

"Right back atcha, birthday girl."

~ ~ ~

"Holy shit!" Kev exclaimed, sitting bolt upright at the table he shared with Billy in the Asian Fusion restaurant at the Cavendish Hotel. "You are *not* gonna believe who just jiggled her ass in here."

Billy started to turn around.

"Don't do that!" Kev warned. "It's your friggin' ex with that director you were always bitchin' about."

"Alex Woods?" Billy said, forcing himself not to turn and stare.

"The very same."

"Just the two of them?"

"Some young dude is taggin' along."

"That's just fuckin' great," Billy said grimly. He was pissed off enough that he couldn't reach Max; now his annoying ex was in town. Why was *she* in Vegas? And why was she with the sadistic Alex Woods, the motherfucker who'd forced him to do every stunt known to man on the movie they'd made together? Alex had almost killed him with his insane demands.

"My luck," he muttered. "Can they see us?"

"No," Kev answered, busily watching. "They're being seated in a booth across the room."

"Then let's get the fuck outta here while we can," Billy said, starting to stand up.

"We just ordered," Kev pointed out. "An' I don't know 'bout you, but *I'm* starvin'. Reminder—we never had lunch."

"Jeez! Is your stomach more important than my comfort zone?"

"Guess so."

"'S long as you're sure they can't see us," Billy grumbled, slouching back into his seat.

"No way, man," Kev assured him. "We're invisible."

~ ~ ~

"Hmm . . . you give great homecoming," Lennie said, lazily stroking Lucky's thigh as they lay on the bed post-lovemaking, sated and at peace after a passionate two hours. Having been involved with a documentary about tantric sex, Lennie was totally into it. Lucky had no objections. Tantric wasn't all about the climax, it was about the slow, steady climb, and the bliss that awaited at the top of the mountain.

When Lennie had first started practicing it a couple of years earlier, she'd been highly suspicious that he'd hooked up with some twenty-year-old yoga fanatic who was teaching him all the moves. But after experiencing it herself, she was into it too. What woman could resist endless foreplay with a man who knew how to do everything right?

She often thought how far Lennie had come from the brash stand-up comedian she'd first met. Age and a series of traumatic experiences had mellowed him into a special and extraordinary man.

She loved him so much that sometimes it scared her. It was always somewhere in the back of her mind that the three people she'd loved the most had all been taken from her. Her gentle mother, Maria. Her brother, Dario. And the love of her life before Lennie—her fiancé, Marco. Each of them murdered on the orders of one man, her godfather, Enzio Bonnatti.

She'd shot and killed Enzio in what was seen as an act of self-defense.

Self-defense. Sure. If that's what everyone believed.

The truth was, she'd set up the appropriate scenario and blown the motherfucker away. He'd deserved it.

True Santangelo justice. And she didn't regret it. Not for one single minute.

"How's little Max?" Lennie asked. "Excited about her party?"

"She's a teenager, Lennie. The only thing that excites teenagers is getting away from their parents or a night of lust with Ian Somerhalder."

"Who's Ian Somerhalder?"

"*The Vampire Diaries* on TV. Sex and vampires. Guaranteed to get any teenager hot."

"I'm in the movie biz—it's a different scene."

"Really?" Lucky drawled.

"Yes, really."

"I'd never have guessed."

"Shut the fuck up."

"Here's what I love about you, Lennie," Lucky murmured softly. "You do exactly what you want to do, and so do I."

"Which is the reason our marriage works so well," he responded. "No ties. No petty jealousies."

"Amen," Lucky agreed.

"*And* we have a daughter who takes after both of us," Lennie said with a grin. "Little Max. She's a maverick. Gotta let her go do her thing."

"Are you intimating that *I'm* stopping her?"

"Well, sweetheart, you *can* be kind of controlling when the mood hits you."

"Ha!" Lucky exclaimed.

"Ha what?" Lennie retaliated.

"Ha! It's amazing that I still love you after all these years."

"All what years?" Lennie questioned. "Seems to me like we've only been together a couple of months."

"Sweet-talker."

"An' doncha love it!"

"Sometimes."

"'Sometimes,' she says," Lennie said affectionately, pulling her close.

"Okay." She sighed. "I'll admit it. All times."

"That's my Lucky."

She smiled, dark eyes flashing. "Always."

~ ~ ~

At the same time as Billy was contemplating leaving the restaurant, Venus was enjoying her time with Alex and Jorge. Two extremely attractive men, generations apart. Jorge was a young stud bursting with testosterone, while Alex was world-weary but filled with stories and life experiences Venus was dying to hear about.

Out of nowhere she suddenly found herself crazily attracted to Alex. He had a Jack Nicholson kind of vibe going, and even though he was getting up there, he was still wildly sexy in a dissolute kind of way.

Of course it was a well-known fact around Hollywood that Alex only went for Asian women. He'd already started hitting on the waitress, a petite girl from Thailand with appealing slanted eyes and a sheet of black hair that hung halfway down her back. But Venus was privy to the information that he'd always had a thing about Lucky. And since Lucky was forever faithful to Lennie, what would be wrong with her taking a shot?

After two extra-strong lychee martinis, she felt the need to share. Jorge was busy stuffing his face with spareribs and seaweed. Young, handsome, and dumb. Why was she even bothering?

Oh yes, sex with a studly stranger. Always a kick.

"You know, Alex," she murmured, leaning toward him, her tone low and seductive. "I never understood why you and I didn't get together when we were making our movie."

"Could it be that you were too busy fucking Billy?" Alex said, arching one of his thick eyebrows.

"Or that *you* had a crush on our producer?" Venus countered, not willing to be outdone. "You know you did."

"If you mean Lucky," Alex said, speaking slowly, "we've always been best friends."

"Hmm . . ."

"What does *that* mean?" Alex said with a deep frown. "Has Lucky ever said anything to you about me?"

"Wouldn't *you* like to know," Venus teased.

"If you've got something to tell me, dear, spit it out," Alex said, his tone tense.

"Why would I have anything to tell you?" Venus replied, delighted that she'd hit on Alex's weak spot. Oh yes, he definitely still lusted after Lucky—the woman he could never have. Typical behavior. Show a powerful man an unobtainable woman, and he wanted her.

"Don't screw with me, Venus," Alex said, still frowning. "I do not appreciate being played."

The edge in Alex's voice attracted Jorge's attention. The young Brazilian put down the sparerib he was nibbling on, turned to Venus, and said, "Everything good?"

"Ah, he speaks!" Alex mocked.

"Yes, Jorge, everything's fine," Venus said, ignoring Alex, while placating her boy toy with a firm pat on his finely muscled arm. "Alex is a major director," she added, speaking slowly as she pantomimed operating a movie camera. "Very important."

"Jesus Christ!" Alex scoffed. "The boy probably speaks perfect English, an' you're treating him like a dummy."

"He's not a boy," Venus said, annoyed that Alex was getting on her case.

"What is he, then?" Alex questioned, raising a cynical eyebrow.

Before Venus could answer, a plump woman in a flowered dress managed to circumvent Venus's bodyguards, who were sitting at a table by the door, and presented herself in front of their table.

"You're just so pretty," the woman cooed, fluttering her hands. "I simply had to tell you. I'm from Kansas, and I seen you on tee-vee, but you are *much* prettier in person." The woman took a deep breath. "And yes, I have to say it—years younger."

"Thank you," Venus said graciously. *And where the hell are my bodyguards when I need them?* She quickly glanced over at their table. The morons were actually eating, and had not noticed she was under attack. Security. What a crock.

"You must get a ton of attention," the woman gushed. "What with your divorce an' all, an' your husband—or should I say your ex—sittin' over there. An' him bein' a young man still. An'—oh." She looked directly at Jorge. "Is this your son?"

Alex burst out laughing.

Venus was speechless with fury. At this point one of her bodyguards stumbled over—red in the face—placed a controlling arm on the woman's shoulder, and moved her swiftly away.

Alex was still chuckling. Jorge looked casual, as if he didn't know what was going on, although of course he did.

"I think it's time to leave," Venus said, cold as ice.

Was Billy really here? In this restaurant?

Damn him. What exactly was he doing in Vegas?

CHAPTER THIRTY-EIGHT

Hyped up on too much coke and ready for action, Armand took a stroll through the casino while he waited for the prostitutes he'd ordered. He was in need of some kind of sexual release while he decided how he was going to deal with the Santangelo bitch.

His surroundings did not please him. The Cavendish was a shit-hole compared to The Keys.

And why was he staying in a shit-hole?

Because of Fouad and Mother Peggy—the whore mother of all time.

It all made sense to him now. Peggy might dress in fancy clothes and stink of expensive perfume, but when the king had discovered her she was probably a prostitute like all the rest of them.

After a while he approached a roulette table and threw down several thousand dollars. In exchange he received a stack of high-denomination chips from an eager croupier.

A steely-eyed pit boss stepped forward and offered to open a private table for his pleasure.

Armand nodded. No need to mix with the sweaty masses. He abhorred crowds.

Roulette was not his usual game of choice, but tonight he felt like playing a different game. Tonight he had a strong feeling that one way or another, he would force Lucky Santangelo's hand. He didn't know how, but it *would* happen, because *he* was all-powerful. Lucky Santangelo might think she had won, but what she didn't realize was that Armand Jordan was invincible.

The more he thought about her, the more he hated her. She was a witch with her dark hair and evil blacker-than-night eyes. The words that had spewed forth from her mouth were unacceptable. She was the devil incarnate. A morally corrupt whore with a black heart.

And then it suddenly came to him like a blinding flash of lightning. SHE DID NOT DESERVE TO LIVE.

The thought struck him like a meteor—a fast-moving meteor that illuminated his mind and told him what he had to do.

Lucky Santangelo had to die. There was no doubt about it.

~ ~ ~

Peggy immediately realized that Gino Santangelo did not remember her, and even though he was quite spry for a ninety-something old man, she was quite surprised that he managed to remember anything at all. She felt sorry for Paige, who was decades younger than her husband. At least Sidney had died before she'd been stuck with nursemaid duties. What a nightmare that would've been. Nurse Peggy. Not her calling in life.

Actually, she hadn't expected Gino to remember her. Why

would he? According to his reputation, he'd had thousands of girls. And such as the circumstances were now, it was better that he didn't recall their one night of fevered lovemaking. As far as Gino Santangelo was concerned, she was a friend of his wife's. Paige had kindly invited her to join them for a quiet dinner at François, and she'd been delighted to accept.

Peggy was embarking on an exciting mission; it gave her mundane existence new meaning. She'd dressed for the occasion. A Valentino cocktail dress. Black Louboutins. Tasteful jewelry. And a large Hermès purse, in which she hoped to stash the evidence she was about to procure. A strand of his hair, his cocktail glass, anything she could get her hands on.

Gino made it easy for her. Fifteen minutes into the dinner, he experienced a major sneezing fit and blew his nose into a napkin. Usually Peggy considered men who did that social outcasts, but tonight she was thrilled.

However, there was a problem—how to maneuver the soiled napkin into her purse before the waiter came over and spirited it away?

Like a true amateur detective, the answer came to her. Without even thinking about it, she nudged her martini glass so that its contents spilled across the table and onto Gino's lap. Confusion ensued, during which Peggy managed to stuff the napkin into her purse. Mission accomplished!

Peggy experienced a moment of deep satisfaction, and even deeper excitement. After all these years wondering who Armand's real father was, soon the suspense would be over.

Earlier that evening she'd visited the computer center at her hotel and Googled Joe Piscarelli. He too was still alive, and had obviously prospered, for he owned a chain of car dealerships and several gentlemen's clubs. Joe was not as old as Gino

Santangelo—nor was he buried in the desert as she'd imagined. Obviously he'd gotten over his criminal tendencies and gone legitimate. He was now a married man with two grown children and two successful businesses.

Peggy had not yet decided how she would approach him and obtain a DNA sample. Right now, Gino was all she could manage.

~ ~ ~

The girl's name was Luscious. She was twenty-two and well jaded for one so young. She'd been around the block countless times, and it showed. Once the prettiest girl in high school in spite of a pronounced overbite, she was now a strung-out erotic dancer and sometime hooker with a criminal boyfriend and her own rap sheet for a variety of offenses ranging from shoplifting to prostitution and two DUIs. Luscious (formerly Sara Smitton from Oklahoma) could care less that she had a rap sheet. Her main concern was keeping the attention of her boyfriend, Randy—a former pro wrestler, con man, petty thug, and porn star. Unfortunately for Luscious, Randy possessed a wandering cock—which she didn't mind when he was using his impressive instrument for work. But she got royally pissed off when she suspected said impressive cock was going elsewhere.

Luscious and Randy. A true Vegas couple, always trying to wriggle out of debt and better themselves, only getting nowhere in a hurry.

Recently things had been looking up. Randy had gone into business with his ex-con older brother, Mikey, and started dealing drugs. Mikey procured the product, and Randy was the deliveryman, which suited him fine. Deliver the order, collect the cash, split it with Mikey, and voilà—money in his pocket.

But all was not so fine as far as Luscious was concerned. She suspected that Randy had a hard-on for Mikey's wife—a fellow dancer who went by the name of Seducta Sinn (formerly Norma Wilkas from Chicago). Luscious considered Seducta major white trash with her enormous fake tits and out-of-control big ass. They performed alongside each other at Dirty Den's, and often vied to see who could score the biggest tips. Even though they were banging brothers, in Luscious's eyes that did not make them friends. However, when Dirty Den himself offered her five hundred bucks to service a john at the Cavendish Hotel, and another five hundred to take along a "friend," Luscious immediately thought of Seducta. Why not? Fantastic money and a chance to see what tricks Seducta possessed that she didn't.

Naturally, Seducta was up for the gig; she was always complaining that she and Mikey were one step away from the poorhouse.

Lying douche, Luscious thought. She was sure that Mikey was cheating Randy out of his fair share of the drug money. Mikey was a slippery character, and Luscious didn't trust him at all. Nor did she trust Seducta, but Randy insisted that Mikey was family and would never cheat him.

Luscious knew a thing or two about family. A mother strung out on crack, a stepfather who was always trying to slip her his limp cock, and an uncle who'd raped her repeatedly when she was twelve.

Family indeed. Luscious knew more about family than anyone. They'd stab you in the back and bury the corpse if they thought they could get away with it.

~ ~ ~

Armand placed a $10,000 bet on number 11. The roulette wheel spun around and 11 came up. He let his original bet ride, and 11 came up a second time.

He'd won $340,000 in less than ten minutes. Time to walk away.

Or stay.

It didn't matter. The money wasn't important; it meant nothing to him. His mind was racing. How could he go about hiring a hit man? Was it like in the movies?

No. Of course it wasn't. He had to be careful and think this through.

He was in Vegas. Anything could be arranged in Vegas.

How much for a hit?

The money was of no consequence. Finding the right person to take care of it was all that mattered.

Where was Fouad? Not that Fouad would approve; he was no longer the loyal lackey Armand depended on. Fouad was a weakling who couldn't arrange anything.

Armand needed another hit of coke. After taking a gulp of scotch from the glass a scantily clad cocktail waitress handed him, he threw a large tip at the croupier and got up. Just as he was about to leave, a girl approached him, a pretty girl in an all-American way. She had long golden-red hair and exceptionally high cheekbones, and acted extremely confident as she slid onto the seat next to him. "Armand," she said, greeting him as if they were old friends. "Long time no see. Are you here for the fights?"

"What fights?" he mumbled.

"Oh please!" The girl gave a tinkly laugh. "I'm sure you have the best seats in the house."

He had no idea who she was, but she obviously knew him.

"Not here for the fights," he said, getting up from the roulette table.

"You know," the girl said, lowering her voice and leaning toward him, "I thought we had a good time together, and yet you never called."

"Ah . . ." he said, trying to recall through a haze of too much coke where it was he'd had her—New York? London? Vegas? Or maybe she was one of the imported call girls who'd been flown in for the king's birthday in Akramshar. "Did I pay you?"

"Pay me?" she said, an uncomfortable expression crossing her face. "Why would you pay me?"

"Remind me," he said gruffly. "What's your name?"

Instead of being insulted, she seemed relieved. "Ah, so many women, such a short memory," she trilled. "Annabelle. Annabelle Maestro."

And then it came to him. Annabelle, the daughter of Hollywood movie stars, one of them brutally murdered. She'd written a book about it, and how—for a time—she'd acted as a madam in New York, and for the right price sold herself on occasion.

Sure, he remembered her now. They'd met at a dinner party in New York and he'd had her in the bathroom between courses. She hadn't minded when he'd ravished her against the cold marble of the vanity. And the next night he'd taken her to the opening of a play, then back to his apartment, where once again the somewhat raunchy sex was consensual.

As far as he could recall, she was up for anything, so of course he hadn't called her. Where was the kick if he couldn't humiliate her? He hadn't paid her either. She was obviously under the impression that he didn't know about her past.

The woman was a reformed whore. The best kind. Maybe she could help him find what he was looking for.

"Would you care to join me for a drink, Annabelle?" he asked, turning to her with a plastered-on smile.

She nodded eagerly.

He had plans for this one.

CHAPTER THIRTY-NINE

Although Denver liked M.J., she wasn't that comfortable with his young, overly ambitious wife, Cassie. The girl couldn't stop talking about herself and her burgeoning career—which as far as Denver could decipher, had failed to take off. She'd had one shot at making a record and a few singing gigs in hotel lounges, but Cassie kept on boasting about how she was about to sign with a new agent, a man who'd promised he could jump-start a fabulous career, making her into the next Rihanna.

This girl has no intention of staying pregnant, Denver thought. *This girl has major ambition on her mind, certainly not babies.*

"I'm younger than Katy Perry," Cassie mused. "*Way* prettier than Ke$ha. And way hotter than Taylor Swift. Which means my chance of making it to the top is *huge*. Right, baby?" she said, turning to M.J., finally acknowledging his existence.

M.J. nodded, although he didn't look too happy about his young wife's enthusiasm for a career that had yet to happen.

Denver could understand why. Surely he knew that there was

no way he could persuade Cassie to change her mind about getting an abortion. She shot a quick glance at Bobby. His expression was impartial. One thing about Bobby—he was not into confrontations unless there was no other way. "I'm going to the ladies' room," she said, rising from the table.

"Me too!" Cassie squeaked, jumping to her feet.

"Talk to her," Bobby mouthed to Denver.

Right, so *that's* why she was in Vegas, to induce a would-be pop star into giving up her dreams and having a baby.

Cassie beat her to it. As soon as they reached the powder room, she threw her sparkly purse on the counter, turned to Denver, and said, "Can you keep a secret?"

Oh no! Denver thought. *Please don't make me your confidante.*

But Cassie was determined. "Can you?" she repeated.

"Uh, not so hot with secrets," Denver managed, quickly ducking into a stall to escape.

Cassie was waiting when she emerged, standing at the counter applying cherry-red lip gloss with her finger. "You're so lucky to be with a dude like Bobby." Cassie sighed. "All the girls in the club are crazy for him."

"Good to know," Denver said, washing her hands while wondering who "all the girls in the club" were. Customers? Staff? What the hell?

"My friend Lindy, well, she says Bobby's into you 'cause you're so smart."

"Also good to know," Denver said dryly.

"I bet he's a total stud in bed."

"Excuse me?"

"Is he?"

"I don't think that's anyone's business except mine."

Cassie giggled. "You're such a lady! I guess that's another reason Bobby likes you. Y'know, he has a big rep for lovin' an' leavin', but you're hangin' in there."

Jesus Christ! Denver thought. *Why do I have to stand here listening to some young girl telling me what a stud Bobby is and how lucky I am to have him. How about he's lucky to have me?*

"I'll see you back inside," Denver said, preparing for a quick exit.

"Wait!" Cassie implored. "I need your help."

"Help?"

"Well, kinda. Y'see, it's like this . . ."

And the story of her pregnancy came tumbling out—all about how there was no way she could have the baby, and M.J. was being stubborn, and what was she supposed to do?

"Look, I'm not a marriage counselor," Denver said patiently. "However, it seems to me you've got a choice here—have the baby and keep M.J., or go the career route."

"I know," Cassie agreed. "But all I want is for M.J. to get it. I can have a baby anytime—the career thing is right now. *Why* doesn't he get it?"

"You should speak to your mom," Denver suggested. "I'm sure she'll advise you."

"Done that," Cassie replied with a careless shrug. "My mom doesn't care."

"Come *on.* I'm sure she does."

"No," Cassie said, shaking her head. "She'd like me *not* to have a kid. She's only thirty-five an' isn't ready to be a grandma."

"Well," Denver said briskly. "I wish I could help you, but unfortunately I can't. All I can say is follow your inner self and work out what you want most."

"Got it!" Cassie said cheerfully. "Knew you could solve it for me."

Denver frowned.

As far as she was concerned, she hadn't solved anything.

~ ~ ~

"I think we gotta hit a strip club," Kev announced as they exited Asian Fusion.

"No way," Billy replied, standing still for a minute. "You think I wanna be all over TMZ with a bunch of strippers tellin' everyone how much I tipped?"

"Where's TMZ?" Kev said, playing dumb. "Don't see 'em hidin' under a palm tree waitin' to pounce, do you?"

"Trust me. They're everywhere," Billy assured him, itching to try to reach Max again. The fact that she wasn't picking up her phone was becoming an obsession. He'd flown to Vegas, for crissakes, screwed up his entire weekend, and now she wasn't answering her damn cell. Could it be that she was purposely blowing him off?

"What're you so edgy about?" Kev questioned. "*I'll* protect you from the paps. I'm an expert at runnin' interference."

"Yeah?" Billy said shortly. "Then where were you when I was gettin' attacked in the casino earlier?"

"Those were *fans*," Kev said, as if that explained everything. "Fuckin' fans who worship at your cock."

"Knock it off, Kev."

"You could've had any one of 'em. You know it, and so do I."

"Thanks," Billy said caustically. "I think my tastes run a little higher than that."

"Not the Billy I know," Kev said with a knowing leer. "Back in the day you would've fucked a log if it winked at you."

Kev was starting to get on his nerves. "Back in the day," indeed. Didn't Kev get it? Things had changed. He'd forgotten how jarring his old friend could be.

They lingered outside Asian Fusion too long, because before he could even think of escaping, Venus stalked out in full star glory, trailed by Jorge and her two bodyguards. Alex had lingered behind, attempting to hook up with the waitress.

Billy realized there was no way they could avoid a face-to-face. "Hey," he managed, caught off guard.

For a moment he thought Venus was about to blank him. But she didn't. She rallied, hung on to Jorge's arm, and threw him an icy "Hello."

So much for remaining friends, which is what she'd said in a recent interview. *"Billy and I are, and always will be, the closest of friends. I wish him nothing but the best."*

Knowing Venus, what she actually meant to say was *"Fuck that son of a bitch. I hope his career implodes and I never have to see him again."*

"You're lookin' good," Billy muttered. It was all he could think of to say. One thing about Venus, she was always in spectacular shape. Too much for any one man to handle.

The dude she was clinging onto was young—young enough to not know what he was getting himself into. At thirty, Billy felt like a veteran of the star wars. Maybe he should warn the poor bastard, help him out.

"Hey, Venus," Kev piped up. "Long time no see."

Venus gave Kev an imperious wave of her hand—her signature move when dealing with an annoying presence. She and Kev had never gotten along. When Kev was Billy's assistant she'd insisted that Billy fire him. He hadn't done so, which had made her resent Kev even more.

Suddenly the theater next door to the restaurant began

hemorrhaging crowds of people. The Gerald M. concert was over, and hundreds of excited fans were on the loose.

Venus's bodyguards closed ranks around their precious star and immediately began moving her off.

Billy decided he'd better get going before he was spotted.

Too late. A gaggle of delirious women descended on him, yelling his name. Soon he was surrounded by screaming fans.

Where was Kev when he needed him?

~ ~ ~

"I get edgy in crowds," Ace said as they fought their way out of the theater. "This is a freakin' nightmare."

"Stay cool," Max whispered as a fat woman inadvertently shoved her in the back. "It'll soon be over. Then we'll go find an In-N-Out Burger. That'll put a smile on your face."

"You got that right," Ace said, grabbing her hand.

"Shouldn't we be heading backstage?" Frankie said, stopping and indicating a side door where select VIPs were being assembled to be escorted back to pay homage to Gerald M.

"Yeah, right," Cookie answered vaguely. She'd hoped he wouldn't notice, but obviously he knew the routine. Major stars always had their assistants gather the people who merited a pass, then bring them back to the luxurious private bar, where they patiently waited their turn for an audience with the star. Such bullshit.

Frankie changed direction and headed for the side door, while Cookie pulled on Max's arm and hissed, "You gotta come with us. *Puh-leeze!*"

"Oh for crap's sake!" Max complained. "This entire night is turning out to be all about you."

"Ten minutes," Cookie pleaded. "Then we'll go wherever you an' Ace want."

"What *he* wants is for us to be by ourselves," Max said, wishing she was anywhere but here.

"You can do that anytime."

"Not really, considering Ace doesn't live anywhere near me."

"He should move," Cookie sniffed.

"Maybe he will. But tonight I have to do what *he* wants. He drove all this way just to be with me. That has to count for something."

"Okay, okay," Cookie said impatiently. "Ten minutes, that's all I ask."

"Fine." Max sighed. "After that, you're totally on your own."

~ ~ ~

It didn't thrill Venus running into Billy. She supposed he must be in Vegas for the fights. He was with his horrible friend Kev—a bone of contention in their marriage. She'd always suspected Kev was a bad influence, therefore she'd never trusted him. She was sure he'd always been trying to hook Billy up with random girls on the side.

Well, at least Billy wasn't with that little tramp, his most recent costar, Willow Price—famous for flashing her snatch at every photographer in town.

Her bodyguards hustled her through the casino and into a waiting limo hovering curbside. Jorge trotted behind them and jumped onto the seat next to her.

"Where to, Miss Venus?" the driver inquired.

"Back to The Keys," she said to the driver, removing Jorge's hand from her thigh. "Stop at the private entrance to Mood." She turned to Jorge. "Do you dance?"

He nodded.

"Excellent, 'cause I feel like letting loose."

~ ~ ~

"You told Cassie about the Bahamas yet?" Bobby asked.

"I'm gonna surprise her," M.J. replied. "Kinda zip her out to the airport from Max's party. She'll never know what hit her."

"Girls don't like surprises," Bobby warned. "They're into preparing and all that crap."

"Preparing *what*?" M.J. said. "I'll buy her anything she needs when we get there."

"If you really think that's the way to go."

"Yeah. She'll love it."

"Okay, she'll love it," Bobby said, although he didn't believe it for a moment.

"Cassie wants me to meet up with some superagent who's considering representing her," M.J. said, signaling for the check. "We're having a drink with him at the Cavendish, then we'll swing by Mood. Okay with you?"

"Sure. I'll hold things down."

"We've got a lot of VIP reservations tonight," M.J. said. "Everyone's in town for the fights on Sunday."

"And you're not staying," Bobby stated. "What's up with that?"

"Yeah, bad timing," M.J. said. "But here's the good news—I'm givin' you my tickets."

"Jeez," Bobby exclaimed. "True love rules."

"Ringside, my man," M.J. boasted. "Primo position. Cannot be beat."

"Problem is, I don't think I can use 'em," Bobby said, watching Denver and Cassie as they walked back to the table.

"Why not?" M.J. asked. "Aren't you listening? Ringside, man."

"I'm not so sure it's something Denver's into."

"Exactly what am I not into?" Denver asked, sliding into the booth.

"Boxing," Bobby said. "Not your thing, right?"

"How did you guess?" she said coolly. "Two grown men beating each other's brains out is hardly my idea of a brilliant time."

"Yeah," Bobby said. "I had a hunch you'd feel that way."

"I'm crazy for the fights," Cassie piped up. "We're goin' Sunday night, right, hon?"

M.J. exchanged a glance with Bobby and nodded. "Course we are. Wouldn't miss it."

Denver wondered what was happening back in L.A. She missed her apartment, her dog, and her work.

So far Vegas was not doing it for her. She couldn't wait to get home.

CHAPTER FORTY

Luscious and Seducta set off in Seducta's 1998 shocking-pink Pontiac, her pride and joy—a wedding present from Mikey after they'd gotten hitched by a Lady Gaga look-alike six months ago after indulging in a drunken orgy with several Scottish footballers. Seducta harbored such fond memories of that special day, she'd even had the date tattooed on her ass.

"How come Mikey bought you an *old* car?" Luscious sneered as she settled in to the passenger seat and attempted to fasten the broken seat belt across her skinny waist.

"Better than that piece of garbage *you* drive," Seducta sneered back, referring to Luscious's used 2008 Toyota. "My Pontiac is vintage."

Luscious wasn't quite sure what vintage meant, so she kept quiet.

"Who *is* this john we're seeing?" Seducta inquired, weaving in and out of traffic with a total lack of concern for other drivers on the road. "What's his deal? Girl on girl? 'Cause if it is, I'm warnin' you—don't go stickin' your tongue in my cooze. You gotta fake it. We clear on that?"

"How the fuck I know who he is?" Luscious said irritably. "It's a job. The jerkoff's payin' top dollar. An' might I remind you to get a life—'cause the last place my tongue wants t' go is anywhere near your fat cooze."

"Fat?" Seducta hissed, tapping the steering wheel with long fake nails—several of them chipped. "If anythin's fat it's your big mouth. Since you had that shit injected in your lips, they remind me of two gnarly worms."

"You're bein' jealous again," Luscious said, refusing to get into a war of words. "Randy gets off on my lips."

"Not what he told *me*," Seducta replied with a knowing smirk.

"Since when did *you* get to talkin' to *my* boyfriend?" Luscious demanded.

"Like I'm not allowed to speak to my own *brother-in-law*," Seducta jeered. "You seem to forget we're related. Randy an' me—we're *family*."

Luscious narrowed her squinty eyes. Seducta was dumb as a sheep, and she wasn't about to take the bait, because that's what Seducta was doing—baiting her into losing her cool. She wished she hadn't thrown this well-paid gig Seducta's way; the fat cow didn't deserve it. She should've picked one of the other girls.

Too late now. The best thing she could do was grit her teeth and put a smile on it.

CHAPTER FORTY-ONE

"I have a yen to surprise everyone," Lucky murmured, sliding seductively out of bed. "I know I said we wouldn't emerge until tomorrow, but it's only eleven and I'm sure they'll all end up at Bobby's club. What do you think? Shall we put in an appearance?"

"My wife," Lennie said, leaning back with a benevolent smile on his face. "Always ready for action."

"Hmm," she said, also smiling. "Tonight I've had enough action to last me until your next visit."

"Jesus," Lennie burst out laughing. "You're making me sound like some kind of randy sailor on shore leave."

"Yeah, that's it," Lucky teased. "My sexy sailor husband—the man with all the right moves."

"If you say so," he said, pulling her back to bed. "Although I'm thinking there could be a few moves we haven't explored yet."

"You think?"

"I do."

"When's your next visit?" she asked, snuggling up close and idly stroking his chest.

"Stop with the visiting crap," he scolded. "I'm away on location making a movie. I'll be home permanently in a few weeks."

"Nothing about you is ever permanent, Lennie."

"Isn't that exactly the way you like it?"

"How well he knows me," she drawled.

"Yeah," he said, scratching his head. "If anyone knows you at all."

"I had a strange meeting this morning," she ventured. "Actually, it was verging on creepy."

"What kind of strange?" Lennie asked.

"I'm not sure, really—it was with some moronic asshole who figured he could waltz right in and buy The Keys. Can you imagine?"

"No shit," Lennie said, his interest piqued. "Who was he?"

"A man called Armand Jordan. Jeffrey set the meeting up; he was under the impression that Armand's company was interested in investing in future projects."

"And I'm guessing that wasn't the case."

"Not at all. This Armand character seemed fixated on buying The Keys for any price. He had this weird vibe about him—it was almost as if he had a vendetta against women."

"Oh yeah, babe," Lennie said dryly. "Just your type. Did you hang his balls on a post?"

"No," Lucky said, smiling because Lennie knew her so well. "But I did have him bounced from the hotel."

"Poor bastard," Lennie said, laughing. "He had no idea who he was messing with."

"I guess not," she said thoughtfully.

"Anyway, you threw him out and he's now history. Right?"

"Exactly."

"So end of that story, and on to other more important things. How's Max doing?"

"The same as ever. Desperate to make a break for it, and get out there on her own."

"You've got to accept that our girl is a free spirit. All she wants is her space."

"She gets all the space she needs, thankyouverymuch. *And* we're throwing her a fantastic party. By the way, Ace drove here to be with her."

"He seems like a good kid."

"Don't you think she's too young to stick with one person?" Lucky questioned.

"Not if he's the right one."

"Oh, you mean like you and me?"

"You got it, sweetheart," Lennie said, laughing.

"I bet you don't remember our first date," Lucky said, deciding to challenge him.

"Is this a test?" Lennie asked, propping himself up on one elbow and giving her a quizzical look.

"Maybe," she teased. "Perhaps I want to see if you can pass."

"Come *on*. As if I could ever forget our first date."

"Go ahead, then," she said, continuing to bait him. "I expect details."

"New York. Chinese restaurant. We killed a bottle of vodka."

"I'm impressed," Lucky said. "You really do remember."

"Did you honestly believe I wouldn't?"

"Well . . . I thought you'd close in on the first time we made love on that raft in the South of France. Now *that* was unforgettable."

"You got that right. We should take a look at reenacting that scene sometime soon. Like as soon as I've wrapped my movie."

"I'm up for it."

"Me too."

They exchanged a long intimate look.

"But hey, I gotta admit—our first date was hot toc said. "After killing the vodka you dragged me off to sor wich Village jazz joint until four in the morning."

"Then *you* dragged *me* to some after-hours dive stayed forever, drinking endless cups of coffee and tall everything."

"And you, my little Lucky, loved every minute of it.'

"I'm not denying it. But even better," she added soft in love that night."

"We did?" he said, feigning surprise. "Now, that I do

"Don't mess with me, Lennie Golden," she said, her eyes in a threatening fashion. "You know you won ate the consequences."

"Okay, okay," he said, grinning. "I guess we did, an at us—an old married couple with kids."

"Easy on the 'old,' mister," Lucky said, throwing hir punch.

"However, Mrs. Golden, you're still as beautiful n were then. Besides, I like a woman with a little sea her."

"'Seasoning,' huh?"

"Oh yeah."

"Fuck you, Lennie Golden!"

With one swift move he rolled on top of her, pinni neath him. "Sure, love of my life. I live to oblige."

~ ~ ~

Most stars conduct a meet and greet after their concerts. Sometimes Gerald M. couldn't be bothered, but in Vegas he was never sure what celebrity could be lurking in the audience, so tonight he hung around to see who might appear. Besides, he was staying in town for the fights, and since he'd recently broken it off with his latest conquest—an ambitious actress (weren't they all?)—he'd decided to sample the local talent.

The last person he expected to see was his almost unrecognizable daughter. Without her trademark dreads, Cookie looked quite different.

"What's up with your hair, chicken?" he asked as she and her group were ushered into his large but crowded dressing room adjacent to the hospitality bar.

"Don't *call* me that," she said, rolling her eyes in horror. "It's *so* uncool."

"This girl is my little chicken," Gerald M. crooned to the assorted gathering. "Hatched her myself. Now look at her—she's all grown up." A lackey handed him a rum and Coke, which he downed in two big gulps. "What you doin' here, sweet thing? How'd ya like the show?"

I hated the show, Cookie was tempted to say. *I hated seeing my father up on stage thrusting his leather-clad dick at a screaming audience of middle-aged loser women desperate to get laid.*

"Your show was phenomenal," Frankie announced, maneuvering himself in front of Cookie and shaking Gerald M.'s hand. "You are the consummate artist. You always rock their fuckin' world—'scuse my language."

"And you are?" Gerald M. said, backing off.

"Frankie Romano, Cookie's friend. Pleasure to meet you, sir."

"'Sir'!" Gerald M. spluttered with laughter. "How the fuck old d'you think I am?"

Oh crap, Cookie thought. *This is so bad. They're bonding already.*

Max hung back. She figured she'd fulfilled her obligation as a friend, and now it was time for her and Ace to duck out.

Cookie was not having it. "You've gotta stay with us," she begged. "Otherwise Frankie's gonna want to hang with my dad, an' there's *no way* I can handle it!"

"But Cookie—" Max objected.

"*Puh-leeze!* I'll never ask you for anything again!"

And so it was that they stayed.

~ ~ ~

Bobby and Denver were sitting at a table in a candlelit poolside cabana at Mood with people swirling all around them. It was almost midnight, the music was loud, and the club was packed. Beautiful girls abounded—even the cocktail waitresses were great-looking in their skimpy uniforms. Denver was feeling out of place and inadequate. Club scenes were not her favorite venues.

"What's with the attitude?" Bobby asked, catching her mood.

"What attitude?" Denver shot back, unable to help herself from taking her frustration out on him.

"You just seem"—he shrugged—"I dunno—kinda uptight."

"As opposed to *not* uptight, like all the girls that keep coming over and talking to you?" she retorted, wishing she didn't sound so damn jealous.

"Hey Denv, you *know* it's only work," Bobby said, stroking her arm. "Since it's my club, what do you expect me to do—ignore them?"

"That's an idea."

"*C'mon*. Drink your wine, loosen up."

"I thought tonight was going to be all about us. Instead it's me trying to talk Cassie out of getting an abortion, and you working the room. Not my idea of a romantic evening."

"Sorry you feel like that. But surely y'know I've only got eyes for you?"

He gave her the look—a look she couldn't resist.

The trouble with Bobby was that he was so damn good-looking, and on top of that, genuinely nice. Then of course there was the rich factor—so naturally women were going to be chasing him. If he was indeed her future, she realized that she'd just have to get used to it.

"Well," she said, softening her tone, "if you put it like that . . ."

"You know where I want to put it," he whispered in her ear.

"Bobby!"

"Half an hour, then we're taking off. That's a promise."

"You mean it?"

"Course I do," he said, leaning in and kissing her.

She kissed him back. "I know I'm behaving like a jealous girl-friend and I don't understand why," she murmured. "It's so not me, you know that."

"I get it," Bobby reassured her.

"You do?"

"I sure do."

"Well then—perhaps you can enlighten me."

He grinned at her again. What a smile. Dazzling.

"'Cause you love me," he singsonged.

She sat up straight, her heart pounding. Had he just men-tioned the L word? And why was he putting it on her? Wasn't it up to him to say it first?

"Excuse me?" she said, slightly breathless.

"L-O-V-E," Bobby said, spelling it out. "And since you're not about to be the first to say it, I'm saying it for you, 'cause I love you too, Miz Jones, and I'm through with holding back. So deal with it. Okay?"

~ ~ ~

Somehow or other Kev managed to lure Billy to a strip club, where the manager—a big fan with caterpillar eyebrows and a smarmy leer—spotted him and immediately sequestered him in a deluxe VIP suite with champagne on the house and two of the club's most popular girls.

Kev was in heaven. If he were by himself he would've been sitting next to the stage staring up at an array of tempting pussy with all the other nobodies. Hanging with Billy was the best. First-class service all the way.

A baby-faced blonde was busily trying to tempt Billy with her wares—shiny new tits, flat stomach, long legs, and shaved pussy. But Billy wasn't buying. "Got a girlfriend," he informed her. Which was news to Kev, because wasn't Billy in the middle of a divorce?

"Sorry about that," Baby-face cooed, adding a cheeky "But just because your dick is occupied, doesn't mean you can't let it out for a run!"

Billy laughed, fleetingly thought about going for it, then hurriedly excused himself, walked outside the club, and tried Max again.

Once again there was no answer, so this time he decided to text her.

"Hey, it's me—Billy. Where r u? Been trying to reach u. I'm in Vegas. Want to c u. Call me."

It was done. He'd contacted her; now all she had to do was respond.

~ ~ ~

Everyone ended up piling into the restaurant area of Mood. Gerald M. and entourage consisted of his two backup singers and his assistant/procurer of female talent.

Then there were Cookie and Frankie (so up Gerald M.'s ass there was no room for anyone else), Max, and a reluctant Ace.

"What happened to ducking out on our own?" Ace said in a low voice to Max as they settled in at the table. He was becoming resigned to the fact that it seemed like he was never getting her to himself.

"This is Vegas, things happen," she answered restlessly. "Besides, we can't be here and *not* see Bobby. He's sitting in a cabana by the pool. Let's go visit."

Before Ace could object, she grabbed him by the hand and began pulling him across the restaurant to the outside club area.

Bobby spotted them approaching. "How to ruin a special moment," he muttered to Denver. "Trust Max to have the worst timing in town."

"She doesn't know," Denver said, feeling light-headed. "Besides, I really would like to get to know her."

"You're sure about that?" Bobby said, standing up as Max descended.

"Hey, big bro," Max said, flinging her arms around him in her usual proprietary fashion. "Remember Ace?"

"Absolutely," Bobby said, giving Ace an amiable nod. "And you all know Denver."

Max threw her a perfunctory nod, while Ace said a polite "Nice to meet you."

"Likewise," Denver replied, thinking that if this was Max's boyfriend, she'd done well for herself.

"Ace drove all the way from Big Bear just to be with me," Max said, hovering by the table.

"How nice," Denver said. "I bet you were thrilled to see him."

As usual Max ignored her. "Guess who's here?" she said to Bobby.

"You know I'm not good at guessing games."

"Your old BFF Frankie Romano."

"Where?" Bobby said. He hadn't seen Frankie in quite a while, not since they'd parted ways after a falling-out about Frankie's addictions.

"We're sitting with him at Cookie's dad's table in the restaurant. You should come over. I know he'd love to see you."

"Maybe later," Bobby said. Once, he and Frankie, along with M.J., had been best friends, but those days were over. "You know," he added sternly, "you're not supposed to be in this area of the club."

"How come?" Max shot back.

"'Cause you're not twenty-one. And that means we could lose our license."

"As if!" Max scoffed. "Besides, we've all got fake ID's."

"Great," Bobby said sarcastically. "That makes me feel so much better."

Then, to his relief, he spotted Lucky and Lennie walking in. Great timing, because it meant that Max was no longer his problem. Let Lucky deal.

"Here come your mom and dad," he warned. "Better skip back

to your table, little girl, or Mommy might give you a smack on your bottom."

"You are *so* mean," Max said, making a face. "I hate you!"

"Not mean, just protective."

"Anyway, what are *they* doing here?" Max said, twisting her head to take a look as Lucky and Lennie approached. "I thought they wanted alone time. So gross!"

"Nice way to talk about your parents," Bobby said.

"They're yours too," Max pointed out.

"Half mine," Bobby said, correcting her.

"Whatever."

Moments later Lucky and Lennie were upon them, and Lennie was giving Max a hug while Lucky was checking out Denver and Bobby was thinking, *Half an hour later and we could've been safely out of here.*

In the club business, the night was only just beginning.

CHAPTER FORTY-TWO

Annabelle Maestro was a talker. She didn't shut up for a minute. Armand had no idea what or who she was talking about. He didn't know and he didn't care. Names came and went as they sat in one of the open lounges drinking tequila on the rocks with *limoncello* chasers—a lethal combination thought up by Annabelle. He liked the buzz the liquor was giving him. He liked the fact that there was no Fouad around keeping a watchful eye on him.

"If you're not here for the fights, what *are* you doing in Vegas?" she asked, rubbing her index finger around the rim of her glass and staring at him expectantly.

"I am buying The Keys hotel and casino," Armand announced. *Yes, that's what I'm doing. Damn you, Lucky Santangelo. You'll soon learn that when Armand Jordan wants something, he gets it. I am unstoppable. And if I say something is going to happen, it will, whether you think you can stop it or not. But how can you stop it if you're dead? Impossible.*

"You're kidding!" Annabelle exclaimed, her eyes widening. This guy wasn't just rich; he was mega rich. Ever since their one date a few months ago, she'd had her eye on him. Although they'd experienced one long wild night of sex, he'd never called. Annabelle did not appreciate rejection, especially as she considered herself semifamous, and he should've been thrilled to date her.

Armand had quite a reputation in New York as being aloof and difficult to pin down. But Annabelle was well aware that he was a major catch, and she craved a steady boyfriend; there'd been nobody permanent since she'd broken up with that sad sack druggie Frankie Romano.

Earlier in the evening she'd had a big fight with her latest boyfriend, Eddie Falcon, the superagent. They'd only been seeing each other a few weeks, but tonight she'd discovered, by scrolling through his texts, that Eddie was cheating on her with not one but three other girls. Apparently he was the Tiger Woods of superagents. What an asshole! She'd been planning on dumping him and flying back to New York, but then, walking through the casino to cool off, she'd run into Armand.

When opportunity beckoned, Annabelle was not about to turn it down.

"I never thought Lucky would sell," Annabelle said. "When's this happening?"

"Soon," Armand replied, feeling the need to get to his villa and indulge in a few more lines of coke before the hookers got there. He'd informed the concierge to alert him when they arrived, and to have them wait in his villa. For a thousand-dollar tip, Armand figured the concierge would fuck them himself.

"Then you must be going to the party tomorrow night," Annabelle ventured.

"What party?" Armand asked, thinking he would invite her back to his villa to see if he could get her to interact with the prostitutes. Now *that* might be worth watching.

"Lucky's daughter, Max, is turning eighteen. There's a big blowout at The Keys," Annabelle said. "Since I told my boyfriend to take a hike, I could go with you. I know the Santangelos; I'm sure they'd be delighted to see me. Bobby and I went to high school together."

"Who is Bobby?"

"Lucky's son. He runs the club Mood in The Keys. We're tight. Maybe we should stop by for a drink."

Tight. What did that mean? This girl spoke a language he didn't understand and certainly didn't want to. However, since she knew the Santangelo family, she could turn out to be useful.

"What do you think?" Annabelle asked, tilting her head to one side.

"I think we should go to my villa first. Spend some private time."

Annabelle considered his offer. She didn't want sex—followed by no phone call. Oh, no, that wouldn't do at all.

On the other hand, Armand *was* one of the most eligible bachelors in New York, and perhaps the timing was right to give him another chance. What did she have to lose?

"One drink," she said brightly. "Then on to Mood. Is that a plan?"

Armand nodded.

Why did God give women the ability to speak? Why couldn't they just keep their stupid mouths shut?

~ ~ ~

Once Peggy captured her prize—Gino's sneezed-in napkin—she was anxious to end the dinner and get back to her suite.

But Paige was having none of it. She was enjoying Peggy's company, and suggested they move on to the Cavendish club for a nightcap.

"I'm a little past nightclubs," Peggy demurred.

"If I can do it, so can you," Gino wheezed. "I'm two hundred years old, hon. You're a spring chicken."

For a moment Peggy was tempted to remind him of their one-night fling all those years ago. But good sense prevailed and she said nothing.

"You see what I have to put up with," Paige said with a complacent smile. "The man is tireless. He hardly ever sleeps."

"What? I should sleep my friggin' life away?" Gino interrupted. "When I go, it won't be quietly in the night, it'll be in the middle of a fuckin' party."

Paige shook her head. "Energy to burn," she said. "If we could bottle it we'd make a fortune."

For a split second Peggy flashed onto a memory of Gino making love to her. Energy to burn indeed. He'd been an insatiable lover. Other men had paled in comparison, especially King Emir, who after a while had suffered from premature ejaculation—something that didn't seem to bother him because he was a king, so who would dare to criticize?

"I suppose one drink wouldn't hurt," Peggy said, removing her powder compact from her purse and checking her appearance.

"Not bad for an old broad," Gino said with a lecherous chuckle.

"I thought I was a spring chicken," Peggy retorted. And for one quick moment she thought she spied a hint of recognition in his dark, all-knowing elderly eyes.

~ ~ ~

Carlos, the chief concierge at the Cavendish, a well-put-together Latin man, personally escorted Luscious and Seducta to Armand Jordan's villa. The two women smelled of cheap perfume, musty sweat, cigarettes, and booze. Hardly a winning combination.

Carlos was surprised to observe such low-rent women. Surely a man such as Armand Jordan expected better than these two?

Luscious pranced around the living room on her cheap six-inch red hooker heels, a cigarette dangling from her overplumped lips. Her legs were bare, and on her left calf was a tattoo of a bodybuilder winking at no one in particular.

"Where's the . . . uh . . . mister?" she asked.

"He'll be here shortly," Carlos replied, deciding it would not be wise to leave them alone in the villa. They looked like the type of women who—if left to their own devices—would steal anything that wasn't locked down. "And this is a no-smoking room," he added. "So if you'd refrain—"

"Fuck that shit," Luscious said, boldly blowing a smoke ring in his face. "If I get cancer an' die I promise not to blame you."

Seducta guffawed as she threw herself down on the couch, one streaky fake-tanned leg casually flung over the side. Her large breasts threatened to fall out of the flimsy top she was wearing, while her red, white, and blue G-string was fully on show. "I could go for a drink while we're waitin'," she said, winking meaningfully at Carlos.

He glanced at his watch. Was he supposed to serve these two creatures drinks? Armand Jordan might be an excellent tipper, but he, Carlos, was nobody's lackey. "Mr. Jordan will be here shortly," he said. "It's up to him if he wishes you to drink."

"For crissakes," Luscious whined. "Lighten up. You're a workin' stiff, just like us. Get the stick out your ass and pour us a fuckin' drink."

"Yeah, I'm parched," Seducta agreed, sitting up. "One drink, an' if you promise to behave, I'll show you my titties."

"I don't—"

"Oh yeah, you do!" Seducta said, peeling down her top and revealing the largest fake boobs Carlos had ever seen.

The women were disgustingly vulgar, but he was a man, after all, and the sudden stirring in his pants reminded him of that fact. He realized that he had to leave immediately before he did something to dishonor his lovely wife of six months. Let them steal; whatever they took, he would simply add onto Mr. Jordan's bill.

"The drinks cupboard is behind the bar," he said, hurriedly backing toward the door. "Help yourselves."

"Bye, honey," Seducta crooned, shaking her enormous bare breasts at him. "See you around!"

~ ~ ~

"What took place between you and the man you came to Vegas with?" Armand asked as he and Annabelle walked through the casino on their way outside to his villa. He wasn't at all interested in anything she had to say, but faking it socially was a talent he'd cultivated over the years. Make them like you, then stick it to them—hard.

"He was one of those hotshot Hollywood jerks," Annabelle complained. "A lying prick who had me figured as a money machine for him to milk. Promised me my own reality show, then when we got here I discovered he'd not only pitched another celeb, but he was sleeping with her too."

Armand made a sympathetic sound in the back of his throat. As if he cared. He didn't. Not one bit.

"Tell me about the party tomorrow night—you say it's for Lucky Santangelo's daughter?"

"That's right," Annabelle said. "Lucky dotes on Max. It's all about ego—Max is like a little version of her mom." She paused for a breath. "Surely you're invited, considering you're buying The Keys? I can't imagine they wouldn't invite you."

"I keep business separate from social occasions," Armand stated. "And since you are one of the few people who know about my imminent purchase of such a prestigious property, I would appreciate your discretion, and trust that you will not mention it to anyone."

"Naturally," Annabelle agreed, quite flattered that she was in the know, although disappointed that Armand obviously didn't have an invite to the party.

She threw him a sideways glance. He was an attractive man—not movie-star handsome like her dad, who was a well-established movie star, but not bad-looking, in a buttoned-down way.

The mustache would have to go, a new haircut might help, and the way he dressed was old-fashioned and too formal. But she could get him into shape. He'd be quite a prize to return to New York with.

Yes. Tonight she would seal this deal. No doubt about it.

CHAPTER FORTY-THREE

If there was one thing that turned Gerald M. on, it was holding court with an attentive audience hanging on to his every word. He reveled in the spotlight—it shored up his escalating fear that his kind of music was becoming irrelevant. Diddy, Jay-Z, and Akon ruled. Plus, every week a new rap sensation hit the street.

Gerald M.'s manager had not so subtly suggested that he might like to try taking a different direction—maybe make a CD of old standards like Rod Stewart had, or perhaps invite some happening rapper to join him on a track or two. But Gerald adamantly refused to even consider the idea. Soul was his thing. Good old-fashioned soul, which got the women hot and horny and the men laid.

In Europe he was still an enormous star. In America—not so much. Although tonight his fans had come out in force and his assistant had collected an array of panties thrown onstage to prove it.

Gerald M. was feeling on top of everything.

Cookie wasn't. Max was so right: Frankie Romano was a major star fuck. He was all over her dad as if Gerald M. was the second coming. She was being ignored, and it was pissing her off big-time.

Max—who was now back at the table—bit her tongue so as not to blurt out *I told you so. Frankie's always been this way. He's a major loser.*

"What's up with his crap?" Cookie complained. "He's all actin' like a freakin' fan. I can't even watch it!"

"Most people get like that around stars," Max offered matter-of-factly. "When Lucky owned Panther Studios, kissing ass was a daily occurrence."

"He's, like, so ignorin' me," Cookie said, her eyes flashing daggers.

Although Max was trying to concentrate on what Cookie was saying, to her horror she suddenly observed Venus making a grand entrance.

Ohmigod. Lucky's best friend. Billy's soon-to-be ex. Ohmigod!

Quickly turning to Cookie, she said, "Y'know what? We should take off, teach your boyfriend to pay you more attention. Besides, Bobby's getting all uptight 'cause he doesn't want us in the club on account of his precious license, so we can't even dance or score a drink, plus my parents are all over me, so whyn't we hit one of those clubs where we can do what we like an' not be under constant scrutiny."

"Yeah," Cookie agreed, still shooting Frankie dirty looks. "Let's go. I'll show Frankie Romano who he's screwing with!"

~ ~ ~

Sitting next to Lucky Santangelo, Denver felt all her insecurities come rushing back. Bobby had just told her he loved her, followed by the instant intrusion of the irritating and rude Max, and now Lucky and Lennie Golden had joined them. She was overwhelmed, even more so because Lucky was extremely friendly and nice, not to mention totally stunning.

Likewise Lennie.

It was all too much.

"So . . ." Lucky said to Bobby, smiling warmly across at Denver. "*This* is the woman you've been keeping a big secret."

"No secret," Bobby replied with a sheepish grin. "You've met, haven't you?"

"Maybe once," Lucky said, sipping a martini. "Very briefly."

"Well, *we* certainly haven't met," Lennie said, extending his hand to Denver. "It's a real pleasure. Where has Bobby been hiding you?"

If she was intimidated before, Denver now felt completely out of her depth. Lennie Golden was a force unto himself. She was a longtime fan of his movies, which only made things worse. How embarrassing to find herself trapped in this situation. Wasn't it enough that they would all be together the following night?

Oh God! Why hadn't she pursued a relationship with laid-back, uncomplicated Sam? Why had she picked Bobby?

Or had *he* picked *her*?

She didn't know. She wasn't sure. She was confused.

"Bobby tells me you're a DA," Lucky said, leaning toward Denver as if she were really interested in hearing her reply.

"Uh, Deputy DA, actually. That's what they, uh, call us."

Oh great, I sound like the idiot girlfriend who comes to Vegas with one dress. And now what am I supposed to wear tomorrow night? And Bobby's mom is too gorgeous for words—slim and sexy

in a sliver of a top and black leather pants, with numerous dia-
mond bracelets stacked up her toned and tanned arm, and a huge
emerald ring on her engagement finger. She looks like some kind
of exotic supermodel.

"You should meet my brother Steven," Lucky said. "He's living in Rio at the moment, but when he visits, we must all get
together."

What the hell—was Lucky trying to fix her up? *Please, no!*

"Steven was a DA," Bobby hurriedly explained, noting her
confusion.

"Really?" Denver murmured.

"Yeah," Bobby said. "You two probably do have a lot in common. Steven started out as a defense attorney, then felt it wasn't
right for him—just like you."

"You were a defense attorney?" Lennie asked, and he too
seemed genuinely interested.

"Yes," she managed. "With Saunders, Fields, Simmons and
Johnson in Beverly Hills."

"And you switched because?"

"I was, uh, one of the defense attorneys for Ralph Maestro. It
became . . . complicated."

God, she was actually sitting in a nightclub in Vegas chatting
away to *the* Lennie Golden.

"I can imagine," Lennie said, reaching for Lucky's hand and
squeezing it.

Apparently they are the perfect couple, Denver thought. *Still*
in love and don't care who knows it.

Could she and Bobby ever achieve that kind of closeness?

Yes! Stop wimping out and embrace what we have together.

Before she could give herself more of a pep talk, here came a
test in the form of a curvy brunette poured into an equally

curvy outfit. The girl approached Bobby from behind, covered his eyes with her well-manicured hands, and cooed, "Guess who?"

To his credit, Bobby didn't panic. He stayed calm, removed the girl's hands, and glanced up at her. "Hey, Gia," he said, without taking a beat. "Have you met my girlfriend, Denver?"

Gia's smile froze. Denver could almost see the thoughts flying through the girl's head. *Girlfriend? What's that about? Bobby's a player. No fun to be had here.*

"No," Gia said at last. "I wasn't aware that you—"

Not allowing Gia to finish her sentence, Bobby was on his feet, walking her away from their cabana.

"Hazard of the business," Lucky remarked dryly, noting Denver's discomfort.

"Excuse me?" Denver said, trying to sound lighthearted.

"Girls throwing themselves at the good-looking boss," Lucky said.

"It doesn't bother me," Denver said, attempting to sound breezy and unconcerned. The last thing she wanted was Lucky feeling sorry for her.

"It doesn't bother me either," Lucky replied. "Girls are always coming on to Lennie. Or at least they used to."

"Hold up," Lennie interrupted, shaking his head. "Whaddya mean, used to? I gotta fight 'em off with a stick."

"Sure, baby," Lucky crooned. "And you better make sure that stick stays in your pants or else!"

"Or else what?"

"You know what."

The two of them giggled like a couple of in-heat teenagers. Denver felt like an intruder on their intimacy; she'd never witnessed two people so into each other.

Bobby returned to the table. Handsome Bobby, so damn hot

in a black shirt and pants. Dark hair, intense eyes, strong jaw-line. Yes, he was a babe magnet, no doubt about it.

"Sorry, sweetie," he said, sitting down.

"Old girlfriend?" Denver questioned, although *old girlfriend* sounded all wrong—shouldn't it be *young sexy girlfriend, who looks like she recently stepped out of a Victoria's Secret catalogue?*

"We went out a coupla times," Bobby admitted. "Nothing se-rious. And I can assure you it was way before you and me."

"You and I," Denver murmured, adding a succinct, "I have ex-boyfriends too, you know."

"I do know that," Bobby said, playing along. "And I've got the urge to smash 'em in the face if they ever put in an appearance."

"You do?"

"If I have to."

They exchanged a knowing smile.

"So what am I supposed to do about *your* exes?" she asked, feeling better already.

"Ignore 'em," Bobby said. "It's you I'm with, and that's the way it's meant to be." He put his arm around her and pulled her close. "I'm hoping you feel the same way."

"Yes," she murmured. "You know I do."

~ ~ ~

Giggling hysterically, Cookie and Max piled into a cab, a dour-faced Ace along for the ride. He wasn't happy about getting stuck with Cookie, but he was pleased enough to escape from Gerald M. and his adoring entourage. Hanging with those kinds of people was not his ideal. "Where we going?" he asked.

"There's this club for under twenty-ones. No alcohol served, but awesome sounds," Max offered, thinking that a riotous time on the dance floor was exactly what they all needed. "Harry's new friend Paco is deejaying there sometime tonight. We gotta go check him out."

"What're we waitin' for?" Cookie said, scrolling through the messages on her cell to see if Frankie had missed her yet.

He hadn't.

Well, he wouldn't, would he? Too busy paying homage to Gerald M.

"Who wants a joint?" she asked, digging in her purse.

Ace shook his head as Cookie found what she was looking for and lit up.

"In a cab? Really?" Ace said to Max in a disgusted tone.

"She's upset," Max whispered. "Besides, it's only one little joint. Nobody's going to throw us in jail for *that*."

"You're unbelievable," Ace grouched. "I drive all this way, and this is what we end up doing."

"Sorry," Max retorted. "But you know I wasn't expecting you."

"Thanks a lot," he said restlessly. "You're making me feel so frigging welcome."

Ace's bad mood was getting to her. Wasn't it enough that she'd gotten dumped by Billy? Now she had to put up with Ace and his complaints.

Why couldn't he relax and simply go with it?

CHAPTER FORTY-FOUR

"Did I just see little Max running out of here?" Venus asked as she joined Bobby's fast-expanding table in his poolside cabana at Mood.

"Don't tell me she left," Lennie said, frowning. "That damn kid—I hardly got to see her."

"Ah, the doting daddy." Venus sighed as she slid into the booth beside him. "And might I say that you, Mr. Golden, are looking great as usual. In all the time I've known you, you *never* change."

"I could say the same for you, Venus."

"Then say it."

"You look incredible for an old—"

"Lennie!" Lucky warned.

"I'm teasing her," Lennie said with a big grin. "She knows it."

"Of course I do," Venus said, smiling. "Lennie and me—we've got a special relationship."

"Not too special, I hope," Lucky said.

"What do *you* think?" Venus said. Turning back to Lennie, she added, "How's your movie going?"

"Two more weeks of hard labor and I'm back in L.A.," Lennie said, picking up his drink.

"For about five minutes," Lucky quipped, joining in. "We all know Lennie—he'll be off again soon. It's impossible for him to stay in one place for long. That's how he rolls."

"And that's how you like it," Lennie retorted.

"My husband the workaholic." Lucky sighed. "But that doesn't mean I don't miss you."

"I know, babe," Lennie said. "But if we were together all the time we'd tear each other apart."

"True," Lucky agreed.

"I wish you'd think of writing something for me," Venus said wistfully. "You know how much I'd love to work with you, Lennie."

"As if I'd trust you and your 'special relationship' alone on location with my old man," Lucky said jokingly. "Surely you're aware what they say about best friends?"

Listening to their banter, Denver was in awe. Not only was she sitting with Bobby's illustrious parents, but superstar Venus was now in the house and had joined them too! It was all becoming a little bit surreal. It wasn't as if she hadn't encountered quite a few stars when she'd worked at Saunders, Fields, Simmons & Johnson—after all, it was a major Beverly Hills law firm, and she'd represented some big names. However, this was different. This was up close and extremely personal.

"We'll leave as soon as M.J. gets here," Bobby said, leaning over and whispering in her ear.

"Can I count on that?" she whispered back.

"Yeah. Sit tight. I just gotta go deal with a couple of things."

And he was gone—lost in the heady mix of loud music, strobing lights, and clinking glasses.

"Hello," a voice said.

She turned to the man who'd moved in next to her. He was model-boy perfect and quite young.

"I am Jorge," he said, with a strong accent. "I am here with Venus."

"Oh, hi," she said, sensing that he felt as out of place as she did. "I'm Denver. I'm with Bobby."

"Bobby?" he said blankly.

"Uh . . . do you know Lucky?"

"Lucky?" He shook his head. His soulful brown eyes had the look of a lost puppy's.

"Lucky, Venus's friend," Denver explained. "She's Bobby's mom, and, uh, Bobby is my boyfriend."

The word *boyfriend* immediately made her feel uncomfortable. It was so straight out of high school. But he *was* her boyfriend—or maybe *lover* would be a better description.

"Ah," Jorge muttered vaguely.

It would be nice, Denver thought, *if Venus introduced her escort to everyone instead of getting all cozy with Lennie Golden.*

Watching Lennie in person, she'd already decided that he did not disappoint. He might be an older man, but he exuded a George Clooney under-the-radar kind of sex appeal. Lucky did indeed have it all. A mega-successful hotel and casino, a great family, and a smart, talented husband. What more could any woman want?

"We go dance?" Jorge suggested in a surprisingly deep voice.

Was he asking her? Was it inappropriate if she said yes?

He was already up and ready to go; she couldn't just leave him standing there.

"Sure," she said, glancing at Venus, whom she hadn't even met. The platinum-blond star was busy talking to Lucky and Lennie. Would Venus even notice her boyfriend was missing?

Probably not.

Without thinking more about it, she got to her feet and followed Jorge onto the crowded dance floor. Bobby didn't dance— early on in their relationship he'd announced it wasn't his thing. At least there was *something* he didn't excel at.

On the other hand, she loved to dance, and since Jorge was no slouch either, the two of them were soon enjoying themselves to the sounds of Bruno Mars and Alicia Keys.

~ ~ ~

The Wonderball was one of the most popular clubs on the strip on account of its no-alcohol, no-drugs policy. For a twenty-five-dollar entry fee, all the under twenty-ones could rave until it was time for a total collapse. The Wonderball featured live bands and guest deejays. It was a major mob scene, and naturally plenty of booze and drugs got smuggled in.

When Max, Cookie, and Ace arrived, the club was filled to capacity. They barely made it through before the fire marshal turned up and posted a NO MORE GUESTS sign at the door.

"This ain't too bad," Cookie allowed, gazing around the cavernous space crammed with writhing sweating bodies, the music so loud conversation was an impossibility. "I could get into this," she yelled, heading for the dance floor. "It's like my kinda crazy."

"We're gonna try to find Harry and Paco," Max shouted above the noise. "If Paco's playing, we can hang out in the booth. See you there."

"Right on," Cookie agreed, dancing and checking her phone

at the same time, which reminded Max she still hadn't taken her phone off plane mode.

She quickly did so, and immediately saw that she had several text messages.

The first one was from her two younger brothers on their European tour wishing her a happy birthday. The second was from Bobby's niece, Brigette. And the third was from Billy.

YES, BILLY!

Her heart jumped. When had Billy texted her? How come she'd missed it?

WHAT THE FUCK?!

Her hands began shaking as she started to read his message.

Hey, it's me—Billy. Where r u?

I'M HERE. RIGHT HERE!

Been trying to reach u.

REALLY?

I'm in Vegas.

OMG!

Want to c u. Call me.

"What're you doin'?" Ace shouted, making himself heard above the noise.

"Nothing," she said, hurriedly clicking her phone off.

"Are we gonna find Harry or what?" Ace asked.

"Yeah, sure," she yelled back, wondering exactly how she was supposed to make a clean getaway. Billy was in town, and seeing him was her number one priority.

~ ~ ~

Bobby met M.J. and Cassie at the door. They were with a man in an expensive suit and tinted aviator glasses. He had slicked-back hair and acted as if he and Bobby were old friends.

"Eddie Falcon," he said to Bobby, proffering his hand. "You and I hung out at Brett Ratner's house. You were diddling with two Playboy Bunnies, an' I was flyin' solo."

Playboy Bunnies were not Bobby's style. He had no idea who this Eddie Falcon was, and he didn't much care.

M.J. filled him in as Cassie and Eddie headed off to a table.

"Eddie's the agent Cassie wants to sign with," M.J. explained. "She says he's hot shit."

"More bad timing, huh?" Bobby remarked.

"I figure if she lands herself an agent, it'll make her happy," M.J. reasoned. "Then she can work on her music stuff while she's sittin' around pregnant. You know she's into writing her own songs, so this could be a way t' go."

Sometimes it amazed Bobby that M.J. could be so dense when it came to his wife. She didn't want to have a baby right now. All she wanted was a career. And Bobby had a strong suspicion that nothing M.J. said or did would change her mind. Signing with a smooth, fast-talking agent would only make Cassie more determined to put her career first.

Not my problem, Bobby thought. *I need to get the hell out of here so that Denver and I can spend some special alone time together.*

And just as he was thinking of exactly how he would take his girlfriend on a sweet ride to ecstasy, a hand clapped him on the shoulder and a familiar voice boomed, "Hey, guys. It's me, Frankie. I'm back in town!"

CHAPTER FORTY-FIVE

Having drinks with Paige and Gino was not where Peggy wished to be. In full detective mode, she was primed to seek action regarding her first DNA sample. Then it occurred to her that she needed something from Armand. He'd told her he was busy with important meetings, so if she could just get into his bedroom and take a few strands of hair from his hairbrush . . .

She already knew where the villas were located, and the sooner she got there, the better. But Gino, at his advanced age, did not seem to be slowing down at all. The man was a freak of nature. And was it her imagination, or as Paige imbibed her fourth glass of wine, was Gino's wife becoming a little *too* friendly?

Peggy feigned a yawn and murmured, "You really must excuse me. I'm still on New York time, and I'm afraid it's catching up with me."

"We're gonna let you go on one condition," Gino said gruffly, winking at her.

"And that would be?" Peggy asked politely.

"Dinner again tomorrow night."

"Gino," Paige said, reminding him. "Tomorrow night is Max's party."

"So Peggy'll come t' the party," Gino said magnanimously, once again giving Peggy the wink.

Was it possible that he *did* remember their one night of lust? It was so long ago, and yet . . .

"I think I'd enjoy that," Peggy replied, getting to her feet.

"I'll call you in the morning, then," Paige said, and just like that, before Peggy could react, Paige kissed her full on the lips. After which Peggy beat a hasty retreat.

~ ~ ~

Carlos the concierge was right about Luscious and Seducta: If it wasn't nailed down, they had an urge to collect.

Seducta carried an oversized fake leather purse she'd recently swiped from K-Mart. It was roomy enough to hold all her favorite things for a rip-roaring night of paid-for sex. Condoms, a double-headed black dildo, and enough lubricant to please an elephant. However, as she flitted around the villa, she still had room to throw in several bars of expensive hotel soap, a couple of crystal shot glasses from behind the bar, and various snacks and several miniature bottles of booze from the minibar, plus two marble ashtrays and a couple of rolls of toilet paper. Every little bit helped. Besides, what was wrong with bringing home gifts for Mikey?

Luscious was more discerning. She raided the bedroom and rifled through Armand's personal possessions, grabbing a silk tie still in its cellophane wrap, and two pairs of what looked like solid-gold cuff links. The dude would never notice; he had a shitload of stuff. Too much.

Luscious wondered who he was. Obviously loaded. Probably wanted a show since he'd requested two girls.

Another night, another pervert.

Luscious was up for it as long as Seducta knew how to behave. They'd never worked together in front of a john. There was a rhythm to making sure the client ended up with a satisfactory happy ending.

Luscious knew exactly how to do it. The question was, did Seducta?

~ ~ ~

When the Cavendish Hotel was built, the team of architects had created a series of on-the-property luxury villas meant for high rollers only, private and discreet—a golf-cart ride away from the main hotel or, if the guests were so inclined, a walk along a series of leafy pathways.

Armand chose to walk, Annabelle by his side.

"How far is it?" she asked after a few minutes of uncomfortable tottering. "These Jimmy Choos are not made for walking."

Armand ignored her; he had many other things on his mind. The concierge had texted him that the women he'd ordered were waiting in his villa. Perhaps sex would clear his head.

He couldn't wait to see Annabelle's expression when she realized they were not alone.

Would she run out on him?

Or would she stay?

He needed her to stay. She knew the Santangelo family, so

that made her useful. Perhaps ignoring her was not in his best interest.

What *was* in his best interest?

His mind was filled with raging thoughts of seeing Lucky Santangelo dead. Shot. The bullet hitting her directly in her loud mouth, the mouth that had dared to insult him.

But how to arrange it?

Fouad would not help. Fouad was a sniveling lackey who thought only about himself. It infuriated Armand that after all these years he could not depend on Fouad.

Enough money would buy him the right person to do the deed, but how to find that person? Would the Internet be of any help? No, probably not.

"I said my feet are killing me," Annabelle repeated, wishing he was a little more attentive.

"Take your shoes off," he suggested, stopping for a moment. "Bare feet can be quite sexual."

"Oh no," Annabelle mock-groaned, hoping to get at least a smile out of him. "Don't tell me you have a foot fetish?"

"Would that bother you?" he asked, testing her.

Annabelle thought for a moment, then leaned up against him while she removed her spike heels. Foot fetish or not, she had him in her sights, and this time she was hanging in there.

Armand seized the opportunity to forcefully kiss her, his tongue darting into her mouth while his hand reached down, making its way roughly up her skirt—heading for ground zero.

She was startled but still game. At least he was interested. This was her shot, and this time she had to make sure it worked out, for unfortunately she had big financial problems. After her somewhat scandalous book was published, her father cut her off, so now money was not exactly falling out of the trees, which meant she needed a man like Armand Jordan to support her and give her credibility. Armand had everything she wanted. Money. Power. Status. And when he became the new owner of The Keys, she would have her own personal playground to entertain her friends. What could be better?

"Easy," she whispered as his thick fingers negotiated a passage past her thong and into her pussy, which was not exactly wet and willing. But she could rally.

Armand Jordan was her major catch of the day.

~ ~ ~

Peggy elicited the help of a willing desk clerk, who for fifty bucks was only too happy to escort her on a golf-cart ride to Armand's villa and then let her in with a passkey. For who would suspect that this well-groomed woman—loaded with expensive jewelry— was anything other than the person she claimed to be. She'd told him she was Armand Jordan's mother, and that she had to pick up some important papers from her son's villa. He had no reason to doubt her.

"Should I wait for you?" the desk clerk asked.

"That would be lovely," Peggy replied, not relishing the long walk back to the main hotel. "I'll only be a minute or two."

She entered the villa and was shocked to encounter two women of extremely dubious appearance. They were lolling around on high stools by the bar, drinking cocktails and smoking.

Luscious and Seducta were equally shocked to see Peggy.

"Where is Armand?" were the first words out of Peggy's mouth.

"Who?" questioned Seducta, adjusting her mammoth breasts, which were fighting to escape from a lime-green halter top that was several sizes too small.

Luscious, slightly quicker on the draw, said a fast "He's on his way. Who're you?"

Peggy stood tall, trying to hide her dismay that this was the type of women her son was associating with. These women were certainly not ladies; they resembled cheap street hookers, the kind she'd observed acting the part on *Law & Order*.

"I am Armand's mother," Peggy said grandly, walking toward what she assumed was the bedroom.

"Kinky," Seducta muttered.

"Shh," Luscious admonished in a hoarse whisper. "Wouldn't think the old bag's here to stay."

"Then what've we got ourselves stuck with?" Seducta said, gulping down her cocktail. "Some sexed-out freaky momma's boy?"

Luscious shrugged. She wasn't sure herself.

After a few moments, Peggy emerged from the bedroom and hurried to the door. She'd gotten what she'd come for, and she had no desire to run into Armand, not with these two dreadful women present. Her disgust was so palpable that she didn't even bother saying anything as she slipped out the door. Tomorrow she vowed that she would sit down with Armand and discuss with him his choice of female companions. He might be a grown man, but it was blatantly obvious that it was time someone gave him guidance.

She was his mother.

She was entitled.

CHAPTER FORTY-SIX

"We could hit another club," Kev suggested.

"Why'd we wanna do that?" Billy responded.

"What the fuck's t' matter with you, dude?" Kev asked, squinting. "You're acting like you don't wanna do nothin'."

"Maybe I don't," Billy replied. He simply wasn't feeling it, and the more time he spent with Kev, the more his old friend was getting on his nerves. Some people you eventually outgrew. Kev was one of them.

"This is Vegas, man. Freakin' Vegas!" Kev said, venting his frustration. "Land of pussy an' cream."

"So go get yourself some," Billy suggested. "Me, I'm headin' back to the hotel."

"Why'd you wanna do that?" Kev complained. "We should be out there rippin' up this town, tearing it to shreds."

"Like I said, you're on your own. You don't need me."

"Why not?" Kev said, sensing that a fun evening of debauchery was slipping away from him. "You're a pussy magnet. The girls cream their panties just lookin' at you."

"Thanks, Kev," Billy said grimly. "Exactly the description of my talent I was jonesing to hear."

"It's a freakin' compliment, man," Kev insisted.

"Yeah, yeah. Pussy catnip," Billy said, getting more irritated by the minute. "Just the compliment I was hoping for."

"Don't take it the wrong way," Kev said, finally realizing he was pissing Billy off and that it was time to backpedal.

"What way should I take it, Kev?"

"Okay, okay, I get it. We're on our way back to the hotel."

"You can stay here an' do your thing. It's not like I need an escort."

"Yeah, I think you do. All those bachelorette parties goin' on in the hotel lobby. You need me t' run interference."

Billy's cell buzzed. Turning his back on Kev, he fished it out of his pocket and answered.

"Hey," said Max, sounding very young and very excited. "It's me. What are you *doing* here?"

~ ~ ~

Although Jorge was quite a dancer, after a while Denver could tell he was dying to talk. She was very adept at reading people, and this poor guy seemed so damn desperate, as if he was in way over his head and didn't quite know what to do.

"How long have you and Venus been together?" she asked, not really interested but making conversation anyway.

"Today. Tonight," Jorge said with a helpless shrug. "Not sure about tomorrow."

"Well, if Venus invited you to Vegas with her, then she must really like you," Denver said encouragingly.

"She ignore me," Jorge said glumly. "In front of people, she treat me like pet. Like little dog."

"Oh dear," Denver said sympathetically. "That's not okay."

"She not even introduce me," Jorge complained. "Like I no matter."

"Venus is a big star. I'm sure she doesn't mean it."

"We see," Jorge said resignedly. "I come long way to be in America, to make success here."

Then, whether she wanted to hear it or not, Jorge launched into the story of his life.

Denver realized she was trapped, but at the same time she felt sorry for him, so she remained on the dance floor and listened.

~ ~ ~

Frankie Romano in all his boastful glory was quite a show.

"What up?" he said to Bobby and M.J., happy to see them.

"Same old," M.J. replied, exchanging a quick fist pump with his old friend.

"Hey," Bobby said, repeating the gesture. "Long time no see."

"You two guys, you never change," Frankie said, his left eye twitching. "Son of a bitch! You both smash it out the park. A coupla studs."

"You're looking good too," Bobby offered, although he didn't think so.

"Didja hear?" Frankie said. "I opened my place in L.A. River. Course, it's nothin' like this setup. Mood is spectacular, with

the pool an' the lights an' the view. But you gotta gimme kudos
'cause I finally got my shit together, an' now I'm runnin' my own
club, an' it's flyin'."

Bobby had heard all about River. It was the go-to club for any
drug you desired. Coke, meth, quaaludes, E, weed, pills. Yeah,
sure it was doing okay. L.A. was an easy town in which to acquire customers for your wares. Everyone had their secret little
addictions—some of them not so secret.

Jokingly, Bobby had once suggested to M.J. that they'd be
better off opening up luxury rehab centers than opening clubs.
It seemed celebrities were willing to pay thousands of dollars a
week just to give the impression that they were clean. More
hooking up and illicit pill popping went on in rehab than anywhere else. Then a week out, everyone was back using.

"It's great seein' you guys," Frankie said. "Missed your smilin'
faces."

"Glad to hear you're doing well," Bobby said, keeping it neu-
tral. Just because Frankie was in his club didn't mean they had
to become close buddies again. Those days were over. In a way,
he missed Frankie, but in another way he didn't. Frankie's coke
habit had gotten out of control, and from the looks of him,
scarey-eyed and emaciated, nothing much had changed.

"You here for the fights?" M.J. asked.

"If I can score me some ringside seats," Frankie said. "Any
connections?"

"As a matter of fact," M.J. said, always Mister Nice, "I might
be able to help you out."

"That's my main man," Frankie said, clapping M.J. on the
back. "You always did have your finger on what's goin' down. An'
speakin' of goin' down—you still married?"

"You bet I am," M.J. replied. "Marriage rocks, man."

"How 'bout you, Bobby?" Frankie asked, taking a swig from the glass of vodka he was holding onto. "You still with that little lawyer piece of ass?"

"If you mean Denver," Bobby said, annoyed that Frankie would be so disrespectful, "we're very much together."

"Hey, that's cool. Me, I can never stick with one of 'em for too long. Annabelle was my last big mistake." Another swig of vodka, and a quick glance back at his table to see if he was missing any action. "Right now my thing is movin' on. Lately I'm hangin' with Gerald M.'s daughter, Cookie. You might've seen our pix online. Cookie's young, hot, an' boy, is she ready to *partee*—if you get my drift."

"Max's friend?" Bobby said, aghast. What the hell was Frankie doing with a teenager? Corrupting her, no doubt.

"'S right. But believe me, she's one horny little tamale. On the ride here she was—"

"Gotta go," Bobby said, itching to move on for two reasons. One, he remembered why he and Frankie had ceased hanging out. And two, what was Denver doing out on the dance floor with some random dude? He'd just noticed, and he wasn't pleased.

Screw it. Was she trying to prove something?

If so, it certainly didn't fly.

~ ~ ~

Eddie Falcon wasted no time in making the move over to Bobby's table and concentrating on Venus, which did not sit well with Cassie, who fell into a major sulk. *She* was supposed to be the center of attention. This was *her* night.

Venus was enjoying the attention. Lately she'd been thinking of seeking new representation, and Eddie's timing couldn't be better. She knew of Eddie's reputation, and it was stellar. He was a comer and hungry, the best kind of agent to have working for you.

"I can get you anything you want," Eddie boasted to Venus. "Any*one* you want. Director, star—Clooney, DiCaprio, Depp— you name who you'd like to work with, and I can make it happen."

"Can you, now?" Venus said, not actually falling for it—she'd been in the business too long to believe everything an agent on the make had to say, but she was liking his enthusiasm. Her current representatives were doing nothing for her moviewise, and she was tired of always having to embark on a world tour every time she put out a new CD. With her divorce almost behind her, she was ready to concentrate on her film career, and Eddie Falcon might be just the man to make it happen. Besides, Billy was huge in movies. It was about time she reclaimed her throne.

"What's going on?" Lucky said, inserting herself into the conversation. She'd known Eddie since he'd worked in the mailroom at Panther Studios. He'd always had big ambitions, and she was glad to see he was working it. "Is Eddie promising you the moon?" she asked with an amused grin.

"And the stars," Venus responded with a smile. "Should I believe him?"

"Well," Lucky said, still grinning, "the day you believe a Hollywood agent is the day you should pack your bags and scoot your fine ass out of town."

"Thanks, Lucky," Eddie said. "Nice to have your full support." The three of them laughed.

"Ah, show business." Lucky sighed. "I do not miss it. Not one little bit."

~ ~ ~

"I need your help," Max said, cornering Cookie in the ladies' room, where a crowd of underdressed and over-made-up girls jostled for space at the mirrors. The room was smoke-filled even though smoking was not allowed, and the smell of cheap perfume and musty sweat overpowered everything.

"Can you believe the a-hole, like, hasn't even texted me to find out where I am?" Cookie griped, once again checking her phone. "He probably hasn't even noticed I'm missing. What a douche!"

"I could've told you that," Max said, grabbing Cookie's arm, attempting to get her full attention. "But this is about *me*."

"No," Cookie argued, applying blush. "It's about *me* havin' to put up with a dumb-ass famous freakin' dad who gets everyone fallin' all over him. You are so right about Frankie. He's a major star-fucker."

"Listen, I have to get outta here," Max said, wishing Cookie would concentrate for once. "It's totally urgent."

"Why? Where're we goin?" Cookie asked, guilelessly.

"*We* are not going anywhere, that's the whole point. *I* have to get out of here and, uh, meet someone."

"Someone like who?" Cookie asked, her curiosity finally aroused.

"Someone I don't want Ace to know about."

"Woo-hoo! *Now* it's gettin' interesting," Cookie said, her brown eyes lighting up.

"The thing is," Max continued, "there's no way I can pull it off without your help. So you've got to tell Ace that I got an important call from Lucky, and that I had to take off. Okay?"

"You're kiddin', right?" Cookie said, curling her lip. "Like what makes you think I'm gonna do this for you an' you're not givin' me the lowdown on who you're meetin'?"

"It's just a boy," Max said, feeling desperate.

"What boy?" Cookie demanded. "Who is he? Is he hot? Hotter than Ace?"

"Please do this for me, Cookie," Max said, her voice rising. "Tomorrow I'll tell you everything."

"I dunno—" Cookie started to say.

"Screw you!" Max yelled, suddenly losing it. "I've been doing what you want all evening—so get it together and do this one thing for me. Tell Ace I'll see him back at the hotel later, and don't make it seem shady."

And with that she stormed off, leaving an openmouthed Cookie in her wake.

CHAPTER FORTY-SEVEN

As they reached Armand's villa, Annabelle was more or less sure that tonight she would be able to cement herself firmly into his life. This time she was not letting him slip away; he was too valuable a prospect.

She'd allowed him to finger-fuck her on the walk to his villa, and now it was time for her to exhibit her considerable bedroom skills. When she was living with Frankie Romano, he'd often told her that her blow jobs were superlative—the best he'd ever had. Now she had the opportunity to show off her technique (learned from a gay friend when she was fifteen) to Armand. Men loved nothing better than a woman going down on them. Annabelle knew that they considered it the ultimate power trip—a beautiful woman on her knees servicing them, his hand pressed firmly on her head. It was the best.

She recalled that when she and Frankie were running their call girl business in New York, the girls were always full of outrageous stories about their clients and the things they were into.

Blow jobs were the number one topic. It seemed that once a man got married, the blow jobs ground to a sudden halt. Too bad, because there were always plenty of working girls ready and able to pick up the slack.

These were the thoughts running through Annabelle's head as they entered the villa, but they came to an abrupt halt when she saw the two half-dressed women lounging on stools by the bar.

"Good evening, ladies," Armand said, not at all surprised that he had company.

"Ladies"! Was he kidding? These two were straight off Forty-second Street on a bad night.

"Hello there," Luscious said, greeting the client in what she considered a suitable manner. "Nice t' meet you."

Seducta, who'd imbibed a little too much free vodka, burped discreetly.

Armand gave Annabelle a sly look. The expression on her face was all that he needed to fuel his sexual desire. He walked behind the bar and opened a bottle of champagne. Had to celebrate, for this was about to be an evening to remember. It was his personal celebration of what he knew was destined to happen to Lucky Santangelo.

Eventually.

It was a done deal.

All he had to do was arrange it.

~ ~ ~

The phone rang in Peggy's suite. She immediately thought it was the messenger service she'd ordered to transport her samples to the DNA testing lab, which, for a price, had agreed to work on a weekend, enabling her to get fast results. Only in Vegas.

However, it was not the messenger service, it was Paige Santangelo.

"I wanted to make sure you got back to your room safely," Paige said, her voice husky and intimate.

"I did," Peggy replied. "And thank you so much for a delightful dinner."

"I'm glad you were able to join us," Paige said. "It's always nice to have new company. Spending time with Gino can sometimes be . . . difficult."

"Difficult how?"

"Gino is old, he's set in his ways. When he was younger he was quite a dynamo."

Oh yes, I know! Peggy thought.

"Anyway," Paige continued with a deep sigh, "Gino's not the man he used to be—if you understand where I'm going."

Where are you going? Peggy wondered.

"Can I be frank?" Paige said after a long pause.

"Certainly," Peggy replied, wondering if the messenger was on his way.

"The sad fact of life is that sexually, Gino no longer satisfies me."

And here it comes, Peggy thought. *She's been heading in this direction all night, and I was too preoccupied to get it.*

"I see," Peggy said calmly.

"Do you?" Paige asked, sounding anxious.

"Do I what?"

"Do you understand that I have needs that are not being fulfilled? I'm getting the feeling that you might be in the same position."

Peggy realized that she was being propositioned, and although it was not by a man, it was flattering all the same. Her sex life had been dead on arrival since Sidney's passing, so what would be wrong with indulging in a little Sapphic lovemaking? It wasn't as if she hadn't experienced another woman before, albeit a long time ago—during her fantasy life in the king's palace. Paige might be older, but so was she. And they were both attractive, well-preserved women.

"Your silence is making me uneasy," Paige said. "So why don't we forget I said anything. I will—"

"No," Peggy interrupted, a sudden recklessness flooding her senses. "I . . . I understand exactly what you're saying." She paused. "If you care to drop by for a nightcap, I would be delighted to see you."

~ ~ ~

"I didn't know you were expecting company," Annabelle said, pointedly waving a stream of smoke away from her face as Seducta blew a series of smoke rings into the air.

"These women are not company," Armand replied, drinking champagne. "They are paid-for whores, here to entertain us. They will do whatever we want. Does that excite you, Annabelle?"

She thought for a moment, realizing that she was heading onto dangerous ground. This was not what she'd expected, not at all. However, if she planned on nailing Armand, it seemed as if she would have to join the party or make a fast exit.

"'Scuse me," Luscious said, hopping off her bar stool with an indignant expression. "We're paid for, but that don't mean you gotta ignore us. We're people too . . ."

"Take your clothes off and keep your mouths shut," Armand ordered. "Do it now."

And without waiting for a reply, he turned to Annabelle and once again stuck his hand roughly up her skirt.

She automatically pushed his hand away. This was all happening too fast.

"More champagne, please," she said, trying to appear cool in the face of such disturbing circumstances.

"I'll offer you better than that," he said, marching into the bedroom and returning with several small glassine bags of cocaine.

"Shall we?" he said, walking toward the glass-topped coffee table.

Damn! Annabelle thought. *Another Frankie Romano scene. I sure can pick 'em.*

Meanwhile, the two hookers were disrobing in a desultory fashion across the room, flinging their clothes in a corner until they were bare-assed naked except for their shoes. Then they hovered, waiting for instructions.

By this time Armand was alternating swigging champagne and snorting lines, feeling no pain, feeling as if he could take control of the entire world. And he would. When he'd disposed of Lucky Santangelo, there would be no one to stop him.

On his alcohol- and cocaine-fueled high, Armand was becoming more and more determined that Lucky had to be . . . what was the word that lingered in his mind? Ah yes—*assassinated.*

The word thrilled him; it revolved in his brain like a mantra. The whore bitch deserved to die. And he would be the one to make it happen.

If they were in Akramshar he could arrange to have her stoned to death. Buried in the ground up to her neck while big jagged rocks were thrown at her until she died a painful and slow death. Unfortunately, that wasn't possible in America. What a shame, because Lucky Santangelo was the slut whore of all women. She deserved many punishments.

Lucky was his dear mother pushing her breasts up against him when he was a child, before beating him with a leather strap while her friends looked on.

Lucky was all the whores he'd ever had sex with, the dirty, filthy, disgusting, money-hungry whores.

Lucky was his dumb wife, who'd given birth to children he'd never wanted.

Oh yes, Lucky Santangelo was the woman who deserved to be punished for all of them.

It was only fitting.

And when she was gone, The Keys would be all his, and life would finally be perfect.

CHAPTER FORTY-EIGHT

The moment Lucky spotted Alex entering the club with an attractive Asian girl on his arm was the moment she decided it was time for her and Lennie to split. By this late hour she knew that Alex would've had quite a few drinks, and when Alex had been drinking, anything could happen, so she figured it was wise to get out while the going was good.

But Lennie had other ideas. He wanted to stay.

Lucky knew better than to try to change his mind. Like herself, Lennie did what he wanted, and he wouldn't budge until he was ready to leave.

He and Alex had an edgy relationship filled with macho posturing, for not only did they both have a thing for Lucky, but they were both director/producer/writers. Not that they were in competition with each other. Lennie made low-budget independent movies, while Alex went the studio route and put together big, high-profile movies—usually controversial and generally critically savaged or acclaimed, depending on the critic. The fact that they both did the same thing always made it interesting. They argued all the time, about other people's movies, politics, books, sports—anything they could think of.

Lennie was well aware of how Alex felt about his wife, but he did not possess the knowledge that once—long ago, during the time he'd been kidnapped and Lucky had thought he was dead—she'd actually slept with Alex. One time. One time only. Alex had never forgotten their one night together. Lucky had tried to put it behind her. In her mind, it was a regrettable mistake.

"There you all are," Alex said, walking straight over to their cabana, the pretty Asian girl trotting behind him. "Can we join?"

"Sit right down," Lennie said, making a magnanimous gesture. "Room for everyone."

~ ~ ~

Prowling around the edge of the dance floor, Bobby was experiencing an emotion that was new to him. Jealousy. He was actually jealous! He could hardly believe it himself. There was Denver, the woman he loved—the woman who professed to love him—and she was dancing closely with another man. A handsome and muscular man.

The deejay was playing some kind of slow smoochy sound, and the dude on the dance floor was taking full advantage. He had Denver pulled in close, and it looked like she was enjoying it.

Fuck it! Bobby was livid. He hit the deejay stand in a hurry.

"What's this slow-assed shit you're playing?" he demanded. "Change it to something fast, now! You're turning this place into a morgue!"

Startled, the deejay switched to Pitbull, and Bobby nodded his approval. He glanced over at the dance floor to watch them separate, but they didn't.

What the fuck? Was the dude deaf? He still had Denver pulled in close, and she was making no move to get away.

Bobby felt a jealous burn he'd never felt before, and he didn't like it. The burn was mixed with a slow-rising anger, an anger that was telling him to do something. But what? He'd never found himself in this position before. Ever since he could remember, girls were always fighting over him. Girls in high school, girls in Greece (where he'd spent the summers with his father's family), girls in college, girls in clubs. Girls, girls, girls. Bobby Santangelo Stanislopoulos. He was always the prize, always the guy they wanted.

So no, he had never actually found himself in this position, and it was a pisser.

He circled the floor, hoping that Denver would notice him. But she didn't, because the dude she was dancing with was talking into her ear while pressing up against her. Meanwhile, everyone else on the floor had split apart.

"What's up, Bobby?" Gia asked, appearing beside him. Sexy Gia, with whom he'd once spent several memorable nights.

"Nothing much," he said.

Gia got it immediately. "Your girlfriend looks like she's having a good time," she murmured with a spiteful gleam in her eye. "Who's the guy? He's cute."

Bobby narrowed his eyes. "Do you know him?" he asked.

"No," Gia replied with a low laugh. "But I'd like to."

In a fit of pure frustration, Bobby took Gia's arm and pulled her onto the dance floor.

Let's see how Denver would like *this* turn of events.

~ ~ ~

Max took a cab to the Cavendish, where Billy had informed her he was staying in one of the high-roller villas. Of course he was—he was a movie star, and movie stars always scored the best accommodations.

She was beyond excited. Billy had come to Vegas especially to see her, and after the gloom and despondency she'd been feeling about their short time together, this was totally unexpected and more than awesome. She couldn't have wished for a better present.

Billy Melina is my birthday present, she thought. *He flew to Vegas just for me.*

OH . . . MY . . . GOD!

Then she remembered that Ace had also made the trek to Vegas to see her, and she started feeling pretty guilty about the way she was treating him. Ace was a cool guy.

But Billy was cooler.

Shivering at the thought of seeing him again, she wished she'd worn a better outfit. She had on leggings, high boots, a cut-off top, and a slouchy sweater. Cute enough, but nothing spectacular.

Thank God Billy hadn't booked into The Keys. Awkward. She could just imagine Lucky's face if she spotted her darling daughter with the soon-to-be ex of her best friend. Even more awkward, Venus was in town and was obviously going to be at Max's birthday party.

Max felt a twinge of guilt, but only a twinge. It wasn't as if she had come between Billy and Venus. Their divorce was well under way when she and Billy got together.

After the cab dropped her off at the front of the hotel, she made her way through the casino and out the back to the leafy paths that led to the villas.

Billy had sounded totally psyched to hear from her, and if he was telling the truth, he'd come to Vegas only to see her. How great was that?

Okay, Billy, I'm on my way! she thought, and once again she shivered with anticipation.

~ ~ ~

Frankie did a line or two with Gerald M. in the men's room. They were bonding big-time.

Frankie had no idea where Cookie was, but he figured she was off doing her thing somewhere, and that didn't bother him because he'd already got what he'd wanted out of the relationship—a strong connection with her famous father. He liked Gerald M. The man was a star, and even better, he acted like one.

If Frankie had to make a choice, it would be daddy every time—girls were crawling all over Gerald M. Pretty girls, sexy girls, girls willing to do anything to get up close and personal.

Cookie was cute, but if he really thought about it, she was just a kid, and he was way out of her league.

He was Frankie Romano, after all. He had to reach higher.

~ ~ ~

Jorge had almost finished his stories of woe—an impoverished childhood, a lack of any adult supervision, begging for food, robbing tourists, sleeping with tourists, and finally his arrival in America and his meeting with Venus.

"She use me," he said vehemently, his handsome face darkening. "I know that."

How about you're using her too, Denver wanted to say. But she didn't, because the more Jorge talked, the more upset he seemed to get.

"Look," Jorge said, gesturing toward their table. "She ignore me. She treat me like ship."

"Shit," Denver murmured, correcting him while thinking that it was time to find Bobby and leave, as he'd promised they would as soon as he'd finished taking care of whatever it was he had to take care of.

Then she spotted him dancing with Gia, and she was rendered speechless.

First of all, Bobby was actually dancing! And not very well at that. Second, why was he on the dance floor with a girl who he'd admitted was one of his exes?

This was unacceptable.

"Excuse me," she said, hurriedly breaking away from Jorge. "There's something I have to deal with."

"I come too?" Jorge asked, a look of dependence in his puppy-dog eyes.

"No," Denver said. "You go back to Venus. I'm sure she misses you."

And she headed toward Bobby and Gia, a determined look on her face.

CHAPTER FORTY-NINE

When Paige knocked on the door to her suite, Peggy couldn't help feeling slightly anxious. Was Paige simply there to talk? Or were matters of sexual gratification on her mind?

Either way, Peggy had decided she would go with it. Why not? She was lonely. She hadn't had sex since Sidney's demise, and she wasn't getting any younger. She also had a son who obviously consorted with prostitutes, a lackluster social life, and no male partners. Besides, she'd never forgotten the softness of the women's lips when they'd exchanged kisses and more in the sanctuary of the king's harem. It was a fond memory.

Although it was late, Paige had changed outfits, and instead of the pale-blue cocktail dress she'd worn earlier, she was clad in leather pants, a black turtleneck, and a brown leather jacket. With her lack of height, pocket Venus body, and cropped copper hair, from a distance she could almost be mistaken for a male. It was obvious Paige was into this. Peggy felt like a novice, and yet at the same time extremely feminine.

She fixed Paige a drink, and they sat on the couch, where Paige proceeded to tell her the story of the time Gino had walked in on her pleasuring his previous wife, Susan Martino. And how, after that, threesomes were quite the norm.

"Gino used to be an amazing lover," Paige confided. Then she gave Peggy a penetrating look and added, "But you already know that, don't you?"

Peggy felt a blush rise on her cheeks. So Gino *had* remembered. "I . . . I didn't think he would recall that night so long ago," she said. "It was only one time, but yes, I have to admit—he *was* an amazing lover."

"Gino might be old, but he has a steel-trap memory," Paige said, toying with a gold bracelet. "As soon as he saw you, he knew."

"That wasn't why I introduced myself to you," Peggy quickly explained. "It was pure coincidence that it turned out you were married to Gino."

"I'm sure," Paige replied. "But what does it matter? It brought you and me together, and here we are, cozy and alone with no one to bother us."

"Doesn't Gino mind?"

"Gino doesn't know. I tucked him up in bed with a couple of Ambien, and he'll sleep through until morning."

"Oh," Peggy responded as Paige leaned toward her and touched her lightly on the cheek. "Then I guess—"

"You guessed right," Paige purred, her hands moving toward Peggy's still very nice breasts.

Peggy closed her eyes and thought of how pleasant it was to once again be the object of someone's desire.

~ ~ ~

Luscious was getting fed up. The dude with the snake eyes and snotty attitude might be paying them a shitload of money, but what was the deal leaving them shivering and naked in the corner while he drank champagne and snorted lines with the girl she'd seen on TV a couple of times? What was that?

The only good thing about it was that she'd had the opportunity to check out Seducta's body—the body she figured Randy might possibly be lusting after. Seducta's tits were ridiculous.

Luscious couldn't help smirking to herself. Why would Randy want to go with that when he had her to come home to? She might not have giant fake tits, but at least hers were the real thing.

Although she would never admit it, Luscious was mad that Seducta had gotten Mikey to marry her. She'd been with Randy for almost a year, and he'd never mentioned the word *marriage*. She waited on him hand and foot, never nagged him, and sucked his dick whenever he wanted. Goddammit, Luscious considered herself the perfect girlfriend.

She glanced over at Seducta, who'd now gotten several miniature bottles of scotch from behind the bar and was going through them at an alarming rate.

Drunken twat. Luscious preferred to stay sober, just in case. A girl never knew when a john could go postal and beat the crap out of her. It had happened to her once, and she carried the scars to prove it. Some old rocker dude with a penchant for girls crapping on his face had beaten her up when she'd refused to do what he'd wanted. She'd ended up in the emergency room getting sixteen stitches under her chin, and several on her forehead. Ever since then she'd worn bangs and plenty of makeup so no one noticed, but she knew the scars were there, and that was enough for her to make sure she stayed alert.

She took another quick peek at the john, still hunched over the coffee table snorting coke with his girlfriend—although the girlfriend didn't seem to be as into it as he was. The girlfriend was definitely hanging back.

Luscious felt like laughing out loud. These rich assholes with their delicate little coke habits didn't know dog shit. The real thrill and a way quicker high was smoking crack cocaine. Yeah. That was the shit, and Luscious should know, for she'd been doing it on and off since she was sixteen.

Randy, on the other hand, was into speedballs; he swore they gave him the best high ever. A line of coke followed by a powerful snort of heroin—Randy called it his dream combination, and it certainly put him in a euphoric state.

Luscious had tried it a couple of times. It frightened her, so she was canny enough to stick to the drug she was used to.

Speedballing led her to another planet.

Planet out-of-your-fucking-mind.

~ ~ ~

"Not for me, thank you," Annabelle said politely as Armand laid out even more lines. She was not a coke freak like Frankie Romano, who'd become so totally dependant on it that it had put her off him. "I would prefer another glass of champagne."

"You would, would you?" Armand replied, slurring his words slightly.

"If it's not a problem," Annabelle said, getting the distinct feeling that maybe Armand wasn't the man of her dreams after all. This entire situation was surreal. The naked hookers in the corner. The mounds of cocaine on the table. Eddie Falcon might have cheated on her, but as far as she could tell, he wasn't into prostitutes and drugs.

She wondered where Eddie was. They'd had a knock-down, drag-out fight and she'd walked out on him, but there was nothing to stop her from walking right back in. It wasn't too late.

Armand was making no move to pour her another glass of Cristal. She could tell the hookers were getting restless, especially the little one with the bad dye job and various tattoos on her skinny body. Where on Earth had Armand found these two freaks? And what were his plans for them?

Annabelle made a quick decision: whatever his plans, she did not wish to be included. A fast exit was in her future.

"Excuse me," she said, getting up. "Just using the little girls' room."

As she walked by the two hookers, she attempted to avert her eyes. But she knew they were staring at her, checking her out, wondering what the scene was.

Her skin crawled.

She made it to the bathroom, locked the door, took out her cell, and called Eddie. Fortunately, he picked up, although she could barely hear him, as there was a cacophony of noise in the background.

"Where are you?" she asked.

"You calmed down yet?" he questioned.

"Have *you*?" she countered.

"I'm at Mood with an interesting group," he said. "You wanna join me?"

"You know what, I think I do," she replied, relieved that he didn't seem to be holding a grudge. She'd yelled some vile names at him, but that's what she liked about Eddie, he was basically a smart guy with a red-hot future. If she could wean him off cheating, they might make it as a couple. "I'll be there soon."

Back in the living room, Armand had finally decided to utilize the services of the two prostitutes. They were not exactly what he'd required—not the usual high-end call girls he was used to—but he was too drunk and coked-out to care.

"The whores are going to dance for us," he announced to Annabelle, patting a place beside him on the couch. "That's before I fuck the life out of them."

Wonderful, Annabelle thought, perching on the edge. *This is exactly where I don't want to be.*

Armand raised his arm, snapping his fingers at Luscious and Seducta. "Over here," he commanded. "Now!"

CHAPTER FIFTY

There were times Denver discovered a boldness within her that usually only came out when she was in full control in the courtroom, a place she loved to be. She considered herself a low-key kind of girl, not prone to outbursts of any kind. However, the sight of Bobby dancing with a vaguely triumphant Gia was enough to spur her into action. After dumping Jorge—who was getting on her nerves anyway—she made it over to Bobby, who pretended not to see her approaching.

"Hey," she said, tapping Bobby firmly on the shoulder. "I thought we were leaving."

"Yeah," he answered, barely looking at her. "We will. Just catching up with Gia. See you back at the table."

"Really?" Denver said coolly. "Is that what you'd like me to do? Go back to the table?"

"Sure, hon," he said, determined not to fold. "Maybe your, uh, friend'll walk you there."

"Friend?" she questioned.

"The dude you were locked on the dance floor with all night."

Oh wow, so that's what this is all about. How dumb.

"I guess you must mean Venus's sad-sack boyfriend," she said sharply.

"I don't give a fuck who he is," Bobby responded, completely out of character for him. "You were with him all night."

Gia, in all her Victoria's Secret sexiness, tugged on Bobby's arm and said, "Are we dancing or not?"

Bobby was torn. Should he stay on the dance floor with Gia, or show Denver that she couldn't get away with dissing him?

Before he could decide, Denver took off.

Shit! He'd called the wrong shot. Denver wasn't into playing games; he should've known that.

~ ~ ~

Ace was not happy about Max running out on him, and Cookie wasn't happy being the one who had to tell him. She was also livid that Frankie had made no attempt to contact her. He was probably so far up her daddy's ass that there was no room for thought. What a major dick. She should've listened to Max.

As soon as she gave Ace the bad news, he told her he was leaving.

"Where're you goin'?" she asked, thinking that it might be a good idea to tag along.

Ace shrugged. He wasn't in the mood for company, especially Cookie's. "I'm taking a walk," he said shortly.

Cookie nodded. Walking wasn't her thing. "See you back at the hotel, then," she called after him as he strode away.

"Yeah," Ace said over his shoulder. "Later."

Cookie wondered who Max was hooking up with. It had to be someone special for her to dump Ace in such a brutal way. After

"I like your girlfriend," Lennie remarked when Bobby finally returned to the table. "She's a smart one, and beautiful too. You should hang on to her. How come I haven't met her before?"

"Could be 'cause you're always away on location," Bobby replied, checking the group out and not seeing Denver. Where was she now? The dude she'd been dancing with was sitting beside Venus, who seemed more interested in talking to Eddie Falcon. "Uh . . . have you seen her?" Bobby said to Lennie, his eyes still searching.

"You're asking *me?*" Lennie said, raising a caustic eyebrow. "She's *your* girlfriend. Gotta keep tabs on this one. She's a keeper."

"*Who's* his girlfriend?" Lucky inquired, leaning over Alex, who'd decided to sit himself down right next to her.

"The smart one," Lennie said. "She gets my seal of approval. How about you?"

"Whatever Bobby wants, Bobby gets," Lucky said with a warm smile at her son.

"Just like you, Lucky," Alex said, nursing a large tumbler of scotch.

"And you know that, do you?" Lennie retorted, putting a proprietary arm around Lucky's shoulder.

"I know it 'cause we're best friends," Alex said, refusing to back down.

Here we go, Lucky thought. *The two bulls are about to go at it. Why couldn't we have left when I wanted to?*

"Y'know, Alex, you're so full of crap," Lennie said. "What makes you think Lucky's your best friend?"

"Does it bother you?" Alex taunted. "Make you anxious that while you're away—"

Lucky stood up. "Both of you, shut the fuck up," she said, her tone brooking no argument. "What's wrong with you, Alex? I told you earlier, you're out of line, so zip it with the childish comments. I gave up having best friends in seventh grade."

Alex scowled and turned to the Asian girl sitting on his other side.

Lennie looked amused.

Bobby left the table, deciding that Denver must be in the ladies' room.

"Can we go now?" Lucky asked, turning to Lennie. "I think this evening has just about peaked."

"You do?" Lennie said calmly. "'Cause I think it's only just beginning."

Damn Lennie. He could be the most stubborn man on the planet. And maybe that's why she loved him so much, because he never jumped at her command.

Well, if he was set on getting into it with Alex, that was his problem.

Lennie could be infuriating, but Lucky knew that she wouldn't want him any other way.

CHAPTER FIFTY-ONE

"Dance," Armand commanded, glaring with unfocused eyes at the two naked creatures who stood before him. The images he had of them were not quite clear.

Were these two what he'd ordered? He vaguely remembered requesting big breasts, but this fat sow was not up to the usual standard of girls Yvonne Le Crane sent over, nor was the thin one.

It didn't matter. Putting Annabelle together with these two would be enough to amuse him; they were only whores, after all. And when he had them all exactly where he wanted them, perhaps he'd join the party.

Right now his mind was taking him on a trip. He was imagining ejaculating all over Annabelle's pert face. He'd pretend she was Lucky Santangelo and defile her in every possible way he could think of. Then he'd make the whores defile her too.

Yes, he'd do all the things to Annabelle that he really wanted to do to Lucky Santangelo, the whore bitch of them all. He'd fuck them over until they begged for mercy.

It was their destiny.

It was his destiny too.

After all, he was Prince Armand Mohamed Jordan, soon to be king of Akramshar. No woman would ever disrespect him again. THEY WOULDN'T DARE!

Armand had his plans, and he was sticking with them.

~ ~ ~

Luscious did not appreciate the john barking orders at them like they were his slaves. They were performing a service, so surely he should treat them better. But he was a man, and early on she'd learned that all men were pigs—there were simply different degrees of piggery.

Seducta didn't give a damn, because by the time Armand summoned them she was so drunk that she couldn't care less how she was treated as long as she got her money at the end of the gig. Dirty Den had informed them that he would hold on to their money until the job was completed, which was okay with Luscious. That way they wouldn't have to wrangle it out of the client, and maybe the john would hand over a fat tip when he was finished with them, which she hoped would be soon, because they'd already been there for over an hour, and it was almost midnight.

She wondered what Randy was doing. At least he wasn't getting the opportunity to go chasing after Seducta and her giant tits. A drunken Seducta was safely here with her, and boy, could she put it away. Luscious hadn't realized what a lush Seducta was. It sort of gave her a stab of satisfaction to know that *she* was the sober one, she was the one in charge.

"We gotta have music if you want us t' dance," she said to Armand, determined to move this show along.

He grunted.

Without waiting for permission, she went over to the music system and activated the sound. Loud sound. Eminem and Rihanna together on "Love the Way You Lie."

Oh yeah, her kind of song. She admired the way the sexy singer who'd gotten herself beaten up had bitch-slapped Chris Brown with this track. It fuckin' rocked.

Seducta was standing in front of Armand and Annabelle like a dumb sack of shit, gazing longingly at the mounds of coke.

"You want some of this?" Armand offered, his bloodshot eyes raking her over. "You want some, come and get it."

Seducta didn't need asking twice. She rushed forward and knelt on the other side of the coffee table to take a snort, and before she knew it, Armand was on his feet, his hand was on the back of her head, and he was shoving her face down onto the table and into the white powder.

Instinctively, Luscious jumped forward and pushed him off her. He spun around and slapped her hard across the cheek.

Seducta surfaced, spluttering and choking, her face a mess of white powder.

"You bastard!" Luscious yelled. "You could've suffocated her."

Armand laughed, an evil laugh. He felt powerful and invincible. He *was* powerful and invincible.

"I'm ready now," he said, sitting back down. "Dance for me, ladies, before I'm forced to punish you even more."

~ ~ ~

Annabelle watched what was going on in horrified silence. She was shocked by Armand's behavior. He was a crazy man, and there was no doubt in her mind that she had to get the hell out.

Fast. Armand Jordan was a definite sicko, and things could only get worse.

It occurred to her that she should've escaped on her first trip to the bathroom, but something had held her back. She'd honestly thought that since he was with her, he would have sent the two women away, but it hadn't happened.

Now he was manhandling them, and forcing them to dance.

It was a horrible, disgusting scene. She wanted out. She wanted to get back with Eddie.

~ ~ ~

To go or stay? That was the quandary Luscious found herself faced with. Her cheek stung where the john had slapped her, and Seducta was a sloppy mess. But the money was too good to risk getting stiffed. Dirty Den might have to give it back if they ran out on this jerk. So since he seemed to have settled back on the couch, Luscious reluctantly started with a few lackluster stripper moves, encouraging Seducta to do the same.

Suddenly his girlfriend rose to her feet, mumbled something about having left her phone in the bathroom, and hurried past them.

Luscious had a hunch that she wasn't coming back, and Luscious's hunches never let her down. At the age of fifteen, while she was blowing a preacher, he'd stopped her mid-blow and informed her she had psychic powers and that what she was doing to him was God's work. "You must visit me every day," he'd insisted. "It is God's will."

So she'd done so, until eventually he'd moved away.

To this day she still believed in her psychic abilities. After all, wasn't it her who'd told Randy he was going to do better this year? And sure enough, Mikey had given him a job. Okay, so delivering drugs wasn't the greatest job in the world, but it was a whole lot better than the lowdown crap he'd been into before.

Yes, she was definitely psychic, and if she knew anything at all, it was that the stuck-up bitch wasn't coming back.

~ ~ ~

After rushing past the dancing hookers, Annabelle made it into the bathroom, where she quickly locked the door and leaned against it, catching her breath. What a nightmare scene. She had to get out now.

Earlier, she'd noticed a large window above the Jacuzzi tub, and rather than get into a fight with Armand—for she suspected that if she told him she was leaving, he would not let her go quietly—she decided the window was the perfect way out.

Removing her high heels and stuffing them in her purse, she gingerly stepped into the tub, and from there she scrambled onto the surrounding marble ledge, opened the window, and, since it was higher than she'd anticipated, tumbled out onto the damp grass outside and into an arrangement of small palms.

Cursing softly to herself, she jumped up, got herself together, and set off down the path toward the main hotel.

The thought of getting back together with Eddie Falcon was looking more appealing every minute.

~ ~ ~

Unable to sleep, Fouad tried, but the tossing and turning would not allow him to fall into a peaceful slumber. He realized that he was so used to being at Armand's beck and call that not hearing from him for at least twelve hours was disturbing.

Armand's words kept playing in his head: *I will see Lucky Santangelo die before she gets the better of me.*

Empty threats, of course, but Armand was definitely veering out of control with his excessive drug use. An intervention was needed, and it had to happen soon.

Then it came to Fouad. He decided that in the morning he would tell Armand's mother everything: the drugs, the prostitutes. He might even tell her about Armand's family in Akramshar, although he knew if he did that, Armand would never speak to him again.

Perhaps it was wise just to inform her about the drugs. Not too much information all at once.

Armand Jordan desperately needed help, and as far as Fouad was concerned, Peggy was the only person he would listen to.

Now Fouad could sleep, for with tomorrow would come the solution.

CHAPTER FIFTY-TWO

Annabelle Maestro was the last person Max expected to run into as she made her way down the leafy pathway heading to Billy's private villa.

Annabelle seemed equally taken aback to see her.

They both stopped, both tried to think of a quick excuse as to why they were there at midnight.

"Hi," Annabelle said at last.

"Uh . . . hi," Max said, thinking that Annabelle did not look like her usually sleek self. She was somewhat disheveled, and for some unknown reason she was carrying her shoes.

"Aren't you at the wrong hotel?" Annabelle asked. "Isn't The Keys where you should be?"

"Just, uh, visiting friends," Max said vaguely.

"Me too," Annabelle replied, equally vague.

"Why are you barefoot?"

"'Cause my shoes are killing me."

"Oh yes, I know the feeling."

There was an awkward pause.

"You've got a birthday coming up," Annabelle remarked. "That's exciting."

"Tomorrow, actually."

"Happy birthday."

"Thanks."

"I hear Lucky's throwing you a big party."

"That's right," Max said, wondering if Annabelle was fishing for an invite, because if she was it couldn't happen on account of Cookie being with Annabelle's ex now.

"How nice," Annabelle said.

"It is," Max agreed.

"Well, uh, have a good one."

"You too."

They both scuttled off in different directions, happy to make their respective escapes.

~ ~ ~

After waiting around outside the ladies' room for a good ten minutes, Bobby tracked down M.J. and told him he was leaving.

"What happened to Denver?" M.J. asked.

"Think she's mad at me. She took off."

"Don't tell me the great Bobby S. got himself dumped," M.J. said, laughing. "Finally! There is a God!"

"Go fuck yourself," Bobby said, shaking his head. "She's probably waiting for me in the room."

"You hope."

"I *know,* man. She's got nowhere else to go."

"She could hop a plane back to L.A. Denver's not one to put up with your crap."

"What crap?"

"Half the club saw you dancing with Gia. She's on the cover of *Sports Illustrated*; she's kinda high-profile."

"C'mon, man, it was nothing."

"Yeah, tell *that* to your girlfriend."

Bobby hurried from the club and out into the main hotel, where he took the private elevator up to their floor.

To his chagrin, their room was empty. No Denver. But the good news was, her clothes were still there, along with her laptop and her phone. It was no wonder he'd never got an answer when he'd tried to reach her on her cell.

Dammit! Was she going to make him sit and wait for her?

Apparently so.

~ ~ ~

Grabbing a cab outside the Cavendish, Annabelle set off for The Keys. She couldn't believe what she'd almost got herself into. Drunken dancing hookers. An excessive amount of cocaine. A crazy sex fiend with cold, hard eyes and a definite cruel streak. What was she thinking?

Oh yeah, right. She was thinking that Armand Jordan might be the catch of the day. How wrong she'd been about *that*.

Then on top of everything else, she'd run into Lucky's daughter. Where was Max going at such a late hour?

Not her concern.

After paying off the cab, she entered The Keys and headed straight for the ladies' room, where she attempted to clean herself up. Her white Chanel skirt had a few streaks of mud on it, and she realized she should've stopped off and changed. Too late now. She didn't want to miss meeting up with Eddie, so after touching up her makeup and brushing her hair, she headed for Mood.

Armand Jordan was just a distant creepy memory.

~ ~ ~

Lennie and Alex were embroiled in one of their favorite arguments—about the death penalty. Alex was for it, Lennie against, and neither of them was prepared to give an inch. Lucky had heard it all before, and since she wasn't prepared to take sides, she moved over to sit with Venus, Eddie, M.J., and Cassie. Jorge was perched uncomfortably at the end of the table.

"So *that's* your little plaything," Lucky observed, checking out Jorge.

"Not so little," Venus replied with a wicked grin.

"You do know you're ignoring him."

"He'll get plenty of attention later," Venus said, fluffing out her platinum hair. "Besides, Bobby's girlfriend was entertaining him."

"She was?" Lucky said, surprised. "How did Bobby feel about *that?*"

"How would *I* know? *You're* his mother. And if you weren't, believe me, he'd be next on my list of things I have to do."

"Calm down, he's way too young for you," Lucky said with a low chuckle.

"Sorry to disappoint, only the way I'm going, Bobby is exactly the right age."

"Yes, I seem to remember that you've always had a crush on him."

"This is true," Venus confessed with an unabashed grin.

"At least you admit it."

"And *you* have to admit that your son is one hot catch."

Lucky nodded. "You got that right, which is why he has to be careful to avoid any girls who happen to be on the make. He's rich, he's handsome, and he's available. What do you think of Denver?"

"Didn't get a chance to talk to her."

"She seems to be making Bobby happy," Lucky mused. "I think I might like her."

"How nice," Venus drawled. "Maybe they'll get married and give you a bunch of sweet little grandbabies."

"Get the fuck outta here," Lucky said good-naturedly. "Bobby's got a lot of living to do before he even *thinks* about settling down."

"Ohhh . . . Momma Bear's *veree* protective," Venus said, laughing, before adding a succinct "And here comes trouble."

Lucky glanced up to observe Annabelle Maestro approaching their table. They all knew Annabelle from her days with Frankie, her famous parents, and her very public confessional book.

"Remember what the late great Andy Warhol said about fifteen minutes of fame?" Venus remarked, slowing sipping a cocktail. "Well, this one is milking it for the number one prize. I feel sorry for her father."

"You feel sorry for Ralph Maestro?" Lucky said, aghast. "Why would you feel sorry for him? He murdered his wife, for God's sake. He should be sitting in jail alongside O.J."

"He *arranged* her murder," Venus pointed out. "It's not the same."

"Damn!" Lucky said, shaking her head in amazement. "You should go sit with Lennie. The two of you can discuss the advantages of having murderers walk the streets. What fun you can have."

"Excuse me, everyone," Eddie said, standing up as Annabelle arrived at the table. "I'd like you all to meet my girlfriend, Annabelle Maestro."

~ ~ ~

"Hey," Billy said.

"Hey," Max responded, standing at the door to his villa, feeling a tad shy.

Loud music was blaring from the villa across from them, a lizard darted in front of her, and there was a brisk night breeze. She shivered, Billy smiled, and all was well in Max's world.

"Can I get a hug?" he said, his intense blue eyes drawing her in.

You can get anything you want, Billy Melina.

"Of course you can," she said, falling into his arms, immediately forgetting how much she'd been hating him.

He hugged her, then led her inside. "Someone's having a party over there," he remarked.

"Sounds like it," she said, breathless at the sight of him.

He shut the door and they stared at each other.

"Sorry about L.A.," he said at last.

"What about it?" she said, keeping it casual.

"Well, y'know," he explained. "I kinda let you get away."

"From what?" she asked, going for the flippant approach.

"Then you took off."

"I told you I was coming to Vegas."

"Why d'you think I'm here?"

"Really? Just to see me?"

"Yeah, really." And he moved in for a kiss that dispelled any doubt that she was doing the right thing.

~ ~ ~

"We're going," Venus announced, standing up and signaling Jorge that it was time to leave. He had a resentful scowl on his boyishly handsome face. She'd ignored him all night, and now she was summoning him to come with her like a pet dog.

He got up anyway, and stood stiffly beside her. He had no alternative.

"I'll be in touch," Eddie said to Venus, jumping to his feet and bowing and scraping a little. Landing Venus as a client would be a huge coup. "We can do great things together."

"I'm sure," Venus murmured. "All you have to do is prove it to me."

"I can do that, all right," Eddie said with a boastful smirk. "You won't be disappointed."

"We'll talk."

"We certainly will."

He sat back down, a satisfied expression on his face.

"Did you just poach Venus from her agent?" Annabelle asked, quite impressed.

"Not yet, but I will," Eddie said, full of confidence, and quite unaware of where his girlfriend had spent the last few hours.

"Congrats," Annabelle said. "I'm proud of you."

"That's a change from calling me a cheating asshole."

"You know I didn't mean it."

"How about I get that in writing?"

"Spoken like a true agent," she giggled.

God! she thought. *It's so nice to be back among normal people.*

She turned to Lucky. "I understand I should be congratulating you too," she said, delighted to have the opportunity to hang out with Lucky Santangelo.

"Why's that?" Lucky asked, looking around to see where Bobby was.

Annabelle lowered her voice. "I know it's supposed to be a big secret and all, but I heard that you're selling The Keys."

"*Excuse* me?" Lucky said, startled.

"Please don't worry. I won't say a word."

"I'm not worried, I'm confused. Who told you this?"

Annabelle glanced quickly at Eddie. He was busy talking to Lennie and Alex. "Uh . . . Armand Jordan. I ran into him at the casino."

"*My* casino?"

"No. Over at the Cavendish. He's staying in a villa there." She paused. "I'm so sorry. I guess I shouldn't have said anything. Armand swore me to secrecy."

"About what?"

"That he's buying The Keys, and the deal will be set tomorrow."

"You *are* kidding me, aren't you?"

"No, I'm not," Annabelle said, feeling a slight shiver of apprehension because the deep anger in Lucky's eyes was unmistakable. "I'm simply repeating what Armand told me."

"Where do you know this man from?"

"New York. We, uh, went out a couple of times."

"How *well* do you know him?" Lucky asked, her dark eyes glowing.

"Not . . . uh, not that well. He's more of an acquaintance than a friend," Annabelle stammered, realizing that she had probably said the wrong thing. Lucky did not seem at all happy about it.

"Then if you know him at all, you know he's a misogynistic, lying, delusional scumbag."

Alex leaned in for the end of Lucky's speech. "Talking about me again," he said with a wry grin.

"You wish," Lucky said, abruptly standing. She beckoned M.J. "I need to make a private call. Take me to the office."

"Certainly," M.J. said, jumping to his feet. "Follow me."

"I think I just pissed Lucky off," Annabelle said to Eddie.

"Well, darlin'," he replied. "Seems you're an expert at doing that. C'mon, let's dance. I'm in a celebrating mood."

CHAPTER FIFTY-THREE

It was a while before Armand realized Annabelle wasn't coming back. By this time he was blurry-eyed from too much cocaine, too much booze, too much of everything.

"Where is she?" he demanded of Luscious, who was using a tall potted palm as a makeshift stripper pole.

Luscious stopped what she was doing and said a ladylike "We gonna fuck or what?"

By this time Seducta had almost passed out. She was slumped on the floor, her eyes half closed.

It was a sorry scene, but Armand was too high to even notice.

"Where is she?" he repeated, rising from the couch, swaying slightly, almost losing his balance altogether.

"Your girlfriend took off an hour ago," Luscious offered, leaving her potted palm and moving over to him. "Least I *think* she did. Either that or she's dead in the bathroom." Luscious snickered. Wouldn't *that* be something. Another psychic revelation. Although if the girlfriend was dead, best not to hang around.

"Bathroom?" Armand questioned. He wasn't thinking straight at all. His heart was pounding, and he felt nauseous.

"Yeah," Luscious said. "She went in there. Want I should take a look?"

"Why?" Armand said, giving her a hard stare.

"See if she's there."

"Do you have a gun?"

"'Scuse me?"

Armand threw her a disdainful look. "A gun?"

Luscious wrinkled her nose. This motherfucker was sicker than she'd thought. Although she preferred him in this state than the way he was when he'd slapped her and Seducta around. "Whaddya want a gun for?" she inquired, thinking it might be smart to humor him.

"Because," Armand stated mysteriously.

"'Cause what?"

"Because I have time to kill," he answered grandly.

Shit! He was off his rocker—something her mom used to say when the old cow was sober enough to say anything at all. What the hell. He was either a stark raving loony or a dangerous psycho.

"You're not lookin' so hot," she ventured. "You'd better sit your ass down."

"Are you aware that I have more money than you'll ever see in your lifetime?" Armand boasted, reaching into his pocket and pulling out a stack of hundred-dollar bills. "You're a whore, you should appreciate money," he added, tossing a handful of bills at her.

The money fluttered around her naked, skinny, tattooed body before falling to the ground.

This nut job with the snake eyes was definitely crazy.

She squashed the urge to bend down and snatch the money up.

Seducta wasn't so patient. After watching the money fall, she began crawling over on all fours to collect.

Luscious wasn't having it. Before Seducta could get there, she quickly bent down and scooped up as much money as she could. *Holy fuck!* she thought, cramming the bills together. *There has to be a coupla thou here. This asshole is loco for sure.*

"A gun," Armand said. "I wish to obtain a hired gun. Do you know where I might find such a service?"

"Why?" Luscious said boldly. "You gonna shoot your girl-friend?"

"What makes you think that you can speak to me in such a fashion?" Armand said, glaring at her, a disdainful look on his face. "Do you not *know* who you are addressing?"

"You di'n't give me your name," Luscious said, noticing a couple of hundred-dollar bills she'd failed to pick up.

"Not a name," he announced with another grand gesture. "A title. Prince Armand Mohamed Jordan, soon to be king of Akramshar."

"Sure, honey," Luscious said, carrying on humoring him while grabbing her purse and stuffing the money inside. "Whyn't I just call you Arnie?"

"A hired gun," Armand continued, nodding to himself. "To kill an enemy of the people. Get me that, and money is no object."

"No object, huh?" Luscious said, a thousand jumbled thoughts running through her head. "Y'know what, Arnie? I gotta hunch you might have yourself a deal."

~ ~ ~

Randy Sorrentino lay back on a lounger (a couch that was about to fall off the back of a truck was being delivered next week), abstractedly stroking his cock and balls while a *Real Housewives* of somewhere episode played on the TV in front of him. Rich pieces of ass with tight faces, plastic bazooms, and stupid fuckhead husbands made it a trip to watch. Plus, he liked checking out their over-the-top houses to see how easy it would be to break in and relieve them of some of their stuff. They all had too much stuff. A little sharing wouldn't hurt.

Randy was done for the day. He'd taken care of business, and now he could relax until Luscious got home.

His girlfriend of almost a year was a piece of work. She catered to him like no other woman ever had before, and that was saying something, because there had been a lot of women. Oh yeah, too many to remember, especially when he'd been into making porn flicks and there'd been an assembly line of fresh gash every week—each girl desperate to make it as the next Jenna Jameson.

Yeah, Luscious was different, and if it weren't for her crazy jealous streak, he might have even considered making it legal between them. But the jealousy thing turned him off. He couldn't help that he'd been endowed with a huge piece of meat. It wasn't his fault that plenty of women wanted to give it a good old chewing.

For instance, Seducta was always coming on to him, rubbing her big tits up against him, whispering dirty messages in his ear, trying to grab a quick feel, suggesting that they'd make a fine team.

No way. She was married to his older brother, and Mikey, like Luscious, was jealous as shit. So Randy attempted to steer clear, but Seducta was relentless. She kept pushing, and lately Luscious seemed to think that it was *him* coming on to Seducta.

It was a fucked-up situation, and if Mikey got wind of it, he'd beat the crap out of him. Which would be a shame, because over the past couple of months he and Mikey had patched up their differences and were getting along fine, which hadn't always been the case. Right now they had a lucrative drug business going, which suited both of them. It was steady money, which made a pleasant change.

Randy was considering whether or not to whack off, when his cell phone buzzed.

It was Luscious.

"What?" he said impatiently.

"Get your ass over here," she said in a hoarse whisper, her voice rising with excitement. "We got ourselves a live one. An' bring the crack pipe, your piece, an' your big old self. We're about to make us some *real* money."

CHAPTER FIFTY-FOUR

Son of a bitch! Lucky thought. *Son of a motherfucking bitch!* What kind of balls did Armand Jordan possess, going around telling people that he was buying The Keys? No fucking way was she letting the asshole get away with it. He was dealing with the wrong woman.

She'd known he was trouble the moment he'd set foot in her office with his "women are inferior" attitude and smug expression. What a dumb prick! And in Lucky's world, if a prick had the temerity to challenge her, she was up for it. Oh yes, nobody got away with this kind of shit. To think that he had the nerve to go around saying that tomorrow The Keys would be his. This was something she had to put a stop to immediately. She didn't care that it was way past midnight, this was too infuriating to wait. It had to be dealt with *now*.

She didn't tell Lennie where she was going, because Lennie— always the voice of reason—would've tried to stop her. And right now she was in unstoppable mode.

Instead she tried calling Danny. But Danny wasn't home—Danny was at a gay club with Buff, dancing the night away. She sent a text message to his cell.

Next she called Jeffrey Lonsdale, who also failed to answer. Jeffrey was in bed with an attractive divorcée he'd met at the blackjack table, and he'd put his phone on vibrate. She didn't bother leaving him a message.

Finally she called Fouad Khan, whom she presumed was at the Cavendish also.

The phone rang in his room and no one picked up. Fouad was standing outside on his terrace smoking a cigarette—a habit he did not often indulge in, but he was hoping it might help him get to sleep. He did not hear the phone because he had the glass door shut lest the smoke make its way into his room and bother him.

Frustrated, Lucky made an on-the-spot decision. She would deal with it herself.

M.J. was waiting outside the office for her to emerge. "Tell Lennie I had to go take care of an urgent problem," she said briskly. "Okay?"

"Is it anything I can help out with?" M.J. asked.

She shook her head. "Nope. It's something I have to do personally. And since I don't want Lennie coming with me, just say that I'll see him back at the apartment."

"Right," M.J. said, wondering what was going on.

"Is Bobby around?"

"I think he left. You want me to double-check?"

"No problem," she said, thinking, *Mr. Armand Jordan, you are about to get a visit from your worst fucking nightmare. A woman—who's going to kick your sorry ass.*

~ ~ ~

Denver soon observed that a woman on her own walking around a casino was fair game. Every man appeared to think he had the right to talk to her.

"Where you from, honey?"

"Here on vacation?"

"How about I buy you a drink?"

These comments came from men traveling alone. However, men traveling in packs were far bolder.

"Nice rack. How much for a night?"

"Wanna go to a slumber party?"

"You got an ass that would stop traffic."

After a while she'd had enough. She probably did look as if she were selling it, wandering around in circles. Still, she wasn't ready to go upstairs. If Bobby was there, they'd probably get embroiled in a dumb fight, and if he wasn't . . . well, she didn't want to think about him *not* being there.

Then her imagination launched into overdrive, and she pictured him in bed with Gia, kissing Gia, going down on Gia . . .

Oh my God! I'm turning into one of those too-much-in-love pathetic idiots!

She determined to do something positive, and spotting an open seat at a blackjack table, she slid onto the vacant stool.

~ ~ ~

It wasn't what Max had intended to happen, but it was inevitable— falling into bed with Billy. He was so sexy and strong, and downright gorgeous, and he smelled so good.

Mister Movie Star—the man who just that afternoon she'd thought she hated—was once again making mad love to her, and this time it was even better than the first.

If that was possible.

Yes, it was possible.

The way he touched her was electrifying. She'd had no idea that actually doing it could feel this good. Wow! If only she'd known, she would've been into it a lot sooner.

Or maybe not. There was a reason she'd waited, and the reason was Billy.

"Couldn't get you off my mind," Billy said in a low voice, gently running his fingers down her back as they lay on top of the bed. "Kept on remembering the beach, an' finding you there like a social outcast all by yourself."

"Social outcast!" she objected, stretching languorously. "It was *my* party."

"And you weren't enjoying it one bit. Not until I came along. Admit it, Green Eyes, you were hiding out."

"True."

"But if you hadn't been hiding, I wouldn't've stumbled across you, and we wouldn't be here together. Right?"

"So right," she murmured, thinking about how happy she was to be with him.

"You do know it's way past midnight, so today's your birthday," he stated. "Makes me pissed that I'm not going to be spending it with you."

"I wish you could," she responded. "But can you imagine everyone's face if I turned up with *you* by my side?"

"I get it," Billy said. "Lucky an' Lennie would throw a shit fit."

"You're not wrong about that. And . . ." She hesitated for a moment. "Venus is in town. I saw her earlier at Mood. She'll probably be at my party."

"I saw her too. Ran into her outside the restaurant where Kev an' I were eating."

"Kev's with you?"

"He came along for the ride. Don't worry, he's not gonna bother us. He's got his instructions."

"It's not that I don't like him . . ." she said tentatively.

"Listen, Kev can be a big pain at times, but the thing about Kev is that he means well."

"Did you *speak* to Venus?" Max asked curiously.

"Briefly. She hates me now."

"She does?"

"Divorce brings out the bitch in everyone."

"Y'know," Max mused, turning over, "Venus has been my mom's best friend since I was a little kid."

"You're *still* a little kid," he teased, lazily tickling her stomach, thinking how luminous and pretty she was with her olive skin and brilliant green eyes. She wasn't just pretty, she was a beauty.

She squealed and rolled away from him.

He laughed and came after her, lowering his lean, bronzed body on top of her, slowly moving inside her until she sighed with pleasure.

Now she realized what Cookie meant when she carried on about how great it was doing the deed instead of holding back the main event.

Once again she realized she was glad she'd waited. Billy Melina was perfect, the birthday present of her dreams.

~ ~ ~

"Where's my little girl?" Gerald M. suddenly demanded, glancing around the crowded table at Mood. He was drinking Jack Daniel's and feeling no pain.

Frankie, who'd managed to insert himself between two buxom

blondes, gave a casual shrug. "Dancin' her ass off," he replied, although he had no idea where Cookie had vanished to, and he didn't much care. The blondes had already invited him to their suite, and he had plans to go, maybe take along Gerald M. if he was so inclined.

"Aren't you supposed to be *with* my little girl?" Gerald M. inquired, a belligerent look in his eyes. "She told me you drove here together."

Cancel the blondes, Frankie thought. *The dude's just remembered he has a daughter.*

"That's right," Frankie said, keeping it casual. "Only you know Cookie—she's a girl who likes t' do her own thing. I wouldn't want to hold her back."

"Go find her," Gerald M. said, scowling. "It's late. I don't like the idea of her wandering around on her own."

"I'm sure she's fine," Frankie said, left eye twitching.

Gerald M. gave him the Big Star look, a look that said *When I want something done—do it.*

"Yeah," Frankie said, reluctantly getting up. "Think I'll go find her now."

~ ~ ~

When Lucky was intent on doing something, there was nothing and no one capable of stopping her. She lived by her own rules, and her rules were stringent. *Never fuck with a Santangelo* said it all.

Armand Jordan was fucking with her, and she would not have it. Oh no, shooting his mouth off that he was buying The Keys might be a minor infraction to some people, but to Lucky it was out-and-out war. She would not allow the fool to go around saying such things. She would put a stop to it instantly.

She made her way down to the private Santangelo parking basement, where she discovered that the attendant was asleep on the job. Instead of waking him, she reached her arm inside his cubicle to the board of keys and collected the ignition key for her Vegas car, a silver blue Aston Martin, making a mental note to have the attendant fired the next morning, unless of course he had a wife and family—in which case she might reconsider.

It felt invigorating to be doing something about Armand Jordan. She hadn't liked the man from the moment he'd set foot in her office that morning. Bad vibes. Very bad vibes.

Damn Jeffrey—he should've known better than to put her in the same room with him. But Jeffrey was going through a divorce, so he probably wasn't thinking straight. Divorces seemed to do that to people, even lawyers.

She drove her car up from the underground garage, adrenaline surging.

It didn't matter that it was almost one in the morning. In fact, it added to the drama.

Armand Jordan was about to find out that nobody fucked with a Santangelo. Nobody.

CHAPTER FIFTY-FIVE

Randy Sorrentino clumsily hauled his big muscled body off the lounger and tried to get his brain around what he should wear. His drug delivery uniform—a light sports jacket over a maroon shirt and pants? Or should he go for more casual wear, such as his prized Guns N' Roses sweatshirt from way back and torn jeans?

Randy Sorrentino did not believe in rushing; he believed in taking his time. His mind worked slowly, so rushing didn't do it for him. He liked to think things through before he left the safety of his apartment.

Earlier in the evening, Luscious had informed him that she wouldn't be dancing at Dirty Den's tonight. Instead she had a high-paying gig at the Cavendish Hotel, and she was taking along Seducta. Randy wasn't sure whether the high-paying gig was for stripping or hooking. He hadn't asked; he didn't need the details. If his girlfriend wanted to open her legs and invite strangers in for money, it was all right with him. As long as she didn't come trotting home with some other dude's stink on her. In the porn business he'd learned a lot about protection and personal hygiene, and thoughtfully he'd passed all the info along to Luscious, who swore she always made the john use a condom.

The money she brought in helped. Eventually they might want to buy a house, or maybe get hitched and start a family. But that was way off in their future. Right now it was all about enjoying themselves, and if there was one thing Randy excelled at, it was enjoying himself.

He considered Luscious's hurried words over the phone. *Get your ass over here. We got ourselves a live one.*

That could mean anything.

An' bring the crack pipe, your piece, an' your big old self.

Was this for a party? Or was he supposed to make a sale?

Randy didn't like it when she called him old. He was only twenty-eight, and yeah, some people might consider him big— 230 pounds of pure muscle—but he was also big in all the right places, something that had always helped him on his journey through life. It was the one thing he had over Mikey.

Thinking of Mikey, he considered whether he should bring him in on this. He had to admit that Mikey was the brains of the family, and he was the brawn. So if—as Luscious had said— they were about to make some real money, wasn't including Mikey the right thing to do?

Yeah, Mikey was the man.

Randy pulled up his pants and reached for the phone to summon his big brother.

~ ~ ~

Armand was slumped on the couch, his mind veering off in all different directions. He'd never combined alcohol and cocaine before, so he was feeling quite disoriented.

The whores weren't dancing, although the music continued, loud and raucous, the harsh beat throbbing through Armand's brain. One of the whores had fallen into a naked, drunken stupor on the couch. She was snoring, her mouth open.

"What's wrong with her?" he muttered to the skinny whore, who for some unknown reason was standing by the bar holding a phone, her scrawny tattooed body nude.

"Got someone on the way," she informed him. "Someone who's gonna do whatever you need done." After a crafty pause, she added, "For a price, of course."

For a price. Armand digested her words. *For a price.*

What was this someone supposed to do for a price?

Then he remembered. They were going to blow Lucky Santangelo's brains out.

Yes, that was it.

And he would pay whatever it took.

~ ~ ~

Randy picked his brother up in his super-charged gold Dodge.

Mikey was standing outside his house, a sinister figure clad all in black, including oblique tinted sunglasses, which he wore day and night.

Mikey and Randy shared a mother, not a father. Mikey's dad, a hardened criminal, was doing life in prison, while Randy's dad—a former bodybuilder—sat at home picking up a disability pension.

Mikey was not big and tall like his younger brother; he was

slight of build and less than five feet eight. To compensate, he wore black snakeskin cowboy boots with three-inch semi concealed heels and a secret compartment where he stashed a six-inch hunting knife.

"What's this shit all about?" Mikey asked as he climbed into the passenger seat.

"Sounds like it's somethin'," Randy said, revving the engine. "Luscious wouldn't steer us wrong."

"She'd better not," Mikey responded. "'Cause if she's wasting my time, I'm gonna slap her sideways till she can't see straight."

CHAPTER FIFTY-SIX

"Is this seat taken?"

Denver didn't bother looking at the man who'd seated himself next to her at the blackjack table. She was fed up with being hit on—enough was enough. Besides, she was doing very nicely, accumulating a tidy pile of chips. Gambling was actually fun, although if she was truthful with herself, she knew she would sooner be with Bobby.

She placed her next bet and waited patiently for the dealer to slide the cards.

The dealer did so—and blackjack! She'd scored again.

"Nice one," said the man seated beside her. She gave him a quick glance and realized it was Bobby.

"Thank you," she said politely, acting as if they were total strangers.

"You're welcome," he said, playing along.

A paunchy man in a Hawaiian shirt sitting two seats away made a triumphant gesture with his thumb and mumbled something about her killing them. "This little lady is picking all my cards," he complained good-naturedly. "But she's way too pretty to get mad at." He nodded at Bobby. "Maybe you'll change the balance."

"I'll try," Bobby said.

They played for fifteen more minutes, until Denver finally lost a bet.

Without looking at Bobby, she gathered up her chips and stood up. "Cashing out," she said, tossing the dealer a generous tip.

"We'll miss you," said Mister Hawaiian Shirt.

Bobby stood too. "Can I buy you a drink?" he asked, addressing Denver.

"Well . . ." she demurred.

"He's not a bad-looking guy; I say go for it," Hawaiian Shirt encouraged. "That's unless he's married. You got to take a look-see at his ring finger. It's always a sure giveaway—you'll see the tan mark."

Denver gave Bobby a solemn look. "*Are* you married?" she asked.

"Nope," Bobby replied, equally serious. "Are you?"

"I recently divorced my third husband," she said.

"Dangerous!" Hawaiian Shirt exclaimed.

"Thanks for all the encouragement," Denver said, smiling at him. "I'll let you know how it turns out."

Hawaiian Shirt nodded eagerly. He loved Vegas—there was always something going on.

"So," Bobby said, still playing along as they walked toward a nearby lounge. "What brings you to Vegas?"

"Like I said, I recently divorced my third husband."

"Did he do something to piss you off?"

"Danced with an ex."

"Really?"

"It didn't sit well with me."

"I guess it wouldn't. Although I'm sure it was perfectly innocent."

"Maybe," she said, shrugging. "Or maybe not."

They reached the lounge and settled in at a corner table.

"What'll you have?" Bobby asked as a pretty waitress came over to take their order.

"A vodka martini," Denver said, getting into their unexpected game. "Make it a dirty double."

"A dirty double, huh?" Bobby said, raising an eyebrow. The Denver he knew was a white wine girl. But this wasn't Denver he was sitting with—this was a stranger, and he found himself getting quite turned on. "Okay then, make it a double vodka martini for the lady, and I'll have a beer," he told the waitress.

"And why are *you* in Vegas?" Denver asked as the waitress moved away.

"Came here for a romantic weekend with my girlfriend, but we kinda got off track."

"You did?"

"Shit happens."

"How true."

The drinks came and Denver downed her martini as if she were celebrating at a Russian wedding.

"Hey," Bobby said, trying not to laugh. "Easy."

"Some men think I am," she murmured provocatively.

"What kind of men would they be?"

She gave a casual shrug. "Oh, I don't know . . . the adventurous kind."

"I'm adventurous."

"You are?"

"Certainly. Uh . . . how about coming upstairs to my room and I'll prove it to you."

"Will your girlfriend be there?"

"My girlfriend's long gone."

"You're sure?"

"Oh yeah, I'm dead sure."

She gave him a bold look. "Then what are we waiting for?"

He threw money on the table, stood up, and offered her his hand. "Nothing I can think of," he said.

~ ~ ~

Lucky did not want Armand Jordan to be forewarned that she was on her way to pay him a visit. Surprise was the name of the game. A nice big fat surprise.

It wouldn't be a physical confrontation, not like the time she'd visited an investor in one of the Santangelo hotels who'd refused to pay up. Ah yes, she'd visited him in the middle of the night while he was sleeping and held the cold steel of a knife next to his balls. The following day, the money was forthcoming.

Lucky smiled at the memory. God, she'd been a wild one—and even though she was now a happily married woman with grown kids, deep down she was still a wild one.

Armand Jordan would soon find out. She'd warn him to stop shooting his mouth off about something that would never happen, and if he didn't comply and she heard any more stories about him supposedly buying her hotel, then he too might experience the touch of cold steel on his precious balls.

~ ~ ~

The instant they hit the elevator, it was on. Throwing Denver up against the wall, Bobby inserted his knee between her legs, rendering her helpless, then began kissing her. Wild, hungry kisses that she immediately responded to.

He had her pinned; she couldn't escape, and since she had no desire to do so, it was fine with her. She kissed him back, loving the taste of his mouth, loving the feel of his body pressed tightly up against her. God! She loved everything about this man.

After a few moments he reached up, roughly ripped the top of her dress, exposing her breasts, then bent to suck and bite her fully erect nipples.

The unexpected excitement of what was happening filled her with fire. His mouth on her breasts, his hard penis jammed against her. Completely forgetting where they were, and that a security camera was probably recording their every move, she quickly unzipped his pants and started caressing him. He felt so damn good.

The elevator was on the move, but neither of them cared.

Bobby's hand crept up her thigh, reached her thong, and tore it off. Then he lifted her so that her long legs were clasped around his waist, and without stopping, he began thrusting inside her.

Sex between them was usually passionate enough, but this was different. This was a sweaty, hot, crazy, out-of-body carnal experience.

The elevator stopped, and the doors opened at a floor. Both of them heard the shocked gasp of a woman before Bobby leaned over and pressed the Close Door button.

"Maybe we shouldn't be—" Denver managed before Bobby pressed his hand over her mouth to stop her from talking. Then he fondled her breasts again, pushing them together, tweaking her nipples, all the while still thrusting into her.

She moaned with pleasure as the thrilling climb began. Nothing mattered except being there with Bobby. He was her soul mate. He was everything she'd ever wanted. She loved him desperately.

"Oh . . . my . . . God!" she cried out as she felt herself approaching orgasm. "This . . . is—"

"Insane!" Bobby yelled, finishing the sentence for her as he shuddered to a mind-blowing climax at exactly the same moment.

The elevator stopped again, the doors opened, and a group of elderly tourists from Florida peered in at them in stunned silence.

Quick as a flash, Bobby zipped up, took off his jacket and threw it around Denver's shoulders, grabbed her hand, and exited the elevator.

"Honeymoon," he explained to the dumbstruck tourists. "Sometimes you just gotta do what you gotta do."

~ ~ ~

Without Billy by his side, Kev was getting nowhere fast. Every time he tried to chat up a girl, her eyes wandered, searching the room for a more likely prospect.

Until Ellie.

Ellie wasn't his dream girl, although she was cute enough in her torn jeans and blue T-shirt, a hooded sweatshirt tied around her waist. She was sitting at a bar he'd stopped at, drinking a beer and doodling on a notepad. Not the type of girl he usually went for, but this was Vegas, so spending the night by himself was not an option.

"Pretty girls should never drink alone," he said, settling himself on the stool next to her.

After giving him a cursory glance, she went back to her scribbling.

"Writing a book?" he joked.

"Working," she snapped, not in a friendly fashion.

Kev did what he did best: he played his trump card. "Me too," he said. "Just left my boss, Billy Melina. What a guy! What a slave driver! Can you believe it's past midnight an' I'm only now off the clock. Movie stars! They dance to their own tune."

Oh yes, surprise, surprise, he had her interest now. Billy's name scored points every time.

"Billy Melina is here?" she said, tapping her pen on the bar. "In Vegas?"

Kev nodded. "'S right," he said. "In all his movie-star bullshit."

She gave him an intent look. "How do I know you're not making this up?"

"Why'd I do that?"

"'Cause."

"'Cause here's the proof," he said, pulling out his phone and clicking on a few choice photos of him and Billy at play. "Take a look at me an' my master."

Ellie scrolled through the photos, then snapped her notebook shut. "How'd you like to make a couple of thousand bucks?" she said.

"Doing what?" Kev asked, his curiosity aroused.

"Nothing illegal."

"Then what?"

"Come with me, and I'll tell you what."

~ ~ ~

"It's not that I *want* to go, but I guess I have to," Max said reluctantly, her head cradled on Billy's bronzed chest.

"How's that?" Billy said, gently brushing a lock of hair off her face. "There's nobody waiting up for you—right?"

WRONG! Ace will definitely be waiting up for me, and what am I supposed to say to him?

"Uh . . . no," she lied. "Only I don't think my mom would be thrilled if she heard about me staying out all night."

"You're eighteen now," he pointed out. "She's got no say anymore, you can do anything you want."

"Yeah," Max said unsurely. "But, uh, being with you is definitely going to create waves."

"More like a tsunami," Billy said, laughing.

"It's no joke," she admonished, sitting up. "You were *married* to my mom's best friend."

"Shit!" he quipped. "How did *that* happen?"

"It's not funny," Max said. "Actually, it's kind of creepy."

"Are you callin' me creepy?" Billy said, mock serious.

"Not *you*," she said quickly. "The situation. I mean, I can't tell them we're seeing each other. You're not even divorced yet."

"Almost."

"Doesn't cut it."

"You're a tough little piece of work."

"*I'm* a piece of work?" she said, indignantly. "*You're* the movie star."

"How does that make *me* a piece of work?"

"'Cause that's how movie stars roll. They're catered to by everyone, and it stops them from acting like normal people. Believe me, I saw it all when my mom owned Panther Studios."

"So now you're tellin' me I'm not normal?" he said, amused.

"You're Billy Melina. How could you be?"

He laughed again and grabbed her leg. "*You're* not normal," he said. "You're too freakin' pretty an' sexy an' hot to even *think* about bein' normal."

"You calling me sexy?" she asked, secretly thrilled.

"Yeah, Green Eyes, I'm callin' you sexy. So forget about runnin' out on me, an' let's see what tricks I can teach you next."

"Don't bother. I got tricks of my own that'll blow you away," she said confidently. "You might've taken my virginity, but I'm not exactly Miss Innocent, so there, Mister Movie Star."

"Feisty. I like it."

"Do you?" She sighed, wondering if this was what falling in love felt like.

"You bet your ass, Little Miss Green Eyes," Billy replied enthusiastically. "I like you a whole damn lot. So we're gonna have to figure out a plan, 'cause I'm not givin' up on you. Okay?"

"Okay," she said. And her heart skipped a beat, because maybe, just maybe, this could be the real deal.

CHAPTER FIFTY-SEVEN

Loud music was emanating from the villa at the Cavendish. Too loud for comfort.

"Sounds like a party," Randy said, standing outside the door, not at all disappointed. One thing about Randy, he was always up for a party.

"No party," Mike growled, narrow eyes behind dark shades checking out his surroundings. "We're here for business. Got it?"

"I got it," Randy said. It was never a wise idea to argue with Mikey. The last time he and Mikey had gotten into a physical altercation, he'd ended up losing two teeth, a painful memory.

Even though Randy was younger, bigger, and stronger, Mikey had moves that came out of nowhere, moves that could flatten a man in less than five seconds, which was why Randy refused to fuck with him. Mikey was the Man.

Randy hammered on the door, and it fell open.

Automatically Mikey reached for his piece. One thing about Mikey, he was always cautious, always alert.

Gingerly, Randy stepped into the room, Mikey right behind him.

The scene that greeted them was quite something. Seducta was sprawled naked and out for the count on the couch. Armand sat next to her in a shirt and tie, no pants, his legs akimbo. Luscious was positioned on her knees in front of him, her mouth and slightly buck teeth enveloping his engorged manhood, her head bobbing up and down.

Loud rap blared on the sound system. Mounds of coke were piled on the coffee table, while empty bottles of champagne, along with miniatures of scotch and vodka, littered the floor.

"This is some shit-hole," Mikey stated grimly, still fingering his piece. "Someone turn the fuckin' noise off."

Luscious stopped what she was doing, turned off the music, and jumped to her feet. She hadn't expected Randy to bring Mikey—with Mikey involved it meant less money for them. She was pissed. Why share when they didn't have to?

Blurry-eyed, Armand took in the new arrivals. Had he invited them? Who were they?

He shook his head, trying to think straight, and stood up.

"For crissakes, put your junk away," Mikey snarled.

Randy was glad Mikey had said it; he was embarrassed by the sight of another man's equipment. Jeez! Some people had no sense of modesty. This wasn't a porno shoot, this was real life.

Luscious wiped her hand across her mouth and snatched up Armand's pants, which she then handed to him.

He put them on and regarded his visitors. "Who are these people?" he demanded of Luscious. "Why are they here?"

"It's only my boyfriend, Randy, an' his brother, Mikey," she said, retrieving her skimpy tank top and short skirt from the corner and slipping them on. "They're gonna take care of that stuff you wanted done. Remember?"

"What stuff?" Armand asked, realizing that if the room didn't stop spinning, he was likely to lose his balance.

"You *know*," Luscious said, nudging him. "Money's-no-object stuff."

"Ah . . ." Armand said, stumbling slightly.

Then it occurred to him that he'd actually done it; he'd hired himself a hit man. Or two.

While they were talking, Randy edged closer to Luscious.

"Why you gotta bring Mikey with you?" she whined.

"'Cause Mikey knows what he's doin'."

"An' you don't?"

"Who d'you need takin' care of?" Mikey said, stepping toward Armand. "An' be aware, it's gonna cost you, friend. Plenty. I don't work cheap."

Once again, Armand attempted to gather his thoughts. This was not the usual way he conducted business. And this *was* business. Urgent business.

Where was Fouad when he needed him? Fouad always took care of the details.

"I have the money," he said. "Whatever the price for your services."

Mikey gave a hollow laugh. "Twenty-five grand for the job. Cash. You got that kinda moola sittin' around?"

"Of course," Armand said with a lofty nod.

"Half up front. The rest when it's done," Mikey said. "Who's the target? You got a picture? And I'll need t' know where to find 'em."

Armand stared at him blankly.

Mikey was beginning to tense up as he waited for an answer.

His body language screamed that he was about to do someone harm for dragging him out of his house and away from his big-screen TV, where he'd been watching a program about killer whales.

He noticed Seducta, moved closer to her, and kicked her off the couch with the tip of his snakeskin boot.

She bounced to the floor and surfaced in a groggy stupor.

"Put your clothes on," he ordered. "We're outta here."

"Huh?" she muttered.

Luscious suppressed a triumphant smirk. Randy could see for himself what a piece of trash his brother had married. Maybe he'd stop coming on to Seducta now that he'd observed what a skank she really was.

"We're goin'," Mikey repeated.

"You can't leave," Luscious said quickly. "Arnie here wants t' make a deal. Doncha, Arnie?"

"A non fuckin' disclosure agreement," Mikey grumbled. "What the fuck. This shit's not for me. This is a handshake deal, or I'm out."

Luscious tugged on Armand's arm. "You told me you wanted somethin' done," she whined. "I got these guys here special. Which means you gotta tell 'em what you want, an' work it out, otherwise they're leavin'. An' you don't want that, do you?"

No, Armand decided, he didn't want that. There was a job to be done, and he understood that money had to exchange hands.

He was a businessman.

A prince.

This could all be settled to everyone's satisfaction.

CHAPTER FIFTY-EIGHT

Emerging from the shower with a towel wrapped around her sarong style and a smile on her face, Denver walked right into Bobby as he let himself into their suite.

"Hey," he said, feigning surprise. "I was hoping I'd find you here."

"That's perfect," she answered brightly. "'Cause I was hoping the same thing."

"Were you now?"

"Yes indeed."

They grinned knowingly at each other.

"So . . ." Denver continued. "Where were you?"

"Well, I finished up at the club," Bobby said, scratching his head. "Then I came directly here."

"Directly?"

"Kinda. Had a little detour on the way."

"A detour?"

"Met this beautiful woman at the blackjack table."

"Really? And who might she be?"

"I think her name was . . ." He thought for a moment. "Uh . . . Chicago."

"Chicago, huh?"

"Right. Gorgeous woman, with real breasts, long silky hair, fantastic legs, and best of all, a taste for adventure."

"Should I be jealous?"

"I dunno. It depends. Where were *you?*"

"Ah," Denver answered mysteriously. "I ran into a tall dark stranger with mad sexy moves and a hard . . . body."

"Sounds exciting."

"It was. We had sex in the elevator."

"Hmm," Bobby said lustfully. "Tell me something—did he make you come the way I'm about to make you come?" And with a deft flick of his wrist, he removed her towel.

They both burst out laughing as the towel dropped to the floor.

"Oh my God!" Denver exclaimed, still laughing. "You're insatiable."

"You bet I am, and don't you just love it," Bobby said, steering her into the bedroom and onto the bed.

She smiled up at him as he began to kiss her very deliberately. Then, at a slow pace, his tongue started moving down her body until he gently spread her legs and began going down on her.

Throwing her head back, she luxuriated in his touch. His hands were on her thighs, holding them apart. Once again she felt deliciously trapped.

After a few minutes, he came up for air. "You're making me forget about Chicago," he said. "That woman is becoming just another distant memory."

"And that's exactly the way it should be," Denver murmured

dreamily, thinking that this was definitely turning out to be a weekend to remember.

~ ~ ~

On the one hand, Kev felt guilty; on the other hand, he thought—screw it—he was entitled to make some decent money. Billy was rolling in it, bathing in it. Billy was a friggin' movie star, and who was he? Poor old Kev who tagged along for the ride, and then got kicked to the curb like some beaten-up old dog, without even a decent explanation. Oh yeah—*So long, Kev. Book yourself a room, Kev. Charge it to me, Kev.*

Was Billy forgetting the months he'd camped out in Kev's apartment when he'd first made it to Hollywood? Billy Melina had not had a pot to piss in, and he, Kev, was the one who'd been paying all the bills, putting food on the table and supporting Billy all the way.

So fuck it. He had a chance of making some real money, and who could blame him for taking it?

It turned out that Ellie was more than just a pretty girl sitting at a bar scribbling in a notebook. Ellie was a freelance photojournalist who was in Vegas to dig up as much dirt as she could on the many famous celebrities flocking into Vegas for the big fight.

"Y'know," she informed Kev after they'd shared a couple of beers, "the right photo of a hot celeb can fetch up to a hundred grand. And with your boss going through such a public divorce, well . . . if I can get an exclusive photo of him with someone new—bingo! We're in the money. You arrange it, and you're in for half."

Who was he to turn down such a lucrative offer?

Screw loyalty. It didn't seem to matter to Billy.

~ ~ ~

Frankie frowned. Where was he supposed to start looking for Cookie? She wasn't on the dance floor, she wasn't in the damn club, so where the hell was she? He had no idea, but he did know that if he wanted to stay on Gerald M.'s good side, he'd better make an attempt to start searching for the little minx.

Gerald M. was the kind of dude he was desperate to hang with. Yeah, Gerald M. might be older, but he was a tried-and-true star—like a Smokey Robinson or a Lionel Richie. Old-school. And Frankie would like nothing better than for Gerald M. to plant his ass in River every night, give the place some star power. He'd even supply him with free drugs for the pleasure of his company.

However, this wasn't going to happen until he produced Gerald M.'s precious daughter.

How precious would Daddy think Cookie was if he'd seen her sucking Frankie's cock on the drive up? Not so precious any-more.

Frankie approached M.J. and was taken aback to observe his ex Annabelle Maestro sitting at the table, right next to Lennie Golden and the red-hot agent everyone was talking about—Eddie Falcon. He and Annabelle hadn't spoken in months, not since he'd threatened to sue her for publishing a libelous, un-truthful book, painting him as some kind of dissolute, lowlife drug addict.

He knew Eddie—the agent had stopped by River on several occasions—so he said a brusque "Hi" and attempted to ignore Annabelle.

Eddie wasn't having it. "You know my girlfriend, Annabelle

Maestro," Eddie said. He paused, then added, "Wait a minute, didn't the two of you used to go out?"

"Briefly," Annabelle said, refusing to look at Frankie.

"Way back," Frankie said, turning to M.J. "You seen Cookie?" he asked.

"Dating juveniles now," Annabelle murmured. "How appropriate."

Frankie pretended not to hear her.

"She and Max were goin' over to Wonderball," Cassie offered.

"Wonder *what?*" Frankie said, wishing he was anywhere but standing in front of this group.

"It's a kids' club on the strip," Cassie said. "Wonderball. Everyone knows it."

Great. His teenage girlfriend had run out on him to go party with the kiddies. Well, at least he could tell Gerald M. where she was.

"Thanks," he said to Cassie.

"No prob," Cassie responded.

Back to his table he went with his newfound information on Cookie's whereabouts.

The table was empty. Gerald M. and his entourage—including the two blondes Frankie had lined up for later—had taken off. All that was left was the check.

His freakin' luck. What the hell was he supposed to do now?

~ ~ ~

Max loved the fact that Billy didn't want her to go; it meant that he really liked her.

"When am I gonna see you again?" he asked, sitting on the edge of the bed watching her as she pulled on her leggings and boots. "'Cause if I'm *not* gonna see you, I may as well hop a flight back to L.A."

"Well . . ." she said, thinking about how she could work it out. "I've got lunch with my family, but after that I don't see why I couldn't come by. Maybe we could do something, go somewhere."

"Sweet dreams, babe," Billy said with a rueful laugh. "If I set one foot outta here, the paps'll be all over me, an' you'll be labeled my new mystery woman."

"Is it *that* bad?" she asked, thinking what a drag it must be to lose your privacy.

"Believe me," Billy assured her, "it's that bad. Even without the divorce thing it was full-on. Now multiply that, an' the situation escalates. I hate it."

"But surely they don't even know you're in Vegas?" she questioned.

"Oh, they know. They just haven't found me yet."

"Does this mean we can't go anywhere together? Even in L.A.?"

"Not unless you're prepared for everyone to find out about us."

Max considered Lucky and Lennie's reaction and shuddered. They would totally *freak*.

"Okay," she said hesitantly. "Then why don't I come back here later and we'll watch TV or something."

"I'm liking the 'or something,'" he said with a lascivious grin. "Your education shall continue."

"Ha!" she said scornfully. "Stop imagining that I'm, like, some innocent little flower you're teaching how to grow. Honestly, I'm not that girl."

"Do not shatter my illusions," he said. "I'm happy that I'm your first. It makes everything very special between us."

"Hmm," she said, trying not to let him see how thrilled his

words made her. She had to play it a little bit cool, couldn't let him see how hooked she already was. "Well anyway, I gotta get out of here," she added, standing up.

"Call me when you get to your room," he said. "I want to be sure you got back safely. I'd escort you, but—"

"Yeah, I know, I know, those freakin' paps."

"Right," he said, grinning. "You catch on fast."

"You'll find out soon enough."

"Lookin' forward to it, Green Eyes."

"So am I!"

~ ~ ~

Lucky knew the Cavendish as well as she knew her own hotel. During the time she was building The Keys, she'd stayed in the villas many times. She was aware of exactly where Armand's villa was located, having gotten the number from the switchboard.

As she drove to the hotel, she decided she'd park in a special spot near the villas. No need to walk through the lobby or the casino. Later, at a decent hour, she'd call Renee, the owner of the Cavendish, and ask her to arrange for Armand Jordan to be thrown out.

But right now she was looking forward to having him exactly where she wanted him. It was a game. A game she excelled at.

CHAPTER FIFTY-NINE

If he hadn't been so stoned, Armand would have been well aware that what he was doing was reckless and beyond stupid. He would have known that he should summon Fouad to make sure that the details were handled properly. And he would also have known that Fouad would put an immediate stop to what he had planned.

Ah, yes . . . Fouad would caution him that he was behaving in an impossible and dangerous fashion. That he was putting himself in distinct jeopardy for dealing with such bad people. Whores and thugs who would do anything for money.

WHORES AND THUGS.

Armand laughed. He didn't care. He had his mind made up.

He walked unsteadily into his bedroom, pulled out the money suitcase and unlocked it. Twenty-five thousand to get rid of an enemy was a cheap price to pay. Twenty-five thousand and good-bye, Lucky Santangelo.

He stared at the neat stacks of bills, organized into bundles of twenty thousand. Cash. There was nothing like it. No paper trails to catch a man out.

Before he knew it, Luscious was standing beside him, her mouth gaping open as she gazed down at the suitcase stuffed full of money. "You rob a bank or somethin'?" she asked, her eyes wide with greed.

"My bank. My money," he replied, vaguely annoyed that she'd followed him into the bedroom.

"You're a rich mothafucker, ain't'cha?" she said, hanging onto his arm. "Rich an' sexy."

"You think I'm sexy?" Armand said, quite pleased that she would say so. He'd never given a woman the opportunity to call him sexy before—he'd always been too busy humiliating them, or telling them they weren't fit to speak.

"Sure you is," Luscious said, still clinging onto him. "An' . . . I got a treat for you all set up in the other room. Somethin' real special."

"What would that be?"

"You ever done crack, Arnie? 'Cause if you never did, then I'm gonna take you somewhere you ain't *never* gonna forget." She pulled on his arm, dragging him away from the suitcase stuffed full of money. Leaving it unlocked and open. "Let's go, big boy. This'll be a night t' remember."

~ ~ ~

Crouching in the bushes near Billy's villa alongside Ellie and her long-lens camera, Kev experienced a pang of guilt. He and Billy went way back. They were longtime friends, and now he was about to sell him out.

But hey—it was all Billy's fault. Billy had decided not to trust him, and that was okay. No trust between friends meant all was fair.

"We could be stuck here all night," Kev muttered, not relishing the thought.

"Okay with me," Ellie replied, perfectly cheerful. "Whoever is in there with him has to come out eventually, and when they do, I've got the shot."

"You've done this before, haven't you?" Kev said, wondering when he should make his move. After all, this was Vegas, and tonight he was definitely getting laid.

"A few times," Ellie replied, a tad sarcastic. "Learned from my dad. Now *he* was one of the greats. He shadowed Jackie O. Captured Elvis fat and thin. Michael Jackson in his pj's. O.J. on the run. Diana and Dodi. Oh yes, my dad nailed it every time. He taught me that the trick is to lie dormant until the exact right moment, then go for it. Kinda like bird-watching. The subject doesn't even know. Night-vision camera, sweet lens. It's a trip."

"I dunno who he's with in there," Kev said for the third time. "Could be Venus for all I know. We ran into her earlier."

"What a shot *that'd* be," Ellie said, adjusting her camera position. "Front page everywhere. Oh my!"

"He's been seeing Willow Price," Kev offered.

"Old news. Besides, everyone knows she's a pussy hound."

"Then there was this young girl in L.A. Max something or other."

"Young is good," Ellie said matter-of-factly. "Or black. Or a porn star. The best would be if he pulled a Charlie Sheen. Always a winner."

"Not Billy," Kev said with conviction. "That's not his scene."

"No? One thing I've learned in this business, anything is possible."

~ ~ ~

"I really don't wanna let you go," Billy said, walking Max to the door, his arm around her waist.

"And *I* really don't want to go," she responded, reaching up to playfully touch the dimple in his chin.

He opened the door, and they stood there, bathed in the moonlight, not ready to part company.

Billy leaned forward and kissed her on the lips, a long sexy kiss. "Night, Green Eyes," he said. "See you tomorrow."

"I guess I should make up a nickname for *you*," she said, reluctant to leave. "How about Dimples?"

"How about that sounds like somebody's pet monkey," Billy said, snorting with mirth. "Dimples, my ass. Think of something macho."

Giggling, Max wrapped her arms around his neck. "What, then?"

"You'll come up with something," he said, hugging her affectionately.

"Oh yes I will."

"Oh yes you will."

And neither of them heard the steady click of the camera lens hidden in the bushes.

~ ~ ~

The euphoria that overcame Armand was like nothing he'd ever experienced before. Sharing hits from a crack pipe with these people—his new best friends—was magical. They *were* his friends.

No. Better than that. They were his loyal subjects, here to do his bidding. Here to help him achieve greatness.

Yes. Greatness. FOR ARMAND JORDAN WAS THE MAN WHO WOULD BE KING.

And when he was the ruler, he would transport everyone to Akramshar, where they would all live in harmony and peace.

He stared at the two women—Luscious and Seducta. These women were not whores, they were beautiful creatures. Exquisite. He wanted to fuck them. He wanted to fuck them both. He wanted to fuck them forever.

They would all float together in a sea of happiness. Their bodies would be filled with wonderment. It was the way it was supposed to be.

His heart was on a crazy trip of its own. It was beating so fast he could hardly keep up. And yet the rhythm was comforting; it made him feel warm and safe.

He could do anything.

Being alive was such a pleasure.

It was heavenly.

He was heavenly.

~ ~ ~

"Do you recognize her?" Ellie asked, keeping her voice low.

"Think it might be the one from L.A.," Kev said, squinting to get a better view. "Max somethin' or other."

"She looks young," Ellie observed.

"She *is* young."

"All the better," Ellie said, clicking away with her long lens as Billy and Max continued to hug and kiss.

Kev wondered if when Ellie had taken enough photos he was going to get laid.

Laid *and* paid. It was a win-win situation.

~ ~ ~

"Seems to me your wife is on the missing list," Alex said, making digs at Lennie as he'd been doing all night.

"My *wife* is at home in bed waiting for me," Lennie responded.

"You mean she leaves you in a club without so much as a good-bye?" Alex taunted, swigging more scotch.

Lennie gave a dry laugh. "Just goes to show how well you know Lucky. She does her thing, I do mine. We never feel the need to check in."

"A modern marriage, huh?"

"Modern, not open."

"Just asking."

"Ask away, Alex. But I think I should tell you—Lucky will *never* be yours. Never. And that's something you can take to the bank." He paused to let that sink in, then added, "Do we understand each other?"

~ ~ ~

"I'm tellin' you," Luscious whispered in Randy's ear. "We gotta forget about the hit. There's a shitload of money in a suitcase in the bedroom—could be more than a hundred thou."

Randy had just taken a solid drag on the crack pipe and he wasn't concentrating, which infuriated Luscious. So did the fact that Seducta was lolling all over him, and he wasn't shoving her off. Her tits were in his face, and he didn't seem to mind.

Sometimes Randy didn't get the bigger picture, but Luscious was sure that Mikey certainly would. She was starting to think that it was time for her to move on.

Mikey was standing by the window smoking a long thin cheroot. He'd pocketed the $12,500 deposit, now he was waiting for the client to tell him who the subject was.

It had crossed Mikey's mind that he could take the money he already had, stick it in his safe deposit box, and do nothing. This visiting prick was so out of it he wouldn't know the difference. And if he did that, there was nothing the john could do. The asshole would be fucked, screwed, caught on a freeway without a ride and no pants.

Mikey gave a grim smile. He didn't do drugs. He smoked. He drank—never to excess. Mikey was a man intent on staying in control.

As he watched them all getting wasted, he felt sorry for them. No willpower. No backbone. Truth was, they were nothing but a bunch of losers.

He observed his wife sucking on the pipe. Dumb as shit. The puzzle was, why had he married her?

Could it be that in a weak moment he'd succumbed to the power of pussy and the lure of big tits? Foolish. Even Luscious—who was no prize herself—was smarter than Seducta.

As if reading his mind, Luscious sidled up to him. "We gotta move fast," she said in a low voice.

"Move fast why?" Mikey said, flicking ash on the rug.

"There's a suitcase in the bedroom stuffed fulla money. I saw it." She indicated Armand. "He's too fucked-up to know anything. What we gotta do is take it an' get the shit out."

"How much money?" Mikey questioned, his interest piqued.

"Go look for yourself," Luscious insisted. "I'm tellin' you—it's worth runnin'."

Mikey didn't need asking twice. He headed purposefully toward the bedroom.

CHAPTER SIXTY

"The time has come," Bobby said. "For us to move in together."

"Don't you ever sleep?" Denver groaned, rolling over in bed. "What's the time?"

"A house, I'm buying us a house," he said decisively. "Half yours, half mine. I'll decorate my half, you can go for it on yours."

"Oh," she said, yawning. "So now you're a decorator."

"I know what I like. I worked with my design team on Mood."

"You're something else, Bobby Santangelo Stanislopoulos." She sighed. "A man of many talents."

"What's your favorite?" he asked, reaching his arms around her.

"Right now my favorite is sleep, plenty of it."

"Then we're agreed?" he said, spooning up against her. "I can buy us a house?"

"I didn't say—"

His hands slid under the oversized T-shirt she wore to bed and began caressing her breasts. "*What* didn't you say?"

"No sex. Sleep," she begged. "You're turning into a horn dog."

"Only if we got a deal."

"Okay, okay, we got a deal," she agreed.

"Is that a promise?"

"Yes, it's a promise."

"Are you a woman of your word?"

"Yes! Yes! Yes!"

"Okay, then," he said, grinning. "You can go to sleep now."

"You're sure?"

"Well . . ." he said, his hands on the move. "Maybe we should—"

"Bobby!"

"Hey—third time for luck."

"Oh my God! Has anyone ever told you you're turning into a sex maniac?"

He grinned again. "Only you."

~ ~ ~

"Was I right or was I right?" Luscious said, addressing Mikey, a triumphant gleam in her eyes.

Mikey, standing in front of Armand's open suitcase filled with nothing but money, let out a long, low whistle. "Yeah," he said at last. "You was right."

Praise from the inscrutable Mikey was praise indeed. Luscious preened.

Mikey began tapping his right foot on the plush carpet, a sure sign that he was thinking. By his quick calculations there had to be at least $300,000 in the suitcase. Maybe more. He'd *never* seen that much money in one place, and he'd been around drug dealers and criminals all his life. This was big-time.

"Who is this prick?" he muttered.

"Dunno," Luscious said, making a helpless gesture. "Just another john with a shitload of cash."

Mikey knew he had to tread carefully as he considered their options. Was it drug money? He didn't think so, for he was familiar with most of the players in town.

Gambling money? Most likely. The john was probably a rich degenerate gambler who came to Vegas for the gambling and the prostitutes.

Luscious was all hyped up and anxious for action. "We gonna take it or what?" she asked, licking her lips in anticipation.

"Yeah," Mikey said slowly. "We're gonna take it. Leave it t' me to work out how."

~ ~ ~

Lucky was not having second thoughts, not at all. It had been a while since she'd had to deal with a situation such as this, and it had her adrenaline pumping.

Mr. Armand Jordan boasting to people that he was buying her hotel. The nerve of him was unbelievable. And she was about to set him straight in no uncertain fashion.

She hoped she was about to catch him asleep in bed so that she could scare the shit out of him. Yes, that would be fun.

She drove her car into the parking section reserved for the villa guests. It was late, no valet on duty, which was good for her, but not so good for the Cavendish. Lucky considered it lax security; she would never allow it to happen at her hotel. Security for the protection of hotel guests was always a priority.

Why are you doing this? she asked herself. *Isn't it beneath you? Calling out some jerk in the middle of the night?*

No. It's a kick. He's a moron who hates women, and I'm about to show him who's boss.

Actually, she was loving it. Kicking butt—her favorite thing to do.

~ ~ ~

"Okay." Max sighed, extracting herself from Billy and his tempting lips. "This is it. I've *really* got to go."

"Really?" he said, teasing her, grabbing her, kissing her.

"Yes, really," she giggled, enjoying every minute. *I love you, Billy Melina!*

"Okay then, go. Leave me wanting more."

"I'll call you when I get to my room."

"You'd better."

"Oh, I will," she said, finally pulling away.

Billy watched her leave, a smile on his lips. She made him feel as if he was back in high school. She washed away all the random girls who'd been giving him blow jobs beside his pool. She obliterated the Venus years and all the crap that went along with being married to a world-class superstar. When he was with Max, he wasn't movie star Billy Melina, he was just a guy having fun with his girl.

Suddenly Max doubled back, rushed past him, and darted into the villa. "Close the door," she gasped, a frantic expression on her face. "I think I just saw my mom!"

~ ~ ~

"Here's what we're gonna do," Mikey decided. "You an' Seducta gonna keep the prick busy while Randy an' me get the suitcase outta here."

"You mean you expect *me* an' your stoned wife t' stay here while you take off?" Luscious said indignantly. "No fuckin' way, Mikey. That's not how it's goin' down."

"Do *you* wanna carry the goddamn suitcase outta here?" he said, stony-faced. "Is that it?"

"No," Luscious said, determined to do things her way. "Randy can take the suitcase while *you* stay here keepin' the mark busy. Me an' Randy'll take it to a safe place."

"An' what's your idea of a safe place?" Mikey said scornfully. "Hidin' it under your fuckin' bed? 'Cause when this prick emerges from his drug haze tomorrow, he's gonna come lookin' for you big time."

"Why'll he be lookin' for me?"

"'Cause you're the slut who was in his room blowin' him."

"I'm not a slut, Mikey," Luscious said, her eyes unexpectedly filling with tears. "You shouldn't call me that. It's your wife who's the slut."

Mikey didn't answer. He was thinking. He was coming up with a plan.

"Got it," he said at last. "You an' me take the suitcase. We leave Randy an' Seducta here. They stay until the john passes out, or whatever the fuck he's gonna do."

"What if he starts lookin' for his suitcase?"

"If that happens, Randy'll deal with it."

"How?"

"How d'you think?"

Luscious preferred not to think. It was one thing to steal the money, but she didn't condone violence.

"I'll fill Randy in on the plan," Mikey said. "You go shut the suitcase, 'cause any minute now we're gettin' outta here."

"What about Seducta?"

"What about her?"

"Are you just gonna leave her?"

"Don't go worryin' about Seducta. She's a big girl. She can look after herself."

"But she's your wife," Luscious felt obliged to point out.

"That don't mean nothin' t' me," Mikey said coldly.

Luscious nodded. Who was she to argue?

Besides, her loyalty was now firmly with the money.

~ ~ ~

"What're you *talkin'* about?" Billy said, quickly closing the door and following Max back inside.

"It's Lucky. I saw her," Max said, almost hyperventilating. "She's walking down the path on her way here. She *knows* about us. What're we going to *do?*"

"First of all, we're going to calm down," Billy said, hiding his own panic. Nobody relished the thought of messing with the infamous Lucky Santangelo. "And second, you're going to think about who knows you're here."

"Nobody. I didn't tell anyone."

"Does anybody know about us?"

"I just told you," Max wailed. "I haven't mentioned you to any-one."

"Did she see you?"

"I don't think so."

"Let's hope she didn't," Billy said, thinking fast. "So here's what we're gonna do. You go hide in the bathroom, an' when she knocks on the door I'll say I don't know what she's talkin' about."

"Oh my God! You don't understand. She's gonna *kill* me. *And* you."

"You're *sure* it was her?"

"For God's sake, Billy, it's my *mom*. Of course I'm sure."

"Then where is she?"

"I dunno," Max said blankly. "Where is she?"

They both rushed over to the window and peered out.

Lucky was there, all right. She was just about to enter the opposite villa.

~ ~ ~

Their plan was in action. While Luscious was blocking Armand's view, Mikey was lugging the money suitcase to the door. It was heavier than he'd expected, too heavy for him to make it to the car. He needed help from Randy, the ox with no brains who was currently in la-la land along with Seducta and the john. But Luscious didn't want that. Luscious wasn't having him and Randy skip out with the money, because Luscious was just about smart enough to know that once they had the money, they weren't hanging around. Well, he wasn't anyway. Randy could do what the fuck he liked. If Randy wanted to stay in Vegas with a crackhead he could do just that. But Mikey had no intention of staying. Once he had the suitcase in the car, he was hitting the road. Too bad about Seducta and Randy; they were on their own.

Luscious was something else. She could be useful. But would she leave without Randy?

Mikey wasn't sure.

He had the money suitcase by the door. Luscious had turned the music back on so that the john wouldn't hear when he opened it. The moment he got it outside the villa, he and Luscious would get it to Randy's car.

Money.

Freedom.

Fuck Vegas.

He opened the door and came face-to-face with a woman. A beautiful woman with deep olive skin and clouds of black hair.

For a second or two Mikey was confused. Was she a late-night call girl the john had ordered?

No. Couldn't be. She didn't look like a hooker. She looked like a fucking movie star.

They stared at each other for a long silent moment. Lucky and Mikey.

Finally Lucky broke the silence. She was cool and collected. Nothing threw Lucky, she always expected the unexpected.

"And who are you?" she questioned, staring down a sinister-looking man with blackout shades covering his eyes and a vicious scowl.

Mikey was not one bit intimidated. "Who the fuck are *you?*" he retaliated.

"I'm here to see Armand Jordan. Where can I find him?"

Mikey indicated the room behind him as he dragged the money suitcase past her. "In there," he said. "Go join the party. You'll fit right in."

CHAPTER SIXTY-ONE

Things were winding down at Mood; it was late, and the music was becoming mellower, while most of the clientele were getting ready to call it a night.

Lennie was mad at himself. He should've left when Lucky wanted to go, but Alex and his attitude pissed him off, so he'd stayed—kind of like a screw-you gesture toward Alex. Yes, Alex Woods was one of the few people who managed to annoy him with his superior ways, and his constant lusting after Lucky.

Ah . . . Lucky. His beautiful, unpredictable wife. Later she would laugh at him, tease him about his ongoing feud with Alex. And they would make love as they always did before sleeping. Lucky was the woman of his dreams. She completed him, she always had.

He sought out M.J. and told him he was leaving.

"Did Lucky solve that problem?" M.J. asked.

"What problem?"

"I'm not sure," M.J. said, realizing he probably shouldn't have said anything. "She made a call, told me she had to take care of something urgent, then left. She wanted me to tell you that she'd see you back at the apartment."

"Thanks for the information," Lennie said, frowning. "How come you didn't wait until tomorrow to tell me?"

"Sorry," M.J. said, a tad sheepishly. "I kinda forgot."

Lennie shook his head. If Lucky had a problem to solve, why hadn't she come to him?

Then again, why would she? Lucky always took care of things on her own terms. She copied Gino in that respect.

The Santangelos. Father and daughter. Two tough birds.

Lennie wouldn't have them any other way. He was proud to be part of the Santangelo family, just as Lucky was proud to be Mrs. Golden.

He wondered if the problem had anything to do with Max. His daughter hadn't seemed too happy earlier. And she should've been ecstatic, considering she was about to turn eighteen. Now it was way past midnight, so she was already eighteen.

He had a surprise present for her, a present he hadn't even told Lucky about because she would accuse him of spoiling Max. But hey, he *wanted* to spoil her. What the hell—eighteen only came along once in a lifetime; why not enjoy it with a brand-new silver BMW?

Lucky would kill him, but death would be worth it when he saw the look on Max's face.

~ ~ ~

"You are *not* coming in!" Cookie shrieked as Frankie tried in vain to get her to open the door of their room.

"Why not?" he demanded. "If I'm correct, it was *you* who ran out on *me*. I'm the innocent party."

"Innocent my ass!" Cookie yelled through the closed door. "You were so far up my dad's butt that you didn't even notice I was gone."

"Sure I did," Frankie answered soothingly. "I missed you like crazy."

"No you *didn't*. If you had, you would've called or texted."

"Maybe you should let me in so we can discuss this like two adults."

"No!"

"You're behavin' like a child."

"Screw *you*."

"Is that all you got to say?"

"Here's somethin' else. Good-bye."

"For crissakes, Cookie, at least let me get my bags."

"No!" she shouted, still steaming. "You made me ruin my hair, and I hate you."

Frankie could not believe he was getting the boot, and from a teenager, no less.

And what had he done?

Nothing.

Scowling, he turned around and headed for the elevator.

~ ~ ~

Peggy had never considered herself a lesbian, but then neither had Paige. They were merely two heterosexual women who found they could enjoy an occasional walk on the wild side. And wild it was.

Peggy could not recall Sidney making her come the way Paige

had. In fact, Paige took her back to the early Vegas days, when sex really mattered and orgasms were a daily occurrence.

Paige knew her way around the female anatomy. She'd taken control, and Peggy had enjoyed every second.

When they were finished, Paige dressed and murmured that she had to get back to Gino before he awoke.

"I wish you could stay the night," Peggy found herself saying.

"So do I," Paige said. "I don't like leaving Gino for too long. He's old; one never knows. However, you'll come to his grand-daughter's party tomorrow, and maybe after that . . ."

"I'll look forward to it," Peggy murmured.

And then Paige was gone, and once again Peggy found her-self alone with her thoughts. Soon she would have to confront Armand about his choice of female companions.

She was his mother, it was her duty.

~ ~ ~

Ellie was clicking away. "Plenty of activity going on here," she remarked, almost to herself. "I'm just taking pictures, we'll see what we've got later. I think we have a definite bonanza."

"You think?" Kev said, attempting to stretch his aching legs. Crouching in the bushes was not for him, although it didn't seem to bother Ellie. She was into all the coming and goings, and there were plenty. It seemed there was a party taking place in the villa across from Billy's, and Ellie was capturing plenty of images as people came and went.

"We need to know who the girl is with Billy," Ellie said. "Think you can find out?"

"I'll do my best," Kev replied. "It shouldn't be a problem."

~ ~ ~

After a while, Ace realized it didn't look like Max was getting back to the hotel anytime soon. Cookie had told him she'd had to meet Lucky, but he wasn't sure he believed her. Now it was past one in the morning and he'd had it. He hadn't driven all the way to Vegas to be treated like this. After all, it wasn't as if Max had acted like she was thrilled to see him. No. He'd had to hang out with her crazy friends all night, sit through a painful concert, and then she'd taken off. To do what?

He didn't know, and he didn't care anymore. She was treating him as if he didn't matter, and he wanted out.

He took the present he'd brought her and placed the box on the bed. Then he wrote "Happy Birthday" on a piece of hotel stationery and left it on top.

After that, he grabbed his overnight bag and took off.

Max was no longer his problem.

~ ~ ~

And still Fouad found it impossible to sleep. He'd tried everything: watching a movie on TV, ordering a hot drink from room service, lying perfectly still and allowing his mind to go blank.

Nothing worked.

Somehow he couldn't shake the thought that something was going on with Armand, something bad.

Over the past few weeks, Armand's drug use had escalated to the point where he did not seem to be in control of his actions anymore. Sleeping with Martin Constantine's wife, then throwing her out of his apartment was a prime example of behavior gone wild. And then there was the embarrassing scene with Lucky Santangelo and the empty threats Armand had hurled at her. Not to mention his ongoing addiction to prostitutes.

Armand was in a bad place, and although Fouad resented the way he'd been treated lately, he still felt a certain responsibility toward Armand. Perhaps this was not the right time to desert him.

On a whim, Fouad decided to get dressed and take a walk.

What harm would it do to stroll past Armand's villa and make sure everything was all right?

CHAPTER SIXTY-TWO

Always expect the unexpected was one of Lucky's mottos, along with *Never fuck with a Santangelo*. So she wasn't surprised to observe the tableau that greeted her when she entered Armand's villa. A man awash in cocaine, a crack pipe, and champagne. That would be Armand. Another man, big and brawny—perhaps a bodyguard—joining in the activities. And a naked woman.

It occurred to Lucky that this was not the perfect moment to tear him a new asshole. He wouldn't understand, he wouldn't get it. Armand Jordan was completely trashed. If asked, he probably wouldn't even remember his own name.

What a shame; she'd been so looking forward to putting him straight.

She stood stock-still, staring at the scene that greeted her. The woman with mammoth breasts noticed her first. "Wanna join?" the woman slurred, waving her over. "Plenny fer everyone."

Lucky shook her head and thought how pathetic Armand

Jordan was. He didn't deserve her wrath. Who would believe anything he said anyway? He was a nothing, a nobody. He wasn't worth her time.

She turned around and started to leave, only to find the man she'd first encountered blocking her way at the door.

He wasn't wasted like the others. He was stone-cold sober, and he wanted to know who she was and what exactly she wanted.

"You first," she said, unable to stare him down because of his dark glasses, which she found most irritating.

"I asked what you want here," Mikey repeated. "This is a private party."

"Didn't you just tell me that I'd fit right in?" Lucky said, noticing the bulge of a gun at his waist.

"Don't get cutesy with me," Mikey said, signaling Luscious. "What'd you come here for?"

Luscious rushed to his side, gave Lucky a filthy look, and said, "Who's this?"

"That's what I'm tryin' t' find out," Mikey said, fast losing patience. "'Cause she don't belong here."

"You're so right I don't," Lucky agreed amicably. "Only I'm beginning to think that neither do you."

~ ~ ~

"Why're you takin' photos of other people?" Kev asked Ellie, who was snapping away. "You've got what we came for; time to split."

"I'm liking this other stuff," Ellie said, concentrating on catching images. "The dude with the sunglasses is classic. And there's some hot woman who just went inside the house."

"Jesus," Kev grumbled. "You're such a voyeur."

"Don't you know that's what real photographers do? They take pictures of interesting people. It's not all about dumb celebs and who they're sleeping with. Those are my money shots. It's the unexpected shots of real people that turn me on."

"I could think of somethin' else that'd turn you on," Kev said, realizing it was time he climbed out of the bushes and got some action going. He put his hand on the back of her neck, and gave her a little rub.

"I'm not sleeping with you," Ellie announced, still clicking away. "So don't go getting any ideas."

"You're not?" Kev said, deflated. "Why not?"

"Because," Ellie answered. "In case you don't get it, I don't play on your team."

For a moment Kev was not sure what she meant. Then it sunk in, and he couldn't believe his lousy luck. Only he would hit on a dyke! Dammit, why hadn't she told him before?

"Don't sweat it," Ellie assured him. "You might not be getting laid tonight, but at least you're making money."

"Thanks a lot," Kev said, wondering if it was too late to score a replacement.

~ ~ ~

"We're takin' care of Arnie," Luscious said, swiping her hand across her nose. "He's havin' himself a good ole' time. I don't remember nobody invitin' you."

"May I ask what's in the suitcase?" Lucky said, pointedly staring at the case Mikey had managed to drag outside the door.

"That wouldn't be your concern, now would it?" Mikey said flatly.

"Maybe I should ask . . . Arnie," Lucky said, her face betraying no emotion. "What do you think?"

"I think you should get t' fuck outta here if y'know what's healthy f' you," Mikey said. "An' forget 'bout anythin' you seen here."

"Is that what you think?" Lucky said, wondering exactly what was going on. "Really?"

Mikey hated the fact that he didn't seem to be getting through to this cunt. She was standing in front of him chill as a fuckin' tall glass of lemonade. She should be running her ass for the hills, not sassing him with her rich-bitch demeanor.

He stepped aside to let her pass through the door. Best to get rid of her; she reeked of trouble.

"Like I told you—get the fuck outta here," he said in his most menacing voice.

"I'm not sure I'm planning on doing that," Lucky replied, cool as an ice cube, still standing in the doorway.

Mikey stepped close to her, so close she could smell his vile breath. "Listen, bitch. Go," he said, adding a threatening "While you still can."

Lucky gave him an implacable look and didn't budge.

This infuriated Mikey, who was shocked that she possessed the gall not to run for the hills—which is exactly what she should be doing. He frightened people; they were supposed to be scared. But not this one. Oh no, fuckin' Miss Movie Star was unafraid.

"I'll go when I've talked to Arnie," she said.

"What're you, his fuckin' wife?" Mikey exploded.

"Would that be a problem if I was?"

Mikey didn't know what to say. If she *were* the john's wife, she'd know about the money—or would she? And if she knew about it, that wouldn't be good, for in Mikey's mind the money was already his, and nobody else was getting their hands on it.

"I don't wanna hurt you," Mikey threatened. "But hear this: if you don't haul your ass outta here, you're likely t' make it happen, an' it'd be a shame t' mess up your pretty face."

Lucky felt her adrenaline rise. Nothing and no one frightened her; she'd been through too much in her life. She'd discovered her mother's brutalized body floating in the family swimming pool when she was five. She'd seen her brother's dead body thrown from a moving car. She'd watched her fiancé, Marco, shot to death in front of her. Did this two-bit punk and his scrawny girlfriend honestly think they were scaring her? No way.

It wasn't that she gave a damn about Armand Jordan and what he'd gotten himself into. But the situation intrigued her. And it had been a while since she'd been faced with an element of danger. She felt invigorated and ready for anything.

"I don't know what scam you're pulling—and believe me I don't particularly care," she said evenly. "Only I'm not leaving until I talk to Armand, so if you'll excuse me, I'm going back inside."

Mikey put his hand on her arm to stop her.

She shook it off and gave him a look that clearly said, *Do not touch me. Or you will regret it.*

There was something in her dark eyes that made him think twice about messing with her. Fuck it. If she wanted to go back inside, let her. He had the money; why hang around? This bitch was about to cause nothing but trouble, so the smart thing would be to get out while things were relatively calm.

"Let's go," he said to Luscious as Lucky moved past them back into the house.

"Huh?" Luscious responded. "You're gonna let her—"

"I told you," Mikey snarled. "We're outta here. Now help me with the goddamn suitcase."

~ ~ ~

Billy and Max stayed by the window, observing the goings-on at the villa across from them. They'd watched as Lucky marched up to the front door and encountered a man dragging a suitcase out. They'd both assumed that once she realized she was at the wrong villa and that Billy wasn't there, she would leave. But that hadn't happened. She'd gone inside, then reappeared at the door and was now involved in some sort of animated discussion with the suitcase man and a woman. Unfortunately, neither Billy nor Max could hear anything except the blaring music.

"What is she *doing?*" Max said, peering to get a better look.

"Beats me," Billy replied.

And then they saw her vanish back inside the villa.

"Where do you think Lennie is?" Max said. "This is, like, so weird."

"Hey," Billy replied. "It's kinda obvious she's not on to us. It looks as if she's got her own thing goin' on."

"What do you mean by *that?*" Max asked, wide-eyed.

"I mean it's a coincidence that we happen to be in the next villa. There's some all-night party goin' on over there, an', uh, Lucky's obviously into it."

"Are you crazy?" Max exclaimed. "Why would my mom be at a party without Lennie?"

Billy shrugged. "Sometimes married couples do things on their own. I dunno, Green Eyes, you just gotta be thankful she's not stalkin' us."

But Max wasn't thankful, not at all. Something was going on, and she was determined to figure out what it was.

CHAPTER SIXTY-THREE

Martin Constantine was not a violent man. Ruthless, perhaps, but when building a business empire one had to be uncompromising and tough. And since he'd come up the hard way, those were two qualities Martin possessed in abundance.

Business, making deals, and accumulating a fortune was Martin's life. That and his exquisite wife, Nona.

Nona and he had been introduced by a mutual acquaintance in New York, and Martin was immediately smitten with the exotic-looking Slovakian beauty queen. So much so that it didn't take long before he'd divorced his wife of thirty years and promptly married the delectable Nona. Martin was sixty-five and Nona was twenty-five. The discrepancy in their ages made no difference to Martin. What was forty years between soul mates?

Eight months into their marriage, Nona had given birth to Martin's one and only son. Since his first wife had only managed to pop out girls—three in a row—Martin was ecstatic. He doted on his wife and his young son. They, along with his business empire, were his life.

Yes, life was very good until the confession.

The confession came one day as they sat at the breakfast table. Nona suddenly broke down in floods of tears. Concerned, Martin asked her what was wrong. In between wracking sobs, Nona told him.

She'd made a mistake. A terrible mistake.

Martin informed her that there was no mistake that could not be rectified.

Secure in the knowledge that he worshipped her, Nona began telling him the story. She told him that she'd gone to Armand Jordan's apartment to view a rare Picasso he'd recently purchased, and that once she was there, Armand had suddenly gone berserk, and viciously raped her in every possible way. Now she suspected that she might be pregnant.

At first Martin had not believed this could happen, that Armand Jordan would dare to commit such a vile act. But once she got talking, Nona insisted on reliving every disgusting detail, including the way Armand had tossed her out of his apartment when he was finished with her as if she were a sack of garbage.

Martin's fury grew. He was not angry at his wife, for she was merely the victim of a perverted monster who had taken out on her his frustration at not getting a building they were vying for. His rage was directed toward Armand.

But Martin Constantine had ways of dealing with rage. And it wasn't long before he took steps to alleviate his anger and his wife's pain.

Nobody messed with Martin Constantine's family and got away with it. Nobody.

Martin knew exactly what he had to do.

CHAPTER SIXTY-FOUR

There was no Lucky waiting for him in their apartment, which right away made Lennie uneasy. It was his first night back, and usually when they'd been separated for a while, they didn't leave each other's side. He blamed himself. Lucky had wanted to depart Mood earlier, and because he was being obtuse about Alex Woods, he'd insisted on staying. Now where was his beautiful stubborn wife, and what problem was she dealing with in the early hours of the morning?

Knowing Lucky, she was probably doing this purposely to get his attention. Not that she needed to do that, she'd always had his attention from the very first moment they'd met. Ah yes, their lives were filled with memories . . . making mad crazy love on a raft in the South of France, falling insanely in love while they were both married to other people, enjoying all kinds of challenging adventures.

So where was she?

He paced around the apartment for a few minutes before picking up the phone and calling Danny.

Danny was at a gay club with his partner, Buff. They were contemplating whether to ask a handsome young barman if he would care to come home with them and spend the night.

Buff was all for it, but Danny was not so sure. He wasn't that fond of sharing Buff with anyone. Why should he?

On the other hand, if it was what Buff wanted, who was he to deprive him?

Danny's phone buzzed. For a moment he panicked. Phone calls in the middle of the night could only mean bad news. His needy mom? His disapproving stepdad? His straight brother who could never hold a job for more than two minutes?

He'd imbibed three cosmos, and decided that he wasn't ready to deal with any kind of a crisis, but he rallied anyway, and answered the phone.

It was Lennie, wanting to know where Lucky was.

"I'm off the clock," Danny sniffed.

"Does that mean you don't give a shit?" Lennie responded, sounding pissed off.

Danny gathered his thoughts. He was speaking to his boss's husband, so maybe he should make out as if he cared. Which of course he did, but he couldn't help noticing that Buff was whispering in the bartender's ear, and that wasn't right, that wasn't sharing. A threesome meant three people, not two.

"Uh, sorry, Mr. Golden," Danny said, throwing Buff a dirty look. "I thought Mrs. Golden was with you."

"She was. But apparently something came up that she had to deal with. Any idea what it could be?"

"No."

"Okay then." He waited a moment, then said, "You're sure?"

"Quite sure, Mr. Golden."

Lennie put down the phone.

Danny clicked off his cell, failing to notice that he had a text message waiting.

~ ~ ~

Frankie could not believe he was out in the cold with his dick in his hand. Cookie had turned out to be a tough little minx. She hadn't even opened the door for him to collect his stuff. Juvie cunt. She had his clothes and, even more upsetting, his drug stash.

And what exactly had he done? Nothing earth-shattering. He'd been polite to her old man, something that should've pleased her. But oh no, nothing was good enough for Gerald M.'s daughter. She was a spoiled brat, although he had to admit she gave great head.

And thinking of head, what was Annabelle doing with Eddie Falcon? Or rather, what was Eddie Falcon doing with her? Strange bedfellows. Eddie Falcon was a comer; he didn't have to settle for used goods.

Frankie made his way back to the casino in the hope that he might find Gerald M. at one of the tables. They could resume their friendship, especially when he was able to tell Gerald M. that his lovely daughter was safely tucked in for the night.

Frankie felt like doing a couple of lines, but he was fresh out and Cookie wasn't opening her door anytime soon.

He had a name and a number. Randy—the deliveryman.

Frankie decided to give him a call.

~ ~ ~

"I dunno what," Max said. "But something shady is going on."

"Hey," Billy said. "Your mom's at a party. No biggie."

"You don't understand," Max said, trying not to lose patience with Billy, who was starting to annoy her. "Lennie came home today. There's *no way* she'd go to a party without him."

"Like I said—in marriages certain events happen. Lucky's doin' her own thing. I know she's your mom, but she's one helluva sexy lady, an' maybe Lennie just doesn't do it for her anymore."

"You are so full of crap, Billy," Max said, suddenly furious. "You don't know anything about my parents, nothing at all, so kindly shut your face."

"*And* she has a temper," Billy said.

"Yes," Max said, shooting him a daggers look. "She has a temper."

"Sorry, babe."

"About what?" Max said, still angry. "Being rude about my parents?"

"I wasn't being rude, I was simply trying to tell you the way it is in some marriages."

"And what makes *you* an expert?"

"C'mon, Green Eyes," he groaned. "I don't wanna fight about this."

"I'm going over there," she said, making up her mind.

"You're doing *what?*" Billy said, frowning.

"I'm seeing for myself what's going on."

"Big mistake."

"Why?"

"'Cause first she's gonna want to know what you're doin' here," Billy explained. "An' second, if she's havin' herself a good time, you're only gonna embarrass her."

"It's a party, Billy. I'll sneak in; she won't even see me."

"Then I'm comin' with you."

"Not a plan."

"Why?"

" 'Cause if she spots me an' then you, well, you know Lucky—she's not stupid."

"And if she *does* see you, what're you gonna say?"

"I dunno. I'll think of something."

"It's not a good idea," Billy warned.

"Well, it's *my* idea, and *I'm* doing it."

CHAPTER SIXTY-FIVE

The pain hit Armand in the pit of his stomach. It startled him, almost made him gag. Not quite, for he had no time to give in to pain. He was enjoying himself too much. He had never experienced such joyous feelings. He was wrapped in a warm cloak of bliss, which might have had a little something to do with the speedball Randy had shared with him—the lethal combination of heroin and cocaine.

Randy and Seducta were his best friends in the world. They cared about him in ways that were so endearing. Seducta had taken her top off again, and he snuggled his face against her mammoth breasts. She reminded him of his mother—dear, sweet Peggy.

Randy snorted coke off her nipples.

Armand smiled. They were sharing. This was exactly the way it should be.

And then suddenly, there was Lucky Santangelo staring down

at him. Words were coming out of her mouth, but he couldn't hear them.

He decided that Lucky was beautiful too. She was his friend. He didn't want her dead, he didn't want anyone dead. They would own The Keys together and exist in perfect harmony.

The pain hit Armand again. He screamed and doubled over. Then everything faded to black.

~ ~ ~

"For God's sake, someone call 911!" Lucky yelled, wondering how she'd gotten caught up in this situation. She was supposed to be reaming Armand a new asshole, not saving his sorry life. How had this happened?

Randy staggered to his feet. He was almost as out of it as Armand, but self-preservation kicked in, and it occurred to him that he'd better get out. He looked around for Luscious.

"Jesus Christ!" Lucky exclaimed, reaching for her cell. "This man could be dying and you can't even make a phone call. What kind of people are you?"

Seducta giggled hysterically. "Fun people," she said, her voice a drowsy slur, white powder decorating her nose. "Arnie loves us."

"While Arnie might love you, he could be dying, you stupid cow," Lucky said, calling 911 and requesting an ambulance.

"Where's Mikey?" Seducta asked, her face crumbling, mascara smudged under her eyes.

Randy flexed his considerable muscles. "Where's the fuckin' money?" he wanted to know.

"You people are the dregs," Lucky said, feeling Armand's wrist to see if he had a pulse. He did.

"We gotta get t' fuck away from this shit," Randy said, suddenly realizing that trouble was looming.

"That's right, run," Lucky said. "You pathetic pieces of crap."

"Where's Mikey?" Seducta whined for the second time. "I want my Mikey."

~ ~ ~

Ten minutes after speaking to Lennie, Danny checked his messages. Sure enough, there was one from Lucky.

He could've kicked himself, for Danny prided himself on always being available to his boss. He quickly scanned her text and experienced a sinking feeling in his stomach.

Armand Jordan is going around boasting that The Keys is his. Off to Cavendish to confront. Care to join?

Yes, he would love to have joined if only he'd known. It was all Buff's fault, flirting with the bartender, taking his mind off work. Threesomes. Ha! Who needed them?

He called Lennie and filled him in on the situation, telling him about the unfortunate morning meeting and what a chauvinistic pig Armand was.

"And you let Lucky go over there alone?" Lennie said, his voice heated.

"I didn't know!" Danny replied, duly chastised. "Besides, have you ever tried stopping Lucky from doing anything? You know it's impossible."

"I'm on my way to the Cavendish," Lennie said.

"I'll meet you there," Danny said.

To hell with Buff and the bartender. Lucky was his priority.

~ ~ ~

"So!" Ellie exclaimed. "Lots of activity at the party house."

"Aren't you supposed to be concentrating on Billy an' the girl?"

"I've got more than enough pix of them together. Anyway, they're back in the villa. Whaddya want me to do, crawl through the keyhole?"

"Don't be facetious."

"Big words coming from a little guy."

"I might be on the short side, but haven't you heard about large surprises comin' in small packages?"

"Lost on me, Kev," Ellie said, shaking her head. "I told you— I'm gay."

"I could turn you."

"Confident, aren't we?"

"Wanna give it a go?"

"No thank you."

"Can't blame a dude for tryin'."

"However," Ellie said with a wicked smile, "if you were to suddenly change into Billy Melina . . ."

"Fuck *you!*" Kev said. Why was everything always about Billy?

"No chance," Ellie said, laughing. "Not unless you cut off your dick and call yourself Daisy!"

~ ~ ~

Danny met Lennie at the top of the pathway that led to the villas. "Villa number four," he said, all business. "Apparently there've been complaints about the noise coming from there."

"Noise?"

"Music. My friend at the desk says there must be a party going on. One more complaint and they're sending security."

"Why haven't they done so already?"

"They don't like messing with the high rollers," Danny explained. "Bad for business."

"So you think Lucky walked in on a party?" Lennie said.

Danny shrugged. "I don't know. Armand Jordan didn't strike me as a party animal, unless it involves hookers."

"Why does Lucky do this?" Lennie questioned.

"Do what?"

"Walk herself into situations she can't control."

"She's *your* wife."

"Thanks, Danny," Lennie said dryly. "I think I know that."

"I'm sure she's fine," Danny said.

~ ~ ~

Fouad hurried down the pathway toward the villas. He had a bad feeling in his gut. Something wasn't right, he knew it. Leaving Armand alone to do whatever he felt like doing was not wise. Armand was too volatile a personality—he had to have some restraints. Fouad had always been the voice of reason, a calming influence. The truth was, Armand needed him.

It was cold out and quite dark, but Fouad could hear loud music ahead of him, and he was sure it must be coming from Armand's villa.

As he got nearer, he suddenly encountered two people, a man wearing sunglasses at night and a skinny, raggedy-looking woman. Fouad might have passed them with a polite nod of acknowledgement, except for one thing. Between the two of them they were lugging one of Armand's distinctive Louis Vuitton suitcases—his initials on the handle.

Immediately, Fouad knew. It had to be the suitcase packed with money that Armand always insisted on bringing to Vegas. Over $750,000 in cash.

"Excuse me," Fouad said.

Mikey stopped for a moment. "What?" he snarled.

"I think you have something that doesn't belong to you."

CHAPTER SIXTY-SIX

On the stroke of midnight, Mr. O arrived in Las Vegas by private plane. A rented town car waited for him at a prearranged spot, the keys under the floor mat as he'd requested.

Mr. O could have been a *GQ* model or a famous actor. He was black and beautiful, a cross between Denzel Washington and Blair Underwood. However, Mr. O had chosen a different profession—a profession that would last as long as he wanted. A profession that paid him top dollar, because he was the best at what he did.

Mr. O was a mechanic. A hit man. A solver of anyone's problem—as long as the price was right.

Mr. O was the best at what he did. And only the best hired him.

This was not the first job he was about to do for Martin Constantine, and it would not be the last.

Mr. O always took care of business.

CHAPTER SIXTY-SEVEN

Mikey was not about to accept shit from anyone. He'd had a try-ing evening, and now he was all set to take off with the prize—a suitcase stuffed full of Benjamins. The last thing Mikey needed was some random ass wipe stopping him and telling him that the suitcase was not his.

Luscious hovered next to him, a shivery presence in her tiny skirt and top. She wouldn't be any help in an argument; she was already a hindrance.

Mikey had decided that when they reached Randy's car, he'd send her back, ostensibly to get the others, then he'd drive off into the night, leaving them all behind. They were a worthless crew—including his big ox of a brother. The truth was, he had no use for any of them.

Mikey took a long steady look at the man confronting him. He did not seem like a threat; he seemed nervous, which was good, because Mikey enjoyed making people nervous.

"You wanna get outta my way, sport?" he said, standing very still. "I won this suitcase legitimate, so back t' fuck off."

"Yeah," Luscious said, joining in, her tinny little voice getting on his nerves. "Back t' fuck off."

Mikey shot her a scathing glare. What were they—a comedy duo?

"I'm afraid I shall have to confirm that with the prince," Fouad said, asserting his authority, although his hands were trembling and he wasn't sure if he could handle this.

"Prince?" Luscious squeaked.

"This is a gamblin' town," Mikey said flatly. "I won this fair an' square. You don't hav'ta check with no one."

"I'm afraid I do," Fouad said, standing his ground.

There was a long moment of silence, then, in a sudden fit of temper, Mikey reached down into his boot and slid out the six-inch hunting knife. He'd had enough jacking around; it was time to go. "Is this what you're lookin' for?" he yelled at Fouad. "You wanna get yourself cut, mothafucker? Is that what ya want?"

"The suitcase does not belong to you," Fouad said, his throat so dry that he could barely speak. "Kindly leave it and get away from here."

"You dumb *fuck*," Mikey snarled, plunging the knife into Fouad's chest. "You dumb, cocksuckin' fuck!"

Fouad staggered slightly, thought about his wife and children for a brief second, then fell to the ground.

~ ~ ~

Standing at the window, Max and Billy watched in horror as the man with the suitcase produced a knife and began stabbing the other man.

"Oh my God!" Max yelled, panicking. "We've got to do something."

"I'll call security," Billy said quickly.

"No, no it'll be too late," Max urged. "We have to help now."

~ ~ ~

Lucky decided there was nothing she could do for Armand except wait for the paramedics. Then she heard yelling, so she ran outside in time to observe Mikey, in a frenzy, stabbing Fouad, who was now on the ground.

She didn't hesitate. Grabbing Mikey's right arm, she twisted it back until she forced him to drop the knife.

Mikey turned on her in a deadly fury. "You fuckin' bitch," he screamed, kicking and punching her. "I'll fuckin' kill you."

"Oh my God!" Max cried out, still by the window. "It's my mom. We've got to help her!" She ran outside and, without thinking, pounced on Mikey's back, clinging tightly around his neck and scratching his face, while Lucky attempted to pick herself up and reach the knife.

With a roar of anger, Mikey sent Max flying, then swooped down and grabbed the knife before Lucky could get to it. At which point Billy joined the fray, springing into action-hero mode, a role he'd played many times on the big screen. He'd had a few fights in his time, and he knew that the best line of defense was attack, so he directed a vicious kick at Mikey's balls.

Mikey doubled over for a few seconds before letting out another powerful yell and striking out with the knife, catching Billy down the side of his cheek.

Blood flowed.

By this time, Lucky was up, and only thinking of protecting

her daughter. She had no idea where Max had come from or what she was doing here, but it didn't matter. All Lucky wanted was to get Max away from the violence, somewhere safe.

"Get out of here!" she yelled at Max. "Run! Go get help!"

"I can't leave Billy," Max cried, sinking to the ground and cradling Billy's head in her lap, attempting to staunch the flow of blood. "He's hurt. Oh my God! He's bleeding."

Fouad was also on the ground, moaning, while Luscious stood to one side—transfixed. Was it? Could it be? Was she looking at Billy Melina, the movie star?

Mikey possessed the strength of a bull. His adrenaline was running strong. Three down. All that was left was the woman, and she wasn't backing away. Oh no. She was staring at him like a black widow spider waiting to pounce.

He had a strong urge to cut the bitch, cut her good. But even more important was taking off with the suitcase.

Where the fuck was Randy?

"Randy!" He roared his brother's name, and the big oaf came lumbering out of the villa, buttoning up his pants.

"What the fuck," Randy mumbled, taking in the chaos.

"We're gettin' outta here," Mikey commanded. "Pick up the fuckin' suitcase, an' let's go."

Lucky stood back and watched them, savvy enough to realize there was nothing she could do, although if she'd had a gun she would not have hesitated to use it. They were the dregs. Criminal dregs. And they were stupid too. She knew without a doubt that they'd be caught within twenty-four hours.

"So long, bitch," Mikey said, throwing her a triumphant look. "Whoever t' fuck you are."

The fight was over. The Sorrentino brothers were on their

way, Luscious trailing behind them, Seducta left snoring on the couch inside the villa.

As soon as they were gone, Lucky took stock of the situation. The sudden violence was over. In spite of everything, Max seemed to be okay. Fouad was not so good, and Billy was still bleeding.

"The paramedics will be here any minute," she said, gazing intently at her daughter. "Are you okay?"

Max nodded, a lone tear trickling down her cheek. "I was so scared for you, Mom. I tried to help. *We* tried to help."

"Yes," Lucky said gravely. "I know you did." Then she added with the hint of a smile, "We make quite a team. Where did *you* learn to kick ass?"

Max gave a wan smile. "From my amazing mom, where else?"

And they exchanged a warm look.

Minutes later Lennie and Danny arrived, followed by the paramedics.

Lucky knew that this was not the right time to ask Max what was going on. There was always another day. And eventually she would find out everything.

CHAPTER SIXTY-EIGHT

Mysteries take place, and sometimes they are never solved.

Take the case of Armand Jordan. The man lost consciousness due to an overindulgence of liquor, heroin, and cocaine. The paramedics arrived in time to save him, but it was not to be, because no one was able to save him from the precise bullet hole right between his eyes.

Prince Armand Mohamed Jordan had been shot execution style, and only two men knew why.

To everyone else it was a mystery that would never be solved.

EPILOGUE
Three Months Later

Everyone was questioned about Armand Jordan's murder, even Lucky. It became quite clear to the investigating detectives that while the melee was taking place in front of the villa, a lone assassin had managed to somehow slip inside the villa and finish Armand off.

It was a professional hit, no doubt about it. The only witness was an exotic dancer commonly known as Seducta Sinn. But Seducta claimed to have been asleep (passed out) at the time, and saw and heard nothing.

~ ~ ~

Within days, Mikey and Randy Sorrentino were arrested outside of Nashville and charged with grand theft and aggravated assault.

They both lawyered up and instantly turned against each other.

Mikey ended up back in jail, while Randy found himself facing ten months' probation.

The money suitcase was eventually returned to Fouad, minus $15,000.

~ ~ ~

Seducta Sinn reveled in a few weeks of minor celebrity. She was the woman in the same hotel room as a murder victim—a well-known New York businessman. She was an exotic dancer, and all the TV shows clamored for an interview.

Her newfound fame did not last long, and eventually she resumed her job at Dirty Den's. A few weeks later she filed for divorce from Mikey, and shortly after that she moved in with Randy.

The two of them decided they'd found true happiness at last, even though Randy didn't have a job, and some nights Seducta was too drunk to make it to Dirty Den's.

But true happiness comes in all different forms, and they were content.

~ ~ ~

Luscious vanished with the $10,000 she'd persuaded Mikey to give her from the infamous suitcase. The moment they'd left Vegas, she'd decided she wanted out. Mikey scared her, and she'd finally decided that Randy was an idiot.

She'd worked on Mikey until he'd agreed to give her some money, then she'd taken it and fled. She hadn't wanted any involvement in what she thought of as the Cavendish Hotel incident. She'd changed her name and taken a bus cross-country to Chicago, where she got a job as a waitress and faded into the background of a mundane life. For the time being, living a mundane life suited her just fine.

~ ~ ~

Paco informed Harry, after one brief awkward encounter in the men's room at Wonderball, that he wasn't (just as Max had suspected) gay after all.

A very disappointed Harry continued searching for the right one.

~ ~ ~

Annabelle and Eddie got married at The Beverly Hills Hotel. It was the first time for both of them, and each of them had their reasons.

Eddie figured marrying Annabelle was somehow or other getting himself attached to Hollywood royalty. After all, her parents were movie stars, even though her dad, the very famous Ralph Maestro, had probably arranged the murder of her very famous mother, Gemma Summer Maestro.

Who cared? This was a Hollywood murder. Ralph Maestro walked free.

And Annabelle decided that marrying Eddie was a good thing because he was a comer with clout and an A-list cluster of clients.

One day Eddie would run a studio, Annabelle was sure of it. And she'd be Mrs. Eddie Falcon, with power up the wazoo. Not such a bad thing.

She never spoke of her evening with Armand Jordan. It was best forgotten.

~ ~ ~

Alex Woods still had lust in his heart for the unobtainable Lucky Santangelo. He moved yet another Asian beauty in with him, and bided his time.

Alex was not a man who gave up easily.

~ ~ ~

Remaining Venus's resident stud for almost three months garnered Jorge a huge amount of publicity. The two of them were all over the Internet, a staple of gossip columns, and of magazines that loved nothing better than putting them on the cover. Together, they made a stunning couple.

The publicity benefited them both. Women were envious of Venus, but they also admired the fact that at forty-something, she was able to attract and keep the attention of such a virile young man.

Jorge became a known name in his own right. So much so that Calvin Klein hired him to be the face and body of the next big underwear campaign.

Jorge was on his way to getting exactly what he wanted.

Fame.

Money.

Recognition.

Love would come later.

~ ~ ~

Meanwhile, Venus met a Venezuelan avant-garde film director who saw her as more than just a blond and beautiful superstar sex symbol who happened to sing, dance, and act. He saw her as everywoman, an earthy creature whose incredible potential had yet to be unleashed on the world.

She saw him as the intellectual savior she had been searching for.

Together they had big plans.

~ ~ ~

Danny and Buff got married in Oregon. The trip was a wedding present from Lucky, who felt Danny deserved some time off.

Danny complained all the way about how ridiculous it was that gay marriage was not legal in California, the most laid-back state of all.

Buff heartily agreed.

And after five wonderful days, they returned to Vegas in full wedded bliss.

~ ~ ~

M.J. never did get to take Cassie on the trip he'd planned, for the night of Armand Jordan's murder was the night she lost their baby, solving all their problems. Although deep down, M.J. couldn't help feeling that maybe she'd done something to facilitate the miscarriage.

He desperately tried to put it out of his mind, but somehow it lingered.

~ ~ ~

Fouad recovered nicely. His wife and children flew to Las Vegas to be by his side, and later, back in New York, they all shared in the surprise that Armand Jordan had split his estate fifty-fifty. Half to his mother, and the other half to Fouad.

It made Fouad sad that Armand had come to such an unfortunate end, for although Armand had been an extremely difficult and challenging man, they had indeed shared many interesting times before the drugs had taken hold.

Strangely enough, Fouad missed him.

To celebrate his newfound position as head of Jordan Developments, Fouad collected all of Armand's sex DVDs and promptly destroyed them.

He determined that Armand's legacy would be pristine, and that his reputation would remain untarnished.

~ ~ ~

Peggy Dunn was all set to organize a spectacular New York funeral for her only son. She had Fouad contact the king and tell him the sad news in case he wanted to attend. The king responded by saying that he wished the funeral to take place in Akramshar. It would be a state funeral, and his people would make all the arrangements.

Peggy agreed, and it was then that Fouad revealed that Armand had a wife and four children in Akramshar.

At first Peggy was horrified and shocked. How could Armand have a family she knew nothing about? Why had he never told her? It was unbelievable.

But as the news settled in, she experienced a strong feeling of excitement and anticipation.

She had grandchildren. Four of them. She was not alone, she had a family.

Peggy couldn't wait to meet them.

On the plane to Akramshar, sitting beside Fouad and his lovely wife, Alison, she reached into her purse and took out the envelope from the DNA sample lab. She had not opened it, and now she decided she never would.

In her mind, Armand was a prince. May he rest in peace.

~ ~ ~

Ace returned to Big Bear, where he hooked up with a young, pretty waitress who came from a similar background to his. He tried to forget Max Santangelo. She wasn't for him; why had he been fooling himself? They lived in two different worlds, and much as he'd tried to fit in, he'd finally realized it was never going to happen.

~ ~ ~

Kev became rich, or relatively so, for Ellie's pictures caused a bidding war among the tabloids, and true to her word, Ellie cut him in for half.

But Kev wasn't happy. He'd betrayed his friend, and not only that, he'd stayed hidden in the bushes like a coward as the dude with the knife had started attacking everyone. He hadn't even emerged to help Billy, and the guilt was killing him.

He took his money and slunk off to New York.

~ ~ ~

Ellie sold her pictures to the tabloids before talking to the police. As a potential material witness she was sternly warned that she should have come forward instead of concealing evidence. She never mentioned that there was someone with her. Kev had begged her not to say he was present, so she'd complied.

Eventually she'd hired a lawyer, pleaded innocence, and handed over all her photos.

All except one.

She'd captured the image of a tall African American man in a black suit, slipping quietly into the villa as Randy emerged.

Was she the only one to see him?

Apparently so.

She placed the photo in a safe-deposit box and wrote a note to her significant other that if anything happened to her it should be given to the police.

Ellie was nothing if not street-smart.

~ ~ ~

Sam's movie came out and was a big hit. Hollywood wanted him, and was prepared to pay for the privilege.

He still sent Denver the occasional text, but she had yet to visit him on the set.

In Sam's mind, there was always tomorrow.

~ ~ ~

Gerald M. took off on a European tour with a Swedish blonde he'd met in Vegas. He was proud to have her accompany him to London, Paris, and Berlin, countries where he was still a certified superstar. The fans appreciated the smooth soul that was the sound of Gerald M. They worshipped at his feet.

He asked Cookie if she'd like to accompany them.

She declined. Having the run of the Bel Air house all to herself was a far more tempting prospect.

Since moving on from Frankie, and hitting the street with a sexy new hairstyle, Cookie had discovered there were far more interesting prospects out there than a coked-out old loser like Frankie.

Cookie decided she wanted to be an actress, and enrolled in acting class.

Young, hot would-be actors were everywhere.

Soon Cookie was having herself a fine old time.

~ ~ ~

Dumped by a truculent, spoiled teenager, Frankie Romano drove back to L.A. determined not to sleep with any girl under twenty-one. He was part of the Hollywood club scene, for crissakes. Pussy abounded. He was a star in his own world.

His drug business was out of control. Supply could not keep up with demand. He'd partnered up with a young Colombian, Alejandro Diego, who had big family connections back in Colombia, and who assured him he could keep the supply coming. Now the money was really rolling in.

Frankie loved his life. He wouldn't have it any other way.

~ ~ ~

Max and Billy. Caught on camera for all to see. Cover of the tabloids along with MURDER AT VEGAS HOTEL—as most headlines screamed. Billy came across as the hero of everyone's dreams. This super-hot movie star had gotten his handsome face cut defending his young girlfriend. Although his PR team immediately denied that Max was his girlfriend—in spite of the intimate photos that appeared everywhere. According to his reps, she was merely a family friend he'd been protecting.

Billy was rushed to the emergency room, and the finest plastic surgeon in Beverly Hills was flown in to consult on his damaged face. The cut on his cheek turned out to be a surface wound, and within weeks Billy was back to his handsome self, a handsome self whose advisers (lawyers, PR people, the studio, etc.) had warned him to stay under the radar until his divorce from Venus was finalized, and not to see Max.

Reluctantly he'd agreed it was for the best. After all, he was getting a divorce from an icon, and already carrying on with a teenage girl was not the image his people wished him to project. "The public can turn on you like a dime," they warned him. "Do not screw with a brilliant career. Not at this time."

He spoke to Max on the phone and told her they should cool it for a few weeks. She wasn't heartbroken; too much was going on and she needed to get her head straight. She was a big girl now. Eighteen. And although Lucky had decided the right thing to do was cancel the Vegas party, she'd been okay with it. Especially when Lucky suggested that they take a family trip to the South of France instead.

Her mom had turned out to be way cooler than she'd ever thought. Lucky didn't berate her about Billy, she merely shrugged and said, "We can't help who we fall for. But maybe Billy wasn't the best choice."

Max still thought about Billy.

She thought about Ace too.

Ace had left her such a thoughtful gift and a sad little note. She knew he had to have seen the photos of her and Billy, and it tore her up imagining his reaction.

Ace had always been her rock, and she'd let him down, but as Lucky said—"We can't help who we fall for."

~ ~ ~

After giving in to the L word, Denver and Bobby returned to L.A. and settled in to the new house Bobby purchased. "No huge megamansions," Denver had warned him. "Something manageable, please. And not in any fancy area. I like normal."

"Normal" turned out to be a one-story house in the Hollywood hills with three bedrooms and a panoramic view of the city. It had a reasonably sized garden and a simple lap pool. Amy Winehouse was in dog heaven!

Denver finally introduced Bobby to her family, not without a great deal of trepidation. Surprise, they all loved him. And as her mom said, "What's not to love? He's a great guy."

Yes, Bobby was a great guy, and she was happy they'd moved in together. She was also happy with her new position in the drug unit. Working closely with Leon was a kick, and they had a lot going on. Leon had been tracking a Colombian drug lord, Pablo Diego, for months, and they were near to closing in on his U.S. connections. Pablo's son, Alejandro, was one of their main targets, along with all the dealers he supplied. A series of arrests was imminent.

Denver was well aware that one of their upcoming arrests would be Frankie Romano. Ethics prevented her from mentioning this to Bobby. What he didn't know, he couldn't do anything about, and even though Frankie was no longer his close friend,

Bobby had an innate sense of loyalty, and could try to warn Frankie, enabling him to skip town.

This could not happen, so silence ruled.

Denver loved Bobby so much. She'd even attended a few of *his* family events, and managed to forge a warm relationship with Lucky—who was not as intimidating as she'd imagined. She also adored Lennie, who was so smart and acerbic in a delightfully clever way. And she and Max were warming up to each other slowly but surely.

All in all, Denver felt nothing but positive thoughts about her future with Bobby.

~ ~ ~

Things were going so well that Bobby had a plan. He'd pulled off buying a house and moving into it with Denver, and now he was thinking he wanted more. Denver was so damn special. Beautiful, smart, sexy, his best friend. What more could he look for in a woman?

He wanted to ask her to marry him, but instinctively he had a feeling she'd turn him down. It had taken him forever to get her to move into a house with him—marriage could send her running.

Or not.

He didn't know.

Help was needed, so he secretly met up with her best friend, Carolyn, who was now part of an extremely content lesbian couple, and asked her advice. Carolyn's advice was sound. "Do not rush her," she said. "When the time is right for both of you, you'll know it."

In the meantime, Bobby went to Tiffany's to purchase a seven-carat engagement ring, which Denver would probably think was way too flashy. But what the hell—it was his prerogative to spoil her.

He put the ring away, and waited patiently for the right time.

~ ~ ~

Lucky Santangelo Golden and Lennie Golden. True soul mates. Who said marriages in Hollywood didn't last?

They dealt with the Max/Billy situation in the only way they knew how, and that was with understanding, love, and a non-judgmental attitude.

The South of France trip turned out to be exactly what everyone needed. They stayed with friends in a magnificent villa above Cannes, and Max hit it off with the son of the family, a twenty-two-year-old French aspiring screenwriter. Nothing serious, just fun. Lucky realized that was exactly what Max needed right now, some mindless fun.

Meanwhile, Lennie had plans of his own. "We're driving to Saint-Tropez for the day," he informed his wife. "Just you and me."

"Let's go," Lucky said, for she knew exactly what he had in mind.

And so it was that they relived the first time they'd made love. They went to the same beach and swam out to the same raft. Making love on it was just as amazing—if not better—than the first time.

Lucky still reveled in Lennie's touch. The excitement between them was still as passionate and intense. But everything had to come to a crashing halt when a couple of kids swam toward the raft and hauled themselves aboard.

Giggling as if they were teenagers themselves, Lucky and Lennie took off, plunging in the sea and swimming back to shore, where they collapsed on the sand, still giggling hysterically.

"Love you," Lennie muttered when they calmed down.

"I know," Lucky replied, her black-as-night eyes gazing into his.

They were two people who had found each other, and nothing and no one would ever split them apart.

Two reckless, passionate people, filled with sensual zest and a hearty thirst for living that would take them wherever they wished to go.

Lucky and Lennie. Two of a kind.